Gabrielle Meyer's *When the* [...] ch
a fresh, creative premise! Th [...] nd
I could not wait to see how it [...] ory,
romance, or time travel will adore this book.

—Julie Klassen, bestselling author

*When the Day Comes* is a historical feast, spanning two centuries and showcasing the burdens and blessings of both the Gilded Age and Colonial America. A seamless blend of choices and chances celebrating the enduring spirit of a woman faced with a remarkable future, this first book in the TIMELESS series is a lovely and memorable time-crossing feat.

—Laura Frantz, Christy Award-winning author of *A Heart Adrift*

With rich historical details and a riveting conundrum, *When the Day Comes* had me glued to the pages, the story tugging at my heart and lingering with me long after the last page. A triumph of a story!

—Susan May Warren, *USA Today* bestselling author of *Sunrise*

A riveting, exceptional hook bolstered by a beguiling authorial voice, *When the Day Comes* eases readers into two startlingly different and brilliantly researched historical periods. Meyer's effective historical voice binds readers to a remarkable woman whose courageous propensity to love is balanced by her decision and willingness to commit to life's truest calling. Fans of Heidi Chiavaroli and Roseanna White will be clamoring for more.

—Rachel McMillan, author of *The London Restoration* and *The Mozart Code*

A unique take on the time-travel novel, *When the Day Comes* will have readers losing track of time in their own lives from the first page until they close the book with a sigh of satisfaction. A guaranteed book-hangover, as the story lingers in the mind long after the conclusion.

—Erica Vetsch, author of the THORNDIKE & SWANN REGENCY MYSTERIES

TIMELESS • 1

# When the Day Comes

## GABRIELLE MEYER

BETHANYHOUSE
*a division of Baker Publishing Group*
Minneapolis, Minnesota

Published by Bethany House Publishers
11400 Hampshire Avenue South
Minneapolis, Minnesota 55438
www.bethanyhouse.com

Bethany House Publishers is a division of
Baker Publishing Group, Grand Rapids, Michigan

Printed in the United States of America

Library of Congress Cataloging-in-Publication Data
Names: Meyer, Gabrielle, author.
Title: When the day comes / Gabrielle Meyer.
Description: Minneapolis, Minnesota : Bethany House Publishers, a division of
    Baker Publishing Group, [2022] | Series: Timeless ; 1
Identifiers: LCCN 2021050662 | ISBN 9780764240171 (casebound) | ISBN
    9780764239748 (paperback) | ISBN 9781493437344 (ebook)
Subjects: LCGFT: Novels.
Classification: LCC PS3613.E956 W47 2022 | DDC 813/.6--dc23
LC record available at https://lccn.loc.gov/2021050662

Scripture quotations are from the King James Version of the Bible.

Scripture quotations marked (NIV) are from THE HOLY BIBLE, NEW INTERNATIONAL VERSION®, NIV® Copyright © 1973, 1978, 1984, 2011 by Biblica, Inc.® Used by permission. All rights reserved worldwide.

This is a work of historical reconstruction; the appearances of certain historical figures are therefore inevitable. All other characters, however, are products of the author's imagination, and any resemblance to actual persons, living or dead, is coincidental.

Cover design by Jennifer Parker
Cover photography by Alexey Kazantsev / Trevillion Images

Author is represented by the Books & Such Literary Agency.

Baker Publishing Group publications use paper produced from sustainable forestry practices and post-consumer waste whenever possible.

22   23   24   25   26   27   28       7   6   5   4   3   2   1

To David,
my best friend and my hero.
Thank you for this amazing life we've built, and for
your endless sacrifice and devotion to our family.
You truly are the best of us.
I love you.

He has made everything beautiful in its time. He has also set eternity in the human heart; yet no one can fathom what God has done from beginning to end.

—Ecclesiastes 3:11 NIV

# 1

**WILLIAMSBURG, VIRGINIA**
**MAY 5, 1774**

For as long as I could remember, my mama had told me that my life was a gift. But at the age of nineteen, I had yet to see how this life I was living—or rather, the *lives* I was living—could be anything other than a burden.

"Libby!" My younger sister Rebecca slammed open the door to the office where Mama and I were working on the weekly edition of the *Virginia Gazette*. "It's that horrid Mister Jennings and the lawyer, Mister Randolph." She was breathless, and her cheeks were red from the heat. She pointed at the window. "They're coming this way. They'll be here any second."

I left the article I had been editing and went to the window. Through the wavy glass, the detestable old merchant was limping with purpose toward our home, his dirty wig askew and his cane digging into the hard-packed soil on Duke of Gloucester Street. Beside him was the formidable Mister John Randolph, lawyer to the governor, and one of the most ruthless men in Williamsburg.

Mama fixed Rebecca's white cap, then calmly laid her hands on Rebecca's thin shoulders. "Did you speak to them?"

"Nay." Rebecca shook her head, and for the first time, I saw that she was trembling. "I started to run the moment I saw them."

I quickly opened my top desk drawer and pulled out the small drawstring bag I kept in the hidden compartment. There weren't nearly enough coins to purchase the weekly necessities for our household of eight, let alone pay off our insurmountable debt. Mister Jennings was not the only person we were indebted to after Papa's death.

"Mayhap we can stall him," Mama said to me, her green eyes revealing the depth of her disquiet, though her voice was steady. "Tell him about the public printing contract we're hoping to obtain."

"We've put him off the last two times." I counted out the meager coins, hoping and praying it would appease the miser for a little longer. "I doubt he'll listen to our plea."

"What will he do, Libby?" Rebecca's large brown eyes filled with worry as she clenched the fabric of her too-small gown.

I put my hand under her chin. "Do not worry." I forced myself to smile, trying to banish her fears. "Mama and I will take care of this matter."

"Mistress Conant?" The men entered the front hall, one of them calling out to us. "We've come about the debt."

Though Mama was only forty-one, she had aged a great deal during Papa's illness. The weight of the debt and the responsibilities of supporting our family pressed upon her, as if she were carrying a physical burden.

I put my hand on her shoulder, wishing I could ease her cares. "This is my debt, as well," I said. "I will speak to Mister Jennings."

I left the office before Mama could protest and greeted the unwelcome visitors. "Good day," I said to them. "How may I help you?"

"I'd like to speak to your mother." Mister Jennings lifted his chin with purpose.

"If this is business concerning the printing shop, you may speak to me." I motioned for the men to enter the large sitting room across the hall.

Mama quietly joined us, closing the office door behind her to keep Rebecca out of sight. "We will both speak to you," she said in her gentle way.

The men moved into the sitting room, taking off their tricorne hats as they turned to us. "I will curtail the formalities," Mister Jennings said. "I have brought my lawyer to show you I am serious, since you have ignored my last two attempts to collect the debt you owe."

"We have not ignored you, Mister Jennings." Mama's patient voice never wavered. She clasped her hands in front of her apron. "We simply do not have the money available. My husband was sick for many years and—"

"That is not my concern." Mister Jennings pointed his cane at her. "He purchased printing supplies from me on credit for years, always making an excuse about his ill health."

"We needed those supplies to operate our business," I said in defense of my father, who had died just six months ago.

"If you do not have the money," Mister Jennings said, appearing not to care about our plight, "then I will give you two options, which my lawyer is here to witness today. You can either be thrown into the public gaol until the sum is collected, or . . ." His eyes glowed with intent as he lowered his cane to the floor. "You can indenture your little moppet to me. The one with the dark hair."

Revulsion climbed my throat as I saw the look in his eyes. "Never," I said, clenching my hands together. "We would never indenture Rebecca to you or anyone else."

"Then it will be the gaol for your mother."

A shudder ran down my spine at the thought of the public

gaol. It was a rat-infested eyesore behind the capitol building, not to mention an embarrassment to anyone cast into shackles there.

Mama stepped forward, putting her hand on my arm. "We are awaiting the burgesses' decision this very day. If we're awarded the public printing contract, we will have your payment for you posthaste. You have my word."

"Your word?" Mister Jennings spat. "What good is the word of a woman?"

I wanted to lash out at his comment, but Mama's grip on my arm tightened and I held my tongue. I had little sway with him or anyone else in Williamsburg simply because I was a woman. Even when Papa had been too ill to run the press and I had taken over, very few people would deal with me. Since his death, it had become even worse.

"You've been warned," Mister Randolph said, handing over a piece of paper. "If you do not pay what is owed by the end of this month, you will either face debtor's prison or be forced to indenture one of your household to Mister Jennings for the sum owed."

"I want the girl," Mister Jennings said to Mister Randolph.

The lawyer didn't respond to his client but merely put his hat on and left the sitting room.

Mister Jennings followed in his footsteps. "You said I could have the girl."

After the front door slammed shut, Mama sat on one of the Windsor chairs and put her face in her ink-stained hands, wilting like a parched flower.

"He cannot do either," I said, trying to alleviate our fears.

"He can and he will." Mama looked up at me. "Where is news of the burgesses' decision? It should have come by now."

I paced to the window, feeling helpless in the face of our debt. With Papa's passing, we had lost many of our newspaper subscribers and advertisers. Yet we were not without hope. Mama had applied for the public printing contract, which would ensure some income. But four others—all men—had also applied for the contract.

"I cannot wait here for the news," I said to her as I left the sitting room and took my bonnet off the front hook. "I shall walk to the capitol and see what has been decided."

Without waiting for Mama to comment, I pushed open the door. She would caution me to stay and await a messenger, but I could not.

The bell on the door rang as I stepped into the warm day. Spring had unfolded its gentle arms around Williamsburg, and like any good embrace, it tried to warm my soul and comfort me. Yet little had given me solace lately—both here and in my other path.

Hundreds of people walked in and out of the businesses lining Duke of Gloucester Street. Coaches, wagons, and single riders clogged the usually quiet capital. Overnight, it seemed, Williamsburg had doubled in size with the arrival of the representatives of the House of Burgesses. The assembly had convened that morning at the governor's request, which was why we anticipated news soon.

Would I even see Henry in this commotion? For surely Henry was the one who would bring me the news.

I walked with purpose toward the capitol, taking note of the people passing me. As the editor of the *Virginia Gazette*, it was my job to know as much as possible about the people and the events transpiring in and around Williamsburg. I had to fight to learn the news, since I was rarely invited to the gatherings my male counterparts attended. But no matter how much they learned, I knew so much more than any of them could ever imagine about the events that would soon transpire.

I knew these things because I lived two lives simultaneously—one in 1774 and one in 1914. When I fell asleep in one path, I woke up in the other, back and forth, with no time passing in either one while I was away. It had been this way since the day

11

I was born. But all of that would change on my twenty-first birthday when I was given the choice to forfeit one path and stay in the other forever.

I already knew which one I would choose.

I approached the Raleigh Tavern, halfway between my home and the capitol, and finally saw him.

Henry Montgomery.

He strode down the street toward me, two other burgesses flanking him. They were deep in conversation and did not see me. I recognized Mister George Washington, who had served in the House of Burgesses for many years, and Mister Thomas Jefferson, who had been added just five years before. They were both powerful men and, I knew from my life in 1914, would both go on to become famous Founding Fathers, American presidents, and important figures in the history of the United States. I still marveled every day that I was here, watching history unfold with my own eyes. And I knew exactly how much work and sacrifice these men had before them.

But I did not know anything about Henry's future. For reasons unknown to me, his name was not one I heard repeated in my other path, and I did not try to discover why. I could not. It was one of the many things Mama had warned me about since I was young: never search for answers about either path. If God wanted me to know, I would know. And I must not, for any reason, try to change either path with the foreknowledge I might obtain. To do so meant I would forfeit the path I tried to alter.

Something I feared almost daily, for I did not want to give up 1774.

"Miss Conant," Mister Jefferson said upon seeing me, his brown-haired tie wig peeking out from beneath his tricorne hat. He stopped and gave me a bow, lifting his hat from his head. Elegance and masculinity emanated from his every move. He was a handsome man, and he wielded it. "It's a pleasure to see you again."

"And you, Mister Jefferson."

Both Henry and Mister Washington offered me a bow as they removed their hats. I curtsied and caught Henry's eye, my heart beating faster at the sight of him.

He stood shoulder to shoulder with these two large and imposing men. His legs and arms were well-formed beneath his tailored breeches and waistcoat. Life on board the merchant schooners his family owned had shaped him into a fine-looking man. But it was his handsome face—or rather, his eyes, which were a shade of blue I had never seen in anyone else—that had captivated me since I was a child.

"I was just on my way to see you," Henry said to me, slipping his hat under his arm. His chestnut-brown hair was clubbed at the back. He was one of the few men I knew who did not wear a wig or hair powder.

"I hope you have good news." Mama and I needed some good news right now, though I held on to my hope with a loose grasp.

"Aye."

He smiled, as did Mister Jefferson and Mister Washington, and I knew it was good news indeed. Relief washed over me, making my legs feel weak and shaky.

"Are you on your way home?" Henry asked. "May I walk with you?"

I nodded eagerly, longing to hear him confirm the news.

"We will meet you back here," Mister Washington said to Henry. "We have much to discuss." He bowed again in my direction. "I hope you'll save me a dance at the governor's ball tonight, Miss Conant."

"The ball?"

"As our new public printer," Mister Jefferson said, "your invitation will be forthcoming."

Mister Jefferson and Mister Washington bowed and left us to enter the tavern.

I turned to Henry. "The public printer?"

"Aye." The grin that lit his face almost made me forget about everything else. "Your mother's petition to become the public printer has been accepted."

I briefly closed my eyes, thanking God for His provision. It could not come at a better time.

"I daresay Washington felt liable for your family, in a way," Henry said as we began to walk. "After all, he was the one who asked your father to leave Maryland and set up his print shop in Williamsburg."

"*I* daresay Mama deserves the contract," I countered, teasing and reprimanding my old friend, not wanting to believe Mister Washington would take pity upon us. "She works harder than anyone I know. I would hope we won the contract on our own merit."

"You have both done well in light of your hardships," Henry agreed. "Though we're well aware she could not do it without you. It was because she listed you as co-owner of the press that your bid won in a tight vote. You've earned the respect of several burgesses, Libby, but there are those who would see you fail."

Emotion clogged my throat as the reality of this decision settled on me. The endless hours I had worked these past months had taken an enormous mental and physical toll, not to mention the toll it had taken on my personal life. There had not been time for courting or pursuing a husband as many of my friends had done. And the one man I would pursue—Henry—had been out of my reach for years.

I straightened my back and lifted my chin. I could not show the strain to Henry or anyone else. I must be as strong and relentless as the businessmen around me—and even more so.

"'Tis good to see you again, Libby."

"'Tis good to see you too, Henry."

"How long has it been?"

"Christmastide, surely," I responded, knowing full well that we had not seen each other since Christmas Day at Bruton

Parish Church. Our interactions were few, but whenever I saw him, all time passed from my thoughts, and I was cast back to our early years together.

"I'm sorry to have missed your father's funeral." Henry's voice was low and filled with concern. "If there's anything—"

"Thank you." I stopped him from making an offer that would embarrass me. Papa had been sick for years, and we had been ready for his death—if one can be ready for such things.

"I heard you put a paper to press the day he passed." Henry didn't hide his admiration or surprise. "A remarkable feat, surely one that would silence any naysayers."

I tried not to think about those who had slandered our good name since Papa's passing. Losing him was a devastating blow, but it was made worse by men who assumed we were incapable of running the press now that he was gone. But what choice did Mama and I have? If we stopped printing, we would be destitute. The very thought of debtor's prison—or worse, my sisters being indentured to the likes of Mister Jennings—had driven me every waking moment. I had much to prove as an editor and businesswoman—and even more as a sister and daughter. I could not fail.

"How was the first session?" I asked, ready to change the subject.

His face turned somber, and his gaze hardened as he stared straight ahead. For almost a decade, tensions had been building with England and had finally come to a head just this past December during the famed Boston Tea Party. Word had arrived within the past weeks that the British Parliament had passed the Boston Port Act and planned to close the port of Boston on the first of June. Parliament would keep it closed until the local merchants repaid the lost revenue from the ninety thousand pounds of tea tossed into Boston Harbor.

"We will show solidarity with Boston," Henry said with certainty.

"How?"

"'Tis not my place to share our plan until we've gained enough support to pass it in the house. But do not fear." He smiled at me. "As our duly-elected public printer, you will be the first to know."

We arrived back at the print shop far too soon.

"Would you like to join us for supper?" I asked, though we had scarcely enough to feed ourselves, let alone a guest.

He shook his head, his gaze resting on my face, and I wondered if he enjoyed seeing me again as much as I enjoyed seeing him. He had always been the kindest boy I knew and had grown into a man of good reputation. I had known since I was young that he would marry someone of his own social standing, and there were rumors that the bride had already been chosen.

"I must return to the Raleigh. Will you save me a dance at the governor's ball tonight?" he asked.

The ball. I had almost forgotten. Mama would be so pleased. "Aye."

With that, Henry bowed and took his leave.

As I watched him walk back to the Raleigh Tavern, slipping his tricorne on his head, I couldn't help the twinge of jealousy that I was not joining him and the others to make history.

The Palace Green was lined with torches as Mama and I walked toward the governor's palace that evening, our hearts a little lighter at the news of the contract, though it would not solve all our problems. It was just Mama and me. Hannah and Rebecca were only eight and nine and were too young to attend. They had been left at home with Mariah, the enslaved woman Papa had bought for Mama upon their wedding twenty-one years ago. Mama's twentieth-century mind abhorred slavery in any form, and she had worked tirelessly to have Papa free Mariah, but it wasn't until Papa's death that Mariah had finally been freed. Upon her freedom, she had chosen to stay with us as a hired servant and had married Abraham, a free black man, who served as our man-of-all-work. They were more like family than employees and lived above the kitchen in the yard behind our house.

Dozens of coaches lined the drive, filled with the wealthiest and most prominent citizens of Virginia. Over a hundred burgesses convened in Williamsburg each spring, and with them, wives, children, and servants. All of the best social events took place in the month they stayed in the capital. It reminded me of the social season I was currently enduring in my other time path in London, 1914. Just the thought of waking up tomorrow to face the daunting schedule Mother Wells had planned made my stomach turn.

"You know," Mama said, "I can always tell when your mind is on your other life."

I couldn't hide much from Mama. She knew me better than anyone.

"Didn't you find it hard to separate the two?" I asked her.

"I did," she conceded.

"And don't you still find yourself thinking about the 1990s?"

She was quiet for a moment as a sadness overtook her. Mama was also a time-crosser. Her second path had begun in the year 1973. Just like me, Mama had gone back and forth between her two lives for twenty-one years. She had chosen which one to forfeit and which to keep on her twenty-first birthday, just as I would, and just as all the other time-crossers in our family had done before us. We were each given just twenty-one years to choose.

Long ago, I had decided to remain forever in the 1700s, though I couldn't make my final decision for over a year. I must endure my 1914 path for thirteen more months. I had no other choice.

"It's been almost twenty-one years since I made my final decision," Mama said with a sigh. "Of course I think about it from

17

time to time. It took me years not to let words or thoughts from my other path slip into my conversations here. What would someone say if I told them to take a chill pill or said 'as if'?" She chuckled and then sighed. "I often wonder what happened to my other mom and dad and siblings, but it all seems like a dream to me now. I'm supposed to be here to guide you and to help the American Revolution. I've been waiting for this all of my life."

I knew exactly how she felt. We couldn't change history, but we did know how it would play out.

We walked in silence past torches that flickered their shadows upon the ground. The sound of horses' hooves clipped on the gravel, and a gentle wind blew through the tops of the trees overhead. I loved that Mama knew all about my other life. She was the only person I could talk to about my troubles. She understood my longing for the modern conveniences I enjoyed in 1914: the electricity, telephones, and automobiles. And she told me about the ones yet to come: televisions, computers, microwaves, and more. I marveled at human inventions, even if I struggled to understand them at times.

If anyone in 1774 ever heard us discussing such things, we'd be labeled lunatics—or worse. So we did not discuss our time paths with anyone else. Not even my little sisters knew about Mama and me—and neither had Papa. Rebecca and Hannah were not time-crossers, so there was no reason to tell them. Only those of us with the sunburst birthmark over our heart were time-crossers. From the stories Mama's marked mother had told her, it had been this way as far back as anyone could remember. We knew there were others outside our family, but they rarely crossed our paths. My grandmother had met one in her second path, in 2022. She had known her from her marking, but they had not shared stories for fear of changing history.

Someday, if I had a daughter, she might or might not have the mark. There was no way of knowing. God was the Author of our lives, and only He controlled who bore the gift.

*If* I ever had a child. I had not yet decided if I wanted to pass this gift on to another generation. Was it right to saddle a child with this kind of existence?

"Hold your head up, Libby," Mama said, reaching out and taking my hand in hers. "And put aside your troubles for tonight. It's not every day we get invited to the palace. You only have thirteen more months until your twenty-first birthday. We've navigated your other path thus far. There shouldn't be any reason we won't continue."

Her words gave me hope and brought a lighter step to my slippered feet.

We arrived at the palace entrance and showed our invitation to the footman, who wore a soft blue livery, and then we passed through the reception room and entered the long hallway leading into the ballroom.

The palace was thick with Virginians laughing and visiting. I knew many of these people by name, though I would consider only a few of them my friends. Most had been subscribers to our newspaper since Papa had started it, though we had lost more than I'd care to admit after his death. I saw George Washington, as well as Thomas Jefferson, Patrick Henry, Peyton Randolph, and several other men whose names would be recorded in history books.

Thankfully, the nasty Mister Jennings wasn't present.

"Mistress Conant and Miss Conant," the footman announced as we stepped into the large blue ballroom. A few people looked our way, but most continued, unaffected by our arrival.

"There's Mister Washington," Mama said. "I must thank him for his support of our contract."

I could have followed her, but I had spied someone else I'd rather speak to.

Henry.

He stood near one of the massive windows, a glass in his hand as he spoke to Governor Lord Dunmore and his wife,

Lady Charlotte. Henry's father, Lord Ashbury, and his mother, Lady Gwendolyn, also stood in the small group. Whatever the five of them were discussing, it looked rather grim, if Henry's face was any indication.

"Have you heard the latest gossip?" a feminine voice asked close to my side.

I turned and found my friend, Sophia Charlton, looking in the same direction.

"I don't believe anything I haven't read in the newspapers," I said with a cheeky smile, torn between wanting to know what she'd heard and not wanting to spread gossip. But I was the newspaper editor, and it was my job to know everything, was it not? "What have you heard?"

"That Governor Dunmore has chosen a husband for his eldest daughter, Lady Catherine." Sophia's dark brown eyes were almost black as she waited for my reaction.

"She's but fourteen."

"Are you not curious who the groom shall be?"

"What does it matter?" I tried to appear uninterested, yet I had already heard the rumors and knew her answer would matter a great deal.

"'Tis Henry Montgomery."

I did not respond for a moment, praying the rumor was not true yet unable to deny what I had long suspected. "But he is three and twenty," I said as a way to cover my true feelings.

"And what is nine years?" Sophia asked, lifting her bare shoulder. "Henry is one of the youngest burgesses ever to grace the house—not to mention a newly elected assembly clerk—and Governor Dunmore has high hopes for him. There are tight bonds between their families that transcend the age difference."

"She's still a child." Even as the words came out of my mouth, I knew they would mean nothing to Sophia. We both knew of younger girls marrying. At the age of nineteen—almost twenty—I was deemed an old maid, but there had been little time to worry about such things while running the printing press.

"I have heard they intend to wait," Sophia said, "for a year or more, until this business with the rebels dies down."

A year? How I wished to tell Sophia that we would not see the end of the rebellion for almost a decade, but of course I could not.

"Do you think they're discussing the terms of the agreement now?" Sophia asked as she tipped her head in contemplation. "He does not look pleased, if they are."

No, Henry did not look pleased. His eyes were hooded, and his forehead was pressed into a frown. How I wished to ask him if it were true. It would make sense for their families' sakes, but it went against everything that made sense to me.

Henry's gaze locked on mine, and his countenance softened. I longed to tell him he did not have to do anything he did not want to do, but I wasn't foolish. How many of us were allowed to do the things we truly wanted? Even in my 1914 life, I was rarely at my leisure to go and do as I pleased. Mama claimed that in the 1990s, things were much different. Women were doctors and lawyers and professors. Some were even in the clergy—had even gone to outer space, though I could hardly believe such a thing. In the future, people were not dependent on one another for their lives like we were in 1774 and even 1914. Marriage was a necessity to boost one's social standing, to solidify family ties, to have security and purpose—all things Henry's family would desire for him.

"It looks as if he's coming this way." Sophia ran her gloved hand down the stiff stomacher of her rose-colored silk gown. It was flawless, just as she was flawless, her curls in perfect order.

Henry crossed the ballroom toward us. The violinist was tuning his strings, and Lord Dunmore was escorting his wife into the middle of the room to open the ball with a minuet.

Henry came to stop in front of us. While he bowed, Sophia and I offered curtsies.

"Good evening," he said. "How do you do, Miss Charlton?"

"I'm well, my lord," Sophia said as she straightened from her curtsy. She addressed Henry properly, though I knew how much he detested such things. He had been born and raised on American soil, and his heart belonged to her cause. Ever since I could remember, he had made his position on the nobility plain—at least to me. He felt, like many others, that there was no place for the aristocracy in America.

I agreed, which made my path in 1914 all the more ironic and disheartening.

Henry turned to me. "I believe I requested the honor of a dance, Miss Conant. Will you allow me the pleasure?"

My smile was quick and, I daresay, radiant. The first dance of the evening was the most important for status and social standing. It would be led by Governor Dunmore and his wife, and each couple would follow them in descending order of importance. Henry would be near the front of the line. To be asked by him was truly an honor. "Indeed, I will."

He took my hand and led me to the center of the room, the full skirts of my gown brushing against his legs as we went. Governor and Lady Dunmore looked in our direction, as did Henry's parents, who had also joined the dance. Governor Dunmore raised his eyebrow at me, while Lady Dunmore's look was more curious than condescending. I was sure they did not know me, since we had not had an occasion to cross paths.

But Henry's parents did know me—had known me since I was a child.

And they did not look pleased to see me on Henry's arm.

# 2

LONDON, ENGLAND
MAY 5, 1914

The following morning, I lay in bed for several minutes with my eyes closed, not wanting to open them and face the day ahead. I languished in the thick feather bed, remembering Henry's brilliant blue eyes as he smiled at me throughout the previous evening. Ours was a deep friendship that had spanned a lifetime and came easily to us both. There were very few relationships I found as easy to navigate as ours.

A knock at the door was all the warning my lady's maid, Edith, offered before she entered my well-appointed bedchamber.

"Good morning," she said in her cheerful Irish lilt. "I've brought the post, and there's a letter from your father."

I opened my eyes at the news. My bedroom in the rented townhouse on Berkeley Square was lavish. The four-poster bed was tall and imposing, yet its size did not dominate the large room.

Edith presented the letter to me with a grin, knowing how much I would enjoy a message from Father. I took it, eager to hear news from home. While I tore open the seal, she brought my breakfast tray to the bed and placed it over my lap, humming an Irish folk song I had heard before. The tray was laden with fresh tea, steaming scones, and strawberry jam. My life in 1914 was so different from my life in 1774. Here, I was waited upon by servants and spent my days pursuing pointless social obligations. Though some might imagine the life I led was delightful, I longed for a purpose like I had in Williamsburg.

As Edith left my bedside to choose the gown I would wear that day, I savored Father's words.

*April 29, 1914*

*My Dearest Libby,*

*I received the telegram that you and Mother arrived safely in London. I am relieved to hear the news. I had so hoped to spend the summer in Newport with you, picking seashells as we used to do when you were small, but I understand your mother's desire to have a season in London after your two successful seasons in New York. We must strike while the iron is hot, so to speak. I hope you enjoy yourself and bring back many wonderful memories to cherish in your heart for all time. Please greet your mother for me and enjoy your adventures.*

*Lovingly, Father*

It was a short note, quickly scrawled. I hadn't seen him in two weeks, not since we left New York City on the RMS *Lusitania*, and I missed him already.

"Is it good news?" Edith asked as she came out of my closet with a gown in hand.

"He wishes me well and is pleased to hear that we've arrived safely."

Her smile was warm as she made her way back into the closet. Edith had a soft spot in her heart for my father, as did most of the staff.

I folded his letter and gently returned it to its envelope. My heart squeezed at the knowledge that in just thirteen months' time, on my twenty-first birthday, I would leave him forever. To those in this life, I would simply die. My 1914 body would remain here, while my consciousness would return to 1774 and stay there for good. It was a strange reality, but one I had been aware of since I was very small.

I didn't want to think about that today—or any other day, for that matter. Father and Edith would mourn my death, but what was I to do? I was desperately needed in 1774. My mama and sisters depended upon me, and I longed to be part of a life that truly mattered.

Unlike this existence, where I was pampered, pressed, and polished to perfection—with little purpose beyond being an ornament.

My bedroom door opened for the second time that morning, and Mother Wells entered. She was my second birth mother, though she was not a time-crosser. She had no idea who I truly was, nor did she ever stop to care. I was her only child, and I had always known I was a great disappointment to her. I should have been born a male to take over my father's business and fortune, but I was not. So she made do with what she'd been given.

I sat up straighter at her arrival. "I did not expect to see you this early."

"Good morning, my pet," she said with a smile that didn't reach her grey eyes. "I'm here to hurry Edith along."

Edith must have heard our exchange, because she exited my dressing room with a pair of shoes in her hands. Her sweet smile had dimmed.

"There you are," Mother said to her. "I need Elizabeth to

be ready in an hour. We have a full schedule today and cannot be late for our first meeting."

"Yes, ma'am." Edith curtsied timidly, the tune gone from her lips. She lifted the gown she had selected. "Will this do?"

Mother shook her head. "I'd like her to wear the pink walking suit today."

Edith nodded once and scurried back to my closet. She'd been afraid of my mother since she'd come to work for us as an orphan at the age of twelve. Mother did not encourage any familiarity or affection with the staff and treated them with the same cool indifference she showed me. Edith had been serving us for over ten years and had become my lady's maid when I turned eighteen.

Mother approached the bed and lifted the breakfast tray off my lap.

I reached for one of the biscuits. "I've not finished my break—"

"We don't have time to dawdle this morning." Mother set the tray on a nearby table and then pulled the blankets off me, tossing them at my feet.

The chill penetrated my thin nightgown. "Where are we going?"

"You needn't worry about that now." Mother went to my vanity and pushed things around until she found the hairbrush. "We don't have time to chat either."

Edith brought out the pink walking suit, the one I hated above all the other gowns Mother had ordered for me before we left New York. Thirty-five gowns had packed my steamer trunks, with matching stockings, hats, gloves, and jewels. They were extravagant and excessive—nothing like my gowns in 1774.

"I detest the pink one," I said as I stepped out of the bed. "I don't think—"

"It's not your job to think, Elizabeth. It's your job to obey."

How many times had I heard her tell me that?

The stark contrast between Abigail Wells and Theodosia Conant, my marked mother, had been jarring as a child. Where one was warm, loving, and understanding, the other was cold, distant, and impenetrable. I struggled to understand how the harsh and demanding Abigail Wells had ever captured the heart of the man I called Father. Adam Wells was as good as they came, a self-made man who had earned his fortune in shipping along the Mississippi River in St. Louis. He had moved to New York to further his interests when he met Abigail and fell in love. By the time I came along, they were already bitter toward one another. And while Father had been working to increase his wealth, Abigail had been working to increase her status. New money was not the same as old money, and no matter how large our homes on Fifth Avenue or in Newport, no matter how lavish our lifestyle, Abigail was still dirt beneath the feet of the old set.

And it drove her to distraction.

I was simply a rung on the ladder of Abigail's success. A pawn to be used to further her ambitions. But I was not a pawn to Father. He adored me and I adored him, which was probably why Mother Wells hated me so much. Though Father was kind to Mother, he no longer looked at her with love. Time and circumstances had hardened their hearts toward one another, which was all the more reason I mourned leaving him behind. He would be alone with her, and the very thought made me want to weep.

Yet how was I supposed to stay when my family and my country needed me in 1774?

Soon Edith had me wrapped in the pink walking suit with a large hat upon my brown curls. The ensemble properly covered me from neck to foot. The dress was well-constructed and of the best quality, but it did not reflect my personality or my preferences. Though I could not deny it showed off every asset I possessed, which was Mother's intent, no doubt. The hobble skirt was so tight, I couldn't imagine walking a great distance in the gown.

I stood in front of the mirror. I looked exactly the same in 1914 as I did in 1774. The same green eyes with heavy lashes, the same curly brown hair, the same cheekbones and slender waist. I was one person, one conscious mind, in a set of identical twin bodies. But what happened to me in one body did not happen to me in the other. If I was sick with influenza in 1914, I woke up perfectly healthy in 1774. If I broke my arm in 1774, I did not have the same affliction in 1914. It was simply my conscious mind that traveled back and forth, accumulating experiences from each time path to create one unique me.

In 1774, my name was Elizabeth Conant, but my mama had called me Libby from birth. In 1914, I was Anna Elizabeth Wells and had been called Anna until I was almost five, when I asked to be called Libby. Father had obliged, but Mother refused to call me anything other than Anna. After years of fighting with her, she had offered a rare concession and agreed to call me by my second name, Elizabeth. It was not what I wanted, but it was more than she usually gave.

I left my room and took small steps down the wide hall to the grand staircase. Our rented townhome was the best that money could buy, as was everything in our lives.

"The driver is waiting," Mother said as she stood by the front door, gloves on, hat in place, and a fierce determination in her eyes. Her clothes were the height of fashion and expertly tailored. She was not a beautiful woman but merely average, which she detested, so she masked her plainness with style.

I still had no idea where we were going, but she would not tell me until she was ready for me to know.

We didn't drive far before we stopped outside a townhouse very similar to our own. It had been less than a mile, but Mother would never deign to walk more than a city block. And with the gown I was wearing, I was thankful. Though my bodices in 1774 were tight and constricting, at least my skirts were full and wide.

The driver helped us out of the automobile, and we crossed the short distance to the front door. Mother rang the bell and then pulled a calling card from her reticule.

"May I ask who we are meeting?" I said.

"Lady Paget, of course."

Lady Paget? She was an American heiress who had married into the aristocracy. Her fame as a London socialite was well-documented in the New York newspapers. But why were we meeting with Lady Paget? Did Mother know her?

A butler appeared at the door and welcomed us into the foyer. He took Mother's calling card and asked us to wait.

We stood in awkward silence, as we always did, and I bore up under her disapproving eye.

When I was a teenager, I had decided that Mother Wells was incapable of love. It was the only way I could ease the ache in my heart from her constant rejection and disappointment in me. I had to remind myself of it even now.

"Wipe that frown off your brow," she told me, "and stand up straight. Really, Elizabeth." She shook her head, her mouth tight with dismay. "Have I taught you nothing?"

I well remembered the straightening rod fashioned for me as a child and strapped to my back for hours on end. I still bore the scars from the chaffing along my lower back. I had often cried myself to sleep in those days—but Mama had always been there, on the other side of each day, to comfort and soothe me, promising that one day it would all end.

That thought gave me courage to endure today.

"Lady Paget will see you now," the butler said as he appeared in the hall.

He led us to a sitting room facing the street. An older woman rose and greeted us.

"Hello, Mrs. Wells," Lady Paget said. "How nice of you to come."

"It was kind of you to agree to meet with us."

"Anything for my American friends." Lady Paget wore a pair of beautiful diamond earrings that looked out of place against the simple style of her morning gown. "And is this Miss Wells?"

"Yes, this is Anna Elizabeth."

I stepped forward dutifully, as I had been trained, and offered a delicate curtsy. "How do you do, Lady Paget?"

"My," the lady said, "she's as beautiful as I've been told."

My cheeks warmed under her praise.

"And I've heard you go by Libby?" Lady Paget asked.

I liked her immediately. "Yes, my lady."

"How very charming."

We were offered tea and enjoyed several minutes of talk about New York. Lady Paget had not been home in some time and seemed to crave our stories. I was having a surprisingly good time when Lady Paget finally landed on the purpose of our call.

"Your mother tells me you're eager to enter London society."

I lowered my teacup but didn't say a word. I was not eager to be here at all. Mother had torn me from the work I was doing for the suffragette movement in New York City. It was one of the only things I truly cared about in this path—not tea parties and balls in London. I had barely tolerated them in New York the past two seasons as Mother paraded me about. But I could not say these things to my hostess.

"I've secured several invitations for you, Libby." Lady Paget looked very pleased with herself. "In no time at all, you'll be meeting the most eligible bachelors that England has to offer."

"What a lovely thought," Mother said.

"You know," Lady Paget continued, "you're not the first American heiress searching to purchase a title." She smiled, as if it were our little secret. "Dozens and dozens of young ladies have successfully integrated into the English aristocracy. Dollar princesses, they're called." She laughed. "One would think the nobility would frown upon such things, but the truth is that our kind have saved the crumbling façades of countless manor houses throughout the commonwealth."

My heart began to pound as she continued to talk about marriages between American women and English lords. To gain social standing, American families had been marrying their daughters into the English aristocracy, while providing their new sons-in-law with lavish dowries to save their estates from ruin. I had no wish to save anything in England. My patriotic heart was fighting a war against this very empire in 1774. These two women were in pursuit of the very thing their ancestors had fought against.

"You need not worry," Lady Paget said to Mother. "With Libby's grace and beauty, plus her father's fortune, she will have no trouble finding an earl or a viscount in need of a wife." She chuckled. "Perhaps even a duke."

I wanted to cry out that she was wrong, that I had no wish to marry anyone in 1914. I was simply biding my time until my twenty-first birthday, and then I would be gone from here forever.

But at the look of triumph in Mother Wells's eyes, the words stuck in my throat. She desired social status, and what better way to achieve it than to have her daughter marry a duke?

⁂

I didn't speak to Mother as we made our way back to Berkeley Square to change for a luncheon, but she didn't seem to notice. Her gaze was fixed outside the automobile as we maneuvered toward our townhouse, and I was certain her mind was concocting elaborate plans.

When we entered the house and the butler had left with our

wraps, I finally turned to her. "Is this why you've brought me here?"

"Of course." She scoffed as if I were an imbecile.

"Why didn't you tell me?" Mother had planned this trip for months, and not once had she mentioned that it would be a husband-hunting adventure.

"So you could moan and sulk about?" She walked toward the stairs. "Really, Elizabeth, do you think I'm stupid? You've made it very clear that you have no interest in getting married. If I had told you my intent for this trip, you would have whined to your father, and he would have been weak enough to give in to you."

"I have a right to choose my own fate."

Mother stopped, her hand on the marble railing. She turned to me, pity and condescension on her face. "I find it humorous that you think so. What woman has the right to choose her own fate? Do you think I like to play these games? Grapple for social status, when I know I deserve it and so much more? This is the hand you have been dealt, and I refuse to let you fold now."

Frustration welled up in my gut, and I balled my gloved hands into fists. In moments like this, I wanted to tell her the truth—that I did have control, and that in thirteen months I would wield that control and never return.

But she would think me mad and send me to an asylum, I was sure of it.

"Why did you make me endure two seasons in New York before coming here?" It had all been a waste of time. There had been wealthy and influential men interested in pursuing me, but she turned her back on all of them. If she was intent on marrying me off, why not stay in America?

"It was an opportunity for you to learn everything you'd need to know for this one glorious London season. The one that truly matters. For it is here that you will receive the title that will open doors for us in New York. It's as simple as that."

Without another word, she ascended the stairs and disappeared into her bedchamber.

Slowly, my anger receded, but it did not disappear completely. No matter what she said, I did have control. I could play the cards she set before me. But this was one game I would not let her win. When she realized I was serious, we would board a ship and return to New York. Perhaps, if I did a good job of frustrating her plans, we could return in time for the end of the Newport season. It was the one bright spot in my otherwise tedious existence in 1914.

I went up to my room and found Edith already laying out my afternoon gown, another tune on her lips. She smiled at me, her hazel eyes as jolly as ever. Tight ginger curls peeked out from under her white cap and made the matching freckles across her nose appear brighter than usual. I marveled that she was always so cheerful when her existence was more tedious than mine. It challenged me to be a better person, though at the moment I struggled.

Her smile disappeared when she saw my face. "Is something wrong?"

Edith was my best friend in this path. It didn't matter to me that she was my lady's maid. We had grown up together, and she had always been a trusted confidante. We were like sisters, when Mother Wells was not present, and I never insisted she treat me otherwise. She was part of my intimate world and therefore knew the ins and outs of my daily life—though she knew nothing about my time-crossing. I had wanted to tell her the truth so many times, but I knew she would struggle to understand. *I* struggled to understand some days.

"Mother is determined to find me an English husband and saddle me with a title."

Edith nodded. "I suspected as much."

My mouth slipped open. "Why didn't you tell me?"

"How could you not know?" She took my gloves and frowned. "I didn't think it necessary to state the obvious."

"I would never have agreed to come if I had known."

She lifted a brow lined with pity. "Did you really have a choice?" I hated seeing her pity—hated seeing the pity on the faces of the other servants when Mother Wells mistreated me. Of course, I didn't have a choice. Once Mother made up her mind, there was little I could do to change it.

With an encouraging smile, she lifted a gown off the chair and presented it to me. "We're here now, so we might as well make the best of it. What do you think of this dress for the luncheon?"

I shrugged, feeling exhausted, though the day was young.

"We have a bit of time." She placed her hand on my arm and squeezed it. "Why don't you have a quick lie-down?"

I nodded, wishing I could fall asleep right now and wake up in 1774, bypassing all the plans my mother had for me today. But if I fell asleep before midnight, I would just wake up in this same time and space. I never crossed over until after the midnight hour. If I stayed awake past midnight, as was common during balls and soirees, I would remain in this timeline until I fell asleep.

When I was little, I had tried to stay awake for as long as possible in the 1700s, hoping I could skip a day in my 1900s timeline, but it never worked. As soon as I fell asleep, I woke up the next day in the 1900s. There was nothing I could do to change my fate until my twenty-first birthday.

On that day, according to Mama, whatever timeline I wanted to remain in forever was the one I could stay awake in past midnight—and I would never wake up in the other again.

I could not wait to ring in the midnight hour on June 19, 1775, and never have to return to the twentieth century again.

# 3

WILLIAMSBURG, VIRGINIA
MAY 6, 1774

The following morning, I opened my eyes and let out a long exhale. A pink glow tinged the eastern horizon just outside my bedroom window, promising another beautiful day in Williamsburg. Beside me, Rebecca and Hannah cuddled on the large bed. Rebecca's feet were wrapped around my legs for warmth. I turned onto my side, laid my arm across her shoulder, and caressed Hannah's soft cheek. They were so sweet and helpless. A scar near Hannah's eyebrow hinted at her penchant for climbing trees and jumping rocks in the streams near town.

I could not stomach the thought of Mister Jennings taking either one of them as an indentured servant. There were no laws to protect them from whatever he had in mind. I would lay down my life for them before I let that happen. Live out the rest of my days in the public gaol, if need be.

Or run the printing press, sacrificing all else, to ensure that the girls and Mama were safe.

Hannah opened her eyes and blinked away the sleep. At eight, she was precocious and curious. Her riotous blond curls refused to be contained, and her dimples charmed even the crossest merchant on Duke of Gloucester Street.

"Morning, Libby," she said with a contented sigh as her green eyes closed again and she seemed to drift back to sleep. Her complete trust in my ability to protect her and provide for her pierced my heart. What if I failed them? The harsh realities of life in the colonies were always close at hand.

"Wake up, little one," I said to her. "You have chores to do, and then Mama will have you work on your sums."

"Must I?" Instead of getting out of bed, she burrowed under the quilt even farther. "I'd much rather play make-believe and paint pictures today."

I smiled, wondering what amazing things Hannah and Rebecca would do with their lives. They were both strong, independent girls. Mama, with her twentieth-century thinking, was quick to let them have their lead. She never squashed their ambitions or dreams—on the contrary, she put ideas into their heads that far surpassed anything I'd ever heard of women accomplishing in the eighteenth century.

Sometimes I questioned if Mama was doing a disservice to our hearts and minds when the world was not ready for our ideas. But time—and life—would take on a course of its own. God had not made a mistake by giving Mama or me this gift. Perhaps it was part of His plan for us to push boundaries in the eighteenth century long before the world was ready.

I tossed the quilt aside and rose to dress. Soon the girls were out of bed, and the three of us joined Mama in the sitting room for breakfast. Mariah had been awake for hours and had a warm meal on the table. A baked Indian pudding, pork sausages, and pickled beets awaited us. She was known as the best cook in Williamsburg. Though we had given her little to work with lately, she still found a way to fill our table with more than enough to eat. She had taught me everything I knew about cooking, though I rarely had time to put it to good use since Papa's illness. I generally spent Monday through Saturday in the print shop, from sunup to sundown most days, editing the newspaper. It went to print on Thursdays, which was the only day my work eased enough to help Mama with the girls.

"Please clear the table," Mama said to Rebecca and Hannah the moment breakfast was done, "and then see if Mariah has any work for you in the kitchen this morning."

Grumbling, the girls obeyed and were soon out of the sitting room.

The moment they were gone, Mama turned to me. "What's wrong?"

As much as I tried to hide things from Mama, she could always see through my façade. I didn't want to burden her with Mother Wells's plans, but my heart was still heavy from the visit we'd had with Lady Paget yesterday.

The Windsor chair I sat upon suddenly felt uncomfortable beneath my padded skirts. "I have discovered that Mother Wells brought me to England to find me a titled husband." I still couldn't stomach the idea. "She introduced me to a woman named Lady Paget who is a matchmaker between American heiresses and English lords."

"And Mother Wells planned this?"

"Yes." I clenched my hands in frustration. "She said the last two seasons in New York were preparing me for this one. Lady Paget has secured several desirable invitations for me during the London season."

Mama nodded slowly, her eyes sad. It had been heartbreaking for her to watch me struggle, powerless to protect me from Mother Wells.

"We've talked about this, Libby," she said gently. "We knew that as soon as you turned eighteen, she would put her plans into action."

"Yes, but I'm almost twenty. I thought she had tired of her plans."

"You cannot believe she would give up so easily. Now it makes sense why she turned down so many of your beaux in New York."

I stood, no longer able to sit on the hard wooden chair. Outside, the world was waking up, and people were beginning their workday. Soon customers would arrive at the office to submit advertisements, articles, and opinion pieces. I would spend much of the day editing them and deciding which ones we would print. We lived by Papa's motto for the newspaper, which was *Open to ALL PARTIES, but Influenced by NONE.* It was a motto I tried to emulate, but I was finding it harder and harder as the revolution drew near. My thoughts and opinions were influenced by many people and events, but especially by the foreknowledge I possessed from the future. How could it not be?

"I have only thirteen months to endure her scheming," I said to Mama, trying to strengthen my resolve and courage. "I can put off her plans until then."

"Can you?" Mama rose from her chair and joined me at the window. "Libby." She paused and looked down at her ink-stained hands, marked with the time and space she occupied. "We've often discussed your desire to stay in 1774, but—"

"There is no *but*," I said passionately, surprising both Mama and myself. "I will not leave you."

Mama put her hand on my arm to calm me, a smile on her lips. "I wasn't suggesting you stay in 1914. I was simply telling you that you must be careful. There are reasons you would choose 1914—"

"I would never choose 1914."

She rubbed my arm and sighed. "Try to push off Mother Wells's plans for as long as possible. Thirteen months is not long, but it can make all the difference for your future."

I wished with all my heart that my twenty-first birthday was next month and not next year. I had been waiting my whole life to live and breathe like a normal human being. The idea of waking up, day after day, on just one path seemed like a dream that was too good to be true. Though I was only nineteen, I had lived for almost forty years.

"Now," Mama said, "it's time to get to work. Louis and Glen are finishing up the forms the House of Burgesses requested yesterday."

Louis Preston was the journeyman who had been Papa's apprentice since he was twelve. He lived in a small room connected to the printing room with Glen, the new apprentice under Louis's teaching. They ate in the kitchen with Mariah and Abraham before we had our breakfast and were already at work in the print shop.

"After the forms have been delivered," Mama continued, "we need to start printing broadsheets for the governor. Louis stayed up late last night working on the proof. You will need to approve it before we make copies."

At the mention of the burgesses, I thought of Henry. Because of his family's merchant business, he spent months at a time away from Virginia. His days in Williamsburg were so few, and I longed to spend as much time in his company as possible. I had a mountain of work awaiting me, but it could wait. "I will run the forms to the capitol."

"There's no need," she said. "It's Glen's job to make deliveries."

"'Tis a lovely day, and I would enjoy stretching my legs. Besides, you know how I love the excitement at the capitol during the assemblies." I had always longed to be a burgess but knew it was out of the question. There had never been a female burgess and would not be a female legislative representative until 1895 in Colorado. Working for the suffragette movement in 1914 made me very aware of the women fighting for a place in politics. Several women were planning to run for state seats, but there had yet to be a woman in a federal position. To even contemplate a place in the 1774 Virginia House of Burgesses was laughable.

"The excitement at the capitol?" Mama asked. "Or the excitement in seeing one burgess in particular? Mayhap the assembly clerk?"

Henry had been elected as the clerk for the 1774 assembly—all the more reason I wanted to take the forms to the capitol. He would be the person to accept the delivery.

I couldn't hide the truth from Mama, though she would not approve. She was aware of Lord Ashbury's plans for Henry's future, and they did not include me.

"His father is a loyalist, Libby," she said, as if I didn't know.

The bell over the front door rang, indicating the arrival of a customer.

Mama moved away from the window and started toward the door. "We have no place in our lives for Henry Montgomery. As much as I want to encourage you to follow your heart, you must see the foolishness in pursuing your friendship with him. You're not children anymore. His family made their feelings toward us known long ago."

She was right, but my heart would not accept her words.

"I can still be his friend," I said. It was enough. It would have to be enough.

Mama sighed. "See if the forms are finished and then deliver them yourself. But be careful, Libby. We're approaching the most difficult years of our lives, and we must be vigilant."

She left the sitting room and greeted the customer in the front hall.

Their voices faded as they entered the office, and I was left alone with my thoughts.

I was walking a precarious tightrope between two very different worlds, with many unanswered questions. Yet there was one thing I knew for certain: my traitorous heart belonged to

Henry Montgomery, no matter how much I tried to deny it or how impossible the situation might be.

The one-story press room sat at the back of our two-story brick home and had a lean-to roof connecting them. Louis and Glen spent twelve to fourteen hours a day wetting the paper, setting type, applying ink, running the press, and then drying the pages after the ink was applied. The room smelled like linen and ink and had all the trappings necessary for running a printing press hanging from the walls or stacked in an orderly fashion around the room. The weekly newspaper was drying on ropes strung from wall to wall.

I didn't spend much time in the press room, since my work required me to be in the office for most of the day, but I loved to watch the process unfold. It was comforting and reminded me of Papa. His handprint was still on the wall near the door, accidentally left when he had tripped and put his hand out to break his fall. He had prided himself on a clean press room, but before he could have the mark painted over, he had become ill, and Mama and I had kept the handprint as a reminder. He had left his mark on our lives and on the lives of all those who lived in Williamsburg.

Would I leave such an indelible mark?

I put my hand over the print, remembering his large presence. He had been kind yet demanding and had ruled our home with a firm set of principles. Mama had her ways of softening him, but he had very much been a man shaped by his time and place. I missed him dearly, though I was proud of the way Mama and I kept his vision and dreams alive.

"Good day, Libby," Louis said when he spied me in the room. He was a tall man, just twenty years of age. He wore spectacles as he set the type, but he took them off and straightened. In one more year, he would be old enough to venture forth on his own and start his own printing shop, if he so desired.

It did not fail to frustrate me that at the age of twenty, in the eyes of society, he was on the cusp of beginning his manhood. Whereas I, at the same age, was considered past my prime and facing a future as an old maid.

Glen was busy putting several small bundles of rags together. We purchased rags from customers and then sold them to the papermakers in England. The plant fibers inside the rags were turned into pulp and used to make paper, which was imported into the colonies. Papa had always purchased all of our supplies from England through Mister Jennings, though I was now purchasing from a different merchant. I hated being dependent on England. There were paper and ink makers in America, but it had always been cheaper to purchase supplies overseas. Soon, we would have no choice but to start relying on other colonies to supply our needs.

"Are you looking for something?" Louis asked me. He wore a leather apron over his breeches and waistcoat. Louis had lived with us for the past eight years, but he was not a member of the family, nor was he treated as such. He ate with us only on very special occasions and spent his leisure time in his room or at a tavern in town. He had been a bit enamored with me when we were younger, and I had spent much of my days trying to avoid him.

"Do you have the forms ready for the capitol?" I asked.

He nodded at a stack of papers on a workbench near the door. "We stayed up most of the night to meet the request. Glen will deliver them when he's finished with the rags."

"There's no need." I walked to the table to inspect the forms. "I have a few errands this morning and am happy to deliver them myself."

"You?" His eyebrows rose high, probably surprised that I would leave my other work to attend to such a mundane task.

"Making a delivery is not beneath my abilities." I tried to

make my voice sound light, though I didn't like to be questioned by my journeyman. "Please have the broadsheet proof ready for me when I return."

Louis stared at me for a moment, and I wondered if he would question me further. I knew he felt the sting of being employed by two women, one younger than him. I'm sure he believed he was capable of being the master of his own printing press, yet he had to answer to me. It was an unenviable position for any man, but for a man like Louis, it was doubly so. His pride was often his biggest stumbling block. But his help was necessary for Mama and me to continue our business, so we tried to pacify him. Perhaps in a year or two, when Mama and I had more experience, we could hire someone else to take over the printing.

"As you wish," he finally said.

I took the forms, which had been tied together with twine, and started to leave the room, but Louis stopped me.

"Libby?"

I turned back to face him and found he had come out from behind the press. "Aye?"

"I was wondering . . ." He wiped his hands on a soiled rag and tossed it onto the workbench. "Mayhap you'll allow me to escort you to the play tonight."

With the arrival of the burgesses and their families, the playhouse located on the Palace Green was offering a nightly performance of *Love in a Village*, a ballad opera I had already seen. I had no wish to see it again, nor did I wish to spend an evening with Louis. Our relationship was that of employer and employee, and it would remain so.

"Thank you for the invitation," I said, "but I must decline. I will be working late this evening."

"Then another night this week?"

Why did he want to take me to the play? I had shown no interest in spending time with him beyond the press room.

He took a step closer to me, and I could smell his body odor, which he had tried to mask with bay rum. It stung my nose, making me long for the deodorants available in my other path. Though not all was pleasant in the twentieth century, the sanitary practices were a vast improvement to life in the colonies. Mama and I both followed good hygiene, understanding that it promoted health and well-being. It wasn't always practical, since a bath required toting water from the well, heating it on the stove, and filling a tub. But we took more baths than our friends and neighbors, who were still under the false belief that frequent bathing could lead to premature death.

"I have tried to find a time to speak to you in private." He glanced at Glen, who seemed oblivious to our conversation. "I would like to court you, Libby. And I would like to start soon. I've waited to speak, since you've been in mourning, but time is of the essence. You're not getting any younger."

My mouth slipped open, but I could not speak.

"It makes the most sense, don't you see?" he asked. "I will arrive at my maturity next year and will be ready to take over the printing shop. You are in need of a husband to guide your hand and your business. I am well-suited to both jobs."

I was still speechless. How long had he been contemplating this proposition?

He studied me as I took a step back.

"I have no wish to marry you, Louis." I didn't want to be unkind, but he must know where I stood on this issue. "I am quite capable of running this business with my mother, and neither of us needs a man's help. I believe we've proven this over and over."

His eyes hardened. I was speaking a truth he was not ready to accept. "Are you not worried about what the others are saying about you?" he asked.

I shook my head, uncertain what he had heard, though it mattered little.

"Your marriage opportunities are dwindling, Libby, and you

have no assurance that you'll be able to care for your mother and sisters much longer. If Mister Archer has his way, you will lose the contract, and he will drive you out of business."

Mister Archer was the owner of the *Williamsburg Weekly Journal*. He had possessed the public printing contract last year, and we had taken it from him.

"When he does," Louis continued, "he has promised me a job." He studied me with his calculating eyes. "That is, unless I have a reason to fight for this print shop."

I pressed my lips together. After all these years, Louis was playing his hand. But I had fought too long and too hard to give up now. I lifted my chin. "Have the proof ready for me when I return."

I didn't wait for him to reply but left the press room and entered the front hall, my heart pounding hard. The forms were heavy in my hands as I exited the house, my bonnet forgotten in my need to be free of the printing shop. I hated that Louis was threatening me and trying to force my hand in marriage. Had I been my father's son, Louis would never have considered pressuring me that way.

My face burned with embarrassment and anger as I strode to the capitol at the end of Duke of Gloucester Street. The ten-minute walk gave me enough time to cool my temper and remember why I had set out on this errand.

As I entered the capitol, the piazza was empty, and disappointment weighed down my spirits. No doubt the burgesses were in session. If Glen had delivered the forms, he could have stepped into the house chamber quietly. If I entered, it would disrupt the entire meeting.

The door to the chamber opened, and my pulse beat at the sight of Henry. His surprise at seeing me was just as stunning. The serious frown upon his face disappeared, and a smile lit up his blue eyes.

"Libby," he said, coming to me as the door to the chamber

closed. "I was just stepping out to get more ink. What are you doing here?"

"I've come to deliver the forms you ordered." I lifted them in my hands.

"You couldn't send your boy to do that?"

"I could—but I was out and decided to bring them myself." There were so many things I longed to ask Henry about the meeting just beyond the closed door, yet it would not be appropriate.

His smile broadened, and he took the forms from me. "I'm happy 'twas you who came. Thank you."

We stood in the quiet for a moment, and neither of us spoke. I should have left, but I didn't want to go so soon.

"How is the assembly progressing?" I asked.

He shook his head, his countenance heavy. "I fear this thing will not end well in Boston, but we cannot allow England's tyranny to prevail."

He glanced over his shoulder at the closed door and then gently cupped my elbow to move me toward a corner in the open-air piazza. The intimate act filled my midsection with warmth.

"You cannot breathe a word of this until we've voted and it's been shared with you through proper means," he said in a low tone, his eyes imploring mine for secrecy.

"Of course," I whispered back. I would hold any secret Henry entrusted to me.

"There's been a call for a day of solidarity with Boston. We've been meeting at the Raleigh Tavern, and we all agree we cannot ignore their troubles, for they are the troubles of all British subjects in America."

"What will you do?"

"As soon as we're able, we will put forth a petition to the assembly, calling for a day of fasting and prayer on June the first, the day the port closes in Boston."

"But if you do that, you will make your positions known, and people will be forced to choose whether they are for you or against you."

"Aye." He nodded, his eyes solemn.

"And what of your father?" I asked, knowing Lord Ashbury did not support the Patriots' cause.

Henry did not respond immediately. I could see the war waging in his heart by the look in his eyes. "I will soon have no choice but to take sides, Libby. I do not believe that God will allow me to stay neutral, nor do I wish to. We are coming to a crossroads, and I will have to choose which way to go." He spoke as if he was trying to convince himself.

I put my hand on his forearm, wishing I could tell him how things would play out. "And what will you choose?" I whispered in the shadowed corridor of Williamsburg's capitol.

"I will have to choose freedom." His voice was heavy with the implications.

"And your father?"

He looked away, and I could imagine he was envisioning his family's country home, Edgewater Hall, and the property that was as much a part of him as the color of his eyes.

"I will try to spare him," he said, "but I must follow my own convictions. I long to please my father, but at what cost to my own beliefs?"

Henry had spent his entire life trying to please his father—which was one reason I was no longer invited to visit his home on the Palace Green. His family owned a beautiful house not far from the Governor's Palace. They stayed there whenever they were in Williamsburg on business, which wasn't often enough.

Our mothers had once been friends, and when Mama went to visit, I went along. But when Henry had turned seventeen and our childhood friendship had begun to change into something more, the invitations stopped. When I questioned Henry, he had told me his father felt it best if we didn't see each other again.

That had been six years ago.

I longed to ask him about Lady Catherine, Governor Dunmore's daughter. Would he try to please his father where she was concerned?

But it was none of my business to ask him such things.

I removed my hand from his forearm. "I'm sure you are needed in the assembly room. I will not keep you any longer. I will not tell anyone what you've told me."

Henry grinned, his earlier troubles vanishing from his gaze. He motioned toward the room behind him. "If any of them knew I was sharing secrets with the newspaper editor, I'd be tarred and feathered."

"Then it will be our secret."

Something sweet and gentle passed between us as we conspired together. As I watched Henry walk back into the assembly room, I wondered what secrets we would share, and my heart picked up that strange beat that echoed only for him.

# 4

**LONDON, ENGLAND**
**MAY 23, 1914**

London's ballrooms had become almost indistinguishable. Loud orchestras, elaborate gowns, fake laughter, and endless dancing greeted me at every turn. Mother Wells had displayed me from one ball to the next, single-minded in her quest for me to make a suitable match. Lady Paget had been true to her word and had secured some of the best invitations, but within the first week, I started to receive them of my own accord.

Tonight, three weeks after we had first met Lady Paget, I entered the ballroom at the Crewe House on Curzon Street, the first with any true distinction. The magnificent home was owned by the recently titled Marquess of Crewe and his wife, the marchioness. It was much larger than the other ballrooms we'd visited, and it dripped with gilded furnishings, ornate decorations, and, by Lady Paget's word, some of the most eligible bachelors in London.

"Tonight is the night," Mother said, moments after we were

formally announced to the assemblage. "I have heard this ball is one of the most significant of the Season. Every person of importance will be here. The Marquess of Crewe is not only the secretary of state for India, he is the Lord Privy Seal and the leader of the House of Lords. He's connected to the most powerful people in England—and you shall meet all of them. You must be on your very best behavior, Elizabeth. If there was ever a night for you to shine, it's this one."

I had done my best to thwart Mother's plans, though I refused to be rude or embarrassing. It was much easier to remain aloof and detached, not encouraging any particular attention. I detested spoiled, simpering debutantes and would not be one of them. Even here, so far removed from Williamsburg and Mama, I could not disconnect from the lessons of kindness and gentility she had taught me. Perhaps it was my only saving grace from the things I'd witnessed and learned at Mother Wells's knee.

"Ah, there is Lady Paget now." Mother led the way through the crush of people. A massive orchestra played on a stage at the far end of the room, and many people were already dancing. Perfume mingled with the smell of alcohol while tiaras, necklaces, and earrings glittered in the light of the chandeliers.

I recognized several people I had met at preceding balls and social events. Winston Churchill, whose mother was an American heiress, stood near the Marquess of Crewe. Lloyd George, chancellor of the exchequer, spoke to the prime minister, Herbert Henry Asquith. And Consuelo Vanderbilt Spencer-Churchill, the Duchess of Marlborough, was currently speaking to the Marchioness of Crewe. There were many others, people I recognized from the local newspapers, which I read every day. They fascinated me, these people in power, as they directed the fate of this nation. Despite my resolve to remain aloof, I couldn't hide my curiosity.

"Mrs. Wells," Lady Paget said as she lowered her fan and let it dangle from her wrist. Large, gaudy jewelry dripped from her earlobes, around her neck, and on her fingers. She turned away from the woman she was addressing to speak to Mother, clinking as she moved. "I'm so pleased you could attend tonight."

"It is our pleasure."

"And Libby." Lady Paget air-kissed each of my cheeks in greeting. "You look stunning this evening. The color of your gown makes your eyes simply shine."

I couldn't deny her compliment. The gown Mother had selected was the most beautiful thing I owned. Made of yards and yards of emerald-green silk with a high waist, a hobble skirt, and a black lace overskirt that flowed to a train behind me. It had a low décolletage and barely skimmed the tops of my black heeled shoes in the front. She had paired it with a black beaded headband and a pair of long emerald earrings.

"Thank you," I said to her.

"We must first present ourselves to the Marquess and Marchioness of Crewe," Lady Paget said to us, "and then I have a few other introductions to make before I hand you off to dance. Does that sound acceptable?"

Mother nodded. "Most acceptable."

As we moved through the ballroom, several people tried to capture Lady Paget's attention, their inquisitive gazes sliding to me, but she seemed just as single-minded as Mother. A part of me wondered why Lady Paget was being so helpful and friendly. She hardly knew us. She couldn't be doing this because of our American connection. Did she stand to gain something if a match was made? Was Mother paying her?

The thought sickened me, but I wouldn't be surprised. My mother had a lot to gain from marrying her daughter to an English aristocrat. I could envision her preening under the approval of Mamie Fish, Alva Belmont, and Theresa Fair Oelrichs, the triumvirate of New York Society, the women who had replaced Mrs. Astor to reign over the famed Four Hundred.

"Oh my," Lady Paget said as she stopped and lifted her fan.

"What?" Mother asked.

"He's here. He's come."

"Who?"

"The Most Honorable Marquess of Cumberland, Reginald Fairhaven." Lady Paget fanned her flushed face, glancing slyly at me. "Could we be so fortunate?"

"Indeed." Mother's voice was low and calculating. She had the latest copy of *Burke's Peerage, Baronetage and Knightage* in her desk at Berkeley Square, and she studied it religiously. The yearly publication was dedicated to the genealogy of aristocracy in England. No doubt Mother knew exactly who this man was, who his ancestors were, and where his ancestral home was located.

"He is one of the most sought-after bachelors in England at the moment," Lady Paget said, "rising in rank and social power. He's currently one of the Lords Commissioners of the Treasury and is at the prime minister's side almost constantly. It's rumored he is being groomed for higher political ambitions. His ancestral home is on the coastal moors near Whitby. It's quite extensive." She lifted her fan to cover her mouth. "It's also rumored that he is on the hunt for a wealthy heiress. Cumberland Hall is facing ruin if it's not saved, and that would reflect poorly upon his political ambitions."

Lady Paget and Mother both looked at me. I met their gazes with disinterest. What Lady Paget was hinting at was Lord Cumberland's need for money, and what better way to acquire it than to marry the daughter of a wealthy American? This Lord Cumberland meant nothing to me—the same as all the others they had introduced me to over the past three weeks. I wasn't interested in his crumbling manor house or his political ambitions.

"Oh, Elizabeth," Mother said, "I do wish you'd stop acting so bored. You stand to gain the most from a prosperous match. And just think—perhaps you could be married to the prime minister of England one day." Her eyes grew wide, and I could almost see the thoughts running through her mind.

What would I possibly gain by marrying a marquess or the future prime minister of England? Gooseflesh raced up my back at the very thought. How could I align myself with the nation we were fighting in my other path? I knew dozens of men in 1774 who were about to put their lives and fortunes in harm's way to seek independence from England—including Henry. It felt treasonous even to consider pursuing a man who represented everything I abhorred.

They were both looking at me expectantly, so I had to say something. I lifted a shoulder. "I have no wish to live on the coastal moors." I longed to say more—so much more—but it would be rude to Lady Paget, and Mother would never understand.

Mother simply turned up her nose and addressed her comrade-in-arms. "Will you introduce us, Lady Paget?"

"I daresay I will." Lady Paget lowered her fan again and smoothed the sides of her gown. A pink tinge of excitement filled her cheeks as she redirected our path.

Lady Paget had not pointed Lord Cumberland out to us, and standing in this mess of humanity, he could have been any number of gentlemen positioned around the room. Some were old, some were tall, some were fat, and some had red noses from too much drink. None of them caught my eye or my attention.

Boredom overwhelmed me, and I found my mind wandering to Henry, as it often did. We had not spoken since I had taken the forms to the capitol. I spent much of my time working and rarely attended the social events around Williamsburg. The burgesses had been meeting for almost three weeks, and their printing needs were more than I had anticipated. They had not yet announced their solidarity with Boston, though there were rumors aplenty.

"There," Lady Paget said under her breath, pulling me from my thoughts.

A gentleman stood alone in a black tailcoat with a white tie near one of the many fireplaces in the ballroom, almost as if he were waiting. The fireplace was not lit but was adorned with a wide garland of fresh-cut flowers and reeked of artificial perfume. He held a glass of dark amber liquid, which he sipped as his gaze found mine. His hair was so light brown that it was almost blond, and he wore a small mustache above his full upper lip. The eyes that watched our approach matched the color of his hair.

He let his dispassionate gaze slip over me from head to foot, as if assessing the purchase of a horse or an automobile, and a spark of interest straightened his spine.

"Lady Paget," he said as he set his glass on the mantel and gave his full attention to her. He took her gloved hand, with its sparkling diamond rings, and bowed over it. "How very nice to see you again."

"My lord." Lady Paget curtsied. "May I present my dear friend, Mrs. Wells from New York City?"

Her dear friend?

Lord Cumberland took Mother's hand and bowed over it. "It's a pleasure to meet you, Mrs. Wells."

Mother curtsied, one eyebrow raised in interest.

"Mrs. Wells, may I present the Most Honorable Marquess of Cumberland, Lord Reginald Fairhaven?"

"I'm honored, my lord," Mother said. "This is my daughter, Anna Elizabeth."

It was my turn to curtsy before Lord Cumberland, which I did as trained, slightly lifting the hem of my hobble skirt to make it easier. "My lord."

"Miss Wells." Lord Cumberland took my gloved hand and

bowed over it as well. "It's a pleasure to meet you. I've heard your name on everyone's lips this season."

"Only good things, I hope," Mother said with a purr.

"The very best." His smile was rakish, revealing a small space between his front teeth.

It was hard to decipher his age, though I would have placed him in his mid- to upper thirties—almost twice my age. He exuded great confidence and a bit of pomposity, though there was nothing distinctive about his appearance other than the small mustache I did not care for and the gap in his teeth.

"I hope you are enjoying your visit to England," he said to me.

"It's been—" How did I tell him it had been tedious and unpleasant? "Educational."

"How very boring." He chuckled, his aristocratic voice sounding snobbish. "Surely there is more to be had in England than an education."

Mother's eyes narrowed at me.

"Of course," I said, not wanting her ire. "We've met many wonderful people and visited several interesting places." I could find nothing else to comment upon and assumed an air of disinterest.

"Perhaps, if you'd allow me," Lord Cumberland said, his voice smooth, "I could plan a few outings for you and your mother, to show you the best that London has to offer."

"That would be marvelous." Mother eyed him openly. "How very kind of you."

"It would be my pleasure." He bowed again. "And, if it's not too much to ask, may I request the honor of a dance or two tonight, Miss Wells?"

I wanted to refuse him, but there was no possible way. "Of course."

"It was good to see you again, Lord Cumberland." Lady Paget's smile held a secret.

"And you." He nodded once, then took his glass off the

mantel, appearing to have completed whatever task he'd been given.

"If you'll excuse us," Lady Paget said, gathering Mother and me to herself like a hen collecting her wayward chicks. "I must present the Wellses to our host and hostess."

As we moved away from Lord Cumberland, I glanced back and found his eyes on me, calculating. He met my gaze, a half-smile on his face.

"Well," Lady Paget asked Mother, "will he do?"

"For my purposes?" Mother's voice was firm and unshakable. "Quite."

I turned back to focus on the path ahead, dread pooling in my stomach.

The automobile ride back to Berkeley Square was quick and silent over the bumpy cobblestone streets. Darkness blanketed us, suffocating me with its oppressive weight. It had rained during the ball, and everything glistened under the streetlamps. The scent of wet earth filled my nose, a pleasant change from the overpowering smells in the ballroom. We passed dozens of townhomes, each one dark and bleak on this cool evening.

Our driver dropped us off at the front door, and we walked up the wet steps to our house. All I wanted was to climb out of the heavy gown I wore, slip into my nightgown, and then bury myself beneath the down comforter on my bed so I could wake up in Williamsburg.

Rogers, our butler, opened the door and silently took our wraps. The front hall was lit with the faintest light, just enough for us to see our way to the stairs.

Not one word passed between Mother and me as we walked up the massive stairway. My room was to the right and hers was to the left, but when I turned to go my own way, her words stopped me.

"I'd like to speak to you." She didn't even look to see if I would follow her.

I hesitated, torn between the comfort of my bed and the cold instructions she was sure to give me for tomorrow. But there was little choice, so I followed her to her room.

Her lady's maid was waiting for her.

"Leave us, Gertie," Mother said. "Return in ten minutes."

"Yes, ma'am." Gertie curtsied and quietly left the room.

Mother's bedchamber was even larger than mine. The dressing room connected to the master bedroom, which Father would have occupied if he'd been with us. I missed him more than ever. He had not always been able to spare me from Mother, but he had softened her blows and given me a reason to smile.

"Sit." She pointed to one of the brocade chairs near the cold fireplace.

I perched on the edge of the chair, remembering how she had instructed my governess to put knives through the slats of my dining chair as a child, forcing me to sit erect. I was never comfortable in Mother's presence. My skin rippled with the chill in the air.

Mother took the seat opposite from me, her back as straight as a rod. She had taught herself everything she had needed to know to enter New York society. Her parents were poor European immigrants, and she had hardly known how to read and write when she met my father, let alone how to maneuver through the inner circles of the upper crust. She had worked tirelessly to be accepted by them but had not yet achieved her ultimate goal: to *be* one of them.

She studied me for a moment, her grey eyes neither hard nor soft. Almost detached. "What is your aversion to marriage?" she finally asked.

My mouth became lax as I stared at her. She rarely asked for my thoughts or opinions. She simply dictated orders that I followed. Mama was the one with whom I shared my heart, my dreams, my ambitions.

"I'm not opposed to marriage," I said slowly, thinking of Henry and how I longed for a life with him, though it was an impossible dream. "I simply have no wish to marry now."

"Why not?"

I wanted to tell her that I would not be here in thirteen months and did not wish to waste what little time I had left on courting or marriage.

Instead, I said, "I'm young."

"That's absurd. Most women who have been through two seasons are married or at the very least engaged. If not, there's generally something wrong with them."

I wanted to roll my eyes at her thinking, longing for Mama's promise of a time when a woman's marital status was not a reflection of her worth or value.

My work with the suffragette movement came to mind as a reason I did not wish to marry, but Mother Wells detested any mention of it, believing the movement beneath me. She thought little about politics and less about the women who were fighting for the right to vote. Her concern had always been personal advancement and social power, thinking a woman had a better chance of controlling her destiny by playing within the bounds of society's rules instead of trying to change them. I wanted to tell her that she could do so much for those less fortunate if she directed her boundless energy and clever mind toward the greater good. She was extremely intelligent and sly. If I was not always on the receiving end of her machinations, I would be in awe. My greatest weakness was that I was no match for her cunning—and she knew it.

I had to think of a reason I did not want to marry, so I said the only other thing I could think of. "I have no wish to leave America."

She waved her hand as if that were of little consequence. "What is one place or another? You would make friends here."

"I already have friends."

Mother finally sighed and pressed her hands against her knees. "I've made up my mind. Lord Cumberland will do quite nicely."

"Lord Cumberland?" I frowned. "I have no interest in marrying him."

"That doesn't matter. He is a marquess, and I have a feeling he will rise in political power. Even if he does not become the prime minister one day, I believe he will serve in a great capacity. *And* he's in need of an heiress. Lady Paget visited him last week and made sure he would be in attendance tonight so he could meet you. He told her he is amenable to pursuing a courtship and marriage—if certain stipulations are met."

By *stipulations*, she meant money.

"No." I stood, my heart pounding hard. "I do not wish to marry Lord Cumberland."

"Sit down, Elizabeth." Her voice was hard and unmoving.

I sat.

"We will allow Lord Cumberland to court you, and if he's agreeable to the match, we will speak of the details later."

I shook my head, my breath coming quickly. "No."

Her eyes hardened. "I've prepared you for this day, Elizabeth. There is no escaping your fate. You were born for a position of importance, and marriage is the only way a woman can gain that power and prestige."

I couldn't stay in her room any longer. I rose again, my arms and legs trembling. "I will not marry him, and you cannot make me." I sounded like a petulant child, but I was desperate for her to understand. "I will appeal to Father."

"Your father." Her laugh was part condescension and part disgust. "He is precisely who I am considering. He knows exactly why we've come here."

I took a step backward, toward the door. "He will not force me to marry Lord Cumberland or anyone else."

She rose and approached me. "Your father needs you to make a good match, just as you do. He stands to gain a great deal if you marry someone within the English government. Just think of all the shipping contracts he could negotiate. I'm only thinking of you and your father."

"Father doesn't care about such things. All you're thinking about is yourself."

Mother's hand snaked out and slapped my face. "Do not speak to me that way, Anna." She hadn't struck me in years, nor called me Anna. "You will do as I say and as your father says."

I put a trembling hand to my cheek.

"When Lord Cumberland arrives tomorrow, you will be here to greet him and to attend to whatever plans he has made. If you do not"—she paused, and my heart slowed—"I will turn Edith out on the street."

"Edith?"

"I know how close you are to that maid." She spat out the word as if it tasted sour. "She'll be the first to go, and I'll tarnish her name so she will be unemployable. Not even the street urchins will want her."

I shook my head. Edith could not be dismissed without a reference. Where would she go, especially here, in England? She had no family and would be destitute and ruined. I couldn't live with myself if I was the cause of her downfall.

Mother must have seen the panic in my eyes, because her smile returned. "I expect you to be ready and eager to please Lord Cumberland tomorrow. If not, Edith will be the least of your concerns."

Her threat hit right where she intended. I had no choice but to attend a few social functions with Lord Cumberland. It didn't mean I must marry him. Perhaps I could use the time to dissuade him from pursuing me. Delay until my time ran out in 1915. I still had options, but fighting Mother Wells was not one of them. I needed to save my strength for what truly mattered. There were other ways to get around her.

"I do not wish to see Edith put out," I said.

"Very good." She turned away, dismissing me with a wave of her hand. "You may go."

I left as quickly as my feet would carry me and arrived in my room moments later, my cheek still stinging from her hand.

Edith was there, tending to the fire, completely unaware of Mother's threats.

"I've laid out your nightgown," she said as she stood, her expression warm and comforting. But her smile quickly disappeared. "Did she strike you?"

I wanted to turn my face from that look in her eyes. It made me feel defenseless and weak. Instead, I held my head high. "Mother has decided upon a gentleman."

"So soon?"

"His name is Lord Cumberland. He's a marquess who lives on the coastal moors in Whitby." I didn't even know where Whitby was located. I'd never seen the moors, nor did I want to see them. They sounded so forlorn and uninviting.

Edith clasped her hands, the firelight dancing across her worried face. "How will you stop her?"

If Edith knew she was the reason I had no choice, she would insist I follow my heart, no matter her fate. But I could not let her sacrifice everything for me. Mother had always proven good on her threats, and she would see that Edith was ruined if I didn't obey her.

"I will rebuff his advances." I sounded more confident than I felt. "I will delay his agenda and convince him that I am not a suitable wife."

I couldn't even imagine marrying Lord Cumberland. There was nothing about him that appealed to me. Nor could I imagine staying in England. If I only had a year left in 1914, I wanted to spend it with my father, doing as much good as I could for the social causes I had adopted. I was wasting precious time here.

"I will help you," Edith said, her voice solemn.

I took her hand and squeezed it, thankful for her friendship.

Not for the first time, I wondered why God had allowed me to be in this time and place. What was the purpose? I belonged in 1774, and my life here was superfluous. Other than Father and Edith and a few friends I volunteered with, I had no one in this path. Mother had prevented me from forming relationships, afraid I would be tempted to stray from the plans she had laid for me. Surely God was aware of my plight and intended for me to leave here.

Edith helped me undress and slip into my nightgown, and then she removed the black headband from my hair and the dangling emeralds from my ears. As she brushed out my curls, all I could think about was tomorrow and waking up with Rebecca and Hannah beside me. They had both grown out of their gowns and shoes. We would have to find a way to make the budget stretch for new ones.

The emerald earrings on the vanity caught my eye. The excess of my life in 1914 mocked my every step in 1774.

Not for the first time, I wished there was a way I could leave the twentieth century early. If I tried to change history, I could forfeit the timeline I tried to change—but there was no way I could change history in 1914. I didn't know what would happen, so how could I change it?

But Mama knew.

A glimmer of hope sparkled in my heart.

Mama had lived from 1973 to 1994. She knew all sorts of things about the future. Did she know something that could help me?

The moment Edith finished braiding my hair, I climbed into my bed and pulled the covers up to my shoulders.

"Good-night," Edith said as she backed out of my room.

"Good-night." I closed my eyes, willing myself to fall asleep.

# 5

## WILLIAMSBURG, VIRGINIA
## MAY 24, 1774

It was impossible to find a quiet moment to talk to Mama until late afternoon. With the prestige of the new public printing contract, we had several new customers come into the print shop to place advertisements for that week's paper. I could hardly keep up with them and still see to the daily needs of the shop. I hoped and prayed it was a taste of the business to come, but there were still people in Williamsburg who would stop at nothing to see us fail.

The extra income was needed, but it did not satisfy all of our financial debts. We were able to pay most of what we owed to Mister Jennings, but there was still the matter of the final portion due in a week. Not to mention the sum we owed to the butcher, the cobbler, and the apothecary, who were all putting pressure on us to pay.

When I finally had a quiet moment near the supper hour, I was ready to close business for the day. My back was stiff from sitting at my desk for the past ten hours, and my eyes were blurry from reading through half a dozen newspapers from

New York, Philadelphia, and other cities. Each week, these papers were sent to us. Some articles and news we chose to print in the *Virginia Gazette* to keep our subscribers informed. We also sent copies of our newspaper to the thirty-five other printing presses in the colonies for the same purpose.

But it was a time-consuming process. On days like today, I thought about how quickly news moved from one source to another in 1914. Telephones, telegraphs, automobiles, airplanes, trains, and even motion pictures made news readily available and almost instantaneous. So much of how we transported information from one person to the next in the colonies was painstakingly slow and arduous. Parliament used this to their advantage, trying to keep the colonies as separate as possible, knowing that if we united as one force, we would be difficult to control. If we were fighting amongst ourselves, better still.

I pushed away from my desk to find Mama. She had left the office hours before to attend to Hannah's and Rebecca's schooling.

I went to the front door and turned over our shingle, indicating that the print shop was closed. Even at this late hour, the capital was still buzzing with excitement. People moved in and out of the blacksmith, the Prentis Store, and the many taverns lining the street. I stood for a moment, reveling in the comfort and familiarity of Williamsburg. Though I had lived equally in two eras and longed for some of the conveniences of 1914, this was where I belonged. Where I felt the most at home. I wanted to stay just as I was and not have to worry about Mother Wells, Lord Cumberland, and the twentieth century ever again.

Just thinking about Lord Cumberland made me step back inside and close the door with purpose. I needed to find Mama.

She was not in the sitting room, so I made my way into the backyard. Mama knelt there, working in one of her flowerbeds while Rebecca and Hannah sat on the grass beside her, each taking turns reading from a primer. No time was wasted on idleness.

The day was warm, and the air was fragrant with the scent of spring. Colorful tulips and irises grew in the cultivated beds. Mama took such pride in her flowers and had often told me that they were one thing that did not change throughout time. Her mother in the 1990s had been a master gardener and had shared her love of flowers with Mama. With Papa's illness and the additional work from the shop, there had been little time for her to devote to the flowerbeds of late, so it did my heart good to see her working there now.

Rebecca glanced up. Her brown eyes were filled with the innocent delight of childhood. She was the only one of us who had Papa's brown eyes. Her hair was also very dark and as straight as Hannah's was curly. Rebecca did not look anything like me or Hannah, but she possessed the same curiosity and confidence that we shared with Mama.

"Libby," Rebecca said in greeting.

Mama's head came up. She sat back on her calves and wiped a piece of hair away from her forehead. Her hands were covered in dirt, and there was a pile of weeds at her side, but she had a wide smile on her beautiful face.

"I've closed the shop for today," I told her, "and I was wondering if I might have a word with you."

"Aye." Mama wiped her hands together as she nodded at Rebecca and Hannah. "Take the book inside and help Mariah get supper on the table."

The girls quickly obeyed, eager to be done with their studies for the day. I brushed my hand over Hannah's curls as she ran past me. She smiled, a giggle on her lips.

Mama stood, her eyes soft around the edges. "They're growing much too fast."

"Aye." The need for new clothes was but one reminder.

A blackbird sang from a branch overhead as Mama took

a seat on the bench under the elm tree and patted the spot beside her.

I could not sit. I had been sitting for most of the day. The question I had for Mama kept me on my feet, pacing the crushed-shell path. I placed my hands on the flare at my hips, and my feet poked out from under my skirt as I walked.

"What's troubling you?" Mama asked.

I glanced around the yard to make sure we were alone. To my left, the kitchen windows were open, but I could hear Mariah singing as she moved pots and pans around. Louis and Glen were still in the printing room, and Abraham was at the York-town harbor, retrieving a shipment of supplies. If I was going to discuss this with Mama, I must do it now.

"Mother Wells has decided upon a suitor for me. His name is Reginald Fairhaven, the Marquess of Cumberland."

Mama lifted her eyebrows. "You're certain this is the one? You thought that once before in New York."

"Lord Cumberland's political aspirations include becoming prime minister of England." I crossed my arms as I continued to pace, feeling the need to shield myself, though Mother Wells and Lord Cumberland were thousands of miles and hundreds of years away. The interest I had gained in New York from some of the wealthiest and best-connected young men was probably the reason Mother Wells had decided to set her sights higher.

"What do you plan to do?"

"I will delay as long as possible. Try to convince him I am not worthy of pursuit. And persuade Mother Wells to take me back to New York."

A noise on the street caused both of us to pause. I strode to the edge of our home and saw it was simply an overturned cart.

When I returned to Mama, she still sat on the bench, her dirty hands pressing down on either side of her, deep in thought.

"Mama," I said tentatively. I could recall all the times I had asked for help leaving my other path, and each time she had told me why it was impossible. But this time I needed her to find a way. "You've often told me that if I ever try to change history, I will forfeit my life in this path."

Her gaze lifted to mine, and concern tightened her eyes. "Aye."

"What about changing the history in my other path? If I intentionally try to change something in 1914, I could forfeit that path, could I not?"

"Libby." She rose to her feet, her concern deepening. "It's not worth the risk. The stories my marked mother told me about time-crossers changing history are alarming. It could have catastrophic results, not only for you, but for the world." She took my hand. "Besides, how would you know what to change?"

"You lived beyond my 1914 path. Mayhap you could help me find a way to alter something."

Mama's eyes grew wide. "What you're asking me to do would not only affect you—it could affect me. If I gave you the information, I would be changing history just as much as you." She shook her head, her white cap securely in place. "I don't know what that would mean for me. It might forfeit my life in this timeline, and then who would be here for Rebecca and Hannah?"

I had not considered that possibility.

"The few things I've told you about my life in the late twentieth century could not possibly affect your life in the early part of the century." She squeezed my hand. "But there are many things I have not told you about wars, pandemics, economic depressions, Prohibition, civil unrest—things I learned in history class that have yet to happen in your other path. I have purposely spared you so that you would not unknowingly change the course of history. To do otherwise would risk both of our lives."

My heart sank. "Then I'm trapped."

"Until June 19, 1915, aye." Mama's voice filled with compassion. "Believe me, Libby, if there were a way out, I would have found it for you years ago. You must endure until your twenty-first birthday, just as I did."

Endure? Mama had never complained about either of her paths. She had spoken so highly of her life in the 1990s that I had always known it was hard for her to forfeit her life there in order to stay here. Yet she took such pride and had such passion living in Williamsburg on the eve of the American Revolution. What had she been forced to endure? Or had she misspoken?

"Keep up your guard," she continued, "and delay as long as possible. That is your only course of action."

"Anyone at home?" a male voice called to us from the side of the house.

It was a voice I would recognize anywhere, at any time.

"Henry," I said to Mama. I lifted the hem of my skirt and moved around the flowerbeds to meet him.

Henry walked toward the back garden, his tricorne hat beneath one arm, a leather satchel in his hand. I paused, admiring the cut of his waistcoat and the way the evening sun made his eyes sparkle—or mayhap it was the smile he offered me, so warm and inviting, that I admired the most.

"I hope I am not disturbing you," he said when we came to a stop along the side of the house. Heat from the day still radiated off the bricks, but it was the purpose and excitement in his gaze that warmed me the most. "I saw that you are closed, but I have urgent news to deliver."

"Public news?"

"Aye."

I motioned to Mama, who joined us.

Henry bowed. "Mistress Conant."

"Good afternoon, Henry." Mama kept her dirty hands behind her back, and her smile was welcoming, if guarded. She knew where Lord Ashbury stood on patriotic matters, but she was uncertain of Henry. And even though I tried to assure her of his dedication to the cause, she wasn't as willing to trust him.

"What can we do for you?" I asked.

He opened the leather satchel and pulled out a piece of paper, which he handed to me. "The burgesses voted today to stand with Boston. We are calling for a day of fasting, humiliation, and prayer on the first day of June and are asking you to print a broadside to be distributed throughout the colony, posthaste."

I stared at the document, signed by Henry as the Clerk of the House of Burgesses. I read it out loud. "'This House being deeply impressed with Apprehension of the great Dangers to be derived to British America, from the hostile Invasion of the City of Boston, in our Sister Colony of Massachusetts Bay, whose Commerce and Harbour are on the 1st Day of June next to be stopped by an armed Force, deem it highly necessary that the said first Day of June be set apart by the Members of this House as a Day of Fasting, Humiliation, and Prayer . . .'"

"We are also asking for members of the house, and those in the capital who so choose, to meet at Bruton Parish Church at ten in the forenoon for prayers and an appropriate sermon given by Reverend Mister Price."

"Has the governor seen this yet?" Mama asked.

"Nay." Henry closed his satchel. "He and Mister Washington left this morning for Governor Dunmore's farm and are not expected back for a day or more."

"And your father?" Mama asked. "Has he heard?"

"Not yet." Henry nodded toward the document I held. "Will you print this?"

"Of course we will," I told him with a bit of importance. "We are the public printer."

"How did you determine this course of action?" Mama asked.

"We have been discussing it for some time, but I met with Thomas Jefferson, Patrick Henry, and several others last night in the Governor's Council chamber, knowing we must take a bold stand with Massachusetts." Henry shifted on his feet as he spoke to Mama. Though he was her superior in every way, he was respectful and deferential as he addressed her questions. "We purposely met there to utilize John Rushworth's *Historical Collections*, which is a documentation of the English civil wars during the Puritan era. We modernized a similar action the House of Commons created in the 1640s to bring down the English constitutional establishment." His voice was serious yet full of passion. "'Tis our desire to implore heaven to keep us from a civil war and to inspire our American brothers and sisters to support our rights. We are asking God to turn the heart of the king and Parliament to justice while showing solidarity to our sister colony. What happens to one of us happens to us all."

His speech moved me, and I wanted to rush into the printing room to set the type myself.

"This is a bold thing you are doing," Mama said, her voice grave. "Do you know the cost?"

"Aye." Henry's blue eyes were filled with determination. "We have all weighed the cost and are willing to pay our share."

"Are you?" Mama studied him. "I pray God spares you from the ultimate cost."

None of us spoke for a moment, but I could no longer withstand the weight of the silence. "We will work on this tonight," I assured him, "and have it ready for distribution on the morrow."

"Thank you."

Mama wiped her hands on her apron and took the document from me. "I will take this to Louis now. Good evening, Henry."

Henry gave her a slight bow, and she left us to enter the house.

"I fear the governor will not be happy," I said.

"I fear the same, but we cannot let this tyranny prevail."

"Will seeing your name affixed to the bottom of the resolution hinder his familial generosity toward you?" I could not help but think of Lord Dunmore's daughter, Lady Catherine.

Henry knew me too well. "Are you asking whether or not he will allow me to marry Catherine?"

It was the first time I had heard it from his mouth, and it stung. I could not look into his eyes as I tried to control my voice and emotions. I did not want him to know how much it hurt to hear him speak of it. "The rumors are true?"

"If you've heard that my father and Governor Dunmore desire a union, then aye. If you've heard that I've agreed to such a thing, then nay."

I lifted my gaze to his, my voice quiet with hope. "You've not agreed?"

"Nay."

I swallowed, trying to understand. "Do you intend to agree at some point?"

It was his turn to study me, his gaze beseeching mine with questions, though what he wanted to know, I wasn't certain. We had not spoken openly of our feelings for the past six years. Did he still harbor any affection for me beyond friendship? I longed to know but had no right to ask.

"I am uncertain of what the future will bring," he finally said, putting his hat back on his head. "I cannot make any promises for now—to Governor Dunmore or to anyone else. To do so would be unwise and reckless."

I nodded, though my heart cried out at his words. The war loomed ahead for the next decade. Would he wait that long to marry?

"I must wish you a good day," he said. "I am meeting my father for supper and should not tarry."

"Will you tell him about the resolution now," I asked, "or wait until he hears it for himself?"

"I have not decided."

"Be safe, Henry."

"Aye," he responded, "and you, Libby."

I did not stay to watch him depart but hurried into the print room to see to the broadside.

"I will not print this." Louis held up the resolution between his thumb and forefinger as I entered the room. He handed it back to Mama.

"I did not ask whether or not you want to print it," Mama said to him, taking the document back. "We were instructed by the burgesses to print it, and we shall."

"It's treasonous." Louis crossed his arms over his leather apron and planted his narrow feet. "Boston should be punished for their reckless actions, and we should not support their cause. It will only incite restlessness and rebellion in our colony."

I had long suspected Louis was loyal to the crown, but this was the first I had heard him speak so plainly.

"'Tis not our job to question the House of Burgesses," Mama told him, her voice much calmer than mine would be. "'Tis our job to print what they ask of us. If we do not, they will rescind our contract, and we will be out of work. I will not toss away everything we have striven for because my journeyman refuses to print a broadside."

"If you want to print it," he said, untying his apron and taking it off, "then you will have to do it yourself."

Mama and I stared at him. We could not operate the print shop without Louis. He knew that as much as we did, and he could take the risk in standing his ground. Hadn't he already tried when he'd proposed to me?

"I will print whatever the burgesses require," Louis said as he hung his apron on its hook, "*within* the bounds of their legal responsibilities. But this, madam, is treason."

"When did prayer, humiliation, and fasting become treasonous?" I asked, stepping farther into the room.

Louis turned his angry glare upon me, disgust in his eyes. "I see Henry Montgomery signed this thing."

"He is the clerk, after all."

"I wonder if that's all he is." He unrolled his sleeves to put on his waistcoat.

I frowned. "What does that mean?"

Louis stared at me, his jaw fixed. "People are talking, Libby."

"Talking?" I shrugged, confused. People were always talking.

"There are rumors that he is spying on Governor Dunmore for the rebels."

"That's preposterous. His family has been close to Governor Dunmore for years. They are friends. Henry's simply a burgess. Nothing more."

"Friends?" He nodded at the document in Mama's hands. "Friends do not sign resolutions in support of rebels."

"What happens to one colony happens to us all." I repeated Henry's words, hoping Louis would feel the same passion I did. "Our brothers and sisters in Boston are suffering. Their plight is our plight."

"Because of their lawlessness and rebellion. They deserve what they get." He buttoned his waistcoat with precise movements. "I do not abide their actions, nor will I stand in solidarity with their cause." He put on his tricorne hat and opened the back door.

He exited the printing room, leaving Mama and me there with Glen, who had blended into the background, his eyes large.

Mama sighed.

I pointed at the door, shocked that she hadn't called him back. "Are you going to let him walk away?"

"I must respect his opinions." She glanced at Glen. "Get some supper and then come right back. Ask Abraham to join us when he returns from Yorktown. We'll be working late tonight."

Glen nodded and rushed out of the room.

Mama went to the workbench and pulled out a wooden form for the broadside type.

"Will you dismiss Louis?" I watched her, uncertain how she would proceed.

Mama paused and turned to me. "We are about to embark on a war for independence, and that will include the freedom of thought, opinion, and belief. I cannot force Louis to do something against his convictions. He has never taken a stand against me before and has printed everything I've ever asked of him. He will continue to do so if it does not contradict his beliefs."

"But our cause is justified. We will ultimately be victorious."

"Stop." She put up her hand. "In this time and place, that is yet to be determined. Regardless, there are always two or more sides to each issue. We cannot force Louis to do something he disagrees with—just as you do not want to be forced to do things you do not want to do. Just because we think—or know—we are right does not mean that Louis is wrong. His life and experiences have led to his own conclusions. 'Tis not my place to be his conscience."

Her admonition convicted my heart. She was right. Of course she was right. Independence from England was not a black-and-white issue. There were several shades of grey intermingled in the argument.

I went to the shelf where we stored the type and pulled down a heavy wooden box. Mama and I knew how to run the press, and though it had already been a long day, it would be a long night, as well. It would take hours to set the type and then several more to print the broadside.

"We will need Rebecca and Hannah's help," Mama said with a sigh. She hated to have them work in the print room. "Tell them to eat their supper and then join us, please."

I left her to find my sisters, a mixture of emotions churning in my spirit. I couldn't stop thinking about Louis's accusations against Henry. Had he heard rumors about Henry spying, or had he simply made it up because he knew Henry and I were friends and he wanted to hurt me?

I could not believe it was true. But if it was, then Henry was in far greater danger than I had realized.

# 6

LONDON, ENGLAND
MAY 25, 1914

The Royal Opera House was magnificent, both in architecture and in the array of glittering occupants the night Lord Cumberland invited us to his box. It was even more grand than the Met in New York City, but it served the same purpose: to see and be seen.

Tonight, *La Bohème* would play on the stage, but the British aristocracy would watch each other.

Mother Wells and I had attended the opera once while in London, as guests of Lady Paget. But this time we were on greater display. In the three days I had been in Lord Cumberland's acquaintance, I had become distinctly aware of his popularity among the upper and lower echelons of London society. The newspapers were already covering our courtship—or, at least, the rumors of our courtship. The morning after the ball at Crewe House, a titillating review of the party made its way into the *Daily Mirror*, and my name was linked to Lord Cumberland's, much to Mother's delight, with claims that we had danced together twice. Today's morning paper reported us riding together in Hyde Park, taking luncheon at the Ritz, and attending a dinner party at 10 Downing Street, the home of the prime minister.

Lord Cumberland had hardly given me a moment's rest, and though I wished to refuse his invitation to the opera, Mother would not allow me.

"We must take what we can get," she had said that afternoon after we had come home from the Victoria and Albert Museum with the marquess. "The newspapers love you, and what better opportunity for your name to be known by everyone?"

It was a marvel that the papers reserved space for such tittle-tattle, though it shouldn't be a surprise. Gossip sold papers, and for those who were on the outside, it was a form of entertainment purchased for a half-penny. But I couldn't help comparing it to the serious newspaper I printed each Thursday in Williamsburg. If I were the editor of the *Daily Mirror*, London's second-largest morning newspaper and foremost authority on the aristocracy, I would fill the pages with things that truly mattered, like the workhouses, the dangerous mills, and the children forced to labor for hours each day.

Lord Cumberland lifted the edge of the red curtain that closed off his box from the hall and motioned for Mother and me to enter. The space was large, with several matching red chairs but no other guests.

"Have you seen *La Bohème*, Miss Wells?" he asked me as I passed him.

I could smell alcohol on his breath, an odor I had smelled every time I'd been in his company.

"I have," I responded. "Twice in New York."

"Do you enjoy the story?"

"I enjoy any theater I have the privilege of viewing." I thought of Louis's invitation to see *Love in a Village* at the modest theater in Williamsburg. The difference between this grand opera house and the tiny open-air theater was laughable.

Though neither Louis nor Lord Cumberland had any chance of winning my affection, I could not help but think that Louis's feeble attempts at wooing me were nothing compared to Lord Cumberland's. Thankfully, Louis had not pressed the issue. I wished the same from Lord Cumberland.

Mother took the seat closest to the railing, and I sat in the middle with Lord Cumberland at my left. The thousands of conversations within the opera house were loud and echoing.

"I hope you don't mind," he said to me, "but I've asked Prime Minister Asquith and Mrs. Asquith to join us, though they will be late."

"Of course not." I had been entertained by Mrs. Margot Asquith at her dinner party the night before. By her own account, she had brought her husband into her sparkling world of society upon their marriage twenty years before. She was vivacious, outspoken, and a tenacious gossip. I had learned more about London society in the two hours I dined with her than in the three weeks we'd been living at Berkeley Square. I was eager to have her join us at the opera, if for no other reason than to take the attention off myself. Lord Cumberland appeared to be infatuated with her and had paid little heed to me the entire time we'd dined with her and the prime minister.

He said quietly, "Mrs. Asquith was quite taken with you, as am I. She has instructed me not to let you get away."

Mother must have heard him, because a self-satisfied smile lifted her lips. For my part, I did not know how to respond to Lord Cumberland's forward statement. It was clear he was serious about me, though I had given him absolutely no encouragement. If anything, I had been distractable and bored in his company. If I said what came to my mind, it would be rude. If I said nothing, I risked him thinking I was playing a coquette.

So I said the only thing I could. "She is a wonderful hostess."

Several people from the other boxes had their eyes on us, some even using their opera glasses to get a better look. No doubt the newspaper would comment on my appearance in public with Lord Cumberland yet again.

It really was a bit unseemly.

"Have I told you how lovely you look tonight?" he asked, speaking for my ears alone.

"Lord Cumber—"

"Call me Reggie, please. All my close acquaintances do."

I could feel myself becoming fidgety, so I repositioned myself in the seat. "Really," I said just as quietly, hoping not to incense Mother, praying that the noise inside the opera house would drown out our words. "We are hardly close acquaintances. We've only just met."

"I would very much like to change that." He leaned close to me—dangerously close. If he came any closer, people would surely talk. It was one thing to lean in to share a comment or observation, but another entirely to *stay* close. "Won't you allow me the privilege, Anna?"

My hair stood on end along my neck. I found myself leaning away from him until Mother grunted under her breath and I realized I was crowding her.

"Lord Cumberland," I said, trying to start over, wishing to dissuade him from his pursuit once and for all. "I am honored by your request, however—"

"Anna would love the privilege," Mother said on my other side.

Heat infused my cheeks. This was hardly the time or the place to have this conversation with her—or him.

"Unfortunately," I said, "I don't know how long we will be in London."

"We'll be here as long as it takes." Mother gave me a warning glare. She had brought up Edith's name again that morning when I protested Lord Cumberland's invitation to the museum. Any time we passed beggars on the streets, she gave me a pointed look. My friend's fate lay in my trembling hands.

"I was under the impression that you were here to stay indefinitely." Lord Cumberland sat upright in his chair, allowing me a bit more room to breathe. "Lady Paget was quite adamant about your desire to live in England permanently, should the opportunity arise."

This was my chance to convince him I did not want to be his wife. I had not anticipated this conversation so soon or in such a public place, but who would hear?

"I do not know what gave her that idea." I tried to laugh off my comment, appearing to be oblivious to my mother and Lady Paget's plans. "I am quite content with my life in America. Do you know, Lord Cumberland, that I have marched in several parades for women's suffrage? And I serve, whenever possible, at settlement houses? I miss my work at home and long to return. I hope to be back before the summer ends."

"I did not know." He looked straight ahead. I had surprised him—though whether it was with my disinterest in remaining in England or with my causes, I wasn't certain. "Mrs. Asquith is quite vocal about her opposition to women voting," he continued. "She was pleased when the House of Lords recently rejected the Women's Suffrage Bill. She, like myself, believes women have no sound reason, have very little humor, and are not honorable enough to vote."

My mouth fell open. It was one thing to hear a man say such things, but far worse to hear that a woman agreed. And the prime minister's wife, no less!

"Anna is being glib," Mother said quickly, her voice rising a notch. "She's trying to be coy, though both she and I long for her to find a place here in England. America is too"—she shuddered—"progressive and vulgar. She yearns for the traditions and ceremonies of a more genteel society."

I stared at Mother, trying to communicate my frustration with my eyes. I wasn't sure what made me more upset: Mother's eternal desire to present me as someone I was not or Lord

Cumberland's comments about Mrs. Asquith's beliefs about women.

"There is work to be done, both here and in America," Mother continued, taking my hand in an unfamiliar show of affection. She petted it, as if I were in need of comfort. "Her heart is sensitive to those in need, and I've long thought her suitable for someone who desires to serve the public's greater good."

Lord Cumberland seemed mollified by Mother's comments. His smile lifted his mustache as he turned to me. "I've thought the same about you, Anna. From what I've heard and witnessed, you would make a fine politician's wife. Mrs. Asquith, who is an expert on such matters, quite agrees with me. The American women in my acquaintance have been well-received by the masses, even if they are a little more outspoken than I would like. You're beautiful, accomplished, and have an unsullied reputation. Perhaps your head has been turned by the fervor of the suffrage movement in America, but you're young and, I hope, trainable. I do believe you possess all the qualities a man in my position could want."

I tried not to frown—tried to pretend I didn't know what he was talking about—but it was painfully clear. He didn't need—or want—to get to know me but had already determined that I would be a suitable match, malleable to his purposes.

It didn't hurt that I would come with a substantial dowry to save his ancestral home. No doubt *that* was my greatest qualification.

I needed to shock him into his place. "I would make a terrible politician's wife. My concern for suffrage will not end upon my marriage."

Mother squeezed my hand so hard that I cried out in pain and pulled it away.

But Lord Cumberland did not seem to notice—or care. "Your humility is yet one more quality I admire."

The lights began to dim, and I breathed a sigh of relief. I prayed that this conversation was over and that Lord Cumberland would think about the things I had said before he tried to revive it.

"You're a fool," Mother hissed in my ear, just loud enough for me to hear as I stared at the stage. "You will find no other man as worthy as the Marquess of Cumberland."

I did not respond to her, my insides crawling with revulsion, even as her words ate at my heart. It hurt to hear her call me a fool or any of the other things she'd called me over the years. I tried to be impervious to her opinions and insults, but it was impossible. Despite all the pain she had caused, I wanted to please her, just as I wanted to please Mama. It was part of my nature.

The opening scene of the opera began in a French flat with four artists struggling to make ends meet in 1830. My heart was not in the opera or the evening. All I could think about was Williamsburg and Mama. How different my life would be if I'd been given a mother like her in this path. She had worked so hard with me to print and distribute the broadside for the burgesses. Governor Dunmore had not yet received the news, but he was expected back in the capital on the morrow and would surely react to the resolution. What would he do?

Now more than ever, I longed to run to a history book and see how the events of 1774 would unfold. I had a general idea of the timeline of the American Revolution but had never studied it to a great extent with my tutors, afraid of knowing too much. It was one of the struggles of my existence.

"Anna," Lord Cumberland said moments after Mother's scolding in my other ear. "I see no reason to prolong our courtship. I know what I want, and I know what you want. I am a man of action and believe you are fully aware of my intentions."

I closed my eyes, willing him to remain quiet.

"I long to speak to your father and see no reason to wait."

"Lord Cumber—"

"If we're to be married, I insist you call me by my Christian name, as I will call you Anna."

Anger and resentment stirred deep within my soul, making me clench my teeth. "My name is Libby."

"A pet name?" He brushed my bare arm with the back of his gloved hand. "I would be honored."

Gooseflesh rose on my skin, and my stomach roiled at his touch. He misunderstood.

"Given the information I've obtained from Lady Paget," he said so close to me that his lips brushed my ear, "I believe your parents will be amenable to our match."

I recoiled, my back stiff, and bumped into Mother's shoulder. There was no place to go. I was imprisoned between them.

"I will call upon your mother in the morning to make my formal proposal and work out the details of our betrothal. I believe we will both be quite pleased."

Panic raced up my legs and hit my heart with a tremendous thud. I couldn't breathe or think and had the intense urge to flee.

But I stayed in place for one reason. Edith.

I had options. I had time. I could still find a way out. But Edith did not have those luxuries. My obedience to Mother was the only thing keeping Edith off the street.

I did not move or hardly breathe as the opera unfolded. But as the tragic love story played out on stage, I could not help seeing the satisfied grin on Mother Wells's face.

The moment the lights turned on for intermission, I excused myself from Lord Cumberland's box. The prime minister and Mrs. Asquith had arrived before the second act, and as I made my way to the lavatory for some space, I was practically trampled by people who were coming to Lord Cumberland's box to present themselves to the Asquiths.

I felt like I was drowning in this sea of society. Several people tried to stop me to converse, but I put my hand to my stomach and shook my head, an apology in my eyes. I was afraid I might be sick right there on the plush carpet.

Perfume and sweat mingled in the stuffy corridors of the Royal Opera House. The lights seemed too bright, the conversation too loud, and the air too thick. The gilded moldings along the ceilings and around the opulent doors reminded me of the thin veneer this crowd of people represented. They were the minority, overshadowing the rest of the population that lived in squalor and desperation. These were the people, like Mrs. Asquith, making decisions that affected every other aspect of society.

I crushed more than one bejeweled hem as I made my way to the ladies' room. When I was finally in the privacy of the lavatory, I pressed my hands against the cool marble walls for support, forcing myself to breathe. I hated that this was the only place I was allowed a bit of respite.

"Miss Wells?" Mrs. Asquith's voice surprised me. "Are you in here, dear?"

I pushed aside the curtain of the stall and stepped out. It was a small lavatory, covered in red tapestry, and no one else had entered.

"I was worried about you." She studied my face. "You left so quickly and looked so ill that I excused myself to see after you."

"Thank you." I tried to smile, but it was difficult. "I will be fine. I get a little light-headed with so many people pressed into such a small space."

She sighed in apparent relief. "I feel the same way. Since Herbert became prime minister, it's always such a crush to be in public. I enjoy social events, but to be surrounded by such exuberant people can make me feel overwhelmed."

This woman was almost three times my age, but she spoke to me like an equal. I'd heard rumors that she was raised like a hoyden, allowed her freedom on her family's country estate. She wasn't a beauty, but her sense of style and confidence made people take notice.

She must have seen something in my eyes, because she stepped toward me and took my hand in hers. "What is troubling you, my dear? Is it truly the crush of people, or is it something more?"

Lord Cumberland's earlier words returned to me, and anger rushed into my chest. Mrs. Asquith did not support women's suffrage. Perhaps if I could convince her I would be bad for Lord Cumberland's political aspirations, she would persuade him to move on.

"My mother brought me here to find a husband."

"That's what most young women are searching after during the Season." She laughed. "It's no reason to be upset, dear. Don't you want a good match?"

My thoughts turned to Henry. How ironic that I was not good enough for him in 1774, yet here I was being pursued by one of the most promising politicians—and a marquess, no less.

"I have no wish to marry."

"Truly?" She frowned. "Why not?"

"I have other ambitions." I took a deep breath, wanting to make sure she didn't misunderstand me. "I've adopted several causes, such as women's suffrage—"

She took a step away from me. "You cannot be serious."

"I believe that all women should be allowed to vote. After all, the men elected to power make decisions for us every day. Shouldn't I have some say in who makes those decisions?"

"You're hardly old enough to understand such things—"

"I am quite certain of my opinion, Mrs. Asquith." I couldn't tamp down the passion I felt in my breast. Mama had raised me to believe in my own mind and abilities. Her experiences in the 1980s and 1990s had taught her to be bold and brave in her convictions, and I was too. Even if it wasn't acceptable to women like Mrs. Asquith. "I believe, with all my heart, that I am on the right side of history in this regard."

She stared at me for a moment. Would she berate me right here in the lavatory?

"Do you know," she said, her voice softening, "I believe the vast majority of women are incompetent and incapable of knowing their own mind?"

I had heard.

"But you, my dear, are different. I can see it plainly in your face. You're intelligent, well-spoken, and not afraid to stand up to the prime minister's wife." She chuckled and smiled affectionately. "I do believe you would make a great politician's wife. It's not easy to stand up to the masses, and women like us are needed to speak our minds—even if we do not agree with each other."

My heart sank. This was not what I had hoped.

She examined me with her approving gaze. "Reggie is carried away with the idea of you, and I can see why. You and he will be the envy of every ambitious couple in England."

The panic returned, and suddenly not even the ladies' room was a safe place.

Hours later, as Mother and I stepped into our cab to make our way back to our townhouse, my head pounded and my stomach was still nauseated. Lord Cumberland had just promised Mother he would call on her in the morning, and I had done everything I could to disregard his advances, even ignoring him during the second half of the evening.

The vehicle's motor rumbled as we pulled away from the Royal Opera House. Exhaust entered the interior, making my head hurt worse than before.

Mother did not waste any time. "Your behavior was abominable tonight. It's a wonder Lord Cumberland still plans to come tomorrow."

"Is it?"

She stared at me. "I really don't know where you came from, Anna. I know dozens of women who would envy your position."

If she only knew.

"He will make an offer for you, I'm quite certain." Her voice had shifted from censure to victory.

Of course he would. He had made up his mind. If he was as influenced by Mrs. Asquith as it appeared, he'd be even more eager on the morrow. "He likes the idea of me and doesn't care much about the reality."

"Your father has given me leave to speak on his behalf, though I'm sure Lord Cumberland will want to make a formal appeal to Mr. Wells." She continued as if she hadn't heard me. "However, that will not be necessary to move forward, and since the wedding will take place in New York, Lord Cumberland can make his formal request when he arrives."

I pressed my hands to my pounding head. If I did not have another life in the 1700s and this was my only existence, I would probably jump at the opportunity to marry someone in England just so I could be an ocean away from Mother Wells. But I *did* have another life, one I did not want to compromise in any way. "There will be no wedding."

Mother Wells sighed, a long and deep sound. "You're tiresome on every level. I refuse to continue playing this game with you."

"I will be twenty in less than three weeks. Old enough to know my own mind. I will marry whomever I want, whenever I want."

The automobile was dark, but I could still feel her steely gaze upon me. "How foolish and vain and self-centered you are."

Her voice dripped with disdain. "You *are* obligated to me and your father," she said. "As your mother, I am the only person who knows what is best for you. And until you marry, your father has legal authority over your life. You may not thank me now, but one day, when you are presiding over England like Mrs. Asquith and people are rushing to your opera box, you will."

"I will not." I spoke with such certainty and conviction that she paused.

Neither of us spoke again until we arrived at the townhouse, but before the driver had come around to open the door for us, Mother's voice reached out and clasped me around the heart.

"I will accept his proposal on your behalf, and you will marry him, mark my words."

She exited the automobile and strode to the door without waiting for me to follow.

# 7

## WILLIAMSBURG, VIRGINIA
## MAY 26, 1774

The sky was overcast on Thursday, matching my mood. Since the paper had gone to press that morning and my work for the following week's newspaper had not yet begun, Mama encouraged me to go to the milliner and mantua-maker's shop with Rebecca and Hannah to discuss the gowns they needed. I had not yet broached the subject of payment, hoping Mistress Hunter would sell them to us on credit, though I detested owing a debt to yet another person. We had scraped together the last of what we owed to Mister Jennings in the past couple of days, but he was not the only one threatening to take action against us.

A low roll of thunder met my ears as we sat in Mistress Hunter's shop, looking at Virginia cotton fabric, buttons, and ribbons. We were the only customers in the store and had come in just as one of the plantation wives had exited, her footman ladened with packages. I wondered if it would start to rain before we returned home, but I was in no hurry and didn't give it much thought. Mama needed a bit of time alone as much as the girls and I needed a distraction and a break from our responsibilities. It helped keep my mind off 1914 and Lord Cumberland's impending visit.

"What do you think of this color?" Mistress Hunter asked Hannah as she held up a dark green cotton. "'Twould match your eyes, miss."

"May I have a pink gown?" Hannah asked me, not even looking at the fabric Mistress Hunter presented. "With lace and ruffles and dozens of petticoats?"

"There will be no lace, I'm afraid." I offered a smile to soften the reality.

"If it's pink the child is wanting," Mistress Hunter said, "then I have just the drugget. It arrived at Yorktown this week, and I haven't had time to bring it out." Her tiny brown eyes opened wide in excitement. She motioned to one of her enslaved women, Martha, to retrieve the material.

Drugget was the cheapest material one could buy next to homespun. Had Mistress Hunter heard of our financial plight? It would not surprise me with the way gossip traveled in Williamsburg.

Another rumble of thunder, this one closer and louder, rattled the windows of the mantua-maker's shop. Mistress Hunter went to the window, looking toward the west. "The clouds are rolling in quickly."

Rebecca hated storms. Her eyes were troubled as she looked from the windows to me. I put my hand on her arm to reassure her, but I wondered whether we should go home now or stay and wait out the storm. There was no telling how long it might last.

"Oh my," Mistress Hunter said, putting her lace-gloved hand to her mouth. "It looks as though there's trouble."

I went to the door to look outside. A great commotion had developed. People were gathering in small groups outside businesses up and down Duke of Gloucester Street. Mister Jefferson and Mister Patrick Henry were standing with several other burgesses just outside the capitol building.

But where was Henry?

"I must find out what has happened," I said to no one in particular. Rebecca and Hannah rushed to the door to look with me. "Return home," I told them. "I will be along shortly."

"But what of our dresses?" Hannah asked.

"We will come back to discuss them later."

The girls did not look pleased, but they obeyed me and left the shop.

I turned to Mistress Hunter. "We will need to return later to make decisions about the dresses, I'm afraid." I offered a quick curtsy and then left.

Sophia Charlton stood with a group of young women on the opposite side of the street, near her father's wig-making shop. When she spotted me, she broke away from the others.

"What has everyone so agitated?" I asked her.

"Governor Dunmore has disbanded the burgesses!" Her dark eyes danced with animation. "He returned this morning from the countryside and was given the resolution. Then, this afternoon, he sent a messenger to inform the assembly that they are to return home until further notice."

"Where did you hear this?"

"'Tis circulating all over town."

"When did they disband?"

"A quarter hour ago, by my knowledge."

Raindrops began to fall from the sky, and several of the men on the street moved toward the Raleigh Tavern, only a few doors down from the mantua-maker. I searched the crowd for Henry, longing to hear from someone who had experienced the event firsthand.

Thunder rumbled overhead again, and I looked up on instinct to assess the oncoming storm. Grey clouds tumbled over each other, building with intensity.

"I must get back to my father," Sophia said, glancing at the sky, as well. "Will you come and tell me if you learn something new?"

"If I am able." I was still searching for Henry. Was he at the capitol? Had he already gone to his house on the Palace Green? Was he inside the Raleigh? Mayhap Sophia knew. She sat by her father's window as she worked and watched the comings and goings of everyone on Duke of Gloucester Street. "Have you seen Henry Montgomery?"

"Not since early this morning, when he went to the capitol."

There were so many people gathered outside the Raleigh that it was impossible to see past them. I stood on tiptoe, but in vain. Mister Archer, the owner of the *Williamsburg Weekly Journal*, was in the midst of the crowd, speaking to several burgesses without noticing me. He had access to the men in ways I never would. He was invited and welcomed into their inner circles, gleaning information and news with little effort.

It forced me to work harder, but I wasn't afraid.

A gust of wind tore down the street, tugging at my skirts and threatening to pull off my cap.

Sophia stepped closer to me. "Have you heard the rumors about Henry?"

I looked at her sharply. Was she referencing the ones Louis had shared? "I've heard some things, but I try not to believe everything I hear." I would never believe it of Henry.

"You've heard that he's spying on the Liberty men for the governor?"

I forgot about the oncoming storm and the gathering outside the tavern. "I've heard the opposite, that he's spying on the governor *for* the Liberty men. Where have you heard these accusations?"

"Customers."

"Rumors abound while everyone is in town. Some people live for the gossip circulating while the burgesses are in session." Both here and in 1914, some things did not change.

"What do you think?"

"I do not think of such things," I said. "Henry is not only

good, he is honorable. These rumors are flying about because he is standing with his fellow burgesses against the crimes committed in Boston. His father is loyal to the crown and to the governor. 'Tis bound to make people question Henry's loyalty, and since he is seen with both parties, the rumors have developed." I wanted to believe what I was saying, but I'd lived long enough, in two different times, to know that rumors were often born from a spark of truth, however small.

"If you think that," Sophia said, ever loyal to me, "then I will think that, as well." She held on to her cap. "I must be off. Father will be cross with me for leaving my work unattended."

She left my side as the rain picked up in intensity. I prayed the girls had made it home as I rushed to the Raleigh, eager to get under the protection of a large elm in its front yard. I did not want to go home without speaking to Henry.

The crowd began to disperse, people rushing off to their houses, businesses, and lodgings. Those who remained started to file into the tavern—with Mister Archer among them.

Mister Jefferson approached the Raleigh with Mister Patrick Henry. They were in deep conversation, but at the last moment, Mister Jefferson glanced my way.

"Miss Conant." He removed his tricorne and offered a slight bow.

"Good day, Mister Jefferson." I gave a quick curtsy, eager to be done with the formalities. "Have you seen Mister Montgomery?"

"Aye." He glanced over the crowd, his brows dipping in confusion. "He left the capitol with us, but we must have lost him in the melee."

My heart sank. "Mayhap he's gone home?"

"I don't believe he would. Not today." Mister Jefferson gave me an apologetic look. "I wish I could be of service to you."

"Thank you."

He and Mister Henry entered the Raleigh. Others soon

joined them, powerful and important men angered by the governor's order, though how could they be surprised? Surely they had known what they were about when they voted on the resolution.

I watched up Duke of Gloucester Street until everyone was gone. If Henry had been inside, Mister Jefferson would have told him I was waiting, surely.

I was just turning toward home when I finally saw Henry. He was running up the street from the opposite direction of the capitol. He stopped momentarily at Mistress Hunter's shop, glanced in the windows, and then continued toward the Raleigh, where he saw me standing under the tree.

He ran the short distance toward me, concern on his face. His chest rose and fell as he tried to catch his breath. "Pray, tell me why you're standing in the rain, Libby Conant."

"I was looking for you."

"Me?" He smiled with surprised pleasure. "I was looking for you." Water dripped off his hat. He began to remove his overcoat, saying, "Here, take my—"

"Nay." I put my hand on his arm to still his offer. "I should be gone."

His brown hair had fallen out of its queue and curled around his shoulders. "The moment we were disbanded, you were the first person who came to mind. I went to your home and was told you were at Mistress Hunter's."

"I was the first person you thought of?" I laid my hand against my stomacher, touched by his consideration.

"You've been so invested in our cause. I knew you would want to hear the news as soon as possible."

His thoughtfulness warmed me, even as the air cooled from the storm. I tried to hide the emotions that welled up at his words. "Everyone has already gone into the tavern. Won't you be missed?"

"Aye, but we'll be in there for hours." He smiled, his entire countenance energized. "This is it, Libby, the moment we've been waiting for. I can feel it."

I nodded, knowing far more than he did.

He ran a hand over his face to wipe away some of the rainwater. "We've been disbanded and told to go home."

"Will you?"

He shook his head. "Nay. I will stay, at least until the first of June, so I can stand with my fellow burgesses."

"Beyond that?"

He shrugged and pointed toward the tavern. "It will all depend on what we decide. There has been talk of holding a colonial convention to discuss the grievances we have against the king."

"Won't that be dangerous? Even treasonous?" I had to raise my voice over the wind and rain. We were being reckless to stand in the elements, though the thick branches and leaves of the tree offered us some protection.

"Meeting to discuss the wrongs committed against us?" He shook his head. "We're British citizens, and we have a right to bring our grievances before the king. That is not treason. We do not have representation in Parliament, and that is wrong."

"Will you participate in the convention?"

"If we agree to hold a convention, and if I am elected, aye."

"What about your father? How has he responded to all of this?" I watched him carefully, remembering what both Louis and Sophia had said about Henry. Was he spying? And if so, who was he spying on?

His enthusiasm dimmed. "He is not happy, but he agrees 'tis too soon to know how this will end. He supports my involvement, hoping I will be a voice of reason in these meetings."

"And will you?"

A bit of devilry lit his eyes. "It depends on which side he thinks I'm supporting."

Instead of making me smile, his answer turned a knot in my

gut. I looked down at my hands, which were clasped over my apron, and then nodded toward the tavern doors. "I should not keep you."

"I wish you could join me."

"Aye." If Papa were alive, he would be there and would bring the news home to us. Just as Mister Archer was sure to do with his family. It was so disheartening to know that my newspaper was read, sometimes out loud, in this very tavern, yet it was not proper for me to enter with these men. The matters they discussed would eventually end up in my newspaper, but I was kept from offering my opinions until everything was settled and decided.

Henry must have heard the longing in my voice, because he said, "If you'd like, I will stop by your home this evening when our discussions have ended."

"Truly?" My spirits lifted. "I'd like that."

"Then I will come." He took a step toward the door. "But it will be late," he warned.

"I don't care if it is the middle of the night. I'll be awake."

Henry smiled, and the look of eager anticipation in his eyes made my stomach fill with butterflies.

Quietness stole over the house as the storm continued to blow outside. Darkness had fallen on Williamsburg hours before, but the wind and rain had not died down. It blew around the eaves and rattled the windowpanes, like a thief trying to find entry. But I was safe, dry, and warm, sitting close to the hearth with Phyllis Wheatley's book, *Poems on Various Subjects, Religious and Moral*.

Mama had gone to bed at the same time as the girls, complaining of a sick headache. I hadn't told her Henry was coming, though I wasn't sure why. Part of me wanted the rare chance to be alone with him. But that wouldn't bother Mama. She often scoffed at the practice of chaperones, telling me that not only had she been free to be alone with gentlemen in the 1990s, but it was socially acceptable. She said women should be allowed to be their own masters.

It didn't really matter what Mama thought, though. If anyone else knew that Henry and I were alone, the gossip would ruin my reputation and could affect our business.

But it was late and stormy. The chances of someone seeing Henry arrive or leave were minuscule. Besides, even if they did, they would have no way of knowing we were alone.

The real reason I didn't want Mama to know was because I wasn't sure of her feelings toward Henry. She had always liked him, but she was leery of him. Both for me and for our family. She had been hurt when his parents snubbed us and she lost her dearest friend, Henry's mother. I was certain she worried I would be hurt by him too, but Henry could never hurt me.

The fire had started to dim, so I rose to put on another log and rearrange the embers. Smoke puffed out of the fireplace, and I fanned it away from my face with my hand. It burned my eyes, which were already tired from the late hour.

It was past midnight. If I went to sleep now, I would return to 1914. I had almost forgotten my troubles with Lord Cumberland in the rush of today's excitement. If he arrived at the townhouse in the morning, as I was certain he would, Mother would set in motion a betrothal. No matter what happened, I would not agree to marry him, and she would have to suffer the consequences. I had told her what I intended to do, and she should not be surprised.

My dogged determination gave me reason to hope, but I usually felt most confident about my path in 1914 when I was in 1774. As soon as I opened my eyes in the townhouse on Berkeley Square, I would probably be a puddle of nerves and uncertainty again.

A light rapping noise at the front door made my heart do a little flip.

Henry.

I left the sitting room and entered the hall to open the door, all thoughts of 1914 slipping away.

He stood with his hat under his arm, his blue overcoat speckled with rain spots, a myriad of emotions playing behind his eyes. "Good evening, Libby."

"Good evening." I opened the door wider. "Come in out of the rain."

He entered the dim hallway. "I hope 'tis not too late. I almost went home—but I didn't want to break my promise."

"Nay." I closed the door to the storm and moved around him, conscious of his nearness, and entered the sitting room. "I would have waited all night."

He followed me, and his gaze swept the sitting room. "Are we alone?"

My heart was still pounding a bit too hard. "Mama had a sick headache and went to bed hours ago."

He was serious as he regarded me. "Would you prefer I leave?"

I shook my head. "I would prefer you stay."

"Does your mother know I am here?"

I clasped my hands as I glanced behind me, toward the hall and the stairs that led up to our bedchambers. "Nay." I looked back at him, afraid he would be a gentleman and leave. "But she wouldn't mind."

He gave me a look that suggested he didn't believe me.

I closed the door, hoping not to wake Mama or the girls. The shutters were closed, and the only light in the room came from the hearth. It offered a soft and intimate glow.

"Are you not afraid to be alone with me, Libby?" His voice was low, and his presence overwhelmed me in the most delightful way, filling up every corner of both the room and my heart.

In answer to his question, I moved across the room and

pulled a chair up beside the one I had used earlier. He did not move out of my way but allowed me to draw close to him, close enough to smell the scents that were uniquely his. Without facing him, I said, "I could never be afraid of you."

He did not speak for a moment, and I could not seem to form a coherent thought with him this close. He had always been a gentleman, never overstepping the bounds of propriety—but for once I wished he would. My heart was so raw from what I was experiencing in 1914, and I longed to be loved—truly loved—by someone who valued me for who I was. Henry understood me, as much as he could, and had always taken pleasure in my company. We were like-minded in all the ways that mattered, and he had no wish to change me.

"'Tis glad I am to hear it," he said quietly.

I turned my head and met his clear, steady gaze. I wished I knew what he was thinking. I longed for him to give me a sign that he cared for me, even a little. I could see yearning in his eyes—at least, I believed I could. There was a connection and a bond between us that I did not feel with anyone else. Surely that meant something.

A sad smile lifted his lips as he motioned to the chair. "'Tis getting late. I should tell you what I've come to say."

If there was ever a time Henry would share his heart with me, surely it would be now, while we were alone. Yet he took a step away from the chairs so I could move around them and take a seat. I tried not to feel frustrated or disappointed.

After I was seated, he sat beside me. Our knees brushed together, so he repositioned himself. I sat up straight on my chair, hands clasped in my lap, willing myself to be content with his time—even if that was all I could have of him.

"I have news you'll want to print." His voice was charged with energy. "We've agreed to call a Virginia Convention. August first, here in Williamsburg. Any burgess who is willing may attend."

"And will you?"

He nodded. "There's talk of calling together a congress of the thirteen colonies at a later date, as well."

I was aware of the two Continental Congresses that would take place in the next year. The second would occur soon after the Battles of Lexington and Concord, in April of 1775. I wished I could tell him these things, but if I did, he would never understand, and I would lose him forever. Not to mention that I would risk changing history.

"For now," he said, "I will stay in Williamsburg until the first of June. Beyond that, I might captain a ship to New York for my father, since the convention won't start until August."

"Must you go?"

He studied me as the firelight flickered in his beautiful blue eyes. "I am afraid so. I'm needed for my father's business."

"Is it safe?"

"Life is a risk, Libby." He smiled, though there was sadness in the depths of his eyes. "I will be called upon to do much more dangerous things before this is all done." He let out a sigh. "I should take my leave."

"So soon?"

"My father will wonder what keeps me."

We both rose at the same time. "Thank you for coming."

"I know how you long to be a part of this cause, Libby. I admire you because of it." Slowly, he lifted his hand and reached for mine.

I allowed him to take it, my pulse beating hard in my wrists. The touch of his skin against mine was unlike anything I'd ever felt before. Warmth flooded my senses, curling low in my belly.

"Libby," he said tenderly, "I count you among my dearest friends and always have. I hope you know that."

I nodded, though I longed for so much more than friendship.

He swallowed as he ran his thumb over the top of my hand,

looking down at it. "I wish . . ." He paused, and I held my breath. "I wish I were free to offer you more."

My face felt flushed, and my legs grew weak at his words. They filled me with hope, yet at the same time dashed that hope against a rock. "I wish for the same," I said barely above a whisper.

"There are things beyond my control." His voice was low and pained. "Things that prevent me from following my heart."

Tears threatened to gather in my eyes, so I had to look away.

He squeezed my hand, forcing me to look up and meet his troubled gaze once again. "But please know that you are dearer to me than my very own life, Libby. It's because I care that I must keep you at a distance." His words pleaded with me to understand.

I stared at him, trying hard to keep the tears from spilling onto my cheeks. I had to press my lips together to stop them from trembling. I wanted to understand him—had thought I did—but if he cared for me, why must he keep me at a distance? Was it because of his father's expectations? Was it because of his uncertainty concerning the events transpiring around us?

Whatever it was, I had to believe he would declare his feelings for me if he could. And if he could not, there must be a very good reason.

"Do not trouble yourself on my behalf." I spoke softly, afraid my voice would crack under my emotions. "You are an honorable man, and you have a difficult burden to carry. My greatest desire is that you would carry it well. I do not want you to be hindered because of me."

"Oh, Libby." He pulled me close.

I buried my face in his chest and closed my eyes, loving the feel of his heart beating against my cheek. The tears did come then. I could not stop them. I had loved him for so long, and this was the closest we had come to sharing our hearts in years.

"You are so very dear to me," he said again. "You always have been, and you always will be."

I'd never known such longing as I did in that moment. Why did God allow such passion and fervor to burn in my heart for Henry when I was not free to act upon my desires?

He kissed the top of my cap and pulled away from me. It was cold without him near.

"Pray, forgive me," he said, his voice choked. "You deserve so much more than I can offer you."

And with that, Henry strode from the room.

I stood near the hearth, but the heat would not penetrate my skin. I was shaking and weak, my heart thudding against my breastbone.

To be so close to him, yet know he was not free to offer me his heart, was one of the greatest misfortunes I could fathom.

# 8

RMS *OLYMPIC*, NORTH ATLANTIC
JUNE 10, 1914

I was finally on my way back to New York, just hours away from docking in New York Harbor, and though I was thrilled to be home, my heart had not been steady since the night Henry and I stood near the hearth. It had been almost two weeks. No matter where I was, in 1774 or 1914, he was never far from my thoughts.

On the first of June, many of us had gathered in Williamsburg at the Bruton Parish Church to pray and fast. There was an awakening in the colonies, and even if I had not been privy to the history of our great nation, I would have felt it. Everyone felt it. The sensation hummed in the hearts and minds of every patriotic colonist.

In the days since then, Henry had remained in the capital at the request of Governor Dunmore and had not taken the trip for his father. I didn't see him often or know why the governor needed his assistance. I also didn't know when Henry would return to Edgewater Hall. For now, he remained in Williamsburg, and I looked forward to the few brief interactions we were able to have. I'd thought it would be awkward to see him again after the evening we were alone, but it wasn't. We'd both shared a bit of our hearts, opening another path of communication—even if it did not lead where I wished to go.

With a sigh, I brought my thoughts back to 1914 and the majestic ship taking me home. I stood on the wide deck of the glorious RMS *Olympic*, the sister ship to the *Titanic*, which had tragically sunk two years before. There were hundreds of other passengers around me. I was watching for my first glimpse of America, allowing the ocean breeze to push any lingering troubles from my spirit. The ship boasted over two thousand passengers and nine hundred and fifty crew members. It was akin to a floating city.

Though Mother Wells and I were returning to New York, we had not come on the terms I would have chosen. Mother had accepted Lord Cumberland's proposal on my behalf and told him we would return to New York to start the wedding plans. It was understood that as soon as we spoke to Father and set a date, Lord Cumberland would travel to America for the nuptials.

But I refused to set a date or acknowledge that I was engaged to be married—no matter what Mother and Lord Cumberland had decided. I had no idea what they discussed behind the drawing room doors in Berkeley Square or what stipulations they had agreed upon, but Mother had come away quite pleased.

Regardless, I was elated that I was almost home. I never wanted to see England again. Perhaps, with time and distance, Mother would accept my decision and we could put the whole matter behind us.

An older gentleman stepped up to the railing beside me, holding his hat so the wind did not tear it away, and I smiled. We'd been introduced early in our voyage, and I had liked him from the start. He was a congressman from Virginia, returning home after representing the US government in conversations with European powers, trying to reduce armies and navies.

We'd dined together at the captain's table, along with the author Sir Arthur Conan Doyle and others. The congressman had sat beside me each time, regaling me with fascinating stories. I'd found him to be a wonderful conversationalist and companion. He was a refreshing change from the stiff Englishmen I'd spent so much time with of late.

"Hello, Miss Wells."

"Good afternoon, Congressman Hollingsworth."

He was warm and congenial with a welcoming smile. "Are you eager to be home?"

I nodded, unable to hide the pleasure from my voice. "I've been gone for six weeks, but it feels like a lifetime."

"I've been gone even longer." There was a hint of longing in his voice. "I miss Virginia. Spring is always my favorite time of year at home."

My own yearning for Williamsburg expanded at his words. Perhaps it was his connection to Virginia that made me feel so at home in his presence. He was a tall gentleman, well-built and handsome for his age, with grey hair at his temples. His interest in me was that of a father or uncle, and when he looked at me, I could see he was genuinely attentive to what I had to say—unlike some people with status who were often distracted by their own importance.

A commotion erupted down the deck, and the congressman and I both looked in that direction. It was nothing more than an anxious woman reprimanding her servant. But at that moment the wind came up, ruffling the hair at the back of the congressman's head and revealing something that made my mouth slip open.

He bore a sunburst birthmark just above his hairline. It would have been almost impossible to see if the wind hadn't moved his hair.

When he turned to look at me, I swallowed hard. The birthmark looked identical to the one I bore over my heart.

Congressman Hollingsworth must have seen the astonishment in my eyes, because he said, "What is it, my dear? You look as though you've seen a ghost."

How did I ask him about his birthmark without telling him about mine? Or what mine meant? Could it be a coincidence that they looked exactly the same? Did his mean what mine meant? Mama said there were other time-crossers in the world, but we only knew of other women. Could this man be one, as well? It seemed too difficult to imagine.

But I had to say something. "Y-Your birthmark. I have one that looks exactly the same, over my heart."

He stared at me for many moments, his gaze penetrating mine.

For a long time we just looked at each other, and the longer it took for him to respond, the more I suspected that his birthmark *did* mean something.

"My father had the same birthmark as me," he said slowly. "And his father before him."

I nodded, trying to communicate with my eyes that I understood—without revealing my secret, in case I was mistaken. "My mother has one, as well," I said. "And her mother, and hers before that. We've each carried the mark, since the beginning of time."

"The beginning of time," he repeated, his face soft with understanding. "What is your other time, Miss Wells?"

Tears gathered in my eyes, and I pressed my trembling lips together. I had never spoken of my other life to anyone in this path before. Nor had I spoken to anyone but Mama about my time-crossing. To do so now felt both liberating and frightening. "It began in 1754," I whispered.

His smile was tender as he said, "Mine began in 1541."

I shook my head, wonder and amazement making me feel a bit faint. "Have you ever met anyone else?"

"Never, though I have heard tales of others."

"Tales?"

"From my grandfather. You might be surprised that some of history's greatest heroes and heroines were time-crossers."

"Truly? Who?"

He chuckled. "Some of them have yet to live, so you wouldn't know them if I told you. But others sacrificed everything for the cause they held dear. They made the world a better place." His smile fell. "But there have also been villains, great and small, who have sought to use their gift for personal gain, at the detriment of humanity."

I stared at him, stunned to learn so much about other time-crossers. I had always sought to live a quiet, peaceful existence. It had never occurred to me that I could use my gift any other way. "But what about changing history?" I asked. "My mama told me it could have cataclysmic effects on the world if I did it intentionally."

"Indeed, and it has. Great wars and disastrous events have brought much pain and suffering to the world through the hands of villains who sought to change history. But, in the end, God's will always prevails."

There was so much more I wanted to know. Excitement bubbled up in my chest. "What about you? Why did you choose this path?"

"Shh." He shook his head and put his finger to his lips. "Let us not share details about our paths. To do so might cause us to unwillingly change a bit of history of our own."

I studied him, wanting so desperately to know everything about him. Was he part of the same family my grandmother had encountered? Were there more families than his and mine? And if so, how many more? I looked around the ship and wondered if there were others, even here.

For the first time in this path, I didn't feel so alone. Even if I never met another time-crosser, at least I knew I wasn't the only one.

I smiled and felt the former tears banished. "I'm so thankful I've met you, Congressman Hollingsworth."

"And I you, Miss Wells. So very thankful." His smile lit up his face.

If Mother were here, I might never have learned the truth about my charming companion. But Mother wasn't with us. She had kept to her berth the entire trip, claiming my refusal to marry Lord Cumberland was making her ill. She was being dramatic and manipulative, so I simply left her to wallow in her despair and enjoyed my leisure time with the congressman and other interesting people I had met on the voyage.

"Miss Libby?"

I turned at the sound of Edith's voice. She stood behind me, her hand on her mobcap so it wouldn't get torn away in the wind.

"Yes?"

"Your mother is asking for you."

My joy at learning the truth about the congressman vanished. I nodded and then turned to the congressman, my heart heavy at the idea of possibly never seeing him again. "I wish we had more time."

"Perhaps," he said slowly, "it's best this way. I think if we'd learned the truth earlier, we might have been tempted to share too much." He took my gloved hand and bowed over it. "It's been a pleasure making your acquaintance. I wish the very best for you, my dear."

"If you'll excuse me, I must see to my mother."

"Of course."

I smiled one last time and then followed Edith to the stairwell, bracing my own large hat against the gusts of wind, even though it was pinned securely to my hair. It took us several minutes to traverse the massive ship to our stateroom, and I could not take my mind off my meeting with the congressman.

The door to Mother's stateroom opened just as I reached out to turn the knob.

I stepped back, surprised, and bumped into Edith.

The ship's surgeon, Dr. O'Conner, exited the room and closed the door quietly behind him. His face was grave. "Miss Wells, may I have a word with you?"

"Of course."

He led me down the hall, away from our cabin, and then stopped, his medical bag tightly grasped in his hand. His heavy white mustache moved as he worked his mouth back and forth a moment before he spoke. "I'm afraid your mother isn't doing well."

My eyes widened in surprise. I thought she was feigning illness to manipulate me. Was she really unwell?

"I am planning to wire ahead to ask for an ambulance to transport her from the ship to your home," he said. "I'm also requesting that her personal physician meet us at the harbor to oversee her care."

Concern tightened my stomach. "Will she be okay?"

His face was severe as he studied me. "I cannot say for certain. She is very ill."

"What troubles her?" She hadn't complained of any particular ailment these past four days, just a general malaise.

"It's hard to tell in situations like this." He shook his head. "The mind is a powerful force, and when one is in such distress as your mother, it can create problems with any number of internal systems but especially the nerves. I've given her a sedative and will administer another before she leaves the ship. It should keep her comfortable until she arrives home."

"Distress?"

"She would not tell me what troubles her, but whatever it is, it's very serious, I'm afraid."

I didn't know what to make of his assessment. Was Mother truly ill or only playacting to manipulate me? If she was sick,

I didn't want to assume she was pretending. It was far too callous.

"Are you certain?" I asked.

He frowned at my question. "Miss Wells, in my long and varied career, I have seen people slip into great despondency. For some, it's a chronic condition of the mind. For others, it's an acute experience. But whatever the cause, it must be taken very seriously, or there are lasting consequences, both mental and physical."

I nodded. "Of course. May I see her?"

"The sedative should be taking effect, but you may go in. We'll be docking soon, so I must take my leave. I'll return when I've arranged all the details."

"Thank you." I offered him an appreciative nod and then allowed him to pass by me.

Edith had stood near me the entire time, listening. When the doctor was out of sight, I said to her, "What do you know of this?"

"Gertie has been worried about Mrs. Wells since our second day at sea." Edith's hazel eyes were huge. "She's never seen your mother like this before."

The entire thing was odd. Mother had always boasted a strong constitution and was not one to give in to weakness. She abhorred it. Even when she had a headache, she refused to let it affect her, as if her body had no right to dictate what she did, when she did it, or how efficiently it was done. For her to be bedridden this long was befuddling.

I entered our stateroom, uncertain how I would find her. Mother's eyes were closed as she lay upon her bed. She looked like she had aged a decade since we'd left London. The wrinkles had deepened around her eyes, her skin was a sickly grey, and her hair had lost whatever luster it boasted.

Was this a nervous complaint, or was it something else entirely?

A twinge tightened my gut. Was this my fault? Was she so terribly unhappy because I refused to marry Lord Cumberland?

And if it was my fault, would she continue to get worse as I continued to refuse?

Within hours, Dr. Payne, Mother, and I were in a boxy black ambulance on the way to our home. Mother seemed oblivious to the bumpy ride, lying flat on the hard bed on one side of the vehicle, not opening her eyes once as Dr. Payne tried to examine her.

My spirits were buoyed as familiar sights and sounds greeted me the closer we came to our brownstone mansion. We passed the famous Washington Arch at the foot of Fifth Avenue and then continued northeast past the Flat Iron Building, one of the tallest structures in Manhattan. There were dozens of mansions along Fifth Avenue, but perhaps the most striking of them all occupied Vanderbilt Row. The impressive mansions from Fifty-Second to Fifty-Eighth Streets were mostly owned by Vanderbilt family members. Our home, on Fifth Avenue and East Fifty-Ninth Street, sat just beyond this famous stretch and across from a golden statue of William Tecumseh Sherman at the east entrance to Central Park.

Seeing our home, I let out a sigh of relief. Father had been informed of our impending arrival, and he would make sure everything was set to rights. If Mother's illness was because of my refusal to marry Lord Cumberland, Father would tell her it was of no consequence. It might take her a while to rally, but she would set her sights on her next challenge, and this whole mess would be forgotten.

Automobiles, bicyclists, pedestrians, and trolleys clogged the road. The day was warm and humid, making the exhaust from the traffic even more suffocating. Edith and Gertie followed the ambulance in a hired cab with our many trunks, though I had lost sight of them somewhere near Thirty-Fourth Street, where the shopping traffic was the thickest.

The ambulance came to a stop, and I exited with the help of the driver. Father was at the open door of the mansion. His blue eyes glowed with welcome as he extended both hands.

I rushed across the sidewalk and up the steps to his tight embrace.

"Libby," he said tenderly as he held me. He, like so many of his class and generation, was not an affectionate man, but when it came to me, he bent his rules. "You are such a sight for my weary eyes, daughter."

I kissed his whiskered cheek, noting the extra lines around his eyes. He was a handsome man, though age and the cares of life had thickened his middle and greyed his hair.

"How is your mother?" he asked as he pulled back to look at me, concern on his face.

"They're just bringing her in on the stretcher." If Mother had been fully aware, she would have been mortified at the idea of entering her home in such a way.

"Is Dr. Payne with her?"

"Yes. He met us at the harbor."

"Good. He'll see to her needs, with Gertie's help."

Though Father and Mother had been at odds with each other for years, it was obvious he still cared for her. How could he not? They'd been married for almost three decades.

The house was just as we'd left it. Its thick, ornate woodwork, heavy draperies, and countless bric-a-brac collected from all over the world made it gaudy. There was no warmth or hominess to the eighteen thousand square feet, but it was familiar, and it felt nice to be back.

The house smelled of fresh polish and lemon oil, though the air was stale as we stood in the entrance hall. There was an echo that had always haunted me as a child and made me feel

113

small and alone. Behind Father loomed the oversized stairway that gleamed from the polish it received daily, making it dangerously slick.

A footman was the first to enter behind me. He held the door open as the ambulance drivers carried Mother in on the stretcher, Dr. Payne close beside her.

A maid materialized from the side of the room and showed the men where to take Mother.

"She's asking to speak to you," Dr. Payne said to Father.

Father nodded and started to follow the entourage. I also followed, but Dr. Payne shook his head. "Only your father, I'm afraid."

I remained in the entrance hall as everyone filed past me, feeling helpless and responsible.

"It's good to see you again, Miss Libby." Pierson, our butler, came to take my hat and gloves. He had always been one of my favorite people.

I smiled at him. "And you, Pierson."

Mrs. Hanson, our housekeeper, also stood nearby with a ready smile for me. "Your room is ready, if you'd like to rest."

"I think I will. Please send Edith up when she arrives."

"Very good."

Pierson bowed, his warm brown eyes kind. "We're very happy you're home."

The house ran on a staff of several dozen. Pierson and Mrs. Hanson had been with us since I was a child. It was like coming home to family.

I walked up the staircase in my mother's wake and went to my room. It faced Fifth Avenue and had a view of William Tecumseh Sherman's statue and the trees of Central Park. There should have been some sort of warmth or comfort in entering my cavernous bedroom, but this home held few good memories. In many respects, it had been an ornate prison, somewhat like the gilded birdcages Mother kept in the drawing room. My surroundings were lovely, but I was not free to fly beyond its confines. I was expected to be beautiful and to perform for the world to see, but I was not allowed to soar as I was meant to soar.

I took off my hat, setting it upon my vanity, and went to the window. Everywhere I looked, there was movement. Even the sky teemed with birds circling above Central Park. I did not love the hustle and bustle of Manhattan, the noise, the smells, or even the view. I longed to be in Williamsburg, looking out at the slower pace of Duke of Gloucester Street. The colors were always brighter, the sounds more cheerful, and the people friendlier. The two cities could not be more different.

A knock sounded at my door.

"Come in," I called, expecting Edith to enter, but it was my father. "Is all well?"

He shook his head. "I'm afraid not."

"Truly?" Deeper concern filled my gut as I walked across my room. "What is wrong?"

"Dr. Payne said she's had quite a shock."

"A shock?"

"She says you've been difficult and petulant, that you have become unruly, undisciplined, and rebellious. She was so ashamed and embarrassed in England that she cut your trip short to bring you home."

I stared at him, at a loss for words. "How could you believe that was true?"

"I don't want to believe such things, but she said you were shameless in your behavior. She was adamant."

"I was unhappy, yes." I swallowed, horrified she would say those things about me, but even more troubled that Father might believe them. "But I wasn't an embarrassment or shameful." I put my hand on his forearm. "You know me. Have I ever been reprehensible?"

"I don't know what to believe. She's quite beside herself, and she cut your trip short. She's been planning it for years."

"That's not why we came home. Did she not tell you? Lord Cumberland made a marriage offer, and she accepted on my behalf. She brought me home to prepare for the wedding."

His frown only deepened. "She mentioned nothing of Lord Cumberland or a proposal."

I did not want to speak ill of Mother Wells. No matter what she had done to me or how she had tried to control me through the years, she was my mother, the woman God had chosen for me in this path, and I could not dishonor her. But nor would I let her get away with her manipulations.

"I have not agreed to Lord Cumberland's proposal, and she is upset with me. I believe that is at the crux of her unhappiness."

He sighed, and his shoulders fell. "Who is this Lord Cumberland?"

I explained that he was the Marquess of Cumberland, a royal treasurer, and a good friend of the prime minister.

"So she has set her sights on a political match instead of just an aristocratic one." He nodded, seeming now to understand what was happening. "I wondered how she would play the game."

"You knew why we went?" The discovery of his knowledge was even more painful than Edith's. "Why did you let her take me?"

"My dear." His face was sad, his voice even more so. "Your mother has known exactly what she planned to do with your life from the moment you were born. There was nothing you or I could do to change those plans. I accepted it long ago, and the faster you accept it, the sooner you will find peace—and an escape."

My heart broke at his words. "You approve of her choice?"

"It hardly matters what I think."

"But it does!"

A clock chimed down the hall, and the sun was starting its descent in the western sky, casting longer shadows into my room.

"Libby, your mother is ill, whether from a real or imagined

116

disease, and her body is weak. I saw her with my own eyes." He searched my face for an answer to his next question. "Do you truly dislike the idea of marrying Lord Cumberland?"

"I do not love him."

"Marrying for love is a girlish fantasy, one that is neither reasonable nor realistic, especially for people like us. Love is fickle." He stopped, and I wondered if he was thinking of his own love affair with Mother and how it had fizzled and died. "Emotions are untrustworthy, and feelings come and go. Marriage is an institution created to form alliances that benefit as many people as possible. I do not wish for you to be unhappy, but even if you married for love, there is no guarantee you'll be happy."

It wasn't happiness I was seeking—at least not in 1914. But Father would not understand, so I had to appeal to his love and affection for me.

"Please do not ask me to marry him," I said.

He sighed and nodded.

Now that I was home, Father would help me.

# 9

## WILLIAMSBURG, VIRGINIA
## JUNE 19, 1774

My twentieth birthday had finally arrived.

I stood in front of the mirror in my room above the printing office to adjust the stomacher of my second-best gown and fluff out the heavy skirts over the pannier I wore at my hips. It had been a long time since I'd had a new gown, but there was no extra money for such things. Mistress Hunter had agreed to make the girls' new dresses on credit, which I despised, but there was little choice.

The extra money we had earned from the increase in advertisements and subscriptions garnered from the public printing contract had not been much, but I had been slowly paying off our other creditors. It didn't feel like enough, but it was better than where we had been a month ago. I just prayed something more would come along to sustain us.

Letting out a heavy sigh, I told myself to set aside such things today. I pinched my cheeks to add color as I heard the first of our guests arrive downstairs. Mama had invited my friends to dine with us, and I would enjoy every moment. She loved celebrating birthdays, and my twentieth was especially worth noting. One year from today, I would stay awake past the midnight hour, and I would never have to wake up in my other time path again.

The thought should have brought a smile, but instead it sent a strange pang to my heart. For Father and Edith, for Pierson and Mrs. Hanson, and for my fellow suffragettes. They would mourn my loss, and I would dearly miss them.

My thoughts shifted to Mother Wells, and though I had always been a disappointment to her, I wondered if she would mourn my loss. It had been nine days since we'd arrived in New York on the RMS *Olympic*, and she had not risen from bed. Her melancholy had begun to scare even me. Our plans to go to Newport had been postponed, and Dr. Payne had visited almost every day to treat her ailments, but nothing seemed to help.

I closed my eyes, trying to push aside the guilt that lay upon me. She had asked me every day if I would reconsider marrying Lord Cumberland, but I could not accept.

And each day she slipped lower and lower, losing weight, growing paler, and becoming so despondent that my heart had begun to ache for her.

Was it really so dire to refuse him?

"Libby!" Mama called from the bottom of the steps. "Your guests have begun to arrive."

I pushed aside thoughts of Mother Wells, determined not to let her ruin this day.

Conversation filled the stairwell as I made my way down. Mama had told me about the birthday parties she celebrated with her family in the 1980s and '90s. Her father had been an important architect in Chicago, and they'd lived a comfortable life. For her twentieth birthday, her parents had taken her on a skiing trip to Vail, Colorado, and she'd been allowed to bring three of her closest college friends. When she spoke of her 1990s life, her face usually shone, and her voice took on a faraway tone that had always charmed me as a girl. Even her accent and word choices changed. Though I would never see that time, I felt as if I had lived part of it with her. I was the only person Mama could share that fragment of her existence with, and I felt it an honor.

Sophia stood in the hall with Constance Meriwether and Emmaline Page. All three women were a year or two younger than me, but we'd grown up in Williamsburg together and had always been friends. Of the three, Sophia was my closest friend, but the other two were equally fun and enjoyable.

"Happiest of birthdays to you, Libby," Sophia said. "You look lovely."

The others complimented me as well, and my cheeks grew warm at their praise. "The party will be in the garden," I told them. "It's much too nice a day to spend indoors."

"Indeed." Sophia linked arms with me, talking all the way as we walked into the gardens.

Constance told us of her upcoming wedding, and we listened intently. She was the first of us to be engaged, though I suspected Emmaline would be next. Her beau had been calling on a regular basis, and the only thing preventing him from making an offer was his apprenticeship with Mister Goodman, the cobbler. But that would end this summer, and then he'd be able to start his own shop.

I wondered how the coming war would change all their plans, but I could not let that daunting knowledge taint my evening, nor theirs.

A beautiful table had been set up under the large elm tree, surrounded by purple irises, yellow daffodils, and pink bleeding hearts. Torches, which would not be lit until it grew dark, were positioned throughout the yard and down the crushed-shell path leading through our property. The printing shop sat on a wide double lot, which was long and deep. On either side of the path that led to the back of the property were vegetable gardens that Mama, Mariah, and Abraham tended. An abandoned stable sat in the back corner of the gardens, which Abraham used to store extra supplies from time to time.

"It's enchanting," Sophia said as she inspected the table, which I noticed was set for eight.

Who else had Mama invited? I turned to ask her, but she had not followed us outside.

Emmaline took a deep breath. "The food smells wonderful."

"Mariah has been cooking for hours," I told my friends, inhaling the delicious scents wafting from the kitchen windows. "Chicken fricassee with mushroom sauce and creamed spinach."

The back door opened, and Mama appeared with several more guests behind her.

Among them was Henry.

I smiled at the sight of him. I had not expected Mama to invite him, nor would I have assumed he'd attend.

He saw me standing under the spreading elm tree, and his face lit with a smile so tender and so sweet that I was certain my legs would fail me. Beside him were three other gentlemen, including Constance's fiancé, Emmaline's beau, and another childhood friend, Thomas Drew. Williamsburg was a small village, with only eighteen hundred people, and everyone knew everyone else, even if they were not intimately acquainted. Thankfully, Henry spent time at his home on the Palace Green and had attended the College of William and Mary. He was familiar enough with my guests and known by all because of his new position in the House of Burgesses. He didn't seem a stranger, as some of the other sailing merchants were often viewed.

I received greetings from everyone before they began talking among themselves.

"Happy Birthday, Libby," Henry said to me when I finally made it to him.

"I'm so pleased that you came."

"When your mother sent the invitation, how could I refuse?" He smiled at Mama, who stood near the kitchen door, admiring the small group before stepping inside to help Mariah.

This was the first time Henry and I had been close enough to talk since the night by the hearth. I had not had the opportunity to ask him why Governor Dunmore had requested that he stay in Williamsburg, though I had been deeply curious. I still couldn't shake the rumors Louis and Sophia had shared. Had he stayed because he was spying for Governor Dunmore?

"Why are you still in town?" I asked.

His smile was teasing. "Why does your question sound like an accusation?"

Had it? Warmth filled my cheeks. What would he think if he knew my suspicions? "Pray, forgive me. It just seems odd, is all. Last we spoke"—I faltered, thinking of that night—"I-I thought you were returning to the sea after the first of June."

"Aye." His face became more serious. "I planned to take a schooner to New York for my father, but Governor Dunmore requested I stay through the summer to aid him in his work."

Was his work spying? I longed to know but could not ask him with the others present.

"It's been good to stay in town, with all the plans we are making for the Virginia Convention," he went on. "As the clerk, I've been tasked with communicating with the other colonies to let them know our intentions. It's kept me quite busy."

"Does Governor Dunmore approve of your involvement in the unlawful meeting you're planning?" Sophia asked, interrupting our conversation.

"The meeting is not unlawful," Henry explained, his voice calm and unhurried. "'Tis not unlawful for British citizens—and elected burgesses—to peacefully assemble."

"Will this be a closed meeting?" Thomas asked.

Henry shook his head. "If you'd like to attend the convention, you may. It will be open to one and all."

One and all, if you were a man. I tried not to let my thoughts show on my face.

Mama came out of the kitchen with a tray in her hands. "Supper is ready."

She'd come at just the right moment, as I could sense growing tension. Sophia's father was opposed to the taxes imposed by England to pay for the French and Indian War, but he was not in support of independence. He was a loyalist, and thus Sophia was a loyalist. At some point, she, like everyone else, would have to choose where they stood on the fight for independence, and I prayed she would side with us. But that day was not today.

It was after seven o'clock, and my stomach was growling. "Shall we sit?" I asked my guests with a bright smile.

I took a seat at the head of the table, and Henry sat at my right, with Sophia to my left.

Mariah exited the kitchen with a tureen of green-pea soup and gracefully served each of us, smiling when she caught my eye. To the outside world, our printing shop appeared to be doing well and prospering. It was an embarrassment that so many of the merchants on Duke of Gloucester Street knew the truth. But here and now, with a feast to celebrate my birthday, I could pretend we were financially stable.

As we ate and visited, laughing and talking of everything but politics, I tried to push aside the thought that before my next birthday, the American Revolution would begin, and next year at this time, though it would be a bright and brilliant day for me, it would be the beginning of a dark and somber decade in the history of America.

Would the gentlemen sitting around my table be here a year from now? Or would they be off fighting alongside General George Washington?

Most important, where would Henry be?

The torches were burning bright as my party drew to a close. I had already said good-bye to all my guests except Henry, who lingered at the table with Mama and me as we talked about fond memories from the past.

"Your mother and I were friends since childhood," Mama told Henry. "Did you know that?"

He shook his head. "I knew you had been friends for a long time, but I didn't realize it went back to your childhoods."

Mama smiled as if she was recalling special memories. She sighed and placed her hands on the table as she rose. All the dishes had been cleared save the noggins, which had been filled with cider and ale. She took a few of the empty ones now. "I believe I will help Mariah clean the kitchen so she can go to bed."

"I should take my leave, as well," Henry said, rising with her.

I begrudgingly stood, unwilling to let the night end but knowing I had no choice. Just one more year, and I would not have to dread waking up in the twentieth century ever again.

"I'll walk you to the back gate," I told him. His home on the Palace Green was easier to access from our backyard, which bordered Nicholson Street.

"Good-night, Henry," Mama said. "Thank you for coming."

"Thank you for inviting me."

Mama slipped quietly into the kitchen.

"I'll fetch your hat." I went into the house, where I found his tricorne hanging on a peg in the entry hall, and then met him out by the tree again.

He was staring into the distance as I approached, his gaze troubled. More than ever, I longed to know if he was spying. But would he tell me even if he was? I didn't think he'd lie to me, but would he tell me the truth? Having such knowledge could put my life in danger as much as his.

He turned at my approach and took his hat, but he didn't put it on his head. Instead, he held it under his arm. "Thank you."

We walked toward the back of our property, along the crushed-shell path between our vegetable gardens.

"It's been good to see you again, Libby," he said, his voice a bit tentative. "I wasn't sure if I should come. I feared you wouldn't want to speak to me again after the last time I was here."

"Of course I do."

Our hands brushed as we walked, and I looked up at him. He was so tall next to me. I felt safe and secure with him in ways I didn't anywhere else. He made me feel seen and understood, though he didn't know all of me. I had a burning desire to tell him the truth—all of it—but I doubted he would believe me. Worse, I feared losing his friendship.

He met my gaze, but I could not read his expression. Whatever he'd been thinking about when I joined him had brought a heaviness to his countenance.

With my twentieth birthday now behind me, I felt bolder than usual in the darkness, the flickering torches offering just enough light to guide our path. I allowed our hands to brush against each other again. This time, he took my hand in his. But instead of looking pleased, his face filled with sorrow.

We were almost to the back gate when he finally paused just outside the circle of light from the last torch. The darkness cocooned us in privacy, though my eyes were adjusted enough to see his face. Pain and longing emanated from every curve and line.

"I should never have shared so much with you the last time we were together," he said. "'Twas unfair."

"Nothing you said felt unfair."

His smile looked sad. "You're too kind to me."

"'Tis easy."

He swallowed as his thumb passed over the back of my bare hand. A shiver ran up my spine, one I could not control.

"I should let you return to the warmth of your home." I felt him pulling away, so I clasped his hand tighter, not willing for him to leave me yet.

"Henry, are you spying?" The words burst from me before I could stop them.

"Spying?" His voice lowered a notch with surprise.

Had I insulted him? I licked my dry lips, trying to read his response. Having come this far, I decided to plunge further. "I've heard you're spying on Governor Dunmore, but I've also heard you're spying on the Patriots. Is there truth to either claim?"

He pulled away from me, dropping my hand. "Who said these things?"

My heart fell. He hadn't denied them, as I hoped he would.

"Are either of the rumors true? Are they both true?" I held my breath, hoping Henry would not lie to me—but also hoping he was not guilty of either offense. Both would put him in grave danger.

"I cannot speak about these things, Libby." He took a step back and ran a hand over his dark hair in a distracted manner I'd seen dozens of times. The curls loosened and fell over his forehead.

"You will not tell me the truth?"

"I cannot tell you what you want to hear, so I will tell you nothing."

I couldn't believe it. He was all but admitting to his involvement—but on which side?

"I do not want to spoil your birthday." His eyes were intense, and they matched his voice when he said, "I want to spare you from pain, Libby. I would rather die than cause you heartache, you must believe me."

He was admitting to something, but I didn't know what it might be.

I stood there, unable to remove the frown slanting my brows. I felt weak and slack and numb as I stared at him.

"Please." He took both of my hands in his, dropping his hat to the path, and entwined our fingers together. He brought my hands up to press against his chest. "Do not look at me that way. I cannot bear disappointing you."

We were close, very close. I could smell the sweet scent of tobacco smoke clinging to his garments. I forced my face to soften. "I'm not disappointed in you," I whispered, looking up to meet his gaze. "I'm worried and confused and uncertain."

"I wish I could make you understand. There are things beyond my control. If things could be different—" He groaned in frustration. "But please know that I do not want to disappoint you, Libby. Your approval means more to me than any other."

My senses were swimming, and I could not think straight with him standing so close. I didn't want this moment to end—didn't want him to leave my side again—especially if it meant he was doing something dangerous.

His gaze fell to my lips, and every inch of my body hummed to life at the look in his eyes. I wanted him to kiss me. I leaned against him, hoping he would.

"Libby." He was breathing hard as he pulled back. "You must trust me." He took several steps away this time, reaching down to pick up his tricorne. "I must go. If I stay, I fear I will tell you more than you should know. I'm very sorry. Forgive me. For everything."

Confusion mingled with my longing as he left.

Was he embroiled in the rebellion deeper than I realized? Was his life in danger? What did he know that I didn't know? What was he afraid to tell me?

A nagging question returned, one I had tried to ignore for years. Why wasn't his name mentioned among the founding fathers in my other path? If he was working alongside Jefferson and Washington and Patrick Henry, men who would go on to great fame, then why hadn't I ever heard his name? Was it because he wouldn't survive the revolution? Was his name lost to history like those of so many others who would die?

Or was it because he was working for the British and wouldn't become an American hero?

# 10

NEW YORK CITY
JUNE 19, 1914

I allowed Edith to take her time helping me dress the next day when I woke in my parents' brownstone mansion. This would be the last time I celebrated my birthday in this path, and the knowledge brought a melancholy I didn't expect, coupled with the pain from Henry's parting. As she styled my hair, I stared at my reflection in the mirror, thinking not about 1914, but about 1774.

It had taken me a long time to fall asleep after Henry left. My heart and mind were troubled. Was he spying on his fellow burgesses for the governor? Was he trying to undermine the Patriots' cause? Was I so blinded by my love and respect for him that I had been a fool? The thought of being deceived and lied to made anger and hurt course through my body.

But what if the opposite was true? What if he was using his position to spy on Governor Dunmore for the Patriots? He would have to betray his father—and his friendship to the governor. It would mean that his passion and zeal for freedom was real, but it would also mean that he was willing to hurt the people closest to him for a cause he felt was more important than his own life. The cost of treason was death—an unspeakable reality I didn't want to think about.

If he was willing to sacrifice his friends and family for freedom's cause, where did that leave me? Was he sacrificing his own feelings for me so he could give himself fully to the revolution? If that was true, then I loved him all the more, but I was angry that God had put me in a time and place where I could not be with the man I loved.

"Does this style displease you?" Edith's face was drawn with concern as she studied my reflection in the mirror. "I can change it, if you'd like."

Her hand came up to remove the pins, but I stopped her. "'Tis beautiful." She looked at me strangely, and I realized I had responded as I would in Williamsburg. I quickly added, "Don't change a thing." I forced myself to smile for her sake, trying to put aside my troubles from 1774.

My hair did look lovely. Edith had styled it full at the sides and back, with a thick, cream-colored ribbon wrapping around the crown of my head. How different it was from the simple style I wore tucked under my cap in Williamsburg.

As she finished, I realized it hardly mattered what I looked like today. With Mother Wells still in bed, there would be no parties to celebrate my birthday. We had turned down all the invitations we'd received since returning to the city. It was the height of the Newport season, yet we could not go there either.

The only thing I could do was volunteer my time. I loved to work at Mrs. Alva Belmont's suffrage settlement house in Harlem. There, I worked with women and children who had recently immigrated to America. As I helped them integrate into the community, I also taught them the importance of a woman's right to vote and her role in teaching her children the same.

Though Mrs. Belmont was a leader in society, the mother of Consuelo Vanderbilt, also known as the Duchess of Marlborough, Mother Wells hated the work she was doing and had forbidden me from participating long ago. Of course, I did not obey. Whenever I had the opportunity, I was either at the settlement house or the National American Woman Suffrage Association headquarters less than a mile down Fifth Avenue from our home. It was there that we organized marches and social events not only to educate, but also to recruit the middle and upper classes to our cause.

Today would be a quiet day, as I had no plans but to dine with Father. He planned to work from home in honor of my birthday.

I rose from my vanity and smoothed out my morning gown. With Mother in bed, I was allowed to wear whatever I chose, and today I was wearing a simple cream-colored gown. Perhaps, after breakfast, I would go on a walk in Central Park.

A knock at my door brought my head up. "Come in."

Gertie, Mother's maid, gave a quick curtsy, but her eyes were filled with alarm.

"What is it?" I asked.

"Dr. Payne is here again, and he's asked to speak to you and your father."

"This early?" We hadn't even had our breakfast. Dr. Payne didn't usually arrive until after lunch to check on Mother.

"I called him, miss." Gertie's eyes were rimmed in red, and she looked as if she hadn't slept all night. "I'm worried."

I hurried out of my room to go to Mother. Father was coming up the stairs as I passed, his own face reflecting his concern.

"What if there's something terribly wrong?" I asked him. "Something the doctor hasn't caught?" What if this wasn't simply Mother overreacting to my refusal to marry Lord Cumberland?

"Let's see what Dr. Payne has to say." Father gently placed his hand under my elbow as he led me to Mother's room. The plush carpet was soft beneath my slippered feet, and the large, framed paintings on the wall made me feel small and vulnerable.

Dr. Payne was waiting outside her bedroom. He was a middle-aged man, with his thinning hair parted on the side and combed over the top. He had a calm, soothing voice and had been my physician since I was born. I had always trusted Dr. Payne, as did most everyone we knew. His reputation with the upper classes kept him in high demand on Fifth Avenue.

"Is it serious?" Father asked.

Dr. Payne let out a sigh. "I'm afraid so. Mrs. Wells's heart is failing. It grows weaker by the day, and this morning she could not be roused by her maid, which is why she sent for me."

Father studied the doctor intently. "What is to be done?"

"I'm afraid I don't know. I've never seen anything like this before. I'd like to take her to the hospital and have some tests done, but she will not let me move her. You must convince her to go, or I fear she will not be long for this world."

Father stared at Dr. Payne. I'd never seen the look that passed over his face, and I realized that he still loved her deeply. He was afraid to lose her, and my heart broke for him. Even if I didn't understand how he could love her, it wasn't my place to question him. This was his wife—my mother—and though she had brought both of us pain, the idea of losing her jarred me out of my self-pity.

"We will speak to her," Father promised Dr. Payne, "and will call you the moment she agrees."

"I will prepare things on my end," he assured us. "Just get her to agree, and I will take care of the rest."

"Thank you."

Dr. Payne started to walk away but then paused. "I believe today is your birthday, Libby."

I nodded, surprised that he had remembered.

"Then I will wish you a happy birthday," Dr. Payne said, "even though the circumstances are so dire."

"Thank you."

Father placed a hand on my shoulder, his face sad. "Happy

birthday, Libby. I do wish this day were different. We should be celebrating in Newport, as we usually do."

"It's all right." I was about to say that we could hope for a better celebration next year, but I would not be waking up on this day one year from now. Instead of celebrating my birthday, Father would be mourning my death.

I swallowed the panicked feeling that thought elicited.

"Let us put on our best faces to greet your mother," he said. "And let us do what we must to get her better."

I nodded. "Of course."

Father pushed open the door to her bedchamber. The room was darker than usual, the heavy velvet curtains closed to the brilliant June sunshine. The smell of antiseptic burned my nose. Gertie was near Mother's bed, her eyes closed as if she were praying. When she saw us, she removed herself from the room and closed the door quietly behind her.

Mother's bed, like the room itself, was oversized and ornate. She lay on her back, her hair lying over her shoulder in a braid. She'd lost even more weight, and the wrinkles under her eyes and around her neck had deepened. Everything in the room was still, and there were no sounds. If the doctor had not been in here moments ago, I would have thought she had already passed on. Her breathing was so shallow, it looked as if she wasn't breathing at all.

That same sickly panic overtook me, creeping up my legs and settling in my chest. I reached for Father and grasped his arm for support. What would happen if we lost her? How could I leave him alone in a year? He would be devastated beyond recovery. I was certain of it.

"Abigail?" Father said softly as he reached for one of her hands.

Her eyelids fluttered open. She looked at him, but she did not respond.

"We've just spoken to Dr. Payne," he said. "Libby and I believe it's best if you go to the hospital."

Mother's gaze flicked to me. I allowed her to look at me without dropping my eyes.

"I don't think I'll make it to the hospital." Her voice was so weak that it was hard to hear what she said.

Father got down on his knees and clasped Mother's hand to his chest. "Don't say such things, my dear. You can't leave us. We still need you."

"You don't need me." She closed her eyes again, as if it were too difficult to keep them open.

"Of course we need you," I said. At least, Father needed her.

Her eyes opened again, and it took a second for her to focus on me. "Elizabeth, all I've ever wanted was the best for you."

"Yes, I know." The best, according to her standards.

"If you do not follow my wishes"—she stopped to take a labored breath—"then I am useless to you."

"That's not true." Guilt weighed so heavily upon me that my legs grew weak, and I was afraid I couldn't hold myself up much longer.

"We both need you," Father said to Mother. "We've always needed you. I'm sorry for how things have become between us, Abigail. My work, my stubbornness, my inability to bend." Tears fell from Father's eyes, and he wiped them away. I had never seen him cry. He'd always been one of the strongest people I knew.

"There is something I must tell you," Mother whispered. "Something very dire, indeed."

Father frowned. "What is it?"

"When I was in England"—her voice broke, but she swallowed and pressed on—"I accepted Lord Cumberland's marriage proposal on behalf of you and Elizabeth."

"Yes, I know, my dear."

"The marquess also had me sign a contract—a binding agreement."

My heart began to pound. "What kind of contract?" I asked.

"If you do not marry him"—she paused to breathe—"he will sue us for breach of contract. And he will ruin us."

Father and I stared at her.

"Don't you see?" Mother asked me. "Why I've been so distraught? If you refuse to marry him, we will lose everything."

"Why would you do such a thing?" Father asked, rising from the side of her bed. "I did not give you leave to be so foolish."

"You gave me permission to act on your behalf." She swallowed again. "I thought I could get Elizabeth to agree—but if she continues to refuse, it will be catastrophic."

"Surely, we can get out of this agreement." My hands and voice trembled as I looked at Father. "There must be something we can do."

Father ran his hand over the back of his neck. "I do not know what your mother signed or how legally binding it might be—but if Lord Cumberland has a written agreement, he has every right to sue us for breach of contract. He can demand whatever sum your mother promised—and more. The legal battle and scandal it would cause could be the end of us."

My throat clogged with alarm. I couldn't agree to marry Lord Cumberland. I needed one more year.

"Adam," Mother said to Father, breathing heavily, "I'm sorry."

Anger and resentment flared in Father's face—but when he looked at Mother, lying in bed, something broke in his gaze. What if she died because of this?

He turned to me, sadness weighing heavily upon his shoulders. "Libby," he said. "I'm so sorry."

My breathing became shallow as I stared at him, hoping and praying he would not ask me to do this thing.

"I don't see any way out of it," he finally said.

I swallowed as I frantically thought through my options. But I didn't have many. There was only one reason I would agree to the engagement, and that was to save my father. But

I would demand we postpone the wedding for at least a year. If we did, I would be gone, and the contract would be nulled because of my death.

I closed my eyes, struggling to use my voice. "I will accept Lord Cumberland's proposal—if you agree to let me postpone the wedding until next year."

Father looked both relieved and dejected, but he nodded his approval, and then he looked back at Mother, contempt in his voice. "Did you hear that, Abigail? Libby has promised to marry Lord Cumberland after all."

Mother's eyes were open, and she nodded. "I did, indeed."

I left Mother's room feeling shaky and uncertain. I had lost my appetite and no longer felt like going on a walk, but I had to leave the house. Father had stayed with Mother to try to convince her to go to the hospital, and I wasn't needed. I had done my part. Father would see to the rest.

An hour later, Edith and I left the brownstone mansion to cross Fifth Avenue and enter Central Park. I had changed into a soft blue walking gown, and Edith had pinned a large matching hat on my head. I'd purposely chosen a hat with a veil, hoping to hide the emotions playing upon my face.

I thought I had always known how I felt about leaving this time path—and I had not changed my mind—but I hadn't allowed myself to truly think about this final year. I was facing a year of good-byes, even if the people around me weren't aware. I just hadn't thought the first good-bye might be to my mother.

The air was hot and humid as we meandered along the shaded paths with no particular destination. Edith walked beside me as we passed through the park's menagerie. I usually conversed with her on walks like this, but today I had nothing to say. She knew I had accepted Lord Cumberland's proposal, but she didn't press me for the details. I wasn't too concerned about the betrothal, but I still didn't want to think about it. With the Atlantic between us and the threat of Mother's death, a yearlong engagement would not only be acceptable, it would be expected.

Even with Edith at my side, my loneliness overwhelmed me, more so than usual. With my impending departure next year, I longed to discuss my other path with her. I thought about Congressman Hollingsworth for the first time since Mother grew ill. Part of me wanted to go to Virginia to talk to him, but the other part knew it was foolish. What good could come from knowing more about the lives of other time-crossers?

All my society friends were in Newport, though they couldn't ease this loneliness I felt either. Perhaps, if I could be by the ocean, it might be a little better. But even if we were in Newport, it would not erase the pain of Mother's illness or the eventual loss of this life.

Birds sang in the trees overhead while white clouds drifted in the bright blue sky. The smell of popcorn mingled with the sound of children laughing and playing. The world I currently occupied was a beautiful one—and I was extremely blessed. I could not deny that. New York City in 1914 was magnificent, especially with the luxuries afforded to me. The life I lived was a charmed one, even if it was tainted by Mother's machinations. If it had been the only one I'd been given, I could have learned how to be content.

But it wasn't the only life I'd been given. The one in which Mama and Henry resided was my true home. Yes, I would miss the motorcars and the indoor plumbing. I would miss the electricity and modern medicine. I would miss the conveniences of the telephone and the elevator—but none of those things could compare to what I was gaining in purpose and pleasure.

We came upon the Lake and boathouse. Edith and I bought peanuts, which we ate as we watched people rowing on the water. All around us, people were laughing and playing—

surrounding me with life—but it only made me feel more iso-lated. I was eager to return home for luncheon.

"Cook has a special surprise for your lunch," Edith said, trying to draw out a smile. "Chicken fricassee."

I did smile, thinking about how different our cook, Mrs. Malone, prepared her chicken fricassee than Mariah.

Since Father was home today, I wouldn't have to eat alone. Perhaps, by the time I arrived back at the mansion, he would have convinced Mother to go to the hospital. The thought quickened my steps.

At home, Edith and I went to my room so I could change for the third time. I would not miss this exhausting ritual when I left this path. I often changed outfits six or seven times a day.

It didn't take long to put on an afternoon gown, and when I finally reached the dining room, Father was already there, waiting for me. He rose from his place at the table and offered me a tight smile.

"What's wrong?" I asked, immediately sensing that he had bad news. "Is it Mother?"

He opened his mouth to reply but was interrupted.

"Elizabeth, I'm so happy you've returned. We have so much to do."

I spun on my heels, my mouth slipping open, as Mother entered the large dining room.

For the first time in weeks, she was properly dressed, though her gown hung off her frame in an appalling manner. Her hair was combed and styled in her usual twist, yet her skin was still a sickly pale. The transformation was remarkable from what she had looked like on her bed, hardly breathing, just this morning.

"Mother." I stared at her. "What? How?"

"It's a miracle," Father said, his voice flat and dry. "I had Dr. Payne come to examine her, and he said he's never seen anything like it before." He leveled Mother with a cool stare. "It appears that whatever was causing her distress has vanished."

"I feel like a new woman," Mother said, ignoring the storm gathering around her. She allowed a footman to pull out the seat at Father's right hand.

Another footman held out a chair for me. As I sat, I could not take my eyes off her. Was she truly on the mend?

As the first course was brought out by the footmen, Mother placed her napkin on her lap. "It feels good to be among the land of the living again." She took a deep breath and gave us a contented smile.

"Perhaps it's not too late to go to Newport," I said, hope in my voice.

"Oh no, we couldn't." Mother shook her head as she picked up her soup spoon to sample the tomato bisque set before us. "We have too much to do."

Father narrowed his eyes, and I noticed he had not touched his food.

"What is there to do?" I asked.

"Plan the wedding, of course." Mother lifted an eyebrow at me. "Now that you have finally agreed."

A cold sweat broke out across my forehead.

"The wedding?" I choked on the word as I looked from her to Father. "We have months to think about that."

"Months?" She laughed. "I've already phoned all the major newspapers to announce the engagement, and I wired Lord Cumberland to tell him the happy news."

"Don't you think that's a bit premature?" Father asked.

"Premature?" She frowned. "How so? We're already behind schedule. The wedding is six short weeks from now."

"Six weeks?" I stood, bumping the massive table with my thighs. Pain shot through my body, but I didn't care. "I will not marry him in six weeks. That's impossible. I said at least a year."

"Yes, you will." She stared at me. "Your father heard you agree."

"She agreed if we postpone," Father reminded her.

Mother frowned. "I didn't hear her say that." She waved her hand. "Besides, it's too late. The newspapers have already been given the wedding date, and Lord Cumberland has already purchased his passage to arrive on July 29th. We cannot postpone now without his consent, or so the agreement says. The wedding will happen in six weeks, whether you want it to or not, my pet."

I couldn't believe what I was hearing. She'd manipulated me. It had all been an incredible act. She'd lost so much weight and had been in bed for weeks. Dr. Payne had even been convinced. I could hardly believe the commitment she'd given to her cause.

I'd been a fool.

"Was all of it a lie?" Father asked, breathing heavily.

"A lie?" Mother lifted her nose at him. "I don't know what you mean."

"Were you truly sick, or was it part of your scheme to get Libby to agree?"

"I was sick at heart at her ungratefulness."

She leveled an icy glare at me, and I knew in that moment that she did not love me. She was incapable of love. All she understood was using people to get what she wanted. Wasn't that why she'd married Father, to get ahead in life? Wasn't that why she had promised me to an English marquess, so she could climb the social ladder?

She took a delicate sip of her soup and closed her eyes briefly, as if savoring the flavor. "It's already been announced. The plans have been laid. Unless you want your family to be humiliated and financially ruined, Elizabeth, you will keep quiet and do your part."

"This was your plan all along, wasn't it?" I threw my cloth napkin down on my bowl of soup. "All this time I thought I had been spared, but you were conniving to get me to agree."

"You're too soft. You must work on that before you're married, or Lord Cumberland will walk all over you." She looked at Father out of the corner of her eye. "Some men are easier to get around than others."

Father also stood and threw his napkin on the table. He strode out of the dining room without another word.

"I refuse to let this happen," I told her.

"Oh, do sit down, Elizabeth. You're making a scene in front of the staff."

"I won't go through with it. You can't make me."

"Well," Mother said, dipping her spoon into the soup again, "perhaps you could try running away, but I fear you would face a far greater calamity if you took to the streets. The staff have already been told to watch your every move, and I still have the power to dismiss Edith without a reference if she's foolish enough to help you. She'll be ruined along with you, and her plight will be even worse than yours." She lifted the spoon to her thin lips and took a sip. "So you must accept your lot in life and look forward to becoming a marchioness in six short weeks. I know I will."

I wouldn't allow it to happen. I had options—surely. Father would not let this happen.

"Remember," Mother said to me as I started to walk out of the dining room, "I can make your life miserable."

More so than she already had? It was hard to believe, but it was true.

I left the dining room to beg Father for his help. Mother had won the battle, but he and I would win the war.

# 11

## WILLIAMSBURG, VIRGINIA
## AUGUST 1, 1774

I sat on one of the Windsor chairs in our sitting room, Mama pacing the floor as I stared at the table. Rebecca and Hannah had been sent to help Mariah and Abraham weed the gardens, and Louis and Glen were already at work in the printing room. That left Mama and me some space and time to talk.

It had been six weeks since I learned about Mother Wells's betrayal. Six weeks of praying and fasting and begging God to spare me from such a fate. Whether I was in New York or Williamsburg, it was all I could think about, especially today. Because tomorrow, in my 1914 path, I would be forced to marry Lord Cumberland.

Father could do nothing to stop her lunacy. He had gone to his lawyer and asked what could be done, but there was nothing. If we canceled the wedding, Lord Cumberland could sue my father for breach of contract. Father had told me that it didn't matter, he'd give everything up for my happiness, but it *did* matter. He'd worked his whole life to establish his business and reputation. I could not be the one to ruin it. So I had continued with the wedding plans, hoping that Mama or Father or I could find another way to stop this from happening.

"Is there no one who could help you escape?" Mama asked, coming to a stop in front of me. "Edith? Mr. Pierson?"

"Mother Wells has threatened everyone, telling them they will be turned out without references if they do." I stopped to swallow the panic climbing up my throat. "Besides, if I ran away, it would only hasten Lord Cumberland's lawsuit, which is the very thing I want to prevent."

Mama sat on the chair next to me and took my hands in hers. Outside the open window, birds were singing as if all was right with the world. Merchants did business on Duke of Gloucester Street, farmers went past with their produce, and children played in the dooryards of the nearby houses.

"I've always felt so helpless, Libby, but never like today."

"What will I do?"

She sighed. "If you are forced to go through with this, keep your husband at arm's length no matter what. You have less than eleven months to go."

I knew what she was telling me. I needed to find a way to stop Lord Cumberland from consummating the marriage. It was the only thing I really feared about marrying him. Though I had no wish to leave America, I could do almost anything for eleven months—anything but that.

To make matters worse, there was a war looming in Europe. I'd already shared all the details with Mama, and she'd told me the little she knew about England's entrance into what she called World War One. Everything had begun at the end of June, when a Bosnian Serb Yugoslav nationalist assassinated the Austro-Hungarian heir Archduke Franz Ferdinand in Sarajevo. Over the course of July, a series of events that I failed to understand had transpired in Europe, and an alliance had been formed by Britain, France, and Russia against

Germany, Austria-Hungary, and Italy. Mama told me that the war would affect not only England, but America as well. She wasn't sure of the dates, but I had a feeling that things would escalate quickly, forcing me to wonder what I was facing if I moved to England. It seemed that no matter where I lived, war was not far away.

"Lord Cumberland arrived in New York two days ago," I said, "but I've only seen him once, very briefly. All he could talk about was the war and how he longs to return to England as soon as possible. He wants to be there with Prime Minister Asquith. He believes war is imminent."

"And he is right. He'll be anxious to take you back to England immediately."

I shook my head, tears threatening to overwhelm me. I didn't want to be in England. I didn't want to be married. And I didn't want to return to that life. But I seemed to have no choice.

A man walked by outside, and the familiar lines of his movement captured my full attention.

Henry.

He'd been at Edgewater Hall for the past two weeks, seeing to his family's business, but had returned to Williamsburg for the Virginia Convention, which started today. I hadn't spoken to him since my birthday, and part of me wondered if he was purposely avoiding me or if events had kept him from my side.

I watched him pause for a moment outside our house, but then he continued down the street, more than likely going to the Raleigh. Men had begun to gather there over the past few days, and though I ached to be a part of their discussions, nothing in 1774 could hold my attention for long.

All I could think about was my impending marriage.

"I don't see any way to avoid the wedding," Mama said to me. "We've thought of every possibility."

I stood, suddenly needing to walk out my apprehension. Work was calling, but I didn't think I could focus. I started to pace.

"Libby," Mama said quietly, "mayhap we should try what you suggested weeks ago."

"What?" My heart soared with hope. Did she have an idea? One I'd forgotten?

"I could come up with something that could help you change the course of history in 1914." Her voice was heavy with implications.

I stopped pacing and shook my head. I couldn't let her risk forfeiting her life to help me. "We don't know what would happen to you. Even if it worked and I was able to leave 1914 for good, what kind of life would I have here without you? What about Rebecca and Hannah?" I couldn't do it.

"But it's possible I would be fine. I don't want you to be forced to choose 1914." She seemed suddenly desperate.

I sat on the chair beside her. "I'd rather take my chances marrying Lord Cumberland and bide my time until my twenty-first birthday. What's the worst thing that could happen?"

She took my hands into hers once again, her voice dropping. "You could be forced to stay in 1914 if you find out you're going to have a baby."

Something caught in my spirit, and I looked at her in a new way. "Is that why you chose this path?" I whispered. "Because you were pregnant with me?"

She didn't meet my gaze. "I love you more than life itself, Libby. Please believe me."

I couldn't say anything as my eyes opened to this new realization.

"I would choose you over and over and over again—but I loved my life in 1994. I dreamed of being an English professor—did you know that? I had a boyfriend named Travis. We were going to the same college, Northwestern University in Illinois." She bit the inside of her mouth as she appeared to fight for control over her emotions. "I adored my parents and my siblings, and the knowledge that I was going to die to them was the most heart-wrenching thing I've ever endured."

"How?" I frowned, confused. "How did it come about that you stayed here?" And why had I never asked?

"When I reached the age of twenty in 1753, my father had died and my mother and I were trying to support ourselves, taking in wash and mending clothes. But then my mother became very ill, and it was up to me. I couldn't keep us going." She lifted a shoulder. "I couldn't let my mother starve. So when your father offered to marry me and take care of us, I said yes. I knew that when I left this path—because I was certain I would choose 1994—he would continue to care for my mother." She looked down at our joined hands. "I didn't even think about the consequences of being married, and when I learned that you were on the way . . ." She let the words trail off.

"You didn't want to stay in this path?" I could hardly believe what she was saying. I'd always thought she chose this path because she loved my father and wanted to be a part of the American Revolution.

"My mother was an angry, bitter woman. She did not guide me like I guide you. I know very little about her other path or why she became so spiteful." Mama shook her head, but then she looked up, passion in her gaze. "But I learned to love your father. It took years, but it grew. And I found great satisfaction in my life with him." She put her hand on my cheek. "And when you came and I knew you were a time-crosser, I was certain I had made the right choice. I would choose you again in a heartbeat. I consider it an honor that I was here to help guide you. And I would never have had your sisters, had I stayed in 1994."

In a matter of minutes, my entire world had shifted. Mama hadn't wanted to stay here, but she had, for me. Her love and sacrifice were deeper than I ever imagined. I hugged her close, tears careening down my cheeks.

"I love you, Libby," she said, "and I will make the final sacrifice for you if it means you can have the life you want."

"No." I shook my head, thinking about how Father Wells had offered to sacrifice everything in 1914 for me, as well. I could not ask either of them to do such a thing. "I will never, ever ask you to make another sacrifice for me. You've done far more than I deserve."

"I've only done what I knew was best. What God asked me to do. And it has worked out just as He planned. I know that with all my heart. The same will be true for you."

I straightened and let out a low breath, ready to accept what appeared to be God's plan for my life. "If you could do what you did, then I can do what I must do."

"I will pray for you," Mama said.

I nodded, thankful God had given her to me as my marked mother. I couldn't imagine walking through this unique life without her. Had she not sacrificed 1994 for me, I would have grown up alone, without a guide, and where would I be? How would I understand this gift?

"I will make us some tea." Mama rose and walked to the door. When she opened it, footsteps hurried down the hall toward the printing room, where the door slammed shut. She looked back at me. "Louis. Do you think he was listening to us?"

My mouth parted at the thought.

"What might he have heard?"

I didn't know, but whatever it was, it couldn't be good.

For the rest of the day, Mama and I tried to decide what to do about Louis. If he hadn't heard us, it would only cause a stir to bring up the subject. If he had, only time would tell what—if anything—he did with the information he'd overheard.

Yet as the day wore on, I couldn't imagine what he *could* do.

He'd overheard things that would make no sense to him. And even if he understood any of it, what would it matter? If he told someone, they would think he was addlepated.

I sat in the office at the end of the workday and stared out the window. Mistress Hunter had sent a runner to collect the money we owed for Rebecca and Hannah's gowns, but I had been forced to send a note telling her that we needed a little more time. There just wasn't enough money left over from our weekly expenses. I prayed she would not be upset, but I knew how I would feel if someone didn't pay me what was owed.

I leaned back in my chair, my stays cutting into my ribs. Some days I wished for the more comfortable styles in the twentieth century—but I would wear stays for the rest of my life if it meant staying in Williamsburg.

The hour was growing late, and the later it got, the closer I came to my wedding in 1914.

Mama stood and stretched as she pushed her chair under her desk. "I will see if Mariah needs help with supper." She paused and looked out the front window. "I wonder when the convention will adjourn for the day." She shook her head and crossed her arms. "'Tis a wonder to me that this day has finally come. I remember learning about the Virginia Convention in grade school in my other path and then again in middle school, high school, and college. So many events transpire to bring about the revolution, but it is the Virginia Convention, which calls for the Continental Congress, that unites the colonies as one for the first time. 'Tis truly a miracle that they will win when you think of the odds stacked against them. To have that kind of faith is admirable."

I watched her with new eyes, knowing what I did now about her choices.

She looked at me, and a smile tilted her lips. "I can almost hear what you're thinking."

I returned her smile—the first one I'd offered in weeks. "You know me better than anyone."

She touched my cheek.

"Mayhap I'll take a walk and see if there's anything to be learned about the convention," I told her, needing an excuse to get out of the office. Regardless of my other path, I still had a job to do here, and I needed information for the newspaper. "There is always gossip to be had in Williamsburg."

I put a bonnet over my mobcap and then stepped out onto Duke of Gloucester Street. Williamsburg had gone back to its normal pace after the burgesses had disbanded in May, but today, with almost all of them back in town, there was excitement and energy in the air. Most of the men were only in town for the length of the convention and had not brought their families this time, but it didn't dim the hum of anticipation.

I walked down the dusty street toward the Raleigh, passing Sophia, who sat in the window, working on a wig. She waved at me and smiled, and I waved back. She pointed at the wig and then shrugged, telling me that she couldn't come out to chat since she was busy. I understood and moved on.

No one stirred outside the Raleigh, so I continued toward the capitol. From down the street, the smells of the market square filled my nose. Dead fish, rotten vegetables, and oyster shells were left in the wake of the farmers and butchers who had hawked their wares since dawn. The clerk of the market would sweep up the mess, but the stench would remain.

All the way to the capitol building, I found myself praying— not for the outcome, but as a way to release my burden to God. I prayed for the convention, though I knew how it would end, and for my life in 1914, because I did not know how it would end.

I had tried everything I could to get out of the marriage to Lord Cumberland, and since I had failed thus far, perhaps it was God's will that it proceed. I didn't know why God would choose for me to marry the marquess, but there had to be a reason—wasn't there? Or was all of my life just a meaningless collection of days and years?

The words of Jeremiah the prophet came to me, and I said them under my breath as I crossed the street to walk down the opposite direction, back toward the Raleigh. "'For I know the thoughts that I think toward you, saith the Lord, thoughts of peace, and not of evil, to give you an expected end.'"

My life was not meaningless. God had an expected end in mind. He had marked out all my days in both paths. Yes, I had choices to make, but I had submitted to His will years ago, choosing to trust Him with all my heart. All I could do was beseech Him to lead me on the right path and trust that He would.

Just ahead, the Raleigh Tavern loomed. It was a large establishment by Williamsburg's standards, but it was even larger in my imagination. It was one of the most important places in American history and would play a part in the outcome of democracy.

A group of men exited the building as I approached, including George Washington and Henry Montgomery, among others. They stood for a moment, chatting, before they disbanded and started to go their separate ways. I smiled at several gentlemen in passing and found Henry standing at the end of the sidewalk, waiting for me.

A genuine look of pleasure filled his face as he removed his hat. "Good afternoon, Libby."

"Good afternoon, Henry." I glanced at the Raleigh. "Have you adjourned for the evening?"

"Aye." He nodded down the street. "May I walk with you?"

"You may."

I recalled, in vivid detail, the last time we walked together on my birthday. I had thought about it so many times that I could have recited our conversation word for word. Had he thought about that evening?

Two of Governor Dunmore's soldiers exited a tavern nearby, their bright red coats blinding in the summer sunshine. They tipped their hats in greeting, and though I didn't know them, they appeared to recognize Henry. He greeted them but did not stop to speak.

We walked in silence for a moment. Finally, Henry said, "I have felt like a fool since the last time we parted."

"A fool?" I stopped under the arm of an ancient oak and faced him. The street was quiet this close to suppertime.

"You asked me a simple question the night of your birthday, and I did not give you a simple answer." He watched me with a gentle expression. "I fear I may have left you feeling uncertain and more confused than necessary."

"'Tis true, I'll grant you," I responded. "But you don't owe me an explanation."

"Nay, I disagree." He continued walking, and I followed at his side. "I hold you in the highest regard, Libby. I want to put your mind at ease and tell you that I am not doing anything I am not proud of."

A smile tugged at my cheeks despite the seriousness of our conversation. "That does *not* put my mind at ease, nor does it eliminate any of my suspicions."

"Nay." He smiled. "I suppose it does not." He grew more serious. "But I must keep my own counsel in these matters. Just know that I will not lie to you."

We had come to the printing shop and stopped on the front walk. There was no one within earshot, but I still said the next words on the breath of a whisper. "Can you answer one question?"

"I will try."

"Are you working for the Patriots or against them?" I held my breath, waiting for his answer.

His eyes were such a magnificent color of blue. "The Patriots' cause is the cause of all men, and I will help win independence or die trying."

I took a step toward him, pride in my heart and in my voice. "Then whatever you are doing, I trust you and I support you, and I will be praying for you."

151

"You cannot know how much your words mean to me." He took my hand in his and pressed it to his lips. "I will carry them with me for as long as I fight."

"Would you like to join us for supper?" I wanted him to stay more than anything.

He glanced down the street toward the Palace Green. As far as I knew, he had come to Williamsburg alone and would not have his family waiting for him.

"Your mother wouldn't mind?" he asked.

"Nay. You could tell us what was discussed at the convention."

A smile lifted his lips, and he nodded.

I returned the smile, thankful to have him near so my thoughts would not dwell on the coming day.

# 12

The wedding was set to take place just four blocks from our home at St. Thomas Episcopal Church at ten o'clock.

Despite my resolve to trust God, and the distraction of Henry's company the day before, I awoke in 1914 with a heaviness upon my chest like nothing I had ever experienced.

Today I would marry the Most Honorable Marquess of Cumberland, and I had no choice in the matter—not if I wanted to protect Father. The newspaper reporters had camped out in front of our house for the past twenty-four hours, trying to get a glimpse of Lord Cumberland or me. They would be ready and willing to smear the Wells name if anything went wrong.

A soft knock at the door preceded Edith's tentative entrance. "Good morning, Libby."

I didn't rise to greet her but stayed in my bed, feeling listless and exhausted, though the day had hardly begun.

She puttered about in my room, opening the curtains to let in the light, picking up my wrapper, which must have fallen off the edge of the bed, and setting something on the vanity. Finally, she came to the bed and looked down at me. Sadness lined her hazel eyes as she took my hand in hers, pressing a handkerchief into my palm. "I will be here for you. I promise."

Warmth filled my heart at her words and the love in her voice. I pulled myself into a sitting position and wiped at the stray tear that had escaped my eye. "Thank you, Edith. You are my dearest friend."

Edith smiled and pointed at the window. "Go and look."

I pushed off my coverlet and allowed her to put my wrapper over my shoulders. I padded on bare feet across the room, tossing my hair behind my shoulder as I looked out at the street.

Hundreds of people lined Fifth Avenue.

"They go all the way to St. Thomas," Edith said. "It's rumored thousands of people will come out to get a glimpse of you."

I didn't do anything but stare at those people for several minutes. None of them knew me. They'd simply read about me in the newspapers, imagining some sort of fairy-tale love affair between Lord Cumberland and me. If they knew the depth of my pain, would they be so quick to applaud and celebrate this travesty brought about by my mother's manipulation?

"We need to get you bathed and dressed," Edith said with forced cheerfulness. "I brought a breakfast tray up for you." She nodded at the vanity where she had set the tray. "Your mother said you're not to go downstairs until it's time to leave for the church. She will be up in two hours to inspect our progress." She paused as she glanced toward the door. "And she's posted extra footmen to keep guard this morning."

More guards? What little appetite I felt vanished. "I'm not hungry."

"You should eat the toast, at least," Edith said. "You'll need all your strength to get through today and make yourself presentable to the marquess."

I grunted in disapproval. It didn't matter what Lord Cumberland thought of me. Since his arrival in New York, I had only seen him for a moment—and not by my choice. Mother had insisted.

"If not for yourself or Lord Cumberland," Edith said, pointing at my breakfast tray, "then do it for me."

I ate the toast dry and choked it down with orange juice. My stomach turned and threatened to expel its contents, but I held it back by sheer determination—and the look Edith gave me.

A bath was drawn for me, though I felt no pleasure in the warm water and soothing lavender soap, knowing guards were just outside the doors. I felt sloppy and weak as I went through the motions of washing my body.

Sooner than I liked, I was back in my room. Mother had chosen an elaborate headdress with a heavy veil as part of my wedding ensemble. Edith curled my hair and then set the headdress in place to style my hair around it. The fresh flower bouquet I would carry had been brought in while I bathed and displayed on my vanity. It filled the room with the scent of roses.

I stared at my reflection, unable to believe this was happening to me. I wanted to run to Father and tell him I had changed my mind, but I couldn't do that to him. I tried to convince myself I was strong enough to face this challenge. In eleven months I would leave it all behind, but a scandal and a lawsuit against Father could devastate him for the rest of his life.

"Now for the gown," Edith said. "Your mother will be here any minute." She looked at a clock on my vanity, her movements getting choppy as her anxiety grew. "And you should be leaving for the church in less than thirty minutes."

Thirty minutes? Despite my resolve, tears started to fall. Would I ever see Father again after today? Would I ever see this house or the servants or New York City? It hadn't occurred to me until now that when I moved to England, I would turn twenty-one before coming back. This wedding would mark not only the start of a loveless marriage I did not want, but also the end of my life here. For good.

With tears falling down my cheeks, I allowed Edith to help me into my elaborate wedding gown, which Mother had chosen. It was sewn out of yards and yards of the most expensive white silk. The train was magnificent, with embroidered flowers trailing along the scalloped edges. It scratched my delicate skin, but that was the least of my worries today.

A knock at the door announced Mother's arrival. She stepped into the room as Edith finished buttoning up the back of my gown.

Mother closed the door and then stood for a moment to inspect me. She had regained the weight she'd lost, and her cheeks held a healthy pink glow. The gown she'd chosen to wear today was simple yet elegant, a soft lavender color, and her hair was perfectly coiffured.

As her gaze traveled up the length of my appearance, I watched her, feeling detached and cold. The moment she saw my tears, impatient annoyance flared to life in her face.

"Really, Elizabeth." She walked to my side and pressed a handkerchief into my hands. "Wipe your face clean and stop acting like a spoiled child. You're not the first bride to marry a man she didn't love. How selfish and ungrateful you are." She nodded at the window. "Almost every woman on that street would change places with you in an instant."

"Let them. Lord Cumberland would probably prefer them over me."

She moved to my mirror and touched her coiffure. "How many of them would give him a hundred million dollars' worth of shares in the Wells Shipping Company?"

I clenched the handkerchief, loathing my father's money and my mother's unquenchable thirst for status.

"After today," Mother continued as she turned back to me, "our names will be numbered with the most important in New

York Society. And when Lord Cumberland becomes prime minister one day, we will surpass them all."

Oh, how I hoped that day would never come. And even if it did, I'd already be gone, and Mother would have no reason to boast. It was one small consolation.

"It's time for Elizabeth's veil and gloves," Mother said to Edith, who stood to the side, her gaze lowered. "And then we must leave for the church. The carriage is outside waiting."

Mother had insisted we pull out our old carriage, which we hadn't used in several years, to drive the six blocks to the church. The top would be down so the onlookers could see us.

In no time at all, my ensemble was complete, and the veil was lowered over my face. The tears returned when Father appeared at my bedroom door to escort me to the carriage and then on to the church. He stood there in his black coattails and white tie, his top hat under his arm, and for several moments we just stared at each other.

"You do not need to do this," he said, his voice heavy with pain.

"I must." I wouldn't let him talk me out of it, knowing what it would cost him.

Slowly, he moved across the room and offered me his arm. "You look lovely, my girl. I am going to miss you with every breath I take."

I hugged him as I wept, knowing I would have few opportunities left.

Why did the sun shine today, of all days? Not a cloud marred the blue expanse overhead as I stepped out of the brownstone mansion on my father's arm.

The crowd of onlookers cheered at my appearance, clapping, shouting, and calling my name. The usual traffic that bustled by our home on Fifth Avenue had been stopped and the road cleared by police officers. Newspaper reporters were there with their cameras, trying to get a glimpse of the newest American dollar princess. To many of the onlookers, I was the closest thing they would see to royalty.

I didn't have it within me to acknowledge any of them, though they'd been waiting for hours. Father nodded at them and raised a hand in greeting. His presence beside me was the only thing keeping me standing.

The black carriage was resplendent with garlands of white flowers. They'd been draped around the sides and back of the vehicle, offering a profusion of scents. Edith walked behind me, helping with my gown as Father handed me up into the carriage. Edith and Mother would ride in the motorcar just behind us.

"Despite everything," Father said as he sat beside me and patted my gloved hand, "I do believe you will be happy, Libby. It is the only reason I've let this continue. I've spoken to Lord Cumberland, and he appears to be an intelligent, reliable sort of man. I know you do not love him, but I believe you could learn to care for him." Hope filled his gaze.

I tried to smile for his sake. If I did not, he would carry guilt from this day forevermore—especially after I was gone.

"And," he continued, "I am relieved that you will be out of your mother's grasp after today. I know it hasn't been easy for you, and for that I am truly sorry."

I leaned close to him, trying to savor this last moment together.

The streets were lined with well-wishers, and the carriage driver took his time. Police officers stood at each intersection, directing cross traffic. As we passed, they doffed their caps at me with big grins on their faces.

Sooner than I would have liked, we arrived at St. Thomas's. The church had recently been rebuilt in the Gothic style, much like the other buildings up and down Fifth Avenue, with a hulking limestone exterior and ornate stonework. It was an impressive structure, and Mother had insisted on using it for our ceremony. Though we were not members of the church, the large contribution given to the rector was much appreciated.

When the driver opened the door for us, Father stepped down and then offered me his hand. His white gloves gleamed in the bright sunshine as I took his hand and stepped out of the carriage. The crowds continued to cheer, and several women tossed flowers onto my path.

Mother and Edith pulled up behind us, and the driver helped them exit their automobile. As Mother was escorted into the church without even looking in my direction, Edith arranged my train and veil, handed me my bouquet, and then gently smiled before she disappeared.

Then it was just Father and me as we faced the large double doors leading into St. Thomas's. I did not try to stop the tears as they flowed beneath my veil. Instead, I looked at the ground, forcing my feet to walk up the steps and down the aisle.

Someone opened a door for us, and we entered the narthex. It took a moment for my eyes to adjust to the dim interior. Mendelssohn's "Wedding March" echoed from the organ, and the nave doors stood open before us.

The massive church was full of people. Mother had invited the height of society, and her invitations had been well-received, placing her in the social position she'd always desired. I recognized many faces, though I only claimed a few as friends. Mrs. Alva Belmont had come, but she was the only person connected to my suffrage work who had been invited.

It hardly mattered to me, since this marriage and wedding were not of my choosing. This was not a celebration in my mind. It was an elaborate business transaction and nothing more.

With one arm anchored to my father, I walked down the long aisle to the altar. The smell of incense penetrated the air, while the massive ceiling and stone walls made the space feel cold, lifeless, and barren. Nothing like the Bruton Parish Church in Williamsburg.

The processional felt like it took an eternity, and then we arrived and Lord Cumberland was waiting with the rector, the Reverend Ernest Milmore Stires.

I didn't even look at Lord Cumberland as my father and I waited for the music to come to an end and the ceremony to start. When the rector asked who gave this woman to be married, I clung to my father's arm as if my life depended on it.

Father looked at me, and I could see the question in his eyes. Was I sure I wanted to go through with this? He would stop everything, if I only said the word.

But how could I do that to him?

I lowered my gaze and let go of his arm. Slowly, he stepped back and went to sit with Mother.

Standing there alone, every instinct screamed for escape. Each exit from the church looked like a beacon of hope—but what would I gain? I'd made my decision, and it was final. I was doing this for Father.

My only consolation was knowing that Mama was keeping vigil over me through the long night in Williamsburg. Though she was not physically with me, I could still feel her prayers and love. They sustained me through the tedious ceremony.

When Lord Cumberland lifted my veil at the end of the ceremony to place a chaste kiss upon my cheek, I saw the shock in his eyes at the sight of my tears, and I felt a measure of gladness that he knew I was miserable.

And then it was over.

I was Anna Elizabeth Fairhaven, the Marchioness of Cumberland. No longer Libby Wells, for I would not give Lord Cumberland the pleasure of calling me Libby. That name was reserved for those I cared most about in the world.

# 13

WILLIAMSBURG, VIRGINIA
AUGUST 2, 1774

Even before I opened my eyes the next morning, tears were wetting my pillow. I had cried myself to sleep in 1914 and woken up with the same tears in 1774.

"Libby?" Mama was sitting near my bed.

I turned toward her voice, and she climbed into the bed to hold me. I clung to her and wept.

She soothed my brow with her gentle fingers and let me cry. "Let it all out, Libby. The girls are sleeping in my bed, so you won't disturb them."

The room was still dim, and the sun had not yet peeked over the horizon. I tried not to let the images and experiences from my wedding day enter my mind, but I could not force them away.

"Tell me what happened," she finally said.

I swallowed, trying to control my tears. "It's too awful."

She continued to hold me, allowing my heart and mind to settle.

When I was finally able to speak, I said, "We were married." I didn't even try to describe the ceremony or the people or the church. None of it mattered. "Afterward, there was a wedding breakfast at the mansion. When everyone left, Lord Cumberland informed me that he didn't have a moment to lose and we would board a ship to return to England by day's end."

"Did he not see your distress?"

"If he did, he did not care. He had come to get his prize, and with all the formalities finished, he saw no reason to linger."

Mama ran a tendril of my hair through her fingers as she listened to me. She'd done it often when I was a child to soothe me.

"We boarded the RMS *Aquitania*." Lord Cumberland had boasted that it was one of the newest luxury ocean liners, and I suspected our passage cost a great deal, but he was no longer a pauper. He had been overly generous in his attention after the wedding, and I wondered if my tears had played a part in his attentiveness, though his behavior later would prove that his memory was short-lived.

Mama did not speak, and as the room brightened enough to see her face, I could tell she hadn't slept all night.

"Did you stay awake for me?" I whispered.

She nodded, a sad smile on her lips. "I prayed for you all night, Libby."

Tears gathered again. I was so tired of crying. It seemed like it was all I had done for days.

"What happened once you were onboard the ship?"

I couldn't look her in the eyes as shame and remorse filled every crevice of my being. But I had to tell her. I couldn't keep it in another moment. "I felt wretched, so I told Lord Cumberland I wanted to go to bed. Edith accompanied me and helped me change into my night clothes, and then she retired to her own cabin. Hours later, after I fell asleep, Lord Cumberland returned, smelling like alcohol." I closed my eyes, trying to forget yet knowing it would be impossible. I swallowed the hard lump in my throat. "I tried to stop him, Mama. I tried to tell him I was tired and ill and that I needed to sleep." I shook my head, embarrassment heating my cheeks. "But he would not listen. I cried for help, but no one came."

I buried my face in Mama's shoulder, my sobs too powerful to contain.

"Oh, Libby," she said, her voice heavy. "I'm so sorry."

It had been the most horrific event of my life, and I despised Lord Cumberland with all my heart and soul.

"I tried to stop him," I said around gasps of air. "I promise I tried."

"I know you did." She ran her hand over my hair, tears in her voice. "It's not your fault."

It felt like my fault. There had to be something I could have done, something I could have said to stop it from happening. Mama had cautioned me to keep him at arm's length.

"You mustn't blame yourself for something out of your control."

Mama's words were comforting, but they did not penetrate the pain and resentment in my heart. I hadn't even said goodbye to Mother Wells when I left the brownstone. I could not.

"What if—?" I choked on the words. What if there was a child? I couldn't accept such a fate. I just couldn't.

"Shh," Mama said again. "Let's take one day at a time. 'Tis all we can do for now."

I lay there, my emotions completely spent. Though the body I possessed in 1774 had not been defiled, my heart had been broken. No matter which body I was in, I felt it in the very marrow of my bones.

"The day is calling," Mama finally said. "I will send Mariah up with your breakfast and tell everyone you're not feeling well. You may lie abed."

I shook my head. "I cannot lie here with my thoughts all day. I'll go mad."

Mama nodded. "Then you must wash your face and dry your tears, for nothing is truly lost yet, Libby. We still have time.

This has never been truer than today, but you must not let one life dictate the other. There's work to be done here, and God is calling us to do it."

I clung to her hope and determined then and there that even if I had to sleep in Edith's cabin, I would not let Lord Cumberland touch me again.

With that resolve, I got dressed for the day. If Mama could stay up all through the night and still face her work, then I could, too. Today was the second day of the Virginia Convention. I needed to be present should there be news.

Breakfast was a hurried affair, since Mama and I were so late to arrive in the sitting room. After we finished eating, she went into the office to start our work, and I went to the printing room to look at the proof for a broadside.

Since it was Tuesday, Louis and Glen would be the only two in the printing room. Abraham was hauling supplies, since a shipment had recently come in at the Yorktown harbor.

But when I entered the printing room, Glen was not present. Only Louis stood over a wooden frame, placing type. He wore his leather apron, and his spectacles perched on the tip of his nose.

"Libby," he said when he saw me enter. He straightened and went to the workbench near the door. "Here is the proof."

I took it from him and examined it closely. Instead of going back to his work, he watched me, and when I could no longer stand his eyes upon me, I looked up. "Do you need something from me?"

"Nay." He took off his spectacles and continued to study me.

"What is it?" I asked, setting down the proof, my irritation high.

"You look unhappy."

I had washed my face as Mama instructed, but I could not shake the heaviness from my spirit. It hadn't occurred to me that Louis would notice.

"I'm fine." I picked up the proof again, trying to pretend what I said was true.

"I didn't intend to hear your conversation yesterday," he said, "just so you know. I had come to inquire about an edit I made. I'm not an eavesdropper."

My pulse ticked in my wrists, and my breathing stilled—but I couldn't let him think he'd heard something he shouldn't. "It's of no consequence."

He studied me again as if trying to piece together some great puzzle. "I disagree. I believe it is of great consequence. Your words troubled me, Libby, though I cannot pretend to understand their meaning. I do not know if you and your mother were playacting or if you truly believed what you were saying. If you did, I fear for your mental state."

Panic swelled in my chest, but I forced my face to remain neutral. "I don't know what you think you heard—or why you would think we were playacting. Mama was sharing a story with me, nothing more." It was true, she had been sharing a story—a story from her past. "Why?" I asked, tilting my head. "What did you think we were discussing?"

Louis was quiet for a moment as he regarded me. I could see the questions swirling in his mind, but he didn't speak them out loud. Instead, he straightened his shoulders and crossed his arms.

I could no longer stand there in his presence. "I will bring this proof back after I've had the opportunity to look it over completely." And, with that, I left the printing room.

"Mama," I said the moment I entered our office and closed the door, "we must be more careful. Louis asked me about our conversation yesterday. He's confused, as I knew he would be, but I don't think I've eased his mind."

"It seems we have spies all around us," she responded.

I frowned. "All around us?"

But she waved aside my question and went back to her work.

Did she know something I did not? Did she know about Henry?

Whatever it was, she didn't appear to want to share.

A light but steady rain commenced that afternoon. It was hard to focus on my work, not only because of the previous day, but also because of the Virginia Convention being held down the street at the Raleigh. More than anything, I wanted to know what the men were discussing. To see history unfold in person—and to know how important it would be in the course of world events—was something very few people experienced. I knew the outcome, but what was it like to be in that room? What did it smell like, sound like, feel like?

I would never know. The closest I could come was hearing a firsthand account from someone who was there. Someone like Henry.

As the day progressed, Mama became more and more exhausted and began to complain of a headache. We were sitting in the office when she finally pushed away from the desk. "I must go to bed. The sleepless night has taken a toll on me."

I noted the dark circles under her eyes and the lines around her mouth. Guilt weighed upon my heart, knowing she was suffering because of me.

She was pale, but she offered me a smile as she placed her cool hand on my cheek. "Do not feel responsible, Libby. I would do it again and again."

"Do you think you're becoming ill?"

"Nay. Just a megrim, 'tis all." She paused and pressed her hands against her temples. "What I wouldn't give for some ibuprofen and a Diet Coke right now." On a sigh, she said, "I'll be fine in the morning once I've had some sleep."

It was rare that she spoke about the things she missed from

her other path, but when she did, it reminded me of all that she had given up for me. "I'll see to the girls."

She patted my shoulder and left the office. Soon I heard her heavy tread upon the stairway.

The day pressed on, and when Abraham appeared at my office door a few hours later, I was surprised to look up and see that the sky was darkening.

"I have the supplies you ordered." He entered and placed a box on Mama's desk. "Mister Tanner will send the bill around."

I tried not to groan, wondering where I would come up with the money to pay the merchant. Instead, I stood to inspect the supplies to make sure Mister Tanner had given me everything on my list.

"There's talk in town that the convention attendees have called for a Continental Congress to meet in September in Richmond," Abraham said. "They've elected delegates to attend from the Virginia Colony, and I've heard several of our local men will be going."

My hands stilled as I lifted a new quill. This was exactly the kind of news our subscribers would want to read. "Do you know who?"

"Nay. I didn't hear any names."

Would Henry attend the Continental Congress? Who else was elected? With the paper going to press in two days, I needed to know. No doubt Mister Archer had been at the meeting and would have all the information he needed. I couldn't compete with that, but I could get my news from another source.

"Could you please ask Mariah to see to the girls this evening? I must go out, and I don't know when I'll be home."

I barely waited for his nod before leaving the office to grab my heavy cloak. I pulled the deep hood over my head to protect me from the rain and curious eyes. If Mama had been awake, she would have asked me to stay home, but I could not. Our newspaper had to compete with Mister Archer's if we wanted to keep the public contract. There were those who would use any excuse to take it from us, and I couldn't let that happen.

It was still light outside, though the clouds were heavy with rain and the sun would soon set. I walked toward the Palace Green. Straight ahead was the College of William and Mary at the start of Duke of Gloucester Street. The stately brick buildings and wide-open lawns were beautiful and set Williamsburg apart in the colony. Many men I knew had attended, including Henry, George Washington, Thomas Jefferson, and others. In my 1914 path, it was still an exclusive men's college, but Mama assured me that one day women would be allowed to enroll. I had often thought about what I would study, had I been allowed. Would I choose to be a newspaper editor? Or would I be a lawyer? A doctor? An architect? It was hard to know. I'd been thrust into my role, but would I have chosen it if given another option?

I took a right turn onto the Palace Green, these thoughts circling through my head, and walked toward the Montgomery home. With the rain, there were few people out, for which I was thankful. I didn't wish for gossip, though I was willing to take the risk.

Henry had come into Williamsburg without his parents, but I didn't know if he'd be happy to see me on his doorstep. I wasn't even sure if he'd be home. It had been many years since I'd been a guest in his house—not since his father had put a stop to our families' connection. I missed the house and those years when our friendship had been welcome. What would his father think if he saw me walking up the steps to the front door now?

I knocked and then stood under the covered stoop, clasping my hands together as I took a steadying breath.

Stanley, the Montgomerys' butler, answered the door.

"Miss Libby," he said with a wide smile. He'd always been a favorite of mine and had often snuck extra treats from the cook for us when we were children, keeping our secrets to himself. "What can I help you with today?"

"Is Mister Henry at home?"

"Aye. He just arrived. Would you like to come in?" He stepped to the side. "If you'd like to wait, I'll tell him you're here."

I entered the foyer and lowered my hood, my hands shaking. To be at Henry's home alone, without a chaperone, was scandalous. I trusted Stanley not to say anything, but what about the neighbors or other servants who might see me? I hoped Henry would not be upset.

The Montgomerys' home was grand and elegant, even though it was much smaller than Edgewater Hall and was only used on occasion. Lady Gwendolyn had redecorated since the last time I'd visited. The entry walls were painted a vivid green, and the trim was a dark cream color. A carpet runner ran up the open staircase, ascending to the second floor.

"Libby?" Henry appeared in the doorway to the front parlor and the study beyond. Concern tilted his brow as he put his hand upon my arm. "Is something amiss?"

I shook my head, trying to find my voice. He must have been at his leisure when Stanley found him, because his coat was askew, his cravat was missing, and the top buttons of his shirt were undone, revealing his neck and part of his chest.

"Nay," I said, forcing my eyes to lift to his face, my cheeks warming at the intimacy of his undress. "'Tis nothing wrong."

He stared at me for a moment, questions in his eyes.

"I'm sorry." I shook my head, suddenly realizing the foolishness of my plan. I started to back toward the door. "You weren't expecting me. I shouldn't have come."

He gently reached for my hand, his face softening. "I'll have Stanley bring us something warm to drink. You're wet."

He let go of my hand and slowly untied the strings of my cloak. My breath caught as his hand brushed the underside of my chin. His touch was soft and tender. This close, all I could look at was his unbuttoned shirt.

"You can't go back out in the rain until your cloak has dried. We'll set it by the hearth."

Stanley entered the hall, and Henry asked for tea. I did not speak a word as Henry took my hand and led me through the parlor and into the study. It was a small, informal room, not meant for company. I'd only been in it once before with Henry, and it had proven to be a mistake. When his father found us, we'd been reprimanded and told never to enter the room again. It was the last time I'd been invited to this house.

Henry glanced at me as he pulled one of the chairs near the fire and spread my cloak over it. His smile was warm and familiar. "Do you remember the last time we were here together?"

"Aye." I returned his smile. "I remember it well."

I had been fourteen and deeply in love with Henry. He had brought me to this room to play a game of chess while our mothers visited, but neither of us had paid much attention to the board. There had been a lot of flirting and teasing and secretive smiles. It was during one of those moments, when my cheeks burned from something sweet Henry had said, that his father found us.

"Will you have a seat?" Henry asked me now, indicating the sofa under the window facing the gardens.

I sat, stiff and proper, and though there were other chairs he could have occupied, Henry joined me on the sofa. He had somehow managed to button his shirt, for which I was thankful.

"'Tis probably foolish of me to come here," I said as I sat on the edge of the sofa, my back straight and my hands clasped in my lap, "but I was anxious to hear news from the convention today—for the *Virginia Gazette*."

"Is that the only reason you've come?" His voice was low.

I looked at him to see if he was teasing me, but he just watched me with a clear, steady gaze.

"Aye, 'tis all."

He leaned back against the sofa, a half-smile on his face,

seeming to take pleasure in my discomfort. "If that is the only reason you've come, then I should get on with the telling. Or mayhap I should wait until you're even more uncomfortable to be here alone with me."

Heat climbed up my neck as I gave him a withering look in return, which made him laugh outright.

It was easy to remember how much fun we'd had as children. No doubt if his father found us like this again, he would be bolder in his dismissal of me.

Henry became serious, though his eyes still smiled. "It was a productive day, and I intended to stop by and share the news with you, but I had pressing matters to attend to here at home. I'm sorry."

"There's no reason to be sorry. You owe me nothing."

"Nay. I feel I owe you a great deal."

His words puzzled me, but he went on to tell me about his day.

"Among other things," he said, "we made a formal call for a Continental Congress to convene on September the fifth in Richmond. We also elected seven delegates to attend."

"Will you be one of them?"

He shook his head. "I was nominated but refused to accept."

"Why?" I finally leaned against the back of the sofa to get a better look at him, surprised he'd turn down the nomination.

"My father has made his feelings known about the congress." He crossed his arms and looked down at his feet. "He knows where I stand on these issues, and surprisingly, he respects my opinions, but he's asked me not to have such public involve-ment. I've agreed to honor his request."

It wasn't difficult to see that this pained Henry. He had been born for his role in this fight. He loved people and drew energy and strength from their presence. To be left out would be ter-ribly difficult for him, but his loyalty to his father was also to be commended—though I guessed it would not stop him from being involved.

"We've also come to a difficult decision." He returned his troubled gaze to me. "One that we've debated each time we've been together, but we all agree that everything else we've tried has not worked. Parliament will not listen to our petitions, nor will they listen to our resolutions or our pleas. Instead, they create more acts to limit our freedom."

He was referencing the Intolerable Acts, passed in Parliament since the Boston Tea Party. The first was the Boston Port Act, which closed the port of Boston, and then there were others specifically aimed at Massachusetts. But the most recent act had affected all the colonies. It was the Quartering Act, which made it legal for a governor to quarter British soldiers on privately held property without the consent of the owner.

Henry watched me closely as he shared the rest of his report. "We are calling for a boycott on all British goods in the colonies until they lift these unlawful acts."

I tried to appear surprised, but I had known this was coming. Boycotting English supplies was one of the tactics the colonies would use to put pressure on Parliament. It would mean paying higher prices for goods produced in the colonies, shrinking my coin purse even further.

"I planned to stop by to speak to you tomorrow," he continued. "The convention has asked that you print a petition asking every merchant and colonist in Virginia to sign, promising to boycott English goods."

"'Twill not be an easy task."

"You're right, but I believe this is the only way Parliament will take us seriously. We must hurt them where it counts, and right now it's estimated that over two and a half million British subjects live in the colonies. If we all boycott, or even a large portion boycotts, we will make a lasting impression."

The idea of a boycott was daunting, but it was the least our family could do when I knew how much more others would give. I nodded, eager to help. "We will print the petition, and we will be the first to sign it."

Though I spoke confidently, dread settled over my spirit. To affix my name to a document in defiance of the governor, Parliament, and the king was daunting. How much harder would it be for the others who did not know the outcome of this act of defiance and who would be putting everything on the line for freedom's call?

"Thank you," Henry said, pride and something more shining in his eyes.

Stanley entered with a tea tray, which he set on the table near us and then took his leave once again without saying a word.

Silently, I served the tea, handing a cup to Henry. Outside, darkness had fallen, and the rain still patted lightly upon the windowpanes. Inside, the fire made the room feel warm and cozy, begging me to stay.

How I longed for this moment to continue, though I knew it couldn't last. I was drawing closer and closer to my return to Lord Cumberland.

Visions of the night before tried to overpower my senses, but I would not let them. I was a different person in 1914— at least, that was what I was trying desperately to believe. Here, in this time and space, I was simply Libby Conant— not Anna Elizabeth Fairhaven, Marchioness of Cumberland. I didn't want my other life to touch me here. Especially now, with Henry.

"I should go," I finally said.

"I will walk you home."

"There's no need."

"I cannot let you walk home in the dark by yourself."

I brooked no argument, and when we rose, he gently placed my cloak about my shoulders before leading me back to the entrance, where he took his own cloak off a hook.

We left the house and walked in silence to my home. The rain was falling harder now, and I shivered.

When we arrived at my back door, I turned to him. "Thank you for seeing me home and for sharing the news with me."

"'Tis a pity you cannot be there to hear it for yourself." He took my hand in his. "Good-night, Libby."

The night was dark, but I could see him well. He lifted my hand to his lips, and I inhaled a breath as he kissed it. And then he was gone, and I was alone with only my thoughts for companionship.

I entered the dark hall, locking the door behind me, and took off my wet cloak. Slowly, I walked up the stairs to the room I shared with my sisters. They were asleep, cuddled together for warmth. Outside, the wind picked up and rattled the windowpanes.

I went to the chair near the window and sat, looking out onto our side yard. I was not yet ready to succumb to sleep and all that would greet me when I woke up.

The darkness was overpowering, and the rain made it almost impossible to see past the glass, but I knew what was out there, even if I couldn't see it—much like my future.

I would need all the strength and fortification God could give me to endure the coming year, both here and away. I was on the cusp of my own great war—a war for my freedom and the choice to live the life I desperately wanted.

# 14

## RMS *AQUITANIA*, NORTH ATLANTIC
## AUGUST 5, 1914

"War has been declared." Reggie handed the telegram to me during luncheon on our fourth and final day at sea. Within hours, we would disembark in Southampton, and our ocean voyage would be over. "Three days ago, Germany demanded passage through Belgium to attack France, but when Belgium refused, Germany invaded Belgium. The next day, Belgium invoked an old treaty with England, which states that England will protect Belgium's neutrality, and England has, therefore, declared war on Germany."

I sat with my back straight as I read the message from Prime Minister Asquith. The other passengers who usually sat with us at luncheon had not yet arrived. With Reggie's status as the Marquess of Cumberland and one of the Lords Commissioners of the Treasury, we had dined with several important people and had been guests at the captain's table each evening.

"What does this mean for you?" I asked as I handed back the telegram, surprised he'd shared it with me. We had hardly spoken a word to each other since we'd come on board. After the first night, I had slept in Edith's cabin and had only seen Reggie during meals. I didn't know what he did with his time, and he didn't ask what I did with mine.

"I will not be able to accompany you to Whitby as we planned but will need to return to London immediately." He folded the telegram and put it into an inner pocket of his suit coat. "London will be no place for you, especially in a time of war. When we disembark, we will take the train from Southampton into London, and then you will proceed without me to Cumberland Hall. I will send my valet as your chaperone. He will see that you are handed over to Mr. Wentworth, the butler, and then he will meet me in London a few days later."

"I'm to arrive at Cumberland Hall without you?" The thought both pleased and frightened me. The sooner I could be out of Reggie's company, the sooner I could relax—yet I was expected to arrive at his ancestral home, without him present, to meet his staff and start the renovations of Cumberland Hall without his guidance. Nothing I'd been taught had prepared me for such a daunting task.

"Mr. Wentworth will see that you're made comfortable." Reggie waved aside my concern as if it was of little consequence. "He and the housekeeper, Mrs. Chadburn, have been at Cumberland Hall for most of my life. They're more suited to showing you about the place than I am."

"How long do you think you'll be in London?" I tried to hide the relief in my voice at the thought of being without him. I could endure almost anything that greeted me at Cumberland Hall if it meant I did not have to be in the presence of my husband. I was already consumed with fear that I was carrying his child, though I wouldn't know for some time.

"There's no way of knowing how long I'll be needed in London." He laid his napkin in his lap as a steward approached to fill our glasses with water. "The prime minister will need my assistance in the days and weeks ahead. It will take a great deal of work to mobilize the nation for war. He'll need all the help he can get, especially from the Lords Commissioners of the Treasury. I'm sure he's anxious for my return."

No doubt he was. I had learned more about Reggie's position in the British government and was surprised at his level of importance. Six men occupied the Lords Commissioners of the Treasury, with the prime minister as the First Lord of the Treasury and the other five men in descending order beneath him. Reggie, as one of the lower-ranking Lords, was considered a whip in parliament. His main job was to make certain that the other men in his party voted according to their party line and did not vote their personal conscience. I could imagine that in a time of war, his party would need all the support possible.

After our brief discussion at the table, I did not speak to him again until the ship was docked and we were waiting to disembark. Because of his need to be at the prime minister's side, we had been moved to the front of the line. With over two thousand passengers on board, it was an honor and a privilege, further solidifying in my mind the importance of Reggie's position.

The next hour was a blur. An automobile waited to transport us to the train station with our many bags and all my luggage. When we arrived at Southampton West Station, there was a heightened sense of frenzy and confusion. We could not turn to the right or the left without reminders of war. Already there were posters up everywhere, calling on men to enlist. It was all anyone could speak of. Thankfully, Reggie's secretary had arranged for our train tickets into London, and we had just enough time to catch the train.

When we were finally settled in the first-class car on our way to London, I could hardly keep my eyes open. It was late, and the day had been arduous—yet I could not fall asleep sitting upright. We would be on the train for several hours before I transferred to a sleeper car in London and said good-bye to Reggie.

He sat across from me, staring out at the darkening countryside of his homeland. I took the opportunity to study him while he was so deep in thought. My initial impressions of him had not changed. His looks were colorless and dull, though he was not unattractive. I suppose a woman might find him appealing—especially with his title and position in the government. He was almost twice my age, a fact that didn't seem to bother anyone but me, although it was hardly the most bothersome thing about our marriage.

Until this moment, I hadn't wondered much about him. But now, as I sat across from him as his wife, his personality and characteristics were all I could think about. Who was this person I had been forced to marry? Was he the jealous type? Did he have a short temper? Was he easily angered? He drank too much, but why? His parents were both dead, leaving him the sole heir of Cumberland Hall, but did he have other family? No one had come to our wedding or sent telegrams. My parents had thrust me off on a stranger and expected me to live happily ever after.

I hoped and prayed I wouldn't have to worry about who he was. The longer he stayed in London, the less I had to concern myself with such things. I had ten months until my birthday, and then I would be gone from here forever.

We rode in silence all the way to London. Reggie had purchased every newspaper available at Southampton and read them from front to back. I did not feel like reading, so I simply sat and looked out the window.

The sun had set and the hour had grown late by the time we arrived at Waterloo Station. Once we had disembarked and Reggie had purchased my train fare to Whitby, we sat awkwardly beside each other in a crowded waiting room. He seemed like he wanted to leave me and go to Prime Minister Asquith, but he did not.

"Is there anything you'll need?" he finally asked above the noise of the other passengers.

I was wearing a grey traveling suit with a hobbled skirt and a short jacket. My head felt heavy from the large hat upon my head, and my hands were clammy from wearing gloves all day. I felt grimy and uncomfortable from traveling, and I wanted to go to sleep so I could wake up in 1774 and have a reprieve from this nightmare. Which meant there was nothing Reggie could give me at the moment that would make things any better.

"No, thank you."

"Well, see that you ask for what you need." He looked at his watch for the tenth time since we'd sat down.

"You may leave me, if you'd like," I said. "Mr. Duncan can see to my welfare from here." Mr. Duncan was Reggie's valet and was sitting on the bench across from us with Edith.

Reggie looked at me then—truly looked at me, as if seeing me for the first time since our wedding day. There was something akin to empathy in his light-brown gaze.

"I do hope you'll be happy, Anna, despite what you may think." His pale brown mustache did not move above his serious mouth as he watched me, his voice low so no one else would hear him. "I'm not a fool, nor am I blind. I'm aware that you did not choose to marry me, nor did you have much say in the matter. But I am pleased with the match, and I hope you'll come to be pleased, as well."

I could not hide my surprise. Did he really care? Nothing to this point indicated that he did. His stiff, pompous personality and careless treatment of me had told me quite the opposite.

"Mr. Wentworth will see to your comfort and your affairs until I can return to Whitby. I've written him a letter, which Duncan will deliver as soon as you arrive at Cumberland Hall. He's been instructed to give you whatever you need or desire."

I didn't know what to say, so I simply said, "Thank you."

Under other circumstances, his words and concern might have been a lifeline in this uncertain time. But a stubborn, angry part of me wanted to lash out and tell him it was the least he could do, given that I was not only forced into this marriage, but his new fortune was, in fact, my father's.

Instead, I simply opened my handbag and pulled out a handkerchief to dab at my nose. His behavior on our wedding night alone was enough for me to justify my resentment. I would not let him assuage his guilt—if he felt any—by showing him warmth.

He looked at his watch again and then stood. "They'll be boarding soon."

I also stood, ready to be done with the awkwardness.

We left the waiting room and found the proper platform. He'd already arranged for all my luggage to be transferred, and I would arrive in Whitby early tomorrow morning. From there, Mr. Duncan would escort me to Cumberland Hall.

What awaited me after that, I wasn't certain.

"All aboard!" the conductor called a few minutes later.

Around us, people were saying their good-byes. The station was loud with the sounds of trains, steam, and passengers coming and going.

Reggie watched me with a strange look of regret. "Good-bye, Anna. I do wish things could be different and I didn't have to part with you so soon after our wedding."

Was he truly sorry to part ways? If he had wanted to make the most of our short honeymoon together, he might have tried to converse with me or seek out my company when he had the chance—not that I would have welcomed such a thing. It didn't matter to me. All I wanted was to be away from him. "Good-bye."

He leaned in and placed a quick, dry kiss on my cheek, and then I turned and boarded the train.

As the train pulled out of Waterloo Station and I had neither my mother nor my husband to dictate every move I made for the foreseeable future, an overwhelming and unexpected sense of freedom took hold of me. Even with a war looming, a staff who would no doubt be unimpressed with their American mistress, and a crumbling manor house to contend with, I still breathed a little easier.

Until I remembered I might be carrying Reggie's child.

## WHITBY, NORTH YORKSHIRE, ENGLAND
## AUGUST 6, 1914

The automobile came to a stop in front of Cumberland Hall, and all I could do was stare up at the majestic stone house. It was three stories tall with a large tower at the front facing the North Sea and a massive glass-encased conservatory at the back. The home had some Italianate influences, as well as Georgian, and it was easy to see that it had been remodeled and added on to several times. The main entrance was under the tower, and at the top were stone-crafted wreaths with weathered brown stains sliding down the façade like age-old tears.

"Welcome to Cumberland Hall, your ladyship," Duncan said as he opened the door of the automobile.

I stepped out and let my eyes wander over the crumbling edifice, the overgrown gardens flanking the house, and the steep cliffs not far away. A strong wind blew over me, bringing the scent of saltwater.

For as far as I could see, the North Sea spread out in front of Cumberland Hall. Behind the house were the moors, with their purple heather, craggy rocks, and barren desolation. It was the strangest countryside I'd ever seen. The only hint of life had been in the small village of Whitby, where we had disembarked from the train and been met by the Cumberland Hall driver, Williams. The red-roofed homes and buildings of Whitby had been built up the hillsides from the sea and the sandy beaches down below and had been very quaint, reminding me of Williamsburg. But the expanse of the North Sea was like an old friend, having spent most of my summers in Newport.

Williams opened Edith's door, and she got out of the automobile, her cheeks pale and her eyes large as she took in the surroundings.

Before I could take a step, the front door opened under a porte cochere at the base of the tower, and an older gentleman emerged, his back straight, his chin up, and his gaze taking me in from head to foot in one sweeping glance. He was very proper, and his coattails were pressed to perfection.

Behind him, a woman stepped out of the house. She was pale and wore her dark hair rolled into a bun. Her appearance was plain, but she carried her chin and shoulders with confidence, as if she knew who was in charge—and it was probably her.

Neither one looked unfriendly, yet they lacked the warmth and familiarity that Mr. Pierson and Mrs. Hanson possessed.

"Hello, Lady Cumberland," the gentleman said. "I am Mr. Wentworth, the butler, and this is Mrs. Chadburn, the house-keeper."

Mr. Wentworth bowed, and Mrs. Chadburn curtsied.

From around the side of the house, half a dozen servants filed into a line. Mr. Wentworth introduced me to two footmen, two maids, the cook, and the kitchen helper.

There wasn't nearly enough staff present to run a manor home of this size and magnitude. It was easily twice the size of my parents' brownstone mansion, and they had twenty-four servants, at least. Where were the others?

"Of course, you've met Williams, the driver," Mr. Wentworth continued, "and Mr. Duncan, Lord Cumberland's valet."

"Yes." I offered him a smile. "It's a pleasure to meet all of you." I motioned toward Edith. "This is my lady's maid, Edith."

"Edith?" Mr. Wentworth said in a slow, almost painful way as he lifted a brow, looking her over from head to foot.

"Yes."

"If it pleases you, your ladyship, a lady's maid is addressed by her last name in England."

A lot depended on this first meeting. He was trying to help me understand how things were done—yet I was not prepared to give up all of my ways. I smiled and said, "I've always called her Edith, for that is her name."

Mr. Wentworth slowly nodded, as if trying to figure out how to respond. Thankfully, he did not. It was clear my American ways would not be accepted easily here, but there were certain things I would not concede.

"If you'll follow me," Mr. Wentworth said, "I will show you to your room, where you may rest from your journey."

"I'd prefer a tour of the house." I was far too curious about Cumberland Hall to take a nap right now. If I was going to spend the next ten months here, then I would like to start on the renovations. Perhaps it would help pass the time.

"As you wish." Mr. Wentworth gave a slight bow. "As soon as the motor truck arrives with your luggage, I'll have it brought to your room."

I followed him under the porte cochere and into the massive great hall.

I had been in many magnificent homes in my life. Our mansion in Newport was larger than Cumberland Hall, yet it was nowhere near as old, and it lacked the charm of a manor house built and remodeled over several centuries. My mouth slipped open as I looked up and found my gaze traveling many stories to a mural painted high on the ceiling. A grand stairway sat on the opposite end of the great hall, and all around were windows letting in the brilliant sunshine.

But despite the grandeur of the room, the disrepair was unmistakable. Peeled paint, crumbling plaster, and cracked windows could not be hidden. The rugs were threadbare, the tapestries faded, and the furniture brocade was glossy with use.

Edith did not join us but went with Mrs. Chadburn to see

to my room and get a tour of the servants' quarters and belowstairs.

"Cumberland Hall's initial construction dates back to the
year 1610," Mr. Wentworth said in an important voice, "when
it was built by the first Marquess of Cumberland." He droned
on as he gave me the dry details of the previous owners and
occupants, the construction, the remodeling, and the additions,
including the walled gardens along the sides and back. It could
have been interesting, if delivered in a tone that begged for questions or conversation, but Mr. Wentworth's tour did neither.
He spoke, instead, of people and dates that didn't matter to
me in the slightest.

We saw an impressive conservatory with a plate-glass roof
inspired by the Crystal Palace in London. It was heated year-
round by warm water running in pipes under the floor. Inside
were many plants and trees, mostly overgrown and neglected.
I thought of Mama and her love for botany. If only she could
be here with me! She would spend hours in this room, tending
to the vegetation all throughout the year. I would need to ask
her advice to return this room to its former glory.

But it was the two-story library facing the sea that took me
by complete surprise and delight.

"The library was an addition in 1771," Mr. Wentworth said.
"The sixth Marquess of Cumberland had a penchant for books."

1771? I could almost imagine this library when it was fresh
and new in the days of my life in Williamsburg. Now it was
ancient and faded with time, reminding me how far removed
I was from my other path. A massive fireplace dominated the
room, and I could see myself curling up with one of the thousands of books come winter.

"The eighth marquess was a student of history," Mr. Wentworth continued, "and he was especially interested in American
history, politics, and literature." He walked over to a section of
the library nearest the large desk. "Over the years, his descen-

dants have added to his collection. Perhaps you'll find some books of interest yourself."

I looked closely at the titles on the shelves, and my eyes fluttered wide. There were dozens and dozens of books I recognized. *Collected Letters* by Christopher Columbus, *The General History of Virginia* by John Smith, *Of Plymouth Plantation* by William Bradford, *Common Sense* by Thomas Paine, and even *Poems on Various Subjects, Religious and Moral* by Phyllis Wheatley. There were historical accounts, as well, but one particular collection of books caught my attention. *A Complete Account of America's Sons of Liberty, Founding Fathers, and Fallen Heroes.* There were thirteen volumes in this collection, one for each of the thirteen original colonies. The book entitled *Virginia* was thick and leather-bound, dusty with age. Inside those pages would be the names of men like Mister Washington, Mister Jefferson, Mister Patrick Henry, Mister Peyton Randolph . . . but would I find Henry Montgomery's name written there? And if I did, would I learn his fate?

My fingers itched to pull out the book and flip through its pages, yet I would not. Was knowing the fate of the man I loved a good thing? What could I do with the information, whether good or bad?

But what if it was good? Wouldn't that put my mind at ease?

"Shall we go into the east drawing room next, your ladyship?" Mr. Wentworth asked.

I couldn't tear my gaze away from the book, yet I had no choice. I could not take the chance that I would learn something alarming or heartbreaking.

"I'm starting to grow tired," I said. "Perhaps we can continue our tour at a later time."

"Yes, of course, your ladyship. I'll show you to your room."

We returned to the great hall and went up the grand staircase. There were cracks in the stone treads, and the red carpet runner was worn thin.

Mr. Wentworth's back was stiff as I followed him through the echoing halls. Dozens of doors lined the corridor, but he stopped near the first door and opened it for me.

The windows in this bedchamber looked out at the sea, and the sunshine illuminated a small, intimate room with an old canopied bed. Edith was there, already unpacking my luggage, which must have been delivered during my tour.

"If you need anything, your ladyship, do not hesitate to call upon me." Mr. Wentworth bowed and then left the room, closing the door behind him.

Edith and I stared at one another. Her face was still pale, and her mouth was drawn. I crossed the room.

"Are you unwell?" I asked.

Edith shook her head and tried to smile, though it didn't reach her eyes. "Don't worry about me, milady."

"Oh, don't. Please." I placed my hand on her arm. I had been brooding over my own discomfort and homesickness, yet I had not once thought about how this move would affect Edith. She'd come all this way to be with me and had not complained once. "Please continue to call me Libby, at least when we're alone."

She shook her head, her hazel eyes wide. "They won't like it. They were appalled that you call me by my first name. Already they've been speaking poorly of you belowstairs. You must call me Riley. And I must call you milady."

Her distress was so alarming that I gave in. "Of course you want to be accepted by all of them. If it will make you more comfortable, I will call you by your last name."

She nodded, relief in the softening of her brow.

There was much I would need to learn if I wanted both of us to be comfortable here for the next ten months—and much I would have to concede.

# 15

## WILLIAMSBURG, VIRGINIA
## AUGUST 16, 1774

When I woke up, I could hardly wait to find Mama and tell her the good news. She was not in the sitting room nor the office when I came downstairs that morning, so I continued my search.

Pushing open the back door, I walked the short path to the kitchen and found her with Mariah, pulling a waffle iron from the brick oven. I wasn't aware of anyone else in the colonies with a waffle maker, but it was Mama's favorite food from the 1990s and she had commissioned the blacksmith to make it for her. Pots, pans, and cooking utensils lined the walls. A work table sat in the center of the room and a bread table in one corner. This was Mariah's domain, and it spoke volumes about her attention to detail, her cleanliness, and her love of order.

Dried herbs hung from the rafters, and hogsheads of salted meat sat in the corner, along with barrels of flour, sugar, and salt. Spices filled several containers on a shelf, and there were crocks of every imaginable shape and size. In the corner near the fireplace lived a pile of split wood, which was never low because Abraham replenished it each day.

"Good morning to you, Libby," Mama said with a smile on her pretty face.

"Good morning." I crossed the kitchen to peek over Mariah's shoulder and see what she was preparing. "Clouted cream?" I couldn't hide the pleasure in my voice. It was one of my favorite things to put in my tea or on my waffles.

"Aye, just for you, Libby." Mariah grinned at me, teasing, since Abraham also loved clouted cream. She said the same thing to him.

"You're just in time to take the sausages in to breakfast." Mama nodded at a platter on the work table. "Are the girls down yet?"

"Aye. I sent them to the sitting room to wait for us."

Mama opened the iron and took out the perfectly baked waffle. She set it on a plate with three others. Mariah put the clouted cream and a jug of maple syrup on the tray, and I placed the sausages next to them.

"Thank you," I said to her as I lifted the tray and followed Mama back outside and toward the house.

The day was already stifling, though the hour was early. It had been one of the hottest months in my memory, and today would be no exception.

"Mama," I said just above a whisper as we traversed the short path from the kitchen to the house. "I have very good news."

She must have heard the excitement in my voice, because she stopped and turned to face me, a smile already brightening her face. "Aye?"

"There's no baby," I said it in the same whisper, though in my happiness, my voice had raised an octave.

Mama grinned. "That's very good."

Relief had flooded me in my 1914 path yesterday at the discovery, and it followed me into today, as well.

"And Lord Cumberland?" Mama asked. "Have you had word from him?"

I nodded. The breakfast tray was growing heavier by the moment, but we could not speak freely with the girls present. "I received a letter from him yesterday. He has no plans to return to Whitby. They are working hard to recruit men for the war effort. He said in his letter that over three thousand men have enlisted every single day, and they are hardly sleeping to meet the demands and needs of the war."

"So he will not return anytime soon?"

In answer to her question, I could not stop myself from grinning.

"We have much to be thankful for and celebrate today, Libby. But first we must get this food to the table while it's still hot."

I followed her the rest of the way, but when I turned to close the back door, I saw Louis. He was walking around the corner of the kitchen, coming from the privy, no doubt.

He met my gaze and stared hard at me. Had he overheard our conversation? If he had, he would have heard the name Lord Cumberland and talk of war. What would he think of that?

Mama and I needed to be more careful.

In the sitting room, we found Rebecca and Hannah waiting for their breakfast. The table had been set, so we laid the food upon it and took our seats. After Mama prayed, we dished up our plates, but a knock at the front door turned our heads.

"Who would come so early?" Mama set down her napkin and began to rise.

I stood. "I'll see to them."

In the front hall, I opened the door and stared in surprise. "Mister Jefferson. Please, come in. We're breaking our fast, if you'd care to join us."

Thomas Jefferson removed his tricorne hat and held it as he entered the hall. In his other hand, he grasped a leather satchel. "I do not want to impose. I'm very sorry to intrude upon your morning, but I must be on my way to Monticello within the hour and cannot delay my errand."

"There's no imposition." I allowed him to enter and then closed the door, touching my hand to my cap on instinct to ensure it was in its proper place. I could not recall Mister Jefferson ever stepping foot within our printing shop. It was an honor I had not expected.

"Could I address both you and your mother?" he asked.

"Aye." I opened the door to the office and said, "If you'd like to wait, I'll call her."

Mama must have heard our interaction, because she appeared in the hall, her face revealing her delighted surprise. "Good morning, Mister Jefferson."

"Good morning, Mistress Conant."

We moved into the office, which was hot and stuffy, having been closed since last evening.

"How may we help you?" Mama asked, going to the window to lift it and let in fresh air. The heat and humidity outside were no better than indoors.

Mister Jefferson opened his satchel and pulled out several pieces of parchment. "I have taken it upon myself to write a summary view of the rights of British Americans to be presented for consideration to the delegates of the Continental Congress, which meets in less than three weeks in Richmond."

He held at least a dozen pieces of paper, written upon both sides. He passed them to Mama, and she took them with great care.

"I am asking you to print sixty copies and to have them ready no later than the first of September. Are you able to accommodate this request?"

"Aye." Mama nodded as she held the pages almost reverently. "We will have them ready for you even sooner, if you need them."

"Peyton Randolph is leaving this city on the first and will

retrieve them at that time. He will deliver them to me in Richmond."

"We will have them prepared in plenty of time."

"Thank you." Mister Jefferson gave a slight bow. "Please address the bill to my home. I am in your debt, madam." He then acknowledged me with another bow. "Good day to you both."

"Good day." Mama walked him out into the hallway, and after he was gone, she came back into the office and closed the door, her eyes wide. "Libby," she whispered, "do you know what this is?" She held up the pages, shaking her head in wonder.

"What?"

Mama set the papers on her desk and looked through them as she spoke to me. "This document will be discussed at great length during the congress, but Jefferson will not be able to attend because he'll be too ill."

It gave me shivers whenever Mama talked about a historical event she knew so much about that had not yet happened. Whereas I tried to avoid learning details so I wouldn't inadvertently change history, Mama had reveled in learning them. Mayhap it was because she hadn't thought she'd stay in this time period but had planned to live in the 1990s and hadn't been as concerned as I was.

"The delegates will be so impressed with this document," she continued, "they will have it reprinted and distributed in New York, Philadelphia, and England. And when they decide to declare independence from England next year, they will ask Jefferson to write up the Declaration of Independence because of how well he wrote *A Summary View of the Rights of British America*."

I stood next to her to inspect the pages that would play such a prominent role in American history.

"And to think," she said in awe, "he asked us to print this. Some days I feel we are not doing enough for the cause, but then I remember how powerful the written word is and how it has made nations rise and fall. We are playing a part in the rise of a great nation."

I placed my hand on her arm, marveling at her comment, and then I paged through the document, calculating the size of the pamphlet we would need to print. "It will be at least twenty or twenty-two pages long."

"'Tis not a short summary," Mama said with a chuckle.

I joined in her laughter, feeling lighter and freer than I had in a long time. If what she said was true, then this pamphlet would make us a good deal of money.

"You and I will have to work on this without Louis's help," she said, "for I fear he will not approve."

I wanted to tell her that I had seen him near the kitchen and that he might have overheard our conversation, but I didn't want to fret. We had enough to worry about. If word started to spread that we were aiding the Patriots, it would bring us more trouble.

After our midday meal, the heat became so oppressive that I could hardly concentrate on my work. The newspaper would go to press in two days, so I didn't have the luxury of taking the afternoon off. A headache had begun to form at my temples, and I needed some fresh air.

I stood from my chair, where I'd been editing a submitted poem for the poets' corner titled *The Soliloquies of a Highwayman*. It was an exceptionally long poem and had many errors, but the content had caught my eye, and I'd decided to publish it.

"I will refresh our water," I told Mama as I picked up our pitcher, needing a break.

"It's days like today that I long for central air conditioning." Mama used a piece of paper to fan her flushed face. "Even a window unit would be nice."

"And I miss the ocean in Newport." I walked toward the door. Artificial cooling techniques were still in their infancy in 1914 and were not widely available, so I couldn't imagine what central air conditioning felt like, though Mama had spoken of it often during the hot Virginia summers. "But I wouldn't turn down an iced glass of Coca-Cola, either."

A flash of red caught my eye at the window, and I paused. A soldier was walking up the short path to our front door, a piece of paper in his hand and a haversack on his shoulder.

"We have a visitor," I said as I set down the water pitcher.

"Oh?" Mama turned to look out the window. "I wonder what he wants."

A moment later, the front door opened, and I met the officer in the hallway.

"Good afternoon," I said. "How may I be of service?"

"Are you the mistress of this home?" He was a tall, handsome man, no more than twenty-five, I would guess, with dark brown eyes.

"Nay, 'twould be my mother."

Mama appeared, a frown on her forehead. "May I help you?"

He gave her a deferential nod and handed her the document he held, quickly taking off his tricorne and putting it under his arm. "I'm Lieutenant Addison."

"'Tis a pleasure to meet you," Mama said.

"Governor Dunmore has identified your property as having an uninhabited outbuilding," the lieutenant said, looking from Mama to me, "which he is claiming for use under the Quartering Act."

The paper shook in Mama's hand, though from nervousness or anger, I wasn't certain. I watched her face as she read the document, which was a printed form that had been produced in our very own printing room. Mama's name and the name of the lieutenant were hand-written in the spaces provided.

Finally, she looked up. "You're welcome to the use of my

outbuilding." She handed the document back to Lieutenant Addison, though she did not offer him a smile. "I'm afraid the building is in poor condition, but it's yours for as long as necessary."

"Thank you, madam."

"Libby, will you show Lieutenant Addison to the outbuilding, please?"

I nodded, assuming she meant the old stable near the back of the property. "Aye. Follow me."

I led the lieutenant through the hall and toward the back door. He glanced into the sitting room and looked up the stairs as we walked, as if he were searching for something. When he caught my eye, he smiled.

Abraham and Mariah were at work in the gardens, and the girls were sitting in the shade of a tree, playing with their rag dolls, as I led the lieutenant into the backyard. Abraham stood with his hoe in his hand, a frown on his face, but he did not question me. Instead, he sent a curious glance toward his wife, who responded with her own perplexed look.

I walked along the path to the back gate, near where Henry had stood with me on the night of my twentieth birthday. The old stable had been built with the same red brick as our home, but the wood shingles had been in disrepair for some time, and the wooden door creaked on its hinges.

"Here is the building," I said. "'Tis not much, I'm afraid."

He walked up to the structure and looked all around it, tapping the wall as if inspecting whether it would hold. "It will do."

Thankfully this building was at the back of the property. Hopefully that meant we wouldn't see much of Lieutenant Addison. I had never seen him in Williamsburg before. Mayhap he'd only just arrived. But that left the question of whether Governor Dunmore had requested more soldiers.

I pointed to Nicholson Street, which ran behind the stable. "This road will take you to the Palace Green."

He looked in the direction I pointed, smiling and nodding his understanding. "Thank you, Miss Conant. 'Tis been a pleasure meeting you."

He hadn't really met me, but I nodded in response and then left, not knowing what—if anything—I should say. I did not want to welcome him or make him feel at home.

When I was near Abraham and Mariah, they stopped their work and met me on the path.

"What is he doing here?" Abraham asked, his gaze hard with suspicion.

I glanced toward the stable. "He's been quartered here by order of the governor."

Abraham frowned. "There's never been a problem housing the soldiers before."

I shrugged, uncertain why things had changed.

Leaving them, I returned to the office, where Mama was staring out the window. She glanced at me when I arrived, her lips pressed together in frustration.

"I have a feeling I know why the governor sent that officer to us," she said.

"You do?" I sat on my chair and leaned forward.

"We printed the resolution for the day of prayer, and we also printed the petition to boycott British goods. And today, Mister Jefferson brought us his pamphlet to be printed for the Continental Congress."

"But we're the public printer."

"None of those things were sanctioned by the governor or his council." Mama shook her head. "Mark my words. Governor Dunmore is putting pressure on us, hoping we'll not assist the Patriots. Lieutenant Addison has been sent to keep an eye on us, and if we're not careful, the governor may rescind our contract."

"Truly?" Alarm finally registered in my gut. The contract was the only thing keeping us out of debtor's prison. "Are we in danger?"

"All of us are in danger, Libby." She crossed her arms, look-ing out the window, up and down the street. "The governor is displeased with us. I'm certain of it. I don't know of anyone else in Williamsburg who has an officer quartered with them—and a lieutenant, nonetheless."

If what she said was true, no one would be free to come and go from our establishment without the governor being privy to the information. Men like Mister Jefferson and Henry would be watched carefully.

"What will we do?" I asked her.

"Nothing. We will do nothing different than we've been doing."

I wanted to share in her confidence, but a niggle of unease twisted in my stomach, and I sent up a prayer of protection.

Our enemy was in our very own backyard, and there was nothing we could do. It would make all of our future work more difficult and dangerous.

# 16

## WHITBY, NORTH YORKSHIRE, ENGLAND
## DECEMBER 16, 1914

A heavy tempest slashed against Cumberland Hall as I sat in my bed, eating my breakfast and looking out the windows at the tumultuous North Sea. It reminded me of the storm that had been brewing in Williamsburg for the past four months as Mama and I lived in constant awareness of the soldier staying on our property—and the heightened tension in the colony. We feared the censure that could be brought upon us if the governor learned of our Patriot leanings. Thomas Jefferson's pamphlet had been a success, as Mama had said, and we had made thousands of copies in the late hours after Louis had retired for the evening. Abraham and Mariah helped us, and the income had been a blessing—though we knew the risk we were taking.

But it wasn't just Lieutenant Addison who was watching our every step. Louis had become increasingly difficult to work with, and I had found him loitering about the kitchen more than usual that autumn. Mama and I were careful in what we said and where we said it. We only spoke of my other path late at night in her room, when we knew we could not be overheard.

A gust of wind shook the windowpanes, bringing me back to the present. I had been in Whitby for over four months now and had grown to love the turbulent weather, even if it meant I must stay inside.

Edith busied herself in my bedchamber, tidying up the secretary where I had spent the preceding evening writing letters. One to my father, one to my mother, and one to Reggie. Each was different from the others. To my father, I spoke of the moors, of a beauty I had not at first appreciated. I told him of the walks I took with Edith, of the sea breeze tugging at my skirts, and how the purple heather had turned brown with the coming of autumn and winter.

To Mother, I spoke of Cumberland Hall, of the addition I had made to the number of servants now that we could afford to hire more help. I told her of the social gatherings, the few I had been invited to attend in Scarborough and Whitby. Of my help for the war effort in rolling bandages, sewing, knitting, and raising funds.

And to Reggie, I wrote the most businesslike letter of all. Surprisingly, I'd come to know him a little better through his weekly letters. Though they were formal in tone, his letters conveyed to me his longing for Cumberland Hall, the North Sea, and the moors. In a way, I connected with him through this place I now called home. Though he was not here with me, I felt bonded to him and his family just by being at the manor house.

It was not hard to feel linked to Cumberland Hall. I had never felt so at home anywhere other than Williamsburg, nor so in control of my own comings and goings. Something about the sea and the moors and the house captivated my imagination like nothing ever had before. It hadn't happened all at once, but over time and in the smallest of ways. Though there was a war raging and the North Sea had gone on alert, with soldiers stationed up and down the coast, I had come to see this place as a refuge.

"Do you want me to have your letters posted?" Edith asked as she set them in a pile on my desk.

"Yes, please. The sooner the better."

My letter to Reggie was full of details about the work I had done on the house. It had not been easy to find individuals to do the repairs. Almost all able-bodied men had enlisted to fight. Even the two footmen who had been here when I arrived left shortly thereafter. The only men on the property were Mr. Wentworth, who was too old; Williams, who had a limp from a childhood injury; and the old gardener, Mr. Ryker. Since I was the only Fairhaven at home, I did not dine formally but took all my meals on a tray in my room. There was very little need for the footmen, a reality that didn't set well with the traditional Mr. Wentworth.

"The carpenters have arrived," Edith said. "Mr. Wentworth has set them to work on the stairs and asks if that is suitable."

I nodded as I buttered my toast. With the war on and the lack of handymen about, I had decided to have only the necessary repairs done for now. The windows and roof had been fixed and the plaster repaired. The decorating could come later, though I didn't think much about that. I was simply biding my time until my birthday. Reggie could decorate however he wanted after I was gone.

But that thought sent a strange longing through me. It wasn't difficult to envision what Cumberland Hall could look like given enough time, attention, and imagination. A part of me was sad that I'd never see it complete.

"What would you like to wear?" Edith asked.

"It doesn't matter. No one but the staff will see me today." I had thought about going into Whitby to purchase Christmas presents, but the weather looked too severe for such an outing. Perhaps I would spend some time in the library or the conservatory. Working with the plants was a delight, connecting me with Mama. The smell and feel of the soil beneath my hands was comforting when I would have rather been in Williamsburg. And the books in the library had been an unexpected gift. I rarely had time to read for pleasure in my path in Williamsburg, though I loved it dearly. The library at Cumberland Hall was one of the most incredible I'd ever had the pleasure of exploring.

Edith pursed her lips in thought. "Perhaps the blue—?"

A strange noise reverberated through my chamber, rattling the windowpanes.

I frowned as Edith looked to the windows.

"Was that thunder?" she asked. "In December?"

The wind blew sleet against the house and tossed up great waves against the cliffs, but surely this squall wouldn't produce thunder.

I set my breakfast tray to the side and removed the blankets. The room was warm, thanks to the fire Edith had lit when she'd come in earlier, but the floor was still cool against my bare feet. I didn't bother to put on my slippers as I moved to the window.

Another boom shook the house, and this time it sounded louder and more sinister, echoing through my chest.

"Edith," I said on a breath.

Clutching my wrapper, she raced across the room and joined me at the window. It was difficult to see, with the wind and rain and waves. But another boom rattled the windows, quickly followed by another.

"It sounds like a bombardment." I swallowed the shock and fear racing up my throat.

"Where are they?" she asked, looking to the right and left, peering out the window.

"It sounds like Whitby." The village was less than a mile south, but the storm made it impossible to see anything on the sea.

"Do you think it's the Germans?" Edith's face had grown so pale that her freckles jumped out in contrast. Her Irish lilt was stronger than usual.

A German air raid on Great Yarmouth a month before had caused much anxiety in the weeks that followed, but we had settled back into complacency, trusting that the Royal Navy was patrolling these waters. Had the Germans decided to attack again?

"I must get dressed and find out." The bombing continued, growing louder.

Edith shook as she helped me dress. I didn't take any time with my hair, leaving it in its braid so I could go downstairs and speak to Wentworth.

"Will they bomb Cumberland Hall?" Edith asked as we rushed out of my bedchamber and down the corridor to the stairway.

"I don't know." We were so close to the edge of the sea that we'd be a prime target. I prayed with all my might that we would be spared.

Mr. Wentworth met us on the stairs, where the carpenter's tools had been abandoned.

"Lady Cumberland," he said, his usually calm and cool demeanor filled with apprehension, "we must get to safety belowstairs. A runner was just here, warning everyone on the coast. The Germans have raided Scarborough and Hartlepool, and they are on their way to Whitby. There were at least six German ships spotted, but there could be more."

"Where is the British Navy?" I asked as I followed Wentworth down the stairway and through the great hall to the servant's stairs.

"I don't know, your ladyship, but they must be out there somewhere."

Edith followed close at my heels. It wasn't even ten in the morning.

The staff was in chaos as we entered the central hall in the basement. I had been down here only twice since I'd moved into Cumberland Hall and was not as familiar with the space as I was the rest of the house.

"This way, your ladyship," Wentworth said, and I followed him and the others into a crowded storage space in the back corner of the manor. My trunks and bags had been placed here with the antiquated luggage of the Fairhaven family. "This is the safest room in the house. It's under the conservatory, farthest away from shore."

There were no windows in this room, and the gaslights were dim. All thirteen of us crowded there together, no one speaking, as the bombs continued to blast nearby. Thankfully the sound was muted, but there was no mistaking the noise of destruction.

"Let us pray," I said to my staff. I didn't know any of them well except for Mr. Wentworth and Mrs. Chadburn, but I was their mistress, and it was up to me to keep them calm.

Everyone lowered their eyes and clutched their hands together.

I led them in prayer, asking for God to spare us and our neighbors along the coast. I prayed for protection, for peace, and for victory in this war that had already drug on for four long months. What I knew from Mama was that this war would last until November of 1918—four more daunting years. Privately, I thanked God that I would not have to endure such a thing—and prayed for those here who would.

The lights went out, and we were cast into complete darkness.

Someone screamed, another began to weep, and soon others were mumbling their own frenzied prayers.

I closed my eyes as I clung to Edith, praying like I had never prayed before.

202

The bombardment ended as suddenly as it had begun, but we stayed in the storage room much longer. Finally, about thirty minutes after it ended, Mr. Wentworth offered to see if there had been any damage and to ascertain the continued threat. He found us several candles, which we lit as we waited.

Edith still sat next to me. She was drawing just as much strength from me as I was from her. What would I do without her? It was a constant worry. What if she chose to return to New York? Now that she was my employee, I would gladly give her a glowing recommendation if she wanted to find employment elsewhere, though I prayed she did not. But with an active war and constant threats, I could not blame her if she did.

Another thirty minutes passed as we waited in the cold, dark room for Mr. Wentworth to return. My back ached from sitting on a hard trunk, but I tried to keep up morale by asking the maids to tell me about their lives before coming to Cumberland Hall.

When Wentworth finally did return, he let out a full breath. "It appears the threat has passed. You may all return to your duties."

The staff slowly left the storage room, talking quietly amongst themselves as they went. I thanked each of them, trying to reassure them, but I wasn't sure how I could encourage them when I wasn't certain what we were facing.

"Is there any damage to Cumberland Hall?" I asked Wentworth.

"None that I can see."

I pressed a hand to my heart. "Good." I was surprised at how much I meant it. I did not wish to see any harm come to this grand home.

I followed Wentworth back up the stairs and into the great hall. The storm continued to rage outside, but all looked as it had before.

"Where are the carpenters?" I asked.

"They've gone to see what has happened. I hope you don't mind, Lady Cumberland, but I told them to convey our wish to help, should the need arise."

"Of course I don't mind," I said quickly. "I'm happy you made the offer. Do you think they'll return with news?"

"I've asked them to do just that." Wentworth bowed. "Is there anything else I can do for you?"

"No, thank you."

Edith was nearby, and when I turned to her, I could see she was still upset.

"Why don't you go lie down?" I suggested. "You've had quite a scare."

She shook her head. "I need to stay busy. If you don't need me, I'll see to the mending."

I smiled at her. "Do as you please."

Soon I was alone in the massive great hall with nothing to occupy my mind or hands. All I could think about was Scarborough, Hartlepool, and Whitby. Were there injured people? How extensive was the damage? Had the Royal Navy driven off the Germans? How had this happened? Wasn't the navy patrolling these waters?

My pacing feet took me to the library. The room was dark and drafty, but I did not want to call Wentworth to lay a fire. I had laid a thousand fires in Williamsburg and was quite capable of starting one myself, but it would be unseemly for the Marchioness of Cumberland Hall to start her own fire.

Wrapping my arms around myself, I walked to the windows that faced the sea, purposely avoiding the shelf near the desk. Almost every day, the volumes of *A Complete Account of America's Sons of Liberty, Founding Fathers, and Fallen Heroes* taunted me. If I pulled the Virginia volume from the shelf, I could easily learn everything I'd ever wanted to know about Henry. But I couldn't do it. Every warning Mama had ever given me warred with my temptation. It was a foolish notion.

Yet I wanted desperately to know. I hadn't seen Henry in four months. From what I had heard, he had been traveling to the other colonies for his father's business. I longed for him more than ever, both here and in Williamsburg. Just seeing his name would draw him near, I was certain.

I stood at the window for a long time, trying in vain to see any ships on the sea. When the temptation to pull out the book became too strong, I left the library to go to the conservatory. Perhaps I could distract myself with some of the plants I had been tending.

Wentworth found me in the conservatory several hours later. "Lady Cumberland?"

Black soil lined my nails as I transplanted succulents from their old cracked pots into fresh, new clay pots.

"I'm here," I called, since I was sitting behind the lemon, orange, and lime trees. I wiped my hands on a cloth and stood to meet him. "Is there word?"

"I'm afraid so." Wentworth's long, narrow face looked even longer today. "The civilian injuries and casualties are high. Some are saying that over five hundred people were injured, and there are several families, especially in Hartlepool, who lost everyone when their homes were shelled."

I put my hand to my throat in horror. "How awful. Where are they sending the injured?"

"I'm not sure, your ladyship."

"We must have as many as possible brought here. Anyone who can travel."

Wentworth frowned. "Are you cert—?"

"I'm quite certain. Please have Williams send word to Whitby, Scarborough, and Hartlepool. Anyone who is in need must come. I will have the staff begin to prepare the great hall and the drawing room. We'll need someone to gather food supplies in Whitby, and I'll have the maids begin to tear apart the sheets for bandages." My mind was already moving ahead of my mouth as I made plans. "We must not hesitate, Mr. Wentworth. There are people in need, and we must do our part."

"As you wish, Lady Cumberland."

I followed him out of the conservatory, and as he left the house to speak to Williams, I went toward the back stairs for the second time that day.

Mrs. Hawthorn, the cook, was rolling out pastry dough when I entered the large kitchen. Her eyes widened as she stopped rolling and straightened. "What can I do for you, milady?"

Long windows lined the top of the kitchen wall, which was at ground level. Though it was stormy outside, their south-facing exposure allowed plenty of light into the tall room. Besides the cook, a kitchen helper was working, peeling potatoes. She also stopped and stared at me, no doubt shocked to see me downstairs for the second time that day.

"There have been heavy casualties along the coast," I told them. "I've instructed Mr. Wentworth to send word that we will take in anyone who needs help. If the reports are accurate, I expect to fill up the great hall and drawing room. We'll need plenty of soup and bread to feed everyone tonight. When we know how many will be here, I'll send Williams for more food and supplies."

Mrs. Hawthorn's mouth hung open as she listened. She was a stout woman with small grey eyes, but she looked sharp and capable.

"Are you able to accommodate my request?" I asked.

Her mouth snapped shut, and she nodded. "Of course, milady."

"Thank you." I offered her and the helper a quick smile, and then I turned, only to find Mrs. Chadburn standing behind me. I startled at her unexpected presence.

"Is there a problem, milady?"

"There is." I quickly explained the situation. "I will need all the maids to help in the great hall and drawing room. We'll need to make room for bedrolls and mattresses, and I'll need a couple of the maids to start cutting up some of the older bed linens for bandages."

Mrs. Chadburn's eyebrows rose as she listened to my instructions. "Are you certain you want strangers traipsing through Cumberland Hall, milady? Who's to say what could go missing?"

"It's of little concern to me at the moment." I was trying not to lose patience. All I wanted was cooperation from my staff. Who knew how soon people would begin to arrive? "We will house everyone on the main level to better keep an eye on things. It will prevent the need to go up and down the stairs with injured people, not to mention food and supplies." I started to move around her. "Please see that it's done. I will go upstairs and start moving furniture."

"You, milady?" Mrs. Chadburn's eyebrows rose even higher.

I didn't bother to respond. We were wasting precious time.

Within two hours, the injured began to arrive at Cumberland Hall. They trickled in at the beginning, but then they came in groups, until the great hall and drawing room were overflowing. At least a hundred injured people had come, including several local artillery volunteer soldiers who had been defending Hartlepool.

Many uninjured villagers also arrived, wanting to help. They brought blankets, food, bandages, and medicine. In addition to supplies, they also brought their energy and assistance, which we needed more than anything.

For hours, we tended to wounds, comforted the confused and scared, and fed those who were hungry. Shock and grief reverberated throughout the house. Stories of great loss weighed each of us down as more and more people recounted their experiences.

"Dr. Aiken is here," Edith said when she found me wrapping the calf wound of a young woman. I had cleaned it with some vodka Wentworth had produced, and for once I was thankful for Reggie's penchant for alcohol. "He's from Sleights."

"Sleights?"

"It's a village about three miles west of here," a middle-aged gentleman with a heavy, greying mustache said as he walked up behind Edith. He nodded at me. "I'm Dr. Aiken. I presume you are Lady Cumberland?"

"I would stand to greet you"—I motioned to the wound I was dressing—"but I'm otherwise engaged." I smiled my thanks at his arrival. "I'm very glad that you've come."

"When I heard that you had opened up Cumberland Hall, I knew I must."

"Please let me know what you need. I or Mr. Wentworth, the butler, will see that you get it."

He nodded and then turned to the nearest patient.

Despite the cold winter day, sweat gathered on my brow as I finished wrapping the calf wound and then moved on to the next injured person. It made me wonder if this was what I would face in my 1774 path, as well.

With the revolution looming, I could see nothing but war in my future.

# 17

## WILLIAMSBURG, VIRGINIA
## DECEMBER 24, 1774

Christmas Eve was grey and dreary as I hung a pine garland over the hearth in the sitting room, thoughts of Cumberland Hall and our makeshift hospital on my mind. I was thankful for a bit of reprieve from the endless work I had been doing in 1914, caring for the sick and injured.

There had been very little sleep for anyone over the past week. Dr. Aiken had stayed with us around the clock, performing surgeries in a small parlor off the great hall. For those eight days, it hadn't mattered our rank or position within the manor. Each of us worked side by side to minister to the patients who had come to Cumberland Hall seeking refuge. We cooked, served food, washed linen, rolled bandages, and simply sat to talk or listen to our guests. A comradery had been built between the staff and me, but it had come at a great cost. There were two dozen patients still with us, those who were seriously injured and many others who had lost their homes.

I forced my thoughts to return to Williamsburg, trying hard to separate my two lives so I could be present for Mama and the girls. It was Christmas, after all. A time to put aside our troubles for even a few hours and reflect upon the joy that had come into the world.

The garland I held was fresh, and the scent of pine was strong. Mama loved to decorate for Christmas, though it was not celebrated in the way she or I were accustomed to from our later paths. No one decorated evergreen trees or hung stockings for Santa Claus to fill. Yet there was beauty, revelry, and excitement in abundance. Wassailers had been traveling up and down the streets of Williamsburg for the past hour, their wassail bowl full of spiced ale and apple slices.

Along with the songs of the wassailers, I found myself humming carols I knew from my other path—ones that had not yet been composed. "Silent Night," "It Came Upon a Midnight Clear," and "Jingle Bells" were three of my favorites.

"What are you humming?" Rebecca asked as she entered the sitting room with a bunch of holly in her hands.

I had been humming "Up on the Housetop" but stopped when she gave me a quizzical stare. "Nothing." I smiled, allowing the season to lift my spirits.

"What present are you giving me?" She redirected the conversation to her favorite subject. "A new hat? A pair of mittens? A doll?"

"You'll have to wait until tomorrow."

With the additional income from Thomas Jefferson's pamphlet, which had paid off the remaining debts we owed, Mama and I had decided to purchase store-bought gifts for the girls. It had been fun to shop for them together, though we hadn't been extravagant. Since the colonial boycott on British goods had begun at the beginning of December, the cost to produce our weekly paper had increased.

Rebecca pressed her lips into a line as she watched me hang the garland. "Do you have to go to the governor's ball tonight?"

"I don't *have* to go," I told her, "but I want to."

The invitation had been a surprise. Surely Governor Dunmore knew we had printed Thomas Jefferson's pamphlet—and the other pamphlets that had come in after his. Lieutenant Addison was keeping a close watch on our activities, spending much of his time on our property. He had been useful, chopping wood with Abraham, toting bushel baskets of vegetables from our harvest, and repairing the shingles on the kitchen after a destructive storm. He seemed always to be present, confirming Mama's earlier suspicions. Which led me to believe that the governor knew about our activities and had still invited us to the ball.

Perhaps to keep his enemies close?

Rebecca's pout was well-rehearsed, but I was immune to it. "But if you and Mama go to the ball, what will Hannah and I do all evening?"

"You will stay here with Mariah and Abraham. They plan to pop corn and heat cider."

"Why do you want to go?" she asked.

"Why, indeed?" I couldn't hide the grin from my face. Henry would be in attendance, and I had not seen him for almost five months. The waiting had been especially difficult with the war approaching and my uncertainty about his fate.

I sent up a prayer, begging God to spare Henry in the war to come. I could not wait to see him again, if only to convince myself that he was alive and well.

A knock at the front door brought my attention back to the task at hand. "Mayhap the wassailers have arrived," I said to Rebecca. "Here. Place the garland over the nails."

She took the garland as I walked into the front hall. I wiped my hands on my apron, trying to get the sticky sap off my fingers, and opened the front door.

Mister Charlton, Sophia's father, stood on our front stoop. He was a large man, and he wore a dark grey wig that was one of the finest in Williamsburg.

"Good day to you, Mister Charlton. Won't you come in?" It had cooled considerably over the past week, reminding me of the weather in Whitby.

Mister Charlton entered the front hall, a gruff demeanor emanating from his person. He was not a jolly man, but he'd been kind to me over the years, especially as one of Sophia's friends. Today, however, he did not offer me any warmth as he turned to face me.

"How may I be of service to you?" I asked, putting a smile upon my face.

"I've come on a most unpleasant errand."

My heart rate picked up at his tone and disposition. "I pray nothing is wrong with Sophia."

"Nay. 'Tis not about my daughter—but about you and your mother and this printing shop."

"Us?" I tipped my head in confusion. "What unpleasant errand involves us?"

He held up Thomas Jefferson's pamphlet, *A Summary View of the Rights of British America*. "Over the course of the past few months," he began, "there have been more and more of these types of publications coming from this printing house. I've been made aware of the increase since your father's passing."

I stared at him, unable to deny his accusation, wondering who had made him "aware." We did not affix our name to all the pamphlets we published.

"As a loyal British subject, I cannot condone such behavior from the public printer." He slapped the pamphlet down on a nearby table. "This is an outrage and a treasonous assault on the king."

"I beg to differ, Mister Charlton." My heart was still thumping hard, and I had to swallow the nerves threatening to make me shy away from him. "As the public printer, we are under contract to print whatever the governor, his council, and the

212

burgesses ask of us—but that does not mean we are limited to printing for the government alone. We have the right—nay, the responsibility—to keep the press free and allow anyone who so desires to publish their thoughts and ideas."

"That does not mean you are obligated to print everything."

"True. But we reserve the right to print whatever we choose."

"Thus, the reason for my visit." His face was red, and his voice had risen to such levels that Mama came down the stairs to see who was here.

"I will not associate with anyone who supports these so-called Patriots." Mister Charlton turned to address Mama, as well. "As long as you persist, my family will not patronize this establishment and will cancel our subscription. I will also be certain to pass this information along to others who will do the same." He looked directly at me. "And no one in my home will darken this doorway until I can be assured of your loyalty to the king."

He was going to keep Sophia from coming to visit? I opened my mouth to protest, but Mama shook her head.

Mister Charlton looked from me to Mama. His jowls shook with the intensity of his words. "That is not my only concern. There has been strange talk circulating about the two of you."

"Strange talk?" Mama came down the rest of the steps to face our guest.

"Some people think you are spies, or at the very least, leading double lives. You've been overheard talking about recruiting men for the war effort—something about three thousand men enlisting every day—and other troubling things."

I frowned, perplexed by his accusations. "Us? Recruiting men for a war?"

And then I remembered that day outside the kitchen when Mama had asked if I had heard from Reggie. I'd said he was busy recruiting men for the war effort and that there were three thousand men enlisting every day.

Which meant that Louis had not only overheard us but had been spreading rumors about us. What else had he been saying?

"When this crisis blows over," Mister Charlton continued, "you will find yourselves without friends, a business, or an income. You put yourselves and the people under your roof in danger. Is that what you desire? To tempt the ire of the governor or the king?" He narrowed his eyes as he stared at me. "Is it worth all that, Libby?"

I didn't respond as I met his gaze. Had I not known the outcome of the looming war, I might have cowered under his threats.

"I've said my piece, and now I shall leave your establishment. But do not be mistaken. I strongly believe the public printing contract should be removed from your business and given to someone who supports the king. I will work toward that end, and others will join my effort."

Men like Louis and Mister Archer, no doubt.

A moment later, the door reverberated with the force of his anger.

"Louis," I said with anger burning in my chest. "He is trying to destroy us from within."

"He is only doing what he thinks is necessary." Mama picked up Mister Jefferson's pamphlet. "He is fighting a losing battle."

"Mayhap, but what might *we* lose in the process?" I couldn't believe how calm she was acting.

Her green eyes were steady as she looked at me. "What makes us different from anyone else? Why must we not pay a cost for freedom? Is it everyone else's job to sacrifice so that we can enjoy the benefits of their payment? Nay. Freedom isn't free, Libby. The price is far greater than anyone realizes." She linked her elbow through mine and led me back into the sitting room. It smelled of orange and clove pomanders and fresh pine. "By the end of this, our lives will look far different than we can imagine."

"What if they succeed in removing the contract from us?"

"The governor has more important issues to address."

I wanted to believe her. "What will I do without Sophia's companionship?"

"Mayhap, as things progress, he'll change his mind." Mama meant as the war unfolded, though she couldn't say such things in front of Rebecca. Instead, she took the garland from Rebecca's hands and touched her younger daughter's cheek. "We can pray he'll have a change of heart. He would not be the only one."

"I hope he'll still allow Sophia to speak to me when not at home. I could not bear to be apart from her overlong."

Mama placed her free hand on my arm. "Much will be required of us, Libby. But let us think of better things today." She put a smile on her face and in her voice. "For tomorrow is Christmas and tonight is the ball. We must take whatever joy can be found from each day and not borrow tomorrow's sorrow."

Rebecca giggled. "That rhymed."

I hugged her close and smiled up at Mama, so thankful for my family and the many blessings God had bestowed upon me.

There was much to be grateful for, even with the troubles surrounding us on every side.

The long-awaited Christmas Eve ball at the Governor's Palace had arrived. Though it was cold, Mama and I walked to the palace, just as we had done in May while the burgesses were in session.

Wassailers and merrymakers were out on Duke of Gloucester Street, singing, dancing, and celebrating from the College of William and Mary all the way to the capitol building. Some were in colorful costumes, with hats and noisemakers. I smiled as we passed a group dressed as court jesters. They wished us health, prosperity, and good tidings.

Mama and I had remade my best gown for tonight's occasion, unable to purchase anything new. The Virginia cotton was a solid green, which complemented my eyes. The back was arranged in box pleats that fell loosely from my shoulder to the floor and had a slight train. The gown was open in front, showing off my decorative stomacher and petticoat. Under the petticoat I wore wide panniers to accentuate my hips, and at the sleeves were scalloped ruffles of elbow-length lace crafted in Virginia. I did not prefer the oversized hairstyles many women chose for formal events. Instead, Mariah had helped me style the top of my hair raised over a wool toque. The rest was waved and curled, with ringlets at the back. It was still fashionable but not gaudy, and I wore a simple green bow at the back instead of the elaborate headdresses I would be sure to see this evening.

"How many patients remain at Cumberland Hall?" Mama asked as we turned off Duke of Gloucester Street and onto the Palace Green.

"About two dozen."

"And has Dr. Aiken returned to Sleights?"

"Yes. He wanted to be home for Christmas."

"Have you heard from Reggie?"

I sighed, thinking about the husband I had not seen in almost five months. "I did not receive his weekly letter, though the post might be slow because of the war." Reggie's letters had come every Monday since we were separated in London. Until now.

"Any news on the war?"

"Daily, but all anyone is talking about now is the raid. Everyone is angry that the Germans were successful. There is an investigation into how the Royal Navy missed the advance notice. The number of deaths is now one hundred and thirty."

"I'm very sorry you've had to endure such a thing." Mama

took my hand in hers. "But God has placed you there for His purposes, and you have done a fine job."

Torches lit the drive up the Palace Green. My heart raced at the knowledge that I would soon be in Henry's company again. It had been much too long.

We entered the palace and were announced by the footmen, who were dressed in pale blue livery. Governor Dunmore and Lady Dunmore were near the door, greeting their guests. Their eldest daughter, Lady Catherine, was with them.

Her presence surprised me. She was not quite fifteen. Had they chosen to present her to society so soon?

"Good evening, Mistress Conant," Governor Dunmore said to Mama as she curtsied before him.

"It's a pleasure to be here, Governor Dunmore," Mama replied. "Thank you for the invitation, and congratulations on your recent victory at Point Pleasant. Your treaty with Chief Cornstalk will ensure peace among the settlers and the Shawnee for years to come."

Governor Dunmore's chest puffed out at Mama's compliment. Over the summer and fall months, the governor had been leading an effort to secure lands in the west for Virginia and had recently negotiated a treaty with a Shawnee chief to protect the settlers in that area.

"And this is your daughter Libby?" he asked.

I curtsied before him and noticed the deep cleft in his chin. It was the most prominent feature on his otherwise plain face. "Good evening."

"I've heard much about you in recent months," Governor Dunmore said as he studied me. His wife turned from the people she had been speaking to, and the governor introduced us to her.

"It's a pleasure to meet you," Lady Dunmore said.

"The pleasure is ours," Mama responded, curtsying.

What had the governor heard about me? And who was

speaking to him? I longed to ask him, but he turned to the next guests who entered.

"Do you think Lieutenant Addison is talking to him about me?" I whispered as Mama and I moved deeper into the palace.

"What could he have said? You've done little else but work."

"But it's the work we've been doing that he might be sharing."

We walked through the entry hall and into a smaller hall that led to the ballroom. The orchestra was playing a lively tune, though no one was dancing yet. They would wait until the governor and Lady Dunmore opened the ball with the minuet. Instead, people milled about the long, narrow ballroom, visiting, laughing, and indulging in festive drinks.

Mama joined a conversation with a group of women, but I did not engage beyond a simple greeting. I scanned the room and almost immediately met Henry's clear, blue-eyed gaze. He smiled, and the months melted away. He was standing with several of the local burgesses, including Mister Peyton Randolph, who had been the president of the recent Continental Congress. While the men around him talked, Henry did not remove his gaze from me, and I could not hide the grin that lit my face.

I had missed him so.

He broke away from the burgesses and walked across the ballroom toward me. I held my breath at his approach, wishing we were alone in the sitting room or at the end of the torch-lit lane. Then we could be open with each other, not worrying about what others heard us say. And there were so many things I wanted to say to him.

It was strange how much had happened in my life while we were parted—both here and in 1914. I felt different after living on the coastal moors these past five months. Yet how could I ever convey that to him?

His smile was for me alone as he wove between the other guests. He looked as if he had much to tell me, too—but then

Governor Dunmore arrived in the ballroom with his wife and daughter.

Henry was stopped by the governor, who said something I could not hear. There was a short pause as Henry turned to Lady Catherine, spoke to her, and then offered his arm.

The orchestra changed its tune, and the master of ceremony announced the opening minuet. Henry offered me an apologetic glance no one else would have noticed before leading Lady Catherine to the middle of the ballroom.

My disappointment was acute. I felt pushed aside, though not of Henry's choosing. I watched as he and Lady Catherine stood next to her parents, who would dance at the top of the minuet as the couple with the highest social standing. They were joined by several others in descending order of importance.

"Miss Conant?"

A gentleman appeared at my side. It was Lieutenant Addison.

"May I have this dance?" he asked, bowing.

I did not wish to stand on the edge of the ballroom to watch and gossip as the others would, so I nodded and offered a curtsy, then reached for his elbow. "I would be honored."

His smile was wide and handsome as he led me onto the dance floor. Though he was often present on our property, helping where he could, I had tried to avoid him whenever possible. To purposely stand beside him now felt daring.

Henry's gaze was upon us, and though I did not wish to make him jealous—if that were possible—I couldn't deny that it felt good to be dancing in the same minuet as he and Lady Catherine.

"It saddens me that our paths do not cross more often," the lieutenant said as we took our positions. "You've quite captivated my attention, Miss Conant. I often find myself admiring you from a distance."

His words surprised me, and I stared at him. All I could think to say was, "Please, call me Libby."

"And I'm James."

James. It suited him.

He was a pleasant young man, though his red uniform was a constant reminder that he would soon become the enemy—if he wasn't already.

The minuet began, and we bowed and curtsied to each other, performing the perfunctory steps to open the dance. Then Governor Dunmore and his wife started at the head of the line and danced their way down, past us, and then back up as we all watched. It was a lengthy process but a necessary part of the evening. Later, we would dance the country dances and the reel, which were much preferred by almost everyone in the room.

Henry and Lady Catherine were the next to come down the line. The minuet required great care and concentration. The footwork and patterns were so intricate that even the slightest mistake could make a person trip.

Lady Catherine had grown quite beautiful. Her cheeks glowed as she danced beside Henry. When they passed, he met my gaze, but I could not read his stormy expression. Was he angry? Jealous? Frustrated at my choice of dancing partner?

It was finally our turn. We danced down and back, and I found James to be an accomplished dancer. He was confident, handsome, and pleasant. I glanced at Henry when we were near him, but he wore the same expression. Anger mixed with something more. Accusation?

The minuet ended, and James led me away from the other dancers to the refreshments table. I would have been elated had Henry's gaze not been so troubling.

"You're a beautiful dancer," James said to me, admiration shining from his face. "I felt proud to stand beside you."

I had to focus on what he was saying instead of trying, in vain, to look for Henry. "You flatter me, Lieutenant."

"James," he corrected with a gentle smile.

"James," I repeated, dipping my head as he handed me a cup. We stood for a moment, watching the next minuet. Henry was nowhere to be seen. I did not want to be rude to James, so I said, "It occurs to me that I know very little about you. Where do you hail from?"

"Whitby, on the North Sea."

"Whitby?" I choked on my punch and stared at him.

"Do you know it?"

I tried to hide my surprise as I set down my cup and wiped my mouth with a handkerchief. How could I explain knowing Whitby to this man? "I'm familiar with the region, aye."

"Have you been there?"

How could I get around this answer without lying? I had been there—as Anna Elizabeth Fairhaven, but not as Libby Conant. "Nay, unfortunately."

"'Tis beautiful and rugged and fierce." He laughed, and I found myself drawn to him despite my reservations. "I miss it dearly. My father is the gardener for the Marquess of Cumberland. I grew up in a little cottage on the estate. 'Twas Lord Cumberland who purchased my commission into the Royal Army."

I couldn't help but stare. "You are familiar with Cumberland Hall?" The words were past my lips before I could think about the consequences.

"Aye." He grinned. "Have you heard of Cumberland Hall?"

I swallowed and nodded. "I have."

"How odd that we should meet," he mused. "I was feeling homesick for the North Sea, and now I feel as if I've returned home for the evening, in a way. It comforts me to know I am not the only one here who has heard of Cumberland Hall."

It was more than odd. All these months, James had been living just behind our house, and I had no idea he was so connected to the very home I was inhabiting in my other path. It sent a shiver up my spine.

"I'm very happy we've had this opportunity to talk," he said to me. "I knew I would like you from the moment we met."

My cheeks grew warm at his words, and I heard someone clear their throat behind me. I turned and found Henry standing close enough to have heard part of our conversation.

"May I have the next dance, Libby?" he asked, not even looking in James's direction.

Butterflies filled my stomach at his sudden appearance, and I nodded. "Of course." I motioned to James. "Have you met Lieutenant Addison? Lieutenant, this is Henry Montgomery."

"Lord Ashbury's son?" James asked as they bowed to one another.

"Aye."

"'Tis a pleasure to meet you." James then turned to give me a slight bow. "And a pleasure to spend time in your company, Libby. I look forward to our paths crossing again soon. I will have to make a point of seeking you out the next time I see you in the yard."

I smiled and curtsied and then turned my gaze back to Henry. He watched James move away before turning those stormy blue eyes on me. It was amazing how they changed in color with his mood. But the look and intensity in his gaze made me frown. Was he angry at me?

As soon as James was out of earshot, he said, "Is it true that Lieutenant Addison is living in your stable?"

"He was quartered there by Governor Dunmore."

"Has it occurred to you that he is spying on your activities?"

I swallowed and nodded, forcing myself to meet his gaze. "Aye. Mama and I are being cautious."

"By dancing with him and playing the coquette?"

"Coquette?" I pressed my lips together in surprise and hurt. "And what of Lady Catherine?"

"What of her?"

"Are you using her to have better access to the governor? Or are you simply playing with her affections?" The moment the words passed my lips, I regretted them. They weren't fair, and they weren't true, but my anger refused to let me apologize.

Henry's jaw clenched, and he offered me a stiff bow. "Good evening, Miss Conant."

And then he walked away.

# 18

## WHITBY, NORTH YORKSHIRE, ENGLAND
## DECEMBER 24, 1914

It was hard to focus on the needs of those in Cumberland Hall the day after the governor's ball. All I could think about was Henry and the words I had uttered. There was nothing as difficult as the time and distance between each path when I was at odds with someone. I longed to run to him and apologize, to put the anger and unkindness behind us—yet he had made me angry too. His words had hurt. I was not playing the coquette with James. Henry, of all people, should know that I was not a flirtatious woman.

What had made him think this? And why had it made me lash out and attack him? It was the last thing I wanted after months of being apart.

"Lady Cumberland." Mr. Wentworth found me woolgathering in the library, where I was standing near a cold window, looking out at the sea. "Luncheon is ready. Would you like to dine with the others in the dining room or take a tray to your bedchamber?"

For the past two weeks I had been eating whenever and wherever I had the opportunity. But now that our patients were stable and the work had begun to decrease, I had been enjoying meals at the appropriate times with some of our guests.

Today, however, I didn't feel like making small talk with the others.

"I will take a tray in here."

"As you wish, your ladyship. I will have it delivered post-haste." His demeanor had warmed toward me as we worked together after the raid. I had grown to appreciate and even like Mr. Wentworth, though he was still stiff and stodgy at times.

I hugged myself as I continued to stare out the window. It was chilly, and the sky was dark and overcast. A fire had been lit in the hearth, but it didn't penetrate the large room. I found myself drawn to the library whenever I needed to get away from the responsibilities and cares of Cumberland Hall. There was something comforting about the deep chairs, the familiar smells of leather and books, and the rugged view. But it wasn't just the room that gave me solace. Knowing that the Virginia book was there somehow made me feel closer to the people and places I loved in my other path.

Even if I didn't open it.

A movement on the road caught my attention as an unfamiliar automobile appeared. Was it someone coming to lend a hand? Or perhaps someone with news? I wasn't aware that we were receiving visitors, though with all the commotion these past two weeks, it wasn't unusual to have unexpected arrivals. Mr. Wentworth would deal with this person and let me know if my attention was required. I lost sight of the automobile as it went around the corner to the main entrance.

My mind wandered back to Williamsburg. Not only had Henry avoided me for the remainder of the evening, but I had also missed Sophia's company. She had been there with her parents, yet she didn't speak to me. When I tried to approach her, she had given me a look of regret and then turned her back on me.

What should have been a highlight of my year had been a crushing and disappointing night. I had so looked forward to being in Henry's company. There was no telling when or if I would see him again.

That thought alone made me want to weep.

The door opened to the library again, and I turned, expecting to find Mr. Wentworth with my lunch tray. But it wasn't the butler standing there, staring at me.

It was my husband.

"Anna," Reggie said as he stepped into the room and closed the door. "Wentworth told me I would find you here." He walked across the expanse of the library to stand beside me.

My heart pounded at the unexpectedness of his arrival, and I realized I had forgotten to breathe.

"Are you surprised to see me?" he asked, watching me closely. I had forgotten how bland his features were and how much I disliked his mustache.

It took a moment for me to find my voice. "Yes. Quite."

His lips turned up in a smile, revealing the space between his front teeth. "I have missed you, Anna, and have regretted our parting since you came to Whitby."

I was speechless. Not only had he been the furthest thing from my mind today, but I had not once regretted our parting. I had reveled in it.

"All these months," he said, "even with all the responsibilities occupying my time and attention, I found my thoughts straying to you. I eagerly anticipated each of your letters."

He'd anticipated *my* letters? They had been formal and stiff, full of nothing personal or private. All I'd spoken about was business affairs.

He reached for my hand, and in my surprise, I let him take it. "You do not know how much I have longed for this trip to

Whitby. I have never missed Cumberland Hall as much as I have these past months, knowing you were here."

"Reggie." My hand was limp in his. "You hardly know me."

His light brown eyes were focused solely on me as he smiled. "Yet what I know is enough to spark my affection."

I took a step back, unprepared for such talk and attention.

He let go of my hand, and I could see the disappointment in his eyes. His gaze hardened ever so slightly, and he bowed formally. "Pardon me for being so forward, Anna. I hoped that your fondness for me had grown while we were apart, but I can see now that it has not."

Remorse and embarrassment filled me at his words. Yet I did not want to make him think I cared when I did not.

"Do not apologize," I told him. "I'm just surprised by your sudden appearance."

"I wanted it to be a surprise."

"You've succeeded admirably."

I took another step away from him, realizing what his arrival meant. For months, I had been at ease, unconcerned about being married. But now the anxiety resurfaced. Would he expect me to make myself available to him? After all, we were married, and he was in need of an heir. Yet I could not let that happen. I would need to find a way to avoid that aspect of our relationship.

"How long do you plan to be at Cumberland Hall?"

"Only until the first of the year. I'm needed back in London as soon as possible. The prime minister did not want to spare me for the holidays, but he understands the great sacrifice you have made since our wedding. He wanted to offer you a gift by allowing me to spend our first Christmas together. It was Mrs. Asquith's idea."

Dread filled me at the thought of him being here for a week.

"As you can see," I said, moving behind a chair to put an object between us, "I'm afraid we have been so busy with our

227

patients that I have not had time to decorate Cumberland Hall for the holidays."

"There's time enough for that." He left the window and approached me. "What you've done for the war effort is admirable, especially after the raid. You made me very proud."

I didn't like the way he was looking at me. His gaze was filled with something akin to awe.

"News of your heroinism reached Mr. Asquith's ears in London. The raid is all anyone could talk about, but your name was mentioned just as often. Everyone marveled at how the Marchioness of Cumberland opened her estate to the wounded and homeless. You brought pride to my family name, and for that, I am grateful. Mrs. Asquith was impressed with your efforts, as well, and sends all her love."

I didn't like this side of Reggie. It was easier to dislike him—resent him—when I thought of him as cold and unfeeling. His public demeanor was so snobbish and aloof that I had assumed his private behavior would be the same. Certainly, his treatment of me on our wedding night and his avoidance of me for the rest of the trip had proven it to be true.

"Do you not like when I compliment you?" He moved a little closer, and I realized I was stuck between the wingback chair and the corner, but this was the first time I had not smelled alcohol on his breath. "Your cheeks are pink, and you look decidedly uncomfortable."

I also felt trapped. "Luncheon is being served. I imagine you're hungry after your journey from London." I tried to move past him, but he did not step back.

"Anna, I cannot recall the last time I apologized to someone for my poor behavior."

I stopped and stared at him, my cheeks becoming warmer by the second.

"But I owe you an apology for—" He cleared his throat and looked down. "Well, I think you know what I'm referring to.

I drank too much that night, though that is no excuse. I am afraid it has caused a rift between us that I would like to repair, if I may."

I closed my eyes, wishing he had not brought up this topic. Mortification filled every inch of my being. I had been trying—and succeeding—at putting it from my mind. "Please," I begged him on a whisper, "do not speak of it."

"I only long for you to know that I deeply regret my actions and hope we can put it behind us."

I finally pushed past him. "Consider it behind us." I walked to the door. "If you'll excuse me, there are things I must attend to."

"Of course." He nodded. "I do hope you'll speak to Mrs. Chadburn about finding a Christmas tree and having a bit of decorations put about the place. I confess, I have been yearning for the Christmases of my youth. Have you arranged for a Christmas feast?"

"I have."

"Wonderful." He smiled. "I look forward to enjoying supper with you tonight. It will be a treat to be in your company."

I turned the doorknob and fled the library, my legs shaking. I did not like this side of Reggie in the least.

That evening would be my first formal meal at Cumberland Hall. While Edith helped me dress, she informed me that Reggie had requested I join him for supper in the library because the dining room was occupied by our remaining patients.

I wanted to feign illness and remain in my room, but I was afraid he would come looking for me. A neutral location would be an easier place to avoid an intimate encounter.

At the appointed hour, I said a prayer and pushed open the library door.

It was dark outside, but the library was illuminated by gas wall sconces. A small table had been set before the crackling fireplace with a candelabra in the center and fresh-cut flowers from the conservatory. Their perfume was pungent and immediately made my head start to pound.

Reggie stood near the fireplace in his black tuxedo. He looked dapper and very much the lord of his dominion. One hand rested on the mantel while the other held a glass of amber liquid. I hoped he hadn't been drinking for long.

"Ah, Anna." He turned and gave me his full attention, taking in my attire from head to foot and then back up again. A pleased expression settled upon his features. "You look stunning."

His praise warmed my cheeks, but not in a good way. I did not wish to increase his ardor. I had chosen a modest evening gown of heather grey and paired it with long white gloves. Edith had insisted on putting a silver tiara on my head, and I had allowed her simply because she took such pleasure in adorning me and hadn't had any reason to for the past five months.

He waited for my response. Not wanting to be rude, I said, "Thank you."

After he set his glass on the table, he pulled out one of the chairs for me. It scraped against the wood floor, further grating on my headache. I took my seat and felt him brush my shoulders in a feather-light touch. It sent a shiver down my spine, recalling his touch on our wedding night. My stomach turned, and I lost what little appetite I had.

Mr. Wentworth chose that moment to enter with a rattling cart and one of the maids. I could tell by the look on his face that he was not pleased with the maid.

"Apologies, milord," he said to Reggie, "but we are without footmen at present, and I am forced to allow this maid to assist me with your meal."

"It's quite all right, Wentworth," Reggie said with a consoling smile. "We must all sacrifice for the war."

I smiled at Mr. Wentworth, as well, thinking of the sacrifices we had already made while turning Cumberland Hall into a hospital. Going without a footman paled in comparison.

He served the first course, vermicelli soup.

"I'm pleased to see that Mrs. Chadburn found a Christmas tree," Reggie said as he watched me lift my spoon to begin eating.

The tree in question had been placed in the great hall and was very impressive. Already the maids had decorated it with the Fairhavens' ornaments. Tomorrow we would light the candles and exchange gifts—though I did not have anything for Reggie, since I had not anticipated his arrival.

I slowly ate my soup, having nothing to say. It tasted bland and unappetizing, though whether from lack of spices or my poor mood, I couldn't tell.

"Perhaps we could go for a walk on the moors tomorrow," Reggie said. "There is much I would like to show you of Cumberland Hall. I only wish I had been here with you from the start."

I finally met his gaze and studied him. Was he being sincere? Was he trying to woo me?

As the meal progressed and he spoke of his childhood memories, his longing for home, and his hope for the future, I noticed one thing he did not address. The war. It slipped in and out of his conversation in a casual manner, but he did not share anything about the past five months of his life. I realized he hadn't shared anything about it in his letters, either. Was it because he wasn't allowed? Or because he didn't want to?

I finally decided to ask him while Mr. Wentworth served the third course, braised beef. "How is your work with the war effort going?"

It was one of the first questions I'd asked since we sat down, and Reggie looked up at me in surprise. But his surprise was soon overshadowed by something deeper and more troubling. He looked down at his plate, almost lost in thought.

"I wasn't planning to tell you this until closer to the end of my visit," he said, "but I believe you should know."

My beef remained untouched on my plate, and I saw Mr. Wentworth pause out of the corner of my eye.

Reggie took another sip of his drink and finally looked up at me, anxiety filling his countenance. "We need more men to enlist, and we've tried every tactic we can imagine. Mr. Asquith believes we need a high-profile member of Parliament to enter the conflict, thereby encouraging the masses." He swallowed and then lifted his chin. "I have volunteered."

I frowned. "But aren't you needed in London?"

"My position can easily be filled. I will be commissioned as a captain in the British Army." He smiled. "But never fear, it will be a mostly ceremonial position. I will be sent somewhere in relative safety and will assist one of the major generals. I will not see any combat."

As he spoke, I could see he was trying to convince himself. Was that why he had become sentimental about Cumberland Hall—and me?

"So you see, I must make the most of this visit, because I do not know when I might have the chance to return." He lifted his glass in an informal toast, then took a long drink.

Empathy filled me in a way I did not expect. Reggie was going to war, and he was frightened.

I laid aside my fork and gave him my undivided attention. It was the least he deserved. "I will pray for you," I said, "and ask that God keep you safe."

"Thank you, Anna." His face softened. "Or may I call you Libby, as you once asked?"

I swallowed, uncertain I wanted him to call me that name. Here, as his wife, I did not feel like Libby. Yet it was my true self. I was Libby Conant, and I always would be, no matter what I was forced to endure in this path.

"You may."

"Thank you, Libby." He smiled, and his anxiety seemed to dissipate. "I have promised myself I would not allow anything to hinder my time with you this week. I hope we can enjoy each other's company."

I picked up my fork once again and began to eat, purposely avoiding his statement.

When supper ended, Reggie stood and pulled back my chair. I could smell the alcohol on his breath, and I had noticed his eyes getting glossy and his speech beginning to slur.

"My head hurts tonight," I said as I moved away. "I will leave you to enjoy a cigar."

"Nonsense." He clasped my hand. "I do not want us to part ways tonight." He motioned to Mr. Wentworth, who was taking the food off the table. "Leave those things until later. I'd like to be alone with my wife."

My heart rate escalated as Mr. Wentworth bowed and then ushered the maid out of the library, closing the door behind them.

"I'm not feeling well," I said, trying to pull my hand loose from Reggie's grasp. "Perhaps I should go—"

"Please don't." He drew me close and pressed his face into my hair, taking a deep breath. "This is all I could think about, Libby. This moment with you. Alone."

I tried to pull away again, but he held me close.

"Please, Reggie," I begged. "My head is pounding. I'd like to lie down."

"Don't deny me, my love," he whispered as he began to kiss my neck.

Goose flesh rose on my arms. My stomach felt like it would toss up its contents. He turned my head and kissed my lips, his mustache poking into the tender flesh above my mouth.

I tried to push him away, but he wouldn't let me go. I wanted to call out, but who would come? Reggie was the lord and master of his home—of me. No one would interfere.

"Don't fight me," he said, between kisses. "I'm your husband, and I want you to know how much I desire you."

"I'm not ready. I don't want—"

My words were cut short as he kissed me again, and no matter how much I protested or fought, he would not let me go.

# 19

## WILLIAMSBURG, VIRGINIA
## DECEMBER 25, 1774

I lay in bed long after Rebecca and Hannah rose on Christmas morning and went downstairs. Snowflakes fell from the dark clouds as I stared out the window at the barren branches. I felt numb. If I allowed myself to cry, I would not be able to stop, so I just stared at the lifeless scene outside my window.

After I left Reggie in the library, I had gone up to my room, where Edith had been waiting. Without saying a word, I had changed into my nightgown and climbed into bed, my body and soul weak and trembling. I suspected Edith knew what had happened, because I saw her tears.

Hours later, Reggie had entered his own bedchamber. He moved about in there for quite some time as Mr. Duncan, his valet, spoke in low, calming tones. Reggie had probably continued to drink long after I left him.

Silently, I had gone to the door that connected our dressing rooms with the intent to lock it but discovered there was no lock. I could not sleep with the fear that he would come to me again, so I curled up on one of the chairs by the fireplace, determined to run if he tried to get into my room.

I must have fallen asleep, because I had woken in Williamsburg to face a cheerless Christmastide.

"Libby!" Hannah ran into our bedchamber and jumped on the bed to shake me. "Are you ill? Why do you lie abed on Christmas morning?"

The last thing I wanted was to ruin her Christmas. It had been a difficult year, first with Papa's passing and then with the onset of the Revolution. My family did not need more to worry about—especially Mama.

I hoped and prayed that there would be no baby, just like last time, and that there would be nothing for her or me to worry about. Why borrow trouble, as she had put it? What had happened to Anna Elizabeth Fairhaven had not happened to Libby Conant—at least, not physically. I thought about Mama's admonition that I should not allow one life to dictate the other. I didn't want anyone in 1774 to suffer because of a life thousands of miles and hundreds of years away, especially my sisters, who had been looking forward to Christmas for weeks.

"I am well," I said as I turned to face Hannah. "'Tis a gloomy day, and I was overtired, 'tis all."

Her mass of curls had yet to be tamed for the day. I placed my hand on her plump cheek and forced myself to be happy for her sake.

"Is Mariah making the plum pudding?"

"Aye!" Hannah's eyes lit up. "And she's roasting a duck. It smells so good in the kitchen. But Mama sent me up to tell you 'tis time for breakfast."

I pushed aside my troubles and quickly got dressed. The last thing I wanted today was for my melancholy to dampen everyone's spirits. I chose my second-best dress. After breakfast, we would attend church at Bruton Parish. Henry would be there, as would Sophia and many other friends and neighbors. Then there would be merrymaking in the streets, a marvelous feast for supper, and presents and games far into the evening. Mama had invited a few close friends to join in our celebration.

What I wanted most of all was to speak to Henry and tell him I was sorry. Even if he had made me angry, there was no cause for me to attack him and his intentions. My weary heart could not handle more pain or disappointment today. If he would not look at me or acknowledge me, I feared I would not have the strength to pretend I was well.

"Good morning, Libby," Mama said when I finally appeared in the sitting room. "And Merry Christmas."

"Merry Christmas, Mama." I put a smile on my face and kissed her cheek.

She studied me for a moment, then turned her attention back to the table. It was laden with many good things to eat. Almond pudding, lemon puffs, strawberry jelly, ham, and boiled eggs awaited us. I forced myself to eat, knowing Mama had woken up early to help Mariah prepare the meal. Thankfully, Rebecca and Hannah were full of conversation and excitement. I simply smiled and listened, laughing with them and enjoying their anticipation.

Soon we were on our way to Bruton Parish Church on the other side of the Palace Green. The bells tolled as a rare Christmas snow continued to fall in a lazy descent. It gathered in the corners of the buildings and along the path.

We greeted friends and neighbors as we walked up the stairs and into the church. I watched for Henry but had not seen him walking down the Palace Green from his home. Had he returned to Edgewater Hall?

The thought made my spirits lag. I could not go for weeks or months without apologizing to him.

Mama glanced at me but said nothing. We were now in the church and must not speak again. We stopped at our box, and Mama followed the girls and me inside. We rented the box, with its white wooden panels and red velvet seats. It was in the center of the church, in a respectable location with a good view of the pulpit. I let my eyes roam over the church and met Sophia's gaze. She watched me from across the aisle, her face sad. Her father whispered something to her, and she turned to look at the front of the church.

The little resolve I had left to be in a good mood completely fled, and I could not force myself to pretend I was happy. Mama gently placed her hand over mine and gave it a tender squeeze. When I looked at her, she offered me an understanding smile, and my heart warmed. She did understand—more than anyone ever could.

As more people entered the church, the choir began to sing "O Come, All Ye Faithful." A familiar figure appeared in the aisle outside our box, and my heart leapt at the sight of him. Henry.

He was so tall and elegant, his dark hair clubbed at the back. He held his tricorne under his arm and stood with confidence in his broad shoulders. When he met my gaze, his blue eyes were just as stormy as they had been last night at the ball, but this time they were not filled with anger, only remorse. I knew him well enough to know he was disappointed in himself.

I longed for him to know I was also upset with my actions, but there was no way we could speak here.

The exchange took place in a matter of seconds, and then he continued down the aisle toward the front, where his family occupied one of the more prestigious boxes in the church. His father and mother were with him, and they sat across the aisle from the governor's box. Governor and Lady Dunmore were there with several of their children, including Lady Catherine, who didn't hide her obvious admiration when Henry appeared.

I tried to focus on Mister Price's homily as I forced the images of the night before in Cumberland Hall from my mind. I was determined to feign illness for the rest of Reggie's visit, regardless of his wishes or his hopes for a bright Christmas in his childhood home. It would not be hard to complain of an ailment when I felt sick just thinking about his actions.

When the service finally ended, we were ushered out of the church to find a world covered in snow. It was coming down faster now, lining the dark branches of the trees, the rooftops of the houses, and the edges of the fence railings. Laughter and conversation filled the winter air. Children played in the snow, throwing snowballs and rolling snowmen. The world was filled with the cold scent of wet earth.

Mister Goodman, a widowed cobbler, stopped our family to inquire after our health. He was a kind man who had been alone for a decade or more since his wife passed away in child-birth with their first child. The infant had also died, and Mister Goodman had spent a long time in mourning. As he spoke to Mama, I watched for Henry.

The governor's family exited the church with Lord and Lady Ashbury. Behind them, Henry emerged at Lady Catherine's side. She was looking up at him from under the brim of her pretty bonnet, and her eyes were shining.

Jealousy twisted in my stomach, and I had to look away. I hated feeling jealous. It was such a hopeless, mean-spirited emotion that made me want to lash out. It was the very emotion that had caused me to say those horrible things to Henry.

"Rebecca, Hannah," I called to my sisters as they stood with their friends in the snowy churchyard. "Let us be on our way."

Their disappointment was evident, but the lure of treats and presents at home overcame it.

Mama was still speaking to Mister Goodman, and I tried to gain her attention so she would know we were leaving. She finally saw me and then smiled up at Mister Goodman, who was quite tall. "Please," she said to him, "come by this eve-ning to celebrate with us. Christmastide is a time for friends to gather."

He nodded, his face filling with joy. "I will, indeed."

"Good." Mama smiled again and then joined me and the girls.

I glanced back at Mister Goodman, and he tipped his hat in my direction.

"Now, don't start thinking there's anything to this," Mama said as she caught my gaze. "Mister Goodman is a kind man in need of companionship. I've simply invited him to join us so he's not alone."

"You've been widowed for over a year," I told her. "I'm surprised he hasn't sought you out sooner."

"Hush." Mama nodded at the girls ahead of us, close enough to hear. "Little pitchers have big ears."

We were halfway home when someone came up behind us. I turned, expecting to find a merrymaker, and found Henry instead. I paused, my heavy skirts swaying around my legs.

"Merry Christmas, Henry," Mama said, stopping as well.

"Merry Christmas, Mistress Conant." He removed his tricorne and looked at me, speaking a little softer. "Merry Christmas, Libby."

"Merry Christmas, Henry."

Mama looked between us and said, "I will leave you. I have much to prepare for our Christmas supper. Henry, you must stop by this evening to celebrate with us. Please say you'll come."

"Thank you," he said. "I will try."

Mama placed her hand on my arm, then continued down the street toward home with the girls.

I stood facing Henry as snow fell around us. My heart was heavy, not only because of what had transpired between us at the ball, but because of everything I had endured at Cumberland Hall. I tried to smile for him, but I could not.

"I did not want to speak to you on the street," he said, "but I cannot let one more hour pass before I apologize for my behavior last night."

"I'm sorry too. 'Twas unkind of me to suggest you are anything but honorable."

"And 'twas boorish of me to suggest what I did about you." He reached for my hand but then appeared to remember we were on a public street and pulled back, squeezing his gloved hand into a fist. "I cannot bear the look in your eyes when I disappoint you, Libby. In the church, when you looked at me, I felt—" He swallowed and shook his head. "'Tis the worst feeling you can imagine."

I longed to smooth away the worry lines around his mouth and eyes with my fingers. I felt my face soften.

"'Tis just—" He paused.

"'Tis what, Henry?" Cold snowflakes landed on my face and melted, but I did not mind. They gathered on Henry's shoulders and the top of his hair, but he did not seem to mind either.

"'Tis just," he started again, "I did not like seeing you in his arms."

A tender smile lifted the edges of my mouth. Henry had been jealous of Lieutenant Addison.

"The way you smiled at him and laughed with him . . ." He looked away for a moment as his blue eyes filled with the storm clouds that had darkened his countenance the night before. "I allowed it to ruin our evening, and I'm truly sorry."

I took a step closer to him, ignoring the other people on the street, and said, "You have nothing to be jealous of, Henry."

The storm clouds cleared as he studied my face, caressing it with his gaze. "Aye?"

I nodded, my heart singing. "Aye."

He reached out and touched my hand for a heartbeat, his smile filling his handsome face. "May I come tonight, Libby?"

I nodded again, unable to find my voice.

"I will see you this evening, then."

My own smile met his. "Merry Christmas," I whispered.

"Merry Christmas."

I turned, not wanting to walk away from him but knowing I was needed at home. My feet felt light as they carried me up Duke of Gloucester Street, and for the first time all day, I truly felt merry.

Our sitting room was full of laughter and good cheer, as mulled cider and ale were shared liberally with everyone who gathered. Mariah had made lemon tarts, apple puffs, minced meat, and figgy pudding, having laid aside the ingredients for weeks in preparation for this feast. Everything was set upon the table, which had been pushed to the edge of the room. Abraham played a fiddle while our guests danced and sang. We played blindman's bluff and other games.

And still, Henry did not come.

I gave Mama a new piece of lace, and together we gave Rebecca and Hannah new dolls. To Mariah, I gave a collection of poems, and to Abraham, a new corn pipe. Louis and Glen were given money, which Mama and I presented to them before the party began.

Our neighbors and friends brought food and small trinkets, and Mister Goodman brought us a whole roasted turkey, which we added to the feast.

Finally, when I thought he would not come, Henry appeared at the door. In all the noise and commotion, I had not heard him knock, but Mariah had.

He entered the sitting room, a bit of uncertainty in the carriage of his shoulders. I was on the opposite side of the room, and Mama went to him first. He was so handsome in his fine blue waistcoat and black breeches. He far outshone anyone else in the room in both presence and style, though he did not appear aloof or proud. On the contrary, he was humble and respectful as he greeted Mama, handing her a bottle of some kind.

Part of me would have been quite content just to sit and watch him all evening—but the other part wanted to be near him, to hear his voice and to look into his eyes.

His gaze circled the room and stopped when it found me. He smiled, and somehow it felt as if everyone had disappeared and it was only me and him in the room.

He walked across the floor to where I was standing near the front window. Outside, the snow continued to fall and was piling up around the house. Wassailers were on the street again, and some had stopped by to sing and greet those within our home.

"Libby." He took my hand. "I'm sorry to be so late. I tried to get away, but Father and Mother are alone, and it was hard to leave them." He didn't let go of my hand.

"Thank you for coming."

"'Tis a lively party." He finally released my hand and turned to survey the room. "Nothing like the quiet celebration I just left." There was something melancholy in the way he spoke about his parents and home.

Abraham started to play a reel, and the others gathered in the center of the room to dance.

"Will you dance with me, Libby?" Henry asked, his mood lightening. "I promise not to insult you this time."

I grinned and nodded.

We danced several reels and country dances. I was breathless and happier than I had been in a long time. Henry was a magnificent dancer and joined in the fun with everyone, regardless of rank or position. He was, by far, the most elevated member of society in the house, but he put everyone at ease with his laughter, teasing, and good nature.

The room grew warm and close as the night progressed. I was ready to step outside for a bit of fresh air when Henry caught my eye. He nodded toward the hallway as if he had read my mind.

We slipped out while everyone gathered for another dance. I took my cloak and bonnet off the front hook, and Henry found his overcoat and hat. Without a word, we stepped out the back door and into the snow-covered yard.

The silence was startling as the still, quiet world opened before us. The stars and moon were hidden behind heavy clouds laden with snow. It fell from the sky in soft, large flakes. Clouds of fog billowed from our mouths, but I was very warm, both from dancing and being with Henry.

Neither of us spoke as we walked along the path that led to the large elm tree in the center of the backyard. The snow crunched beneath our feet.

Henry stopped and wiped snow off the bench. When he was done, I took a seat, and he sat beside me. Anticipation filled me as I looked at him. It didn't take long for my eyes to adjust to the darkness, and the white snow all around seemed to reflect whatever light touched it.

He took my hands in his. Neither of us was wearing gloves, and our skin pressed together. His hands were warm and firm and much larger than I had realized. I felt tiny and fragile, yet safe and protected. My heart beat an erratic rhythm as he ran his thumbs over the backs of my hands. We had been alone together before, but this time it felt different.

"I've missed you," he said, his voice low and soft, somehow matching the cadence of the falling snow. "I could think of little else while I was away."

"Five months is too long."

He lifted one hand and brushed his thumb over the ridge of my cheekbone to remove a snowflake. "Five hours is too long, Libby."

My heart soared at his words and his touch. "Henry," I said on a soft breath, leaning into his hand, marveling at how he made me feel. I placed my hand over his. I wanted his touch and his love, had yearned for it since I was fourteen.

"Libby," he said my name again, almost reverently, "there is so much I wish to tell you, so many things I long to say."

"Then say them." I wanted him—all of him—his secrets included.

He lifted his free hand to my other cheek and looked into my eyes. There was so much restrained emotion there, as if he were warring within himself. "Do you remember the first day you came calling with your mama to our house on the Palace Green?"

I nodded. I was young, but I remembered it like it was yesterday.

"We were just children," he continued, "but I knew then, and every day since, that you are the only woman I'll ever love."

I held my breath, almost unable to believe what he was saying. Tears gathered in my eyes. "I've loved you too." I spoke the words, though they didn't seem like nearly enough to convey how dear he was to me.

A smile tilted his lips. "Truly?"

"Is it not obvious? You are my heart, Henry."

He kissed me then, lowering his lips to mine in the gentlest caress I could have imagined. Love and hope mingled together, filling me with a thousand wishes and a million dreams as snowflakes danced upon our cheeks.

Henry pulled me close, deepening the kiss. I wrapped my arms around him, holding him, wishing for it never to end. The more he kissed me, the more I wanted. I'd never known anything like it.

When he broke away, he still held me close, and I rested my cheek against his chest. All I could do was marvel at his touch. Everything else seemed to slip away. He was warmth and strength and everything good.

He whispered, "Do you know why I left Williamsburg in August?"

I shook my head.

"Because I could no longer hide my love for you. Every time I was with you, it became harder and harder. When we walked along the garden path, when we were alone in the sitting room, and even when we stood in the rain. You mean more to me than life itself, and if I had stayed, I would have done something foolish, like declare my love for you and steal a kiss. Like this."

He kissed me again as I clung to the folds of his cloak.

"You do not have to steal something I would give to you freely," I whispered when we parted.

He held me for a long time before he said, "I could not stay away, Libby. I tried—truly. I was going to stay at Edgewater Hall through Christmastide, but I couldn't keep myself from you. It was agony."

I pulled away from him. "Why would you even try?"

He swallowed and looked down at our hands. He took mine in his, and I clung to him. "I'm not free to marry you." His words were painful to hear, and I knew they were even more painful to say.

"Because I'm not good enough?" I whispered.

"Nay." He touched my face, his voice filled with disbelief. "'Tis I who am not worthy. I do not deserve your love, nor your faith in me. You asked me last summer if I'm spying, and the answer is aye, for the Sons of Liberty. I am part of a network up and down the coast, collecting information and passing it along between the colonies as I work for my father. I know things—things I wish I didn't know."

His voice was hoarse with emotion, and I placed my hand on his cheek to let him know I understood. I truly did.

He finally met my gaze again. "You don't know how many times I have prayed to God, asking Him to spare me from this mission, yet I know I was born for such a time as this. I long for freedom, to live a life of my own choosing. But I cannot deny my destiny."

"That doesn't mean you can't marry me," I said, trying to convince him as I was trying to convince myself. "I would not hinder your—"

"Nay." He shook his head. "You would never be a hindrance. But there is a war coming. This thing has taken on a life of its own. I will be asked to risk everything I hold dear, a sacrifice I am willing to make, but I cannot ask you to sacrifice along with me." He turned his head and kissed the inside of my palm, pressing his lips there for several moments before he said, "I love you too much to risk making you a widow."

"I would rather know one day as your wife than none at all." I longed to tell him that the fighting would not begin until spring and we would have several months together before he was called to go. "And even if we go to war, we would pray God's protection upon you. We would hope and trust that He would bring you back to me."

Even as I said the words, I wondered if they were true. Would Henry survive the war? More now than ever, I wanted to look inside the book in the library at Cumberland Hall. Yet what would I gain in knowing his fate? Would it change my love for him or my desire to be his wife?

"Oh, Libby," he said, groaning as he pulled me close again. "How I long to make you my wife." He kissed me again, this time with more passion than before.

I met his kiss with my own aching desire, drawing him close, taking from him whatever he was able to give me.

We were breathless when we pulled apart.

He ran his thumb over my cheek again, a sad smile on his lips. "This is why I left, because I knew it would break our hearts to speak so plainly. But I could not deny it any longer, and when I saw you dancing with that officer last night"—his jaw tightened—"I have never been so jealous."

I smiled. "I didn't like seeing you with Lady Catherine either."

"She is nothing to me, Libby." He frowned. "But my convictions are strong, and I do not think it wise to marry before we know what will happen. 'Twas pure selfishness of me to declare myself when I couldn't offer you everything."

I closed my eyes as I bit the inside of my mouth. I *did* know what would happen. Would he truly make me wait a decade? "And what if there is a war?" I asked, unable to hide the frustration in my voice. "What if it takes years and years to win? Will you make me wait for you?"

He didn't respond right away, though he removed his hand from my face. There was something he wasn't telling me. I could see it in his eyes. "I will not make you wait for long," he finally said. "But, please, let us wait for a bit longer, until I can be certain."

"Certain of what?"

"That 'tis wise to marry."

I looked deep into his eyes. "I will wait as long as it takes."

His smile returned as he kissed me again. And in that moment, nothing else mattered. Knowing that Henry loved me was enough. For now.

# 20

It had been five weeks since the raid on Whitby, Hartlepool, and Scarborough. *Remember Scarborough* was now a common phrase in England. Posters featuring the motto had been hung all over the country to recruit soldiers. The raid marked the first time a British soldier had died on English soil in over two hundred years—and the first civilian casualties of the Great War, as it was called. It had impacted us deeply but was not limited to our region. All of England suffered with us.

Reggie had left Cumberland Hall on New Year's Day, and I was not sad to see him go. I had spent Christmas week in bed, nursing an illness that was more emotional than physical. He'd only spoken to me twice before he left and had not written to me since returning to London. I suspected he regretted his actions that night in the library, and that alcohol had played a part again—but it did not excuse his behavior, nor ease my trauma.

The last of our patients had left Cumberland Hall the week before. Slowly, we had restored order to the manor, though I missed the commotion.

A bright blue sky domed over us as Edith and I rode in the automobile to Whitby. Williams drove along the coast until we came to the small town on the seashore. It was cold, but there was beauty in the starkness of the moors and the cliffs. And when I saw the jaunty red roofs climbing the hillside, it made me smile.

"We will first assist in the soup kitchen," I told Edith, "and then I have some shopping to do."

"As you wish, milady. Williams will take us wherever we need to go."

Williams glanced over his shoulder to smile at Edith, and her cheeks turned bright pink. I had noticed a growing attraction between the two of them but hadn't said anything. Some felt that servants should remain single to stay employed—after all, it was more convenient for all involved. But I would never hinder Edith or the desires of her heart. Nor would I send her away. She was a dear friend, even if we had to maintain our social differences.

Instead, I simply turned away from them and looked toward the sea, allowing myself to think about Henry. I indulged in the memory of Christmas night and the stolen kisses in the garden. He'd left soon after he'd told me he loved me and then returned the next day to tell me he was taking another trip to New York under the guise of his father's shipping interests. He'd learned things while in Williamsburg that he had to pass on to the other spies on his route. I wanted to ask him not to go, but I didn't have that right. He must do what he felt best, so I had wished him Godspeed and told him I'd be praying.

It had been four weeks since I'd seen him last, and though I missed him terribly, the memory of his kisses and his love kept me warm when I missed him most.

Williams pulled the automobile to a stop at the base of the hill where the Church of St. Mary stood proud on the east cliff, overlooking the River Esk and the town of Whitby. A daily soup kitchen had been set up in the church since the raid.

"You don't mind the steps, milady?" Williams asked as he put the automobile in park and then came around to open the door for me.

"I am glad for some exercise," I told him. "Please return at three for us."

"As you wish." He tipped his black driving hat.

Edith and I gripped the picnic baskets we'd brought full of cakes and pastries from Cumberland Hall and started the ascent up the stone church steps. There were one hundred and ninety-nine of them, and they wound around buildings all the way up the hillside.

Halfway, a sudden bout of dizziness took me unaware. I became winded and had to stop for a rest.

"Are you unwell?" Edith asked as she put her hand on my back while I caught my breath.

"I'm fine." I tried to smile. "I should take more walks in the fresh air, and perhaps I won't tire so easily."

"You're pale." Concern tightened her voice. "Perhaps we should turn back."

"I confess, I feel a little queasy." I looked out over the red-roofed town and toward the sea beyond and had to close my eyes because of the dizziness. Nausea soon followed, and I gripped the handrail. "Perhaps it's the height. I've never done well with heights."

"But we were just here two days ago, and it didn't bother you." She wrung the picnic basket handles as she looked up the remaining steps and then back down.

"I will be fine in a moment." I pressed my hand against my head until the dizziness passed. "See, I'm feeling better already."

Edith didn't look convinced.

I straightened and stared up the daunting stairway. People were coming and going, no doubt to the soup kitchen. To one side of the stairway was a steep, stone-covered road, where a lady with a white handkerchief leaned against a building to watch the people going up and down the stairs. She had her eye on me but made no move to help.

The smell of the sea floated past me as I gripped the cold handrail, making the nausea feel worse. I would not be sick on these steps.

I pushed myself until we reached the top and was rewarded with a magnificent view of the North Sea and the old ruins of Whitby Abbey behind the Church of St. Mary. For as far as I could see, the sea and the cliffs and the rolling moors filled my senses. I regained a sense of normalcy and felt the nausea pass.

Several people from Whitby that I had come to know in the past few weeks were present. Kind, thoughtful people who had endured unspeakable hardships since the raid. But as I entered the church, with its white-painted wood and dark-stained pews, I recognized another familiar face.

"Dr. Aiken! How nice to see you again."

"And you, Lady Cumberland." He motioned toward the basket I was carrying. "I see you are not taking a rest, even though your home is now empty."

"I will not rest until everyone is healthy and properly housed."

Edith offered to take my basket, and I handed it to her so she could take it to the tables where they were serving the meal. Several dozen people waited in line for their lunch.

"What brings you here?" I asked the doctor.

"I came to check on some of the patients I cared for at your home. I was invited to stop by the soup kitchen to enjoy the meal."

I smiled. "Are *you* not tired and in need of a rest?"

"A doctor? During a war?" He smiled, and his eyes wrinkled at the edges. "Not likely."

Another wave of dizziness passed over me, and I had to latch on to the pew at my side. The nausea followed, and I pressed my lips together as sweat broke out on my brow.

"Are you unwell, Lady Cumberland?" Dr. Aiken set down his plate while his gaze narrowed on me.

"I—" I paused, unsure. My hand went to my stomach, where the nausea was threatening to upend me. "Will you excuse me?" I looked desperately for an escape from the church and rushed toward the door we had entered. People watched me with concern and curiosity as I passed, but no one said a word.

I almost didn't make it to the churchyard before I lost the contents of my stomach. A gravestone nearby seemed to taunt me as I retched in the tall grass. My eyes watered, and I had to force myself to take a deep, shuddering breath.

"Lady Cumberland?" Dr. Aiken had followed me and extended a handkerchief for my use.

With shaking hands, I took it from him and pressed it against my mouth, mortified at what had happened—afraid it might happen again.

Edith had also followed us, her eyes wide with alarm.

"Please get Lady Cumberland a glass of water," Dr. Aiken said to her.

She nodded and disappeared inside the church.

"Why don't you sit down?" Dr. Aiken put his hand under my elbow and led me to a stone bench overlooking the cliff and the town below. The cold air felt good against my warm cheeks.

I took the seat, thankful to ease the strain on my weak legs. "I'm so sorry. I don't know what came over me."

"There's no need to apologize. How long have you been feeling this way?"

I shook my head. "Not long—just today, really. It came on so suddenly."

Edith returned, out of breath from rushing. She handed me a glass of water, which I took thankfully.

"Perhaps you should return to Cumberland Hall," Dr. Aiken said.

"I think you're right." If I was getting sick, the last place I wanted to be was in the soup kitchen.

"Would you mind if I visited you later? When I'm done here?" he asked.

"Oh, I don't think it's necessary. I've been sick before. Surely it will pass soon enough."

"I'd feel better, all the same."

Edith nodded, imploring me with her eyes to accept his offer. How could I deny both of them?

"I believe you'll be wasting your time," I said in a lighthearted voice, "but if you would like to come, I will not turn you away."

He smiled. "Thank you."

Edith sent a young man to find Williams, and twenty minutes later we were on our way back to Cumberland Hall. The nausea continued, though it wasn't nearly as bad.

"All I need," I said to Edith as the car rumbled over the country road leading to Cumberland Hall, kicking up dust in our wake, "is a good lie down. I'll be better once I can rest."

She didn't look so sure.

By the time Dr. Aiken arrived at Cumberland Hall, I was in a nightgown and under the covers of my large four-poster bed, with a fire crackling in the hearth, feeling better. I was tired and found when I lay down, the nausea subsided. It also helped with the dizziness.

"Perhaps I'm getting influenza," I told Edith, who had appeared in my room to tell me she had seen Dr. Aiken's automobile on the road. "Though I don't feel feverish."

Edith plumped up my pillow and moved a tendril of hair off my cheek. "How about we let him determine your ailment?"

I smiled at her motherliness. She had been kinder and more thoughtful to me than Mother Wells ever had.

A few minutes later, Dr. Aiken appeared at my door. "How is our patient feeling?"

"Better," I told him. "When I lie down, the nausea and dizziness are almost gone, but as soon as I stand, they return."

"And no other episodes?"

"Do you mean, have I retched again? No." Thankfully. There were few other sensations as distressing.

He set his black bag on my side table. "Do you mind if I examine you and ask a few questions?"

I shrugged. "I won't say no after you've come so far."

Edith stayed in the room, watching as the doctor took my temperature, ran a candle before my eyes, looked in my mouth, my nose, and my ears, and listened to my heart and lungs.

He glanced at Edith, a question in his eyes, and I nodded. "She's welcome to stay."

"Very well." He sat on a chair next to my bed and smiled. His face was so kind and gentle. "Lady Cumberland, may I ask a few, er, delicate feminine questions?"

My mouth slipped open to respond that I didn't mind, but I suddenly knew what he was going to ask.

It had been three weeks since Reggie left Cumberland Hall. Four weeks since he had forced me to stay in the library with him after supper.

My breathing slowed until I felt like I wasn't breathing at all, and everything came to a halt. I looked at Dr. Aiken as if he were far away and I couldn't reach him. I swallowed as realization settled like a boulder in my gut. It was soon followed by panic like I had never known in my life.

"Lady Cumberland?" Dr. Aiken looked at me with a bit of alarm.

I couldn't focus on anything or anyone. A strange feeling rushed up my legs and into my heart, making it pound uncontrollably. I shook my head and put my hands over my face. The sensation to run came over me, but where could I go to get away from the truth?

"No," I said. "This can't be."

"Lady Cumberland." Dr. Aiken put his hands on both of mine and pried them away from my face. He was only a few inches from me, forcing me to look him in the eyes. "What is the matter?"

"I can't be pregnant," I said, the panic making me feel like I might die. "I simply can't be."

"I don't know for certain," he said, "but your symptoms are consistent with pregnancy. I will need you to answer a few questions, and then I'll perform a thorough examination to be sure."

I nodded, hoping and praying it wasn't true. Edith's face had gone pale at my reaction, but she didn't leave the room or shy away.

Patiently, I answered the doctor's questions and then allowed him to examine me. The entire time, all I could do was pray. I couldn't have a baby in this path—I just couldn't. Each time I thought about the consequences, the panic returned. And then I would calm myself and try to reassure myself that it just couldn't be true.

I had a life I wanted in 1775. I had a man I loved with all of my heart who loved me. I had a mother and sisters who relied on me. A newspaper that depended on me. I had a cause I was willing to die for. I couldn't leave any of it behind.

When the doctor had finished, he slowly put all of his instruments back into his bag. It felt like it took forever for him to finally turn to me. I held my breath as I waited for his diagnosis.

"Lady Cumberland," he began slowly, "everything points to pregnancy."

A loud sound pulsed in my ears, and my stomach turned again. This time, I could not hold back the contents as Edith rushed a pan to my bedside. Sobs wracked my body as wave after wave of nausea rolled through me.

"Lady Cumberland." Dr. Aiken's voice sounded far away

and commanding. "You must not behave this way. You'll hurt the baby with the way you're carrying on."

I couldn't stop crying. With one sentence, my entire existence was shaken to the core. All of my hopes and dreams were torn away, and everything I'd ever longed for was pulled from my grasp.

I was going to have a baby—possibly a marked baby—and she would need me, just as I had needed my mama.

Mama. Tears continued to flow as I thought of her. I knew in an instant that I had lost 1775 for good. How would I tell her? How would I live in this path without her?

And what of Henry? I wept uncontrollably at the thought of him. But I could not explain to Dr. Aiken or Edith. They tried to console me, to drag me from the abyss, but they could not.

Finally, Dr. Aiken pulled a vial from his medical bag. I was vaguely aware of him filling a syringe. But when he stabbed the needle into my arm, the sharp pain pulled me back to the present, and I lay back upon my bed, completely spent from my tears.

"Lady Cumberland," Dr. Aiken said, standing over me, "I do not know why this pregnancy has come as such a shock. Surely you knew it was a possibility. You're a properly married woman, and it's only right to produce an heir for your husband. He will be pleased when he hears of this happy news. And, in time, I know you will be pleased, as well."

My eyes began to grow heavy as my limbs relaxed into the mattress. A warm, cloudlike feeling overcame me, and my tears stopped. It almost felt like I was floating and nothing mattered anymore.

"There, now." Dr. Aiken put a gentle hand on my shoulder. "In a moment you'll be asleep, and when you wake up, you'll realize that all is well. A baby is a blessing. A true miracle from God. Each child is God's way of telling us He wants the world to go on." He patted my shoulder. "You'll see. Soon, you'll come to love this baby unlike anything you've ever loved before, and you'll be willing to lay down your very life for him. I promise."

A baby. I was having a baby.

I could no longer lift my head off my pillow as my eyelids drooped closed.

# 21

WILLIAMSBURG, VIRGINIA
JANUARY 24, 1775

I opened my eyes to find myself in Williamsburg. Hannah and Rebecca were asleep beside me, cuddled up close to stay warm. It was still dark outside, but I could not stay in bed. I needed to speak to Mama, to get her reassurance and help. I refused to believe that it was over—that I was without a choice. My twenty-first birthday was six months away—surely we could think of something to save me from 1915 by then.

There was no time to waste on tears or panic. I dressed in the cold room and rushed across the hall to Mama's bedchamber.

Her door creaked as I opened it, and I found her kneeling beside her bed. She was already dressed, her white cap covering her head and her black shoes peeking out from the hem of her full gown. She was praying.

I paused, not wanting to interrupt her, but I could not wait. "Mama," I whispered.

Lifting one hand to quiet me, she continued to pray silently.

Impatience pushed me into her room. I closed the door and

then stood next to her. "Mama," I said again, desperate to speak to her.

After a moment, she finally stood and looked at me.

"I'm sorry," I told her as I took her hands, "but I couldn't wait."

"I know, Libby." She turned my hand over and pressed our palms together.

"You know?"

"I know what you're going to tell me."

"How?" I hadn't told her about Reggie's behavior the first night he'd returned to Cumberland Hall.

She put her hand on my cheek, her face filled with sadness. It was dark, but I could still see her. "Christmas morning I knew something had happened with Reggie." She wiped a tear from my cheek that I hadn't even realized was there. "You're going to have a baby, aren't you?"

A sinking sensation filled my stomach, and all I could do was nod.

"I've known from the moment you told me that Mother Wells had chosen Reggie to be your husband." Her voice was heavy when she lowered her hand as if she had no strength to hold it up. "I hoped and prayed 'twould not happen, but I had a feeling. 'Twas much the same for me."

"But I can't have a baby," I told her, desperation weighing down my words. "I don't want to stay in 1915. I want to stay here with you."

"I know." She stood and put some space between us. "But I also know that our hopes and dreams are not always God's. Sometimes He has a plan that looks much different from ours."

"But how can that be?" My voice was filled with anger and despair. "Why would He allow me to want this life when He didn't intend for me to keep it?"

"I won't pretend to have all the answers. God is concerned with the state of your heart more than where you live or what time you occupy. He wants to know that He has your heart, Libby. All of it. He wants to know that you trust Him no matter what happens." She came back to me and took my hands again. "You've long had your path all planned out. You knew exactly what you wanted and how to go about achieving it. But just because *you* want something doesn't mean God does. You are here, and in 1915, because He chose to send you. It's not just about what you want but how you can best serve God for His purposes."

"Are you saying I don't have a choice?"

"You have a choice—you always have a choice. You could leave 1915 and stay here—but think of the consequences. The baby will be due after your twenty-first birthday, correct?"

I nodded.

"Then if you left 1915, your body would die and your baby along with you." She pressed her lips together and shook her head. "I cannot tell you how much I want you to stay. The thought of never seeing you again, knowing that you are alive in a time and place I will never see, tears my heart in two. But, darling, our days are never guaranteed. Our paths are never certain. I know that full well." She looked down at our hands, her voice filled with a sadness so deep and penetrating that it made my heart clench. "I gave up the man I loved and the parents I loved to stay here with you. And though I mourned in ways that you could not imagine, I have never once regretted giving everything up for you. I would do it all again. Someday I promise you will feel the same way about your child."

Tears flowed freely as Mama took me into her embrace and held me close.

"Mayhap there is still time," I told her, trying to grasp onto hope. "I could still lose the baby."

She pulled back from me. "Libby." Her voice was hushed. "You do not want that."

I swallowed the blackness in my soul, knowing I should not

want such a thing, yet feeling desperate and afraid. I could not consciously allow my baby to die along with my 1915 body, but if something should happen to prevent the pregnancy from proceeding, I wasn't certain I would mourn the loss.

"I promise you will love your baby," she said, "and you will do anything within your power to protect and shelter her, to keep her safe and healthy. You will move heaven and earth to see to her well-being. And one day you will wonder how you ever lived without her—or how you will go on once she is no longer a part of your daily life."

"Oh, Mama." I hugged her again.

"It will be fine, my darling," she said, running her hand over my back. "We still have some time together, and we will cherish every single moment. How many people know the day and hour of their parting? We are blessed, Libby. Blessed beyond measure."

I did not feel blessed. I felt wretched and dejected.

But Mama's words planted a seed of hope, small and deep. I clung to that hope, knowing that if I did not hold on tight, I would be lost in a sea of sorrow and melancholy. We still had six months until my birthday, and anything might happen.

And if I could not be spared, then Mama was right. As hard as it was to face the truth, my life was not my own. It never had been. Being in the center of God's will was where I wanted to remain. If that meant living in 1915 and leaving Williamsburg behind for good, then I had to trust that God had a better plan.

And yet . . .

I closed my eyes as visions of Henry filled my heart and mind. It was one thing to say good-bye to Mama, for she understood completely. We would mourn each other for the rest of our lives, but at least she knew where I was going.

'Twas another thing to say good-bye to the man I loved more than the very air I breathed.

I didn't think I could do it.

It was cold later that day as I walked out the back door to help Mariah get our midday meal on the table. The temperatures had fluctuated since Christmas, causing most of the snow to melt, but there were still piles of it in the corners of the buildings and along the pathways.

A strange sight caught my eye as soon as I closed the back door. Lieutenant Addison and Louis stood near the woodpile beside the kitchen, speaking in hushed voices. They did not notice me at first, but then James caught sight of me, and they both straightened their shoulders and nodded an acknowledgment.

I should not have cared what they were discussing, but I was not pleased to see them speaking in such a manner. Louis was our employee, and James was a guest, if an uninvited one. Were they conspiring against us?

Louis left James and walked past me, only meeting my eyes briefly as he returned to the printing room. James removed his tricorne and came toward me. His red coat and white trousers gleamed fresh and bright under the January sun. We had not spoken since Christmas Eve, though we saw each other in passing from time to time.

"Libby." He bowed. "'Tis a pleasure to see you again."

I glanced over my shoulder toward the printing room, unable to contain my anger. "I was not aware that you and Louis had become friends."

James shrugged. "When you live as neighbors, you're bound to get to know one another."

"Yet you and I have not become friends."

"Haven't we?" He frowned. "I hoped we were more than acquaintances."

"One trusts one's friends." I was feeling bold and mayhap a

little reckless today. The knowledge of my pregnancy in 1915 made me feel impervious to any more threats.

He studied me. "You don't trust me?"

"There are very few people I trust these days." I started to walk away, but his words stopped me.

"Do you trust Henry Montgomery?"

I paused and looked back at him but did not respond.

"You do know he's working against Governor Dunmore, do you not?" He took a step closer to me. "And treason is punishable by death."

Words failed me as I realized what he was saying.

"I like you, Libby. And because I like you, I will tell you something I should not." He looked around and then lowered his voice. "If you want Montgomery to live a long and prosperous life, you should tell him to quit his activities immediately and swear fealty to the king. 'Tis his only hope."

I did not want to implicate Henry by asking questions, but I desperately wanted to know if Governor Dunmore was aware of his activities. How much evidence did they have against him? Was it enough to convict him of treason?

"And keep an eye on Louis," James continued. "He has told me some bizarre things about you and your mother that are too preposterous to believe. From what I've gathered, I'm not the only one he's told."

"What has he told you?"

"'Tis not worth repeating." His brown eyes were kind and gentle. "He believes that he and I are friends, and so he confides in me, but I suspect he would like nothing more than to run you out of business and take over your printing press."

I swallowed the words that wanted to be spoken. Harsh, angry words. Papa had taken Louis under his wing as a child, and we had provided him with a home and a job for the last nine years.

James took another step closer to me, and I was forced to

look up into his face. "He, like many others, is aware of your work in aiding the Patriots' cause." His voice was low as he studied me. "Believe it or not, I understand your heart, Libby. This is your home, and you want the freedom to live as you choose. I would feel the same about Cumberland Hall." His voice was serious. "But Louis does not see things that way. You would be wise to let him go as soon as possible."

Would Louis really try to get rid of us? I did not think him capable, but I had no reason to believe that James was lying.

"Thank you," I said, truly grateful.

"I do hope you'll consider me a friend, Libby." He smiled, and I could see the genuine request in his eyes. "You are the first person I've met in America who has spoken to me of Whitby, and I do not want to lose that connection."

"You've told me all of this because of Whitby?"

His cheeks took on a bit of color. "That, and I think you're pretty."

It was my turn to blush. "Thank you."

James grinned and took his leave.

---

Several hours later, when the supper dishes had been cleared, I sat near the hearth in the sitting room with Mama. Hannah and Rebecca had gone up to bed, but it was still early, and I had no wish to hasten back to Whitby.

Mama was mending, and I was staring into the flames, thinking about the baby. We had discussed it several times that day in stolen moments, but now I had nothing left to say. I'd also told her what Lieutenant Addison had said about Louis, but neither of us were certain how to proceed. If we let him go, we would need to run the press ourselves until someone could be hired to take his place. Mama said she would write some letters in the morning to friends in other colonies who might know of a printer looking for a job. But until then, we would need to watch him closely.

A knock sounded on the front door, bringing me out of my melancholy thoughts.

"Who might that be at this hour?" Mama asked.

"I'll go."

I entered the hall and opened the front door. It was dark, but I could never mistake the person standing on our front stoop.

"Henry," I breathed as I went into his arms.

He made a surprised sound, and I was certain he hadn't expected my response. But my heart was sore, and I needed his comfort. I didn't even care if anyone saw us, though it was dark enough that it would be unlikely.

"Libby." He said my name like a gentle caress as his arms enfolded me in a hug. He smelled of bergamot and pipe tobacco, and the folds of his coat were coarse against my cheek.

"I've missed you," I said.

"I've missed you too."

I looked up at him, and he lowered his mouth to kiss me.

It was everything I'd remembered and more. My pulse pounded, and my stomach filled with butterflies. I loved him so dearly.

Finally, he pulled back and whispered, "Your mama will wonder why there's a draft."

I smiled, though my heart was heavy. It was bittersweet to be in his arms again, knowing what I did about my 1915 path and the choice I would need to make in six months.

"Come in." I stepped back and allowed him to enter the house, then closed the door behind him. He took off his hat and cloak, and I hung them on the hooks. "Mama is in the sitting room."

"Good," he said with a gentle chuckle, placing his hand upon my cheek. "I wouldn't trust myself to be alone with you."

My cheeks warmed, and I placed my hand over his. I didn't want to share him with Mama, but we could not stay in the hallway all evening. And after my discussion with James, there were things I needed to tell him.

"Henry." Mama smiled in surprise when we entered the sitting room. "What brings you here?"

He looked at me with a tender gaze, and my cheeks warmed.

Mama's smile fell, and I knew she was now fully aware of our feelings for each other. It was impossible to hide them any longer.

"I've returned to Williamsburg on request of the governor," he said, "but I am not expected at the palace until tomorrow. 'Tis cold and lonely at my father's house, so I thought I would come for a visit. I hope I am not intruding."

"Not at all," I assured him as I pulled a chair near the fire, my mind spinning with unanswered questions. Why had the governor called him? To question him? Charge him with treason? My heart pounded with fear, but I could not voice these concerns with Mama present, so I simply said, "Please have a seat."

"Aye." Mama seemed to pull her wits about herself again. "Sit and warm yourself." She set aside the apron she was mending and stood. "I will go to the kitchen and make some tea."

Henry or I should have tried to stop her, but neither of us did as we watched her walk from the room. The moment the back door closed, I sat beside Henry and reached for his hands.

He grasped mine, his face shining on me. "'Tis a wonder I survived the past four weeks away from you. My mind is so restless and my thoughts are so scattered that I can hardly put two words together or perform even the most mundane task."

I wanted to smile at his teasing, but being with him only reminded me of the baby and the horrible decision I would have to make. Tears gathered in my eyes before I could stop them.

"Libby," he said gently, his voice dipping with concern, "why are you crying?"

I wiped at the tear that fell down my cheek and tried to stop the others. I could never explain to him why I was so upset, but I had to tell him something. "I've just missed you."

He gathered me in his arms and kissed my temple. "'Tis no need to cry, love."

The words I had uttered under the elm tree returned to me. I had told him that one day as his wife was better than none, but now it could never be. I could not marry Henry, not even for one day. There could be no possibility of another child. I was committed to the child I carried in 1915. Her life was now more important than any other. It was more important than my love for Henry—it had to be.

I could no longer carry on with Henry. It would only cause him more pain. In six months, when I was forced to stay in 1915, my body would die on this path, and Henry would mourn. If I could spare him even the slightest pain, I would do whatever it took. I would have to put space between us and no longer allow him to kiss me and declare his love. Because the more he did, the deeper our bond became, and the harder it would be to say good-bye.

I pulled away from him. He handed me a clean handkerchief, and I wiped my wet cheeks. "There's something I must tell you."

Uncertainty clouded his eyes. "I don't like the way that sounds."

I pressed my hands against my knees and took a deep breath. "Lieutenant Addison spoke to me today—"

"I would not listen to a word that man says." Anger lit up Henry's face in a flash. "He is not to be trusted, Libby. He's one of the king's officers."

"But he is also a man," I countered, "and he is kind and good."

"I cannot trust a loyalist."

He would not listen to me if he was angry, so I put my hand on his arm to calm his fears. "I have always been a good judge of character. After all, I knew you were honorable from the moment I met you."

His shoulders eased as he put his hand over mine.

I swallowed, loving the feel of his touch yet knowing I could not encourage it anymore. I did not want to pull away so suddenly that he would be hurt and confused, but I could not, in good conscience, initiate it any further. It made me feel shallow and flighty, falling into his arms one moment and turning him away the next. Yet I knew of no other way to spare him from heartbreak.

It wasn't fair. I'd waited years for him to love me, and now I was meant to turn him away.

I slowly eased my hand away from his and stood to put another log on the fire. "I must speak to you about what the lieutenant said."

He crossed his arms and leaned back in his chair. "Whatever he said, it sounds as if it frightened you."

"Very much." I was so restless that I could no longer sit, so I remained by the hearth. "He knows you are working against Governor Dunmore. He said that if you value your life, you must cease all your treasonous activities and swear fealty to the king."

Henry didn't speak for a moment as his eyes filled with questions. "Are you suggesting I give up the cause of freedom, Libby?"

I swallowed and clasped my hands. "Of course not. But they know what you're about, Henry. They know you're working against the governor. If they have enough evidence, they will convict you, and you'll hang. Mayhap that's why the governor has sent for you."

"I cannot stop now."

"But how much help can you be to the Patriots when the governor knows of your activities?" I felt desperate to stop him, for him to see reason. "Is there nothing else you can do to help the cause?"

"I thought you understood."

"I know you long for independence and that you're willing to sacrifice whatever it will take. But be reasonable, Henry. Whatever activities you're involved in have been compromised."

"And how does Lieutenant Addison know these things? Was he fishing for information? Did you confirm his suspicions?"

"Nay. I said nothing about you." I returned to the chair next to Henry. "I do not think Lieutenant Addison means you harm. I truly believe he was warning me, for both our sakes. He also told me that we should let Louis go. I suspect Louis is the one working against us, not the lieutenant."

Henry stared into the fire for several moments before turning his attention back to me. "I will consider what you've told me, but I cannot promise I will heed the advice of Governor Dunmore's spy. He is a British officer. His job is to suppress us into submission. I do not believe he means to spare either of us from harm or trouble."

"But you will consider what I've said?" I couldn't hide the distress from my voice. "You'll consider changing tactics, at least?"

"I will." He nodded, and his countenance softened. "But I did not come here to speak about these things." He took my hands into his again. "There are much more pleasant things to discuss."

I bit the inside of my mouth as I looked down at our hands. For so long, I had known Henry was not within my reach— and for one short month, I had held on to the hope that he was finally mine. I had soared on the wings of a dream, but then I had crashed to the earth. My love for Henry would never die, but the reality of being his wife was something I had started to mourn.

The back door opened, and Mama's feet could be heard on the hardwood floors. Henry let go of my hands, and we turned at her entrance, saving me from any difficult conversation. For now.

There was no way to ignore the truth. Henry was lost to me, and I needed to start the process of letting go. For his sake and mine, but especially for the child that would change my destiny forever.

# 22

WHITBY, NORTH YORKSHIRE, ENGLAND
JANUARY 24, 1915

The following morning, I sat in the warm conservatory of Cumberland Hall, surrounded by the lush greenery of the plants and trees I had been tending for the past six months. Overhead, the great glass ceiling arched toward the sky. Grey clouds covered the expanse, and droplets of rain ran in rivulets down the windows. I occupied a chair with a view of the moors and a glimpse of the sea. I wore a shawl around my shoulders and watched the waves roll across the massive body of water, disappearing from view before they crashed against the cliffs beyond the manor house.

A cup of tea had gone cold in my hand, and the wrought-iron seat beneath me had grown uncomfortable. But this room had become a sanctuary to me since the library was no longer a place of refuge. I had not returned there since the night Reggie had come home, and I did not think I could visit it again.

"Lady Cumberland?" Mr. Wentworth appeared at the entrance to the conservatory with a letter on a silver tray. "The post has arrived."

I felt groggy as I reached for the letter. The sedative Dr. Aiken had given me was still running through my body. My stomach was unsettled, and I was unable to eat anything, but I had not wanted to lie abed all day. So Edith had helped me dress, saying very little to me, and I had come into the conservatory. She'd brought me the cup of tea, but even that had not been appetizing.

"Thank you," I said to Mr. Wentworth, taking the letter opener off the tray to slit the envelope. It was from Reggie.

I set the letter opener back on the tray, and Mr. Wentworth straightened, his left hand behind his back. "If I may," he said· tentatively, concern in his tone, "how are you feeling, your ladyship?"

A quick glance in the mirror that morning had told me all I needed to know about my appearance. My face was pale, and my gaze was dull. There were dark smudges beneath my eyes and deep lines around my mouth. No doubt he thought I was quite ill indeed. "I am not well," I admitted, allowing him to see a glimmer of my true feelings. "Things have not gone at all how I hoped."

He nodded. "I understand perfectly."

Did he? I had never asked Mr. Wentworth about his life before coming to Cumberland Hall. Had he always aspired to be a butler? Or had his life not gone as planned, either?

"If that will be all?" he asked.

I nodded, and he took his leave.

The letter from Reggie sat like a rock upon my lap. I had no wish to open it. No desire to hear from him, especially now that I knew about the baby. He hadn't written since he left Cumberland Hall, and I knew nothing about where he had been sent. Perhaps he was still in London. Or maybe he was on the battlefield already. It didn't matter. I never wished to see him again.

But I could not ignore the letter. From time to time he sent instructions for the staff to deal with certain aspects of Cumberland Hall's upkeep. He had dealt with several issues during his Christmas holiday, and still others needed to be addressed. I opened the letter for no other reason than my concern for the home I occupied.

*January 10, 1915*

*Libby,*

*I don't know how to begin this letter. I have given you no reason to trust me and every reason to hate me. I would not blame you if you tore it up and threw it into the fire without reading further. But I hope you do not. It has never been easy for me to talk about my feelings, especially in person. It is my hope that I can do so on paper, so I will try.*

*Ever since leaving Cumberland Hall, I have been plagued by guilt, and I cannot face the battlefield without writing to you first. I haven't been able to sleep or eat, knowing that I have hurt you deeply. My behavior, on our wedding night and when I visited for Christmas, is inexcusable. I don't expect you to forgive me, but I hope you will try.*

*You might not believe it, Libby, but even before Lady Paget introduced us at the Crewe House, I had already noticed you. I remember precisely the moment you entered the ballroom, wearing that green gown. At the time, I didn't know you were the one Lady Paget had told me about. You moved with such grace and quiet dignity, sadness in your lovely green eyes. When Lady Paget introduced us, I could not believe my good fortune.*

*You are aware that I had no choice but to take a wealthy bride. It was the only way to save Cumberland*

Hall. Perhaps, since you've been living there yourself, you understand my consuming desire to preserve her for future generations. I would have done almost anything for her—would have married almost anyone. Imagine my pleasure when it was you that I could marry. Not only would I save my ancestral home, but I would be the envy of every man in England.

Everything happened so quickly. I had my own purposes and intentions in mind and did not consider how you might feel. It was my understanding that you wanted the marriage as much as I did. Lady Paget had assured me this was the case. The morning I went to Berkeley Square to make my offer, your mother claimed you were in full agreement. The contract she had written felt unnecessary, but she insisted.

Until I lifted your wedding veil and saw the tears in your eyes, I foolishly believed you approved of the match. That moment will forever be etched into my mind. Your weeping slayed me, but it was too late. Everything had been done. All the papers signed. If I had backed out then, your mother's contract ensured I would lose what little I had left.

I swear that our wedding night was not what I intended. I left you in our stateroom after we boarded the ship feeling like a cad. I knew what I had done to you, what I had taken from you by going through with the wedding. I tried to drown my guilt and shame with too many drinks. When I returned to you that night, I was not myself. And for the rest of the voyage, I could not bear to speak to you, knowing what I had done. I was embarrassed and ashamed.

When I returned to Cumberland Hall for Christmas, I truly hoped to put all of it behind us. I had tried to convince myself that you might have forgotten what I *did, but it was evident as you pulled away from me that you had not. That night in the library was not meant to happen. I was upset and worried about going to war, and I overindulged again. Please believe me when I say that I did not intend to hurt you, though I know I have. I have done something inexcusable and unforgivable, and I'm not sure how I can ever face you again.*

*But I am now a captain in His Majesty's Army, working as an aide to the commander of the 1st Army of the British Expeditionary Forces. I could not face the battlefield knowing what you must think of me, but I am under no illusion that you will easily forgive me. This letter isn't meant to make you forget or even to forgive, but to understand my intentions. It is my prayer that one day I will have the opportunity to make things right. I don't deserve a second or third chance, but I'm hoping you can give me one. I will do everything I can to be worthy of the right to be called your husband.*

*Reggie*

I stared at the letter, numb and confused. If I were not familiar with his handwriting, I would have thought someone else had written it. Reggie had never given me reason to believe he cared about my feelings. There was so much I didn't know about him, but everything he said in the letter felt genuine. I wasn't under any illusion. I knew he had written because of his fear of facing death on the battlefield. Would I have listened if he tried to share his feelings with me in person? He had hurt me deeply, in ways that might not be repairable.

Yet I was now committed to this path because of the baby. For better or worse, Reggie would be my husband for the rest of my life. If he was even half the man he claimed to be in his letter, did he deserve a second or third chance, as he had put it? Was it possible to give him another opportunity to prove himself? Could I trust him?

And what of his claim that it had been Mother Wells who insisted upon a marriage contract? She had said it was Reggie who made *her* sign one—yet his letter stated differently. This whole time, I had thought Reggie was threatening to ruin Father, but it had been part of Mother's manipulations. Would Reggie really have let me call the whole thing off?

None of it mattered anymore. There was no room in my life for regret. The child I carried was as much a part of him as it was a part of me. If nothing else, the baby deserved parents who could find a way to move forward. I could not abide raising a child in a home like the one I had grown up in with Father and Mother Wells.

I put my hand to my stomach as the first sense of maternal affection came over me. My baby had not asked to be born, to be brought into this world, yet she was here. And I could not leave her or do anything that would harm her. I had a beautiful home, a substantial bank account, and a good name. My child would be born into a life of luxury and refinement. She would have all the advantages available to a woman in the twentieth century—and she would have me and, one day, her father.

Tears gathered in my eyes at the realization that I loved her dearly, though I did not yet know her. And if she was marked, though I prayed she was not, I would be here to guide her through whatever lives God chose to grant to her. It was the gift my mother had given me, and it was the gift I would give to my child.

I was tired after sitting in the conservatory all morning and ready for a lie down. Already, my body was experiencing changes due to my pregnancy, and it was exhausting.

Edith helped me change into a nightgown and then pulled back the covers on my bed so I could climb in. My eyelids were heavy as I laid my head upon the pillow.

A light knock sounded at the door, and Edith went to see who had come. One of the chambermaids stood outside my room. Edith spoke to her in low tones and then came back to me.

Her eyebrows were pulled together in disapproval. "Mary would like to speak to you. She says she has something you might like to have, but she won't tell me what it is. Should I send her away?"

Curiosity made me sit up as I motioned for Mary to enter the room. I had only seen her a few times, since she usually cleaned downstairs before I left my bedchamber in the morning and then worked upstairs while I was on the main floor. My path rarely crossed with those of the chambermaids.

She was a quiet woman, small and pale, with big eyes and light brown hair. On the morning of the raid, as I had spoken to the maids to try to calm their fears, Mary had told me her mother was a local healer but that Mary's older sister would take over her mother's practice. That left Mary without an income, so she had come to Cumberland Hall to make something of her life. She had made her family proud and would do anything to keep her job.

Now she entered my bedchamber tentatively, looking about as if she'd never seen it before, though she cleaned it every day.

"Mary?" I offered a welcoming smile so she wouldn't feel uncomfortable. "Is there something I can do for you?"

"I'd like to speak to you alone, milady, if I may."

"Of course."

Mary looked to Edith, who made an exasperated face and then left the room.

"Please speak freely." I was sitting with my back against the pillows and my arms over the blanket. I was tired, but my interest had been piqued, and I felt a surge of newfound energy.

She stopped about two feet away from the bed and glanced around again, as if looking to see if anyone was listening. "I don't mean to be impudent or presumptuous, milady, but I heard you were upset after Dr. Aiken left yesterday."

I stared at the maid, uncertain how to respond. I knew word spread quickly in a house like this, but how much did she actually know? And how much should I allow her to know? "Go on."

She pulled a vial from her apron pocket. "My mum gave this to me." She placed the vial in my hand and took a step back. "When I told her the distress you were feeling about the—" She nodded at my midsection. "She gave me this remedy."

I stared at the vial. The dark, thick fluid slid down the glass like oily mud.

"She said to put the contents into warm water and drink it down. In a day or two, you'll feel awful sick, but it will take care of your . . . problem."

Revulsion filled me as I realized what she was suggesting, and I quickly handed the vial back to her, shaking my head. I could never do what she was suggesting. "Please leave," I told her, "and destroy the contents of that vial immediately."

Mary's eyes widened, and she took a step back. "I'm only trying to help, milady."

"I know your intentions were—" I couldn't think of the right word. "But I have no wish to do as you've suggested. If you'll please leave, I'd like to rest."

Backing up, Mary bumped into a chair and then the vanity. She hurried from the room, closing the door behind her.

I lay back upon the pillow again, my heart pounding. I placed my hand on my flat stomach, imagining the child growing within. If she was a time-crosser, then somewhere in a different time and place, another mother was learning about her impending arrival. It was so hard to fathom, even though I had lived such a life for over twenty years.

I found myself praying for the other life my daughter might

live, for the mother and father who would help me raise her. My mind wandered, thinking of what she might see and do, the people she would know, and the experiences she would have. Would they be good? Bad? What if her second life was as challenging as mine? Or more so? What if she was meant to do something extraordinary?

I thought about Congressman Hollingsworth for the first time in a long time and smiled. What if my daughter was meant to be one of the great heroines in history?

Without a doubt in my mind or heart, I knew that this child's life was important, and I would have the privilege of being her mother. It was an awesome and frightful thing to imagine, bearing and nurturing a child, but it also gave me the strangest feelings I'd ever experienced.

Hope mingled with the broken places in my heart, binding them together into a new vessel to hold a new kind of love, the love I would have for my child. I felt inadequate and unprepared but also very much in awe of the miracle of her life.

I had not chosen to bear this child, but for some reason, she had chosen me. Making the decision to keep her would mean losing almost every person I cared about and loved—yet Mama's words rang true in my heart. I would love this baby more than life itself, and I would give up everything for her, over and over again. It was the power and the miracle of life. It was the same love that Christ had shown for me when He gave up His life on the cross. He had laid down his life so that others could live. I would be asked to do the same for my child.

I closed my eyes as tears slipped down my temples, pondering the great mysteries of life, and my thoughts strayed to Henry. My heart ached with a longing that would never ease. Yet I had made my decision, and it was final. Unless God intervened in a way I could not fathom or expect, I would stay in 1915 upon my twenty-first birthday.

It gave me but five short months to say good-bye.

# 23

WILLIAMSBURG, VIRGINIA
APRIL 20, 1775

Spring had returned to Virginia on the breath of warm sunshine. As I walked along Nicholson Street, three months after learning about the baby, I admired the sight of green shoots poking through the black soil. I loved spring in Williamsburg. It was my favorite time of year, and knowing that this would be my last somehow made the colors brighter, the smells stronger, and the noises louder.

While my body changed in 1915, my heart had begun to change in 1775. I still mourned with each passing day, and Mama and I still cried together when we were alone. I prayed for a miracle to spare me, yet the longer I knew my growing child, the more I loved her and wanted her.

But it didn't make me want Henry any less. I hadn't seen him in three months, though he had sent several letters. His responsibilities had taken him to Philadelphia and then Boston, and though he claimed it was business for his father, I suspected he was also working with the Sons of Liberty. I prayed fervently that he would come home soon, if for no other reason than to remove him from the dangerous region where the first shots of the American Revolution had been fired just yesterday.

Though news had not yet reached Virginia, I knew the Battles of Lexington and Concord had transpired the day before. Mama and I had prayed for all those involved. What Williamsburg would soon learn was that British troops had marched from Boston to Concord, Massachusetts, to destroy a store of ammunition held there by the local militia. Men like Paul Revere and William Dawes learned of this march and rode ahead to warn those in Lexington and Concord. By the time the British arrived, a group of minutemen had assembled on the village green in Lexington as a first line of defense. Shots were fired, and the British continued their march toward Concord. The local militia fought back, hiding along the road and confronting the soldiers in combat. At the end of the day, the British had lost almost three hundred men and the Americans had lost almost a hundred. It would be considered the first American victory.

But Williamsburg would not know any of this for several more days.

I passed Peyton Randolph's red house and nodded a greeting at his wife, and then I was at my own back gate.

The stable in the corner of the property had been empty for the past two months, since Lieutenant Addison had been called away to Boston. It would not surprise me if James had participated in the march into Lexington and Concord. I hoped and prayed he had survived.

I passed Abraham and Mariah, who were cultivating our large gardens in preparation for planting. Rebecca and Hannah were sitting on the bench under the elm tree, doing sums, and Glen and Louis were busy in the printing room. I bypassed all of them and went into the house, planning to get a head start on next week's paper, but I paused in the hallway when I heard a male voice coming from the sitting room.

The door was open, so I entered. Mama and Mister Goodman, the widowed cobbler, were sitting close together, and when I appeared, they both stood quickly.

Mama's cheeks blossomed in color. "You're back so soon, Libby. Did you enjoy your walk?"

Mister Goodman was a tall man, and he made Mama look much shorter by comparison. He had been visiting us regularly since Christmastide, and we had enjoyed his company, Mama most of all.

"I did, indeed," I told her. "'Tis a beautiful day to be outside—or in."

"Aye." Mister Goodman moved away from Mama and toward the door. "I should be getting back to the shop. I left my apprentice to work on his own, but with the warm weather and his impending wedding, I doubt he's been productive. Good day, Libby." He nodded at Mama, a special smile lighting his face. "Good day, Theodosia."

"Good day, Alpheus."

Mister Goodman walked past me to the hallway and then let himself out.

I stared at Mama, who busied herself pushing the chairs back to the table. "Do you plan to work this afternoon?" she asked, avoiding eye contact.

"Is there something I should know about Mister Goodman?" My question was tender yet challenging. If she was growing close to him, shouldn't I know?

She finally stopped fussing with the chairs and gave me her attention. "Alpheus is a wonderful man. He's kind and good, and he loves the Lord with all his heart. His business is doing well and—" She paused as she swallowed and ran her hand along the back of the chair. "He could provide well for the girls and me when—" She paused again without looking at me, yet I knew what she intended to say.

"When I'm gone."

"We only have two months left." Tears glistened in her eyes. "I've been thinking and praying a lot, and I have some hard decisions to make."

I moved across the room to stand in front of her. "Why haven't you been discussing them with me?"

"To what end, Libby? Every time we discuss these things, we both end up weeping." She moved to the door and closed it, then came back and said quietly, "When you are gone, I will have to move on with my life, and I will not have you here to help make decisions for our family."

A pang of grief hit as I realized Mama was starting to push me away. Not because she didn't love me, but because she was trying to mourn her loss apart from me. I couldn't fault her. She would need to mourn in whatever way she felt best, just as I would.

But it still hurt.

"Have you come to any decisions?" I asked just above a whisper, afraid my voice would crack if I spoke any louder.

"I believe I have." She took a deep breath. "Alpheus has asked me to marry him. He doesn't know you'll be leaving us, so he fully believes that you and the girls will come with me."

"You're leaving the printing press?" I couldn't believe what she was saying. The print shop had been her life for so long that it seemed unimaginable she would no longer be a part of it.

"I cannot run it without you, Libby, and to be honest, I don't want to." She clasped her hands together and paced over to the window. "This was your papa's dream, and then yours. You two had the passion for it, not me. I quite like the idea of simply running Alpheus's home and not his business." She turned back to look at me. "I will have more time for Hannah and Rebecca."

My spirit caught on those words. *More time for Hannah and Rebecca*. It was what we all wanted. But more than that, if Mama married Mister Goodman, then she and the girls would be provided for once I was gone. They wouldn't need to worry about finances anymore. The girls could have new gowns without going into debt.

"And what of Mariah and Abraham?" I asked, the fight going out of me.

"They're free to come or go as they like. Alpheus has said they can continue working for us if they want. His business does very well, and he's in need of another man."

I placed my hands on my hips and stared down at the floor, trying to control my emotions. It was difficult to think about my family moving on once I was gone. Of giving up the press and moving into someone else's home.

"I haven't wanted to burden you with these things." Mama walked back across the room and put her hand on my shoulder. "You have enough to contend with on your own."

It took me a moment to find my voice. "And who will take over the press?"

"I will offer to sell it to Louis."

I closed my eyes, struggling with the idea that Louis would continue our legacy. "But what about his threats? Have you not inquired if there is someone else?"

"No one has shown an interest. But it matters not to me. I simply want to be done, Libby. I'm tired and heartsore. If he is in a position to purchase the press, who am I to stop him?"

"Are you certain that's what you want?"

"I do not care for Louis as a man," she confessed, "but as an employee, he's been faithful to us. I know he will make changes—"

"He'll run this as a Tory press." The words were vehement as they came out of my mouth.

"Aye," she conceded, "but not for long. You forget the war will be over one day, and men like Louis will have to decide if they want to go to England or if they want to become an American. There will be no middle ground."

"And until then?"

"Until then, each of us must make the decisions we feel led to make."

I wrapped my arms around my waist, trying to accept yet another change. "And you feel this is the decision you must make?"

"Aye. I do."

"Have you told Mister Goodman?"

She nodded. There was something bittersweet about the way she looked at me. "I told him we will marry at the end of the summer. It will give the girls and me time to grieve before we move on."

*Move on.* I closed my eyes, unable to stop the tears from coming again. I was so tired of crying. So tired of feeling this constant ache. Part of me just wanted it to be over, while the other part wanted to hold on as long as possible.

Mama pulled me into her arms and held me tight. "I love you, Libby. Please know that everything I decide is because of you and not in spite of you."

"I know." Her sacrificial love was never in question. She had done more for me than I deserved. "I want you to be happy. And if Mister Goodman makes you happy, then you have my blessing, Mama."

She pulled away and smiled through her tears. "He does make me happy." A soft giggle lifted off her lips, and she covered her mouth in embarrassment. "I haven't been this in love since . . ." She let the words trail off, but I knew the answer.

"Since 1994?"

"Oh, Libby." She squeezed my hand. "I didn't know such love could ever exist for me here."

Joy filled my heart at her words, and I smiled. "Truly?"

"Truly." Her cheeks colored again. "He's returning for supper tonight. He'll be pleased to know I've told you the truth. It's become very difficult for us to hide our feelings."

My mama was still a young woman, just forty-two years old. I hoped and prayed she would have many wonderful and happy years with Mister Goodman.

Even if I wasn't there to witness them.

That evening, I walked into the house carrying Spanish peas, asparagus, and green apricot tarts. Mama and Mister Goodman were already in the sitting room with Hannah and Rebecca, waiting for our evening meal. The beef steak pie and almond cheesecake on the table were a gift from Mister Goodman. I set down the other dishes and took a seat.

"Shall we pray?" Mama asked.

I laid my hands in my lap and nodded.

"Alpheus, will you do the honors?"

He looked at Mama with a question in his eyes, and she nodded. It was customary for the head of the home to pray, so for her to ask him told all of us a great deal about his new position in our lives.

Now that I knew how serious their relationship had become, I wondered how I hadn't noticed it before. Was I so wrapped up in my own concerns that I was missing out on the events unfolding around me?

After Alpheus prayed, we began to pass the dishes. Mama didn't like to serve meals in courses, much preferring the simpler family-style meals she was accustomed to from her life in the twentieth century.

A knock at the door signaled the arrival of a visitor. I stood to answer it as Mister Goodman addressed the girls. "Your mama tells me that you've always wanted a pony."

Rebecca's and Hannah's cries of delight followed me as I opened the front door and found Henry.

My heart leapt at the sight of him—and then it crashed,

like the sea upon the cliffs at Cumberland Hall, shattering in the next second.

He stood on the stoop, wearing a fine suit of clothes and holding his tricorne under his arm. His dark hair was clubbed at the back, and his blue eyes were bright at the sight of me. Sun had kissed his cheeks, giving him a boyish charm.

"Libby," he said. "My eyes will never tire of seeing you."

I wanted to throw myself into his arms, but I was reminded of the task ahead of me. I had to say good-bye to him, and it would be so much harder if I allowed myself the warmth and affection of his touch. It took every shred of willpower I possessed to stay where I was standing. But I allowed myself the pleasure of smiling at him.

"Good day, Henry. Won't you come in?"

He hesitated before stepping into the hallway. As he passed me, he paused. His eyes searched mine, and I swallowed, then took a step back to put space between us.

His smile fell as I closed the door.

"Mama is entertaining Mister Goodman, and we've just sat down to supper," I said. "Would you like to join us?"

I could see his uncertainty in the way he held his shoulders and in the way he watched me. "Could we speak alone for a moment?" he asked, his voice low.

"Aye." No doubt they could hear us within the sitting room and probably knew who had come. "Shall we go out back?"

He nodded and then followed me down the hall to the back door.

The sun was low in the sky, but it was still warm, and I did not need a shawl. Beneath my feet, the shells cracked, and ahead, the bench beckoned us with memories from Christmastide.

He took my hand, guiding me to sit next to him. "What troubles you, Libby?"

I sat, my back stiff. The last thing I wanted was to make him feel angry or frustrated with me. He didn't deserve anything but my complete heart for as long as I could offer it to him. Yet was that wise? Would it only hurt more?

"I have a lot on my mind," I told him. "But you didn't come here to hear about my worries."

He took my other hand in his and rubbed his thumbs across my skin. Just like Christmas, it sent a warm sensation up my arms and into my chest. I longed to lean into him and let everything else fade away. With him this close, the constant ache from the previous months felt heavier somehow.

"I have a lot on my mind, as well." He let out a sigh. "I'm sorry I haven't been back since January. I've wanted to be with you and hold you again."

He tried to draw me into his arms, but I pulled away and stood, my heart pounding against my chest.

"I received your letters." I wrapped my arms around my waist. "You've been in Boston?"

He watched me for a moment, a frown marring his handsome face. "Aye. I've only just returned. I'm expected at Edgewater Hall, but I could not go home until I saw you." He stood and came to me. "What's wrong, Libby? I cannot bear to see you unhappy. Is it me? Have I hurt or offended you in some way?"

I turned away, uncertain of myself and my emotions. I was making a mess of this whole thing. I was supposed to be kind yet distant. I was supposed to let him go gently and not draw more questions. I'd planned it for months. Yet, standing here with him, I realized I could never willingly let Henry Montgomery go—not until I absolutely had to.

When I looked back at him, the pain in his eyes was so intense that I could not restrain myself any longer. With a soft cry, I went into his arms. Anyone might see us, but I didn't care. The whole world could know I loved Henry, and I wouldn't mind.

He was warm and solid and familiar.

"I've missed you," I said. "'Tis been too long, and I've been worried about you."

He held me tight, kissing the top of my head. "I'm sorry. This is why I knew it was best not to tell you how I felt. I knew it would be too hard for us to bear."

This would be hard even if I didn't know he loved me.

"What were you doing in Boston?" I pulled back to look at him.

"Work for the cause." He took my hands in his and sighed. "After you told me what Lieutenant Addison said, I spoke to some of the Liberty men, and they agreed I needed to cease my work in this colony. You were right. My spying had been compromised. So I was sent to Boston to aid them there. I met with several of the Sons of Liberty and shared the information I had gained, and they shared what information they had with me. I was then sent back here, communicating with several different men along the way and with an extended stay in Philadelphia. I plan to make the trip again at the end of May."

"The end of May?" I pressed my lips together as grief stole over me. "And how long will you be gone?"

He shrugged. "It might be another three months—unless I'm needed longer."

That meant that I didn't have two months left to say good-bye to Henry. I only had about a month—and much of that time he might be at Edgewater Hall. Beyond that, the colonies would be fully engaged in war with Britain, and Henry would be needed.

I let go of his hands and paced away, but he did not follow me. Mama's flower beds were just coming to life, and I walked around the one containing her tulips, which were yet to bloom. I could not stop Henry from being involved in the war. The cause was as much a part of him as I was. It was just as near and dear to his heart. To ask him to stop would be akin to asking him to quit breathing. Yet I knew the horrors to come.

I turned to face him again. "Please," I begged, "be careful, Henry."

There was something deep and heavy in his countenance, a weariness that I recognized and leaned into. "I will try. But, Libby—" He paused as his hand came up to caress my face. "If something should happen to me—"

"Do not speak of such things."

"I must." He lowered his hand. "If we are parted, please promise me you'll find happiness and joy in my absence."

If we were parted. We would be, though it was my death he would mourn, not the other way around. But could I promise that I would find happiness and joy in the life I was left to live? I swallowed, choking back the pain. "I promise," I whispered. I would try for his sake, if not for my own.

We stood there for a long moment before he nodded. "I do not want to rush, but I've heard rumors that Governor Dunmore has plans to move the ammunition from the magazine in Williamsburg tonight, under the cover of darkness. I need to do more investigating and then spread the word."

I frowned. "Why would he do such a thing?"

"War is imminent. He doesn't want the ammunition to land in the hands of the local militia, so he plans to move it to a Royal Navy ship called the *Magdalen*. It's docked in the James River, not far from Edgewater Hall."

"But how will he move it? None of the soldiers have returned from Massachusetts."

"I should not be telling you these things, Libby. I do not want you to get hurt or to be questioned, should something happen to me." He touched my cheek again. "I promise I will come again before I leave for Massachusetts." He lifted his other hand to my face and lowered his lips to mine in a sweet and tender kiss.

I grasped his hands, holding onto him as if he were an anchor in a storm-tossed sea. He was the only thing that made sense to me, the only person outside my family who truly mattered anymore.

When he finally pulled back, I felt adrift.

"I must go. But I love you, Libby, with all my heart."

"I love you, too, Henry."

He placed his tricorne on his head and took the path to our back gate, no doubt starting his alarm at Peyton Randolph's house. I watched him walk down the path, his steps long and confident, his movements sure, and his destination certain. I wished with all my heart that I could walk into my future with such conviction and passion, even knowing the dangers and the uncertainties.

Before he went through our gate, he turned back and waved. I returned the wave, watching as my heart left me once again.

# 24

Five long weeks had passed since I stood with Henry in Mama's garden. After the Gunpowder Incident in Williamsburg, he had made himself scarce, and I was certain he didn't want his name connected to the alarm that had been raised the night of the event. After Governor Dunmore's soldiers had removed all the ammunition from the magazine and transported it to his ship, the local militia had been mustered, and Patrick Henry had marched into Williamsburg to retaliate. The threat to the governor and his family had been so great, the governor had taken his family to their country home on the James River but had recently returned to the palace in a show of reconciliation.

Tensions had continued to escalate as men left the colony for the Second Continental Congress, putting everyone on edge. The governor said that he had fought for Virginia, but he was also ready to fight against her. He wasn't afraid to turn Williamsburg to ashes.

I sat in the little study I used at Cumberland Hall and looked out the window, thinking about the events transpiring in Williamsburg. The closer I came to leaving, the more I worried about Mama and the girls and all that faced them during the revolution. I felt so helpless, but what could I do? Knowing Mister Goodman would be there to protect them alleviated some of my concern.

The study was on the first floor with a view of the moors. Everything was lush and green, with craggy rocks protruding from the carpet of cotton grass and heather. Sheep grazed lazily on the hills behind the manor. Overhead, the bright blue sky had nary a cloud in sight. It was the most beautiful time I'd yet experienced in North Yorkshire.

I stood to stretch my back, knowing that Reggie's latest letter begged for a response. He was still in the Champagne region of France working as an aide to Lieutenant-General Sir Douglas Haig. He could not tell me much about where he was or what occupied his time, so he shared instead memories of his childhood at Cumberland Hall and his hopes for the future. After that initial letter in January, he had not spoken again of his feelings for me or of his actions in the library. He had returned to less vulnerable topics, for which I was grateful. I did not want to address those issues, not when my heart was so tender and raw. We would have years to deal with such things once he returned home after the war.

"Lady Cumberland." Wentworth appeared at the open door. "Would you like your tea in here today?"

"Yes, thank you."

He nodded and then gestured for a maid to enter the room with a cart laden with tea and biscuits. My daily newspapers were also there. Early in my time at Cumberland Hall, I had asked Mr. Wentworth to subscribe to several newspapers, both in London and in Whitby. He'd been surprised but had not questioned me. My work on the *Virginia Gazette* had taught me to seek information from more than one news source, and I continued that here in 1915.

After Wentworth and the maid had left, I reached for the pile of newspapers. Today I was especially interested in the *London Evening News*. They had been willing to publish an article I wrote about my experiences during the raid. Though it had been several months since it happened, the public was still hungry for news about the civilian losses, the military presence, and the work done at Cumberland Hall. My words were being used to help recruit more soldiers, men who took offense at civilian casualties.

A movement within my womb brought my hand down to my growing midsection, and I felt the baby roll beneath my fingers. It brought a smile to my face as a wave of affection filled me with warmth. Pregnancy was like nothing I'd ever experienced. I finally understood the glow that some women exhibited, as I'd never felt so feminine nor had such purpose in my life. To know that this child was dependent on me and solely me for nourishment, love, and protection was both an honor and a privilege. I loved knowing I was responsible for protecting her precious life.

As I nibbled on a tea biscuit, thankful my sickness had finally passed, I noticed a section of the paper that made me pause. It was a list of men killed in action during the Battle of Gorlice-Tarnow, which had happened earlier that month. As I read the list, not recognizing any of the names, I thought about all of the family and friends mourning their losses. It caused my thoughts to turn back to the troubles plaguing the American colonies in 1775.

A siege had been laid in Boston after the Battles of Lexington and Concord. Militiamen were not allowing British soldiers to leave the city by land or by sea. Henry had sent a note saying he planned to see me tomorrow, because he was needed in Boston and would be leaving soon. Since the Second Continental Congress was meeting in Philadelphia, I was certain he would stop there to pass along any information he had gathered.

Dread filled me at the thought of him returning to the middle of the fight. But even worse was the knowledge that tomorrow I would say good-bye to him for the last time.

I'd been trying to push our farewell from my mind, busying myself with my work on Cumberland Hall, but it refused to be silenced. What little appetite I had for tea fled, and I set my biscuit on the tray.

I would never see Henry again after tomorrow. I would never be held in his arms, never know the sweet kiss of his lips, and never hear the cadence of his voice.

The baby moved again, causing my stomach to lift at the force of her somersault.

Suddenly, I could not be still any longer. I needed to find something to occupy my mind.

Leaving the study, I walked down the corridor to the great hall, where stone masons were repairing the cracks in the wall high above. Sunshine poured in through the tall windows, illuminating their work.

I observed them for a moment, but my loneliness overwhelmed me. My pregnancy caused me to stay home more and more. No longer could I serve at the soup kitchen or visit the people who had become friends during their recovery at Cumberland Hall. Dr. Aiken visited regularly and suggested I keep to light, easy activities. He had some concerns about my pregnancy, though he said I didn't need complete rest. The last thing I wanted was to hurt my baby, so I had heeded his advice and stayed close to Cumberland Hall this past month.

But it had caused a deep, gnawing isolation, especially with the impending loss in 1775. Once I left Mama, I would have no one to talk to about my time-crossing. That in itself made me feel like a castaway on a deserted island.

Not for the first time, I thought of Congressman Hollingsworth, and a bit of the loneliness lifted. There was one other person on this planet who understood, and even though I could not contact him now, perhaps I could after my twenty-first birthday. There would be no history to change then.

The door to the library was open, and I caught a glimpse of the maids cleaning inside. I had not entered that room since Reggie had visited and had no desire to do so now. Yet the Virginia book called to me. More than ever, I wanted to look through the pages to see the familiar names and places I would soon be leaving forever.

I stopped outside the door, wondering if the memories of Reggie's visit would overshadow the comfort I might take in seeing the book again. Perhaps I could slip in, grab the book, and then go to the conservatory. I didn't need to actually read the book; just having it with me felt like enough.

Taking a deep breath, I stepped into the library. The two-story room immediately brought back the memories of that night five months ago when Reggie had forced me to stay with him. An uneasy, panicked feeling settled in my chest. I laid my hand on my stomach and felt the baby press against my palm, reminding me that there was beauty among the ashes. I quickly located the Virginia book and then rushed out of the library.

Pressing the book to my chest, I felt as if I had found a friend once again. I ran my hands over the leather cover as I entered the conservatory. It was bright and welcoming, a refuge among the rubble of my sorrow.

I sat in my favorite chair, with a view of the moors and the sea. The conservatory was warm and humid, but I didn't mind. For the first time in a long time, I wasn't alone. Part of me wanted to open the book to find the names of people I knew. Yet part of me was frightened. Would I have the willpower to stop myself from looking up Henry's name? But what if the news was good? Might the book tell me where he would live, if he married, and how many children he'd have?

Did I want to know?

Somehow, the thought of him moving on with his life after I

died felt like too much. Maybe one day I would have the strength and desire to learn the truth, but was that today?

"I wish you could know him," I said to the unborn child in my womb. "But I'm afraid all he'll be to you one day is a name from a distant time and place that bears no significance. Just like the name Travis from Mama's path is to me."

The book was large and heavy, so I set it on the table beside me—but I missed the edge, and it fell to the stone floor, landing facedown with the pages splayed open. I bent to pick it up and turned it over, afraid I'd hurt the spine or damaged some of the old paper. A smudge of dirt marred one of the pages, and I wiped it away, but then my eyes fell on the words.

The book had opened to the *r*'s, and Peyton Randolph's name jumped out at me. He'd served as the speaker of the House of Burgesses in Williamsburg and the President of the Virginia Convention and the First Continental Congress. But I paused when I read the date and circumstances surrounding his death. He would die of apoplexy on October 22, 1775, while dining with Thomas Jefferson during the Second Continental Congress in Philadelphia.

My heart lagged as I thought of his wife and children, who would soon be bereft. He'd already left for Philadelphia, which meant they'd probably never see him again.

I was so far away from the *m*'s that I decided to look at the other names near the *r*'s. Some of the biographies surprised me, others made me sad, and still others made me smile. I was honored to know some of these men and proud to be a Virginian.

I spent the afternoon reading the book, purposely avoiding the *m*'s, and that was where Mr. Wentworth found me when it was time for supper.

"Would you like your meal brought to you here?" he asked.

I stood and stretched, sore from sitting for so long but happy I had spent time with so many people I knew and cared about.

"I'll take supper in my bedchamber tonight," I told him.

I was exhausted and would retire with my book after I was done eating. It would take me hours and hours to get through all the information contained within this volume, and then I'd have twelve others to read when I was done. I looked forward to learning more about the colonists who would aid in the American Revolution.

An hour later, after I was done eating and Edith had helped me into a nightgown and wrapper, I went to the chair near the fireplace. It had been lit to contend with the spring chill that had settled inside the house that evening.

I brought the book with me and opened it to a random page, ready to keep reading, but realized I was looking at the *m*'s.

Henry's name stared at me, and before I could stop myself, I was reading the information the book contained.

Henry Montgomery was a merchant, burgess, and American Patriot. He was born on August 16, 1750, at Edgewater Hall along the James River near Williamsburg, Virginia. Montgomery served as a spy for the Committee of Correspondence, first in Williamsburg, using his connection to Governor Dunmore, and then on two separate missions from Virginia to Massachusetts, gathering and sharing intelligence among the colonies to aid in preparation for war. It was on this second mission, at daybreak on June 17, 1775, during the Siege of Boston, that Montgomery was captured by the British army. The papers he was carrying conveyed a message from Colonel William Prescott to the Second Continental Congress at Philadelphia, revealing the plan to occupy the hills around Boston and prevent the British from fortifying the city. This alerted the British of the colonists' plans, and the Battle of Bunker Hill ensued. Though the British won the battle after three separate attacks and the colonists were forced to retreat after running out of ammunition, it demonstrated that the inexperienced American militia were able to fight regular army troops in battle. Henry Montgomery was held as a prisoner and hanged for treason on June

19, 1775. He became the first American spy executed during the Revolution.

I stared at the words on the page as my body grew cold and numb with disbelief. This couldn't be true. Henry couldn't die on my birthday. He couldn't die at all. He was meant to live a long and happy life, bearing the fruit of his sacrifice and labor for decades to come.

Grief, deep and debilitating, settled over me as I reread the short paragraph. This was what Henry's sacrifice would amount to? This was what his death would produce? A brief mention in an old book? It wasn't right or fair. How could God allow such a tragedy? It was a waste that defied comprehension.

Anger soon replaced my grief. I could not let this happen. Henry couldn't die, not this way and not this soon. He had so much to offer the Patriots—so much to offer the world.

I wouldn't let him go to Boston. When he came to see me tomorrow, I would tell him not to leave Williamsburg. I would think of a way to prevent him from going.

There was still time to change history, to save him from this fate, and I was the only person who could.

# 25

## WILLIAMSBURG, VIRGINIA
## MAY 29, 1775

The second I awoke in Williamsburg, I rushed out of bed. It always took me a moment to adjust to the differences in my body and remember that my child was not with me in this time and place. I ached for her while I was here, my hand often going to my flat stomach out of habit.

I dressed quietly, not wanting to wake Rebecca and Hannah, and slipped out of my room.

A dim light filled the eastern horizon as I tiptoed toward the stairs. Mama was probably awake, saying her morning prayers, but I did not want her to know I was leaving the house. If she knew what I was doing, she would try to stop me. I was about to change history, and I knew the consequences.

Henry was carrying papers that would alert the British to the American activities on the hills around Boston. It would lead to the Battle of Bunker Hill, a defining moment in American history. Would the battle not happen if Henry didn't go? And what about the other information he passed along before he was captured? Would that affect the war or the outcome? Would it have a ripple effect that prevented America from winning? I couldn't even imagine what that meant for the world.

I'd wrestled with these questions all night in 1915 and come to the conclusion that it was worth the risk to save Henry's life. One small change couldn't possibly affect so much. The knowledge that I was forfeiting my path in 1775 three weeks before my birthday was harder to accept. Tonight, when I went to sleep in Williamsburg, I would wake up in Whitby and never return.

The thought stopped me as I put my hand on the railing. My legs became weak, and I sat down hard upon the first step. Did I have the courage to do this?

"Libby?" Mama's door opened, and she peeked out of her bedchamber, a frown on her face. "What's wrong?"

I couldn't gather the strength to rise and address her. My words stuck in my throat, and I tried to swallow them.

She stepped out of her room and walked down the hall, joining me on the top step. It was crowded, with both of us sitting there, but it also felt safe and secure.

"What's wrong?" she asked again. "Is it the baby?"

I shook my head as tears gathered in my eyes. "It's Henry. He's going to die." I couldn't keep the information to myself. It was too much to carry on my own.

"How do you know?"

"I read about it in a book in Whitby. He's going to be hanged for treason on my birthday—in Boston."

"What?" Mama frowned. "Are you certain?"

I nodded as the tears fell down my cheeks and dripped off my chin. "I've known about the book for nine months, but I wouldn't allow myself to look—until yesterday. Oh, Mama."

I laid my cheek against her shoulder and wept like I'd never wept before. She put her arm around me and held me tight, whispering soft, reassuring words, though none of them made me feel any better.

"I love him," I said when my tears had subsided.

"I know, Libby. I know."

"What will I do?" I kept my cheek on her shoulder, staring down the stairs and at the path before me. "How can I stop this from happening?"

"You can't."

"But I must." I sat up straighter and used my apron to wipe my cheeks. "I can't let him die."

"Only God is in control of our destiny. He alone is sovereign. When we try to control the people and events around us, we are telling Him He doesn't know what's best for us. We're setting ourselves up as our own gods, elevating ourselves above Him. It's a dangerous game, Libby."

"But you said I always have a choice."

"You do, but is that truly the choice you want to make? Doesn't He know what's best for Henry?"

"Death?" I shook my head until it ached. "How can death be the best thing for Henry?"

"I don't know, Libby, but we must trust God. There are some things too mysterious for us to understand. We are not meant to know all the answers. Only God is, and He calls us to trust and believe that He is doing what is best."

I couldn't accept what she was saying. It didn't make sense.

Mama took my hands. "Libby, please don't do this. I know what's on your mind, but you'll forfeit this life—today. If you try to stop Henry, all you'll accomplish is your own death before its time."

"I'm only losing three weeks." But as the words fell from my mouth, I knew how wretched they sounded.

"Three weeks is three weeks." She pressed my hands tight, as if she wouldn't let me go. "You have work to finish here—and I'm not ready to say good-bye."

My hands trembled and my heart pounded, but I knew what I must do. "If it means sparing Henry from a horrible death, then I must sacrifice those three weeks. It's the least I can do when so many others are doing so much more."

"It's not just your own sacrifice. We don't know what else might happen. If Henry doesn't go to Boston, how will that affect the rest of history? What will change if he isn't there?"

None of it mattered. I couldn't let Henry die this way, not if I had the power to stop it.

I rose on trembling legs and pulled my hands from Mama's grasp.

"Libby," she pleaded, tears streaming down her cheeks, "don't do this."

"I'm sorry." I walked down the steps and stopped at the bottom to look back at her. "I must."

The sun had just crested the horizon when I stepped out our front door. As I walked, I pulled my shawl tighter around my shoulders, feeling the early morning chill deeper than usual.

I hadn't been to Henry's home on the Palace Green since that rainy evening so many months ago, and I wasn't certain I would be welcome if his father or mother was there. The House of Burgesses had not been called to convene this year, but many people had still come into Williamsburg for the spring activities. I wasn't even sure Henry was home. His note said he'd come by to see me today before he left for Boston, but that didn't mean he was already in Williamsburg. Yet I could not sit around the print shop all day and wait for him. This was too important to put off, and if I had stayed at home, Mama would have found a way to convince me not to do this.

My heart ached for her, but it ached for Henry more. He didn't deserve to die, and if I could prevent it from happening, I had to.

There was little movement on Duke of Gloucester Street as I walked toward the Palace Green. A stray dog trotted across my path, and a rooster crowed in a nearby coop. Someone stepped outside to shake a rug, and a man ambled down the street as if he'd been drinking all night and hadn't yet gone home.

Soon I turned onto the Palace Green. The Montgomerys' house was on the left, near the Governor's Palace. My heart pounded as I walked up the steps to the front door. My courage almost failed me when I reached up to knock, but then I thought about Henry hanging from the end of a noose, and I banged hard upon the door.

It took several minutes, but Stanley finally answered the door. "Miss Libby! How can I help you this morning?"

"I've come to see Henry. Is he at home? It's very important."

He nodded quickly. "He's at home, but I don't know if he's prepared to receive visitors."

"Could you please tell him I'm here to see him? I'll wait outside until he's ready."

"You don't want to come in?"

I shook my head, not wanting to risk seeing Lord and Lady Ashbury.

Stanley seemed to understand, and he nodded as he closed the door.

I stepped off the stoop and paced along the dirt road in front of the grey house, my hands on my hips. I didn't allow myself to think about why I'd come, afraid I would lose the courage to talk to Henry.

The palace was quiet. Across the green, the open theater was empty, and up and down the road, there was nothing but birds and squirrels to keep me company. I was happy for the lack of activity. I needed to speak to Henry in private—especially because this would be the last time I'd ever see him.

I stopped to catch my breath as emotions overwhelmed me. How would I say good-bye to him?

A few minutes later, the front door opened and he was there, concern tilting his eyebrows together. It struck me that if I didn't do something, he would only be alive for three more weeks. Anxiety compelled me toward him.

"Libby," he said as he came down the steps, adjusting his waistcoat, "what are you doing here?"

"We need to speak." I looked around for a place of privacy, but seeing none, I asked, "Will you walk with me?"

He glanced back at the house for a moment, then nodded. "Of course."

"Do you have somewhere you need to be this morning?"

"Nay. I planned to eat breakfast with my parents and then come see you in a few hours. After that, I was prepared to leave for Philadelphia at noon."

"Noon?" I ran my clammy hands down my skirt as I walked toward Nicholson Street. It would be quieter than Duke of Gloucester, and we'd have more privacy.

Henry stopped and took my hand. "Libby, you're scaring me. What's wrong?"

In my haste to get to him, I hadn't contemplated how I would convey my request or convince him without telling the truth. He'd never understand or believe me if I tried, and I could not leave him thinking I was mad.

I took in a calming breath and steadied my thrumming pulse. If ever I needed to keep my wits about me, it was now. I forced myself to continue walking, drawing him along with me. "I'm sorry, but I need to tell you something very important, and I must beg you to take me seriously."

"Of course."

This was the moment. I could not go back from here. Once I told him, I would forfeit my life in 1775. But with one look at him, I knew I could not let him die, no matter how much I wanted to stay here for the next three weeks.

"I have learned something very disturbing, and it involves you."

His head jerked back with surprise. "Me? Something I've done?"

"Nay." I prayed I could find the right words, knowing that I could not beseech God for help. Not this time. "I have learned that your mission to Boston has been compromised." It wasn't necessarily the truth, but it would be. "You cannot go. If you do, you will surely be caught and face dire consequences."

He forced me to stop, concern deep within his eyes. "How do you know these things? Who have you talked to? Lieutenant Addison?"

I struggled to meet his gaze. "I cannot tell you."

"Then how am I to believe what you're saying?"

His words hurt more than they should have. "Have I ever lied to you?"

"Of course not."

"Then why would I lie now?"

"I'm not suggesting 'tis you who's lying. If I don't know your source, how can I believe the person who has told you this thing? Mayhap it's a trap to keep me here."

"Nay." I placed my hand on his arm. "Henry, you must trust me and believe me. If you go, you will be caught, and if you are caught, you will be executed."

He stared at me, his blue eyes filling with a range of emotions that were hard to track.

"Promise me you won't leave today," I said, my hand still on his arm. "Promise me you'll stay in Virginia."

"Libby, you don't know what you're asking me to do."

"I'm asking you to save your life."

"'Tis not as easy as that. There are things set in motion that I cannot control. I must go to Philadelphia and then to Boston. I'm needed for the cause, and I fully understand the dangers and risks I'm taking."

My desperation rose with every word he spoke. "But how can you go, knowing that this mission has been compromised?"

"I have to trust and believe that God is in control. He alone will decide my fate."

I couldn't understand him. I was offering him a lifeline, yet he wasn't taking it. "What if I'm sent here to stop you? What if you're supposed to listen to me?"

He swallowed and took my hand in his. It was a long moment before he spoke. "You're right, of course. If you have been given information to help me, I should heed your warning."

Hope took root within me. "You believe me? You'll not go?"

He lifted my hand to his lips and kissed it as he drew me close, though I could see he was still struggling with the information I had given him. "I would be a fool not to listen to you."

We started to walk again, but neither of us said a word. My emotions had swung like a pendulum that morning, and I was now weak with relief yet heartsore with the weight of my sacrifice.

Soon we arrived at my back gate. Slowly, we followed the path between the gardens and stopped at the bench beneath the elm tree. There we sat, side by side.

"I was coming to say good-bye today," he told me, still holding my hand. "But it seems I don't need to anymore."

I clung to him, knowing it wasn't true. He did need to say good-bye to me, because tomorrow he would learn that I had died.

"Are you certain you won't go?" I asked.

He nodded.

I felt like weeping, but I had to force myself not to reveal my emotions. He would know something was wrong if I wasn't careful. So instead, I smiled at him.

He returned the smile, but it was clouded with something deep and troubling. No doubt he was still thinking about what I'd said and how he could remove himself from his responsibilities to the correspondence committee.

We sat for a moment in silence until Abraham came out of the kitchen. He seemed surprised to see us sitting there, but he simply tilted his hat at us and then moved on to the gardens.

"Everyone will soon be stirring," I told Henry. "Would you like to break fast with us?" Even as I said the words, I knew I wouldn't eat a thing. I had no appetite.

"Nay, but thank you. I should return home to deal with some business. Father is planning to return to Edgewater Hall this evening, and if I'm not leaving for Philadelphia, I should escort him. He's been ill, had you heard?"

I shook my head.

"He had a fit of some kind this week." His voice was heavy. "I was already hesitant to leave him, so mayhap this will work out better for everyone."

I nodded, eager to hear him say such things. He would survive, and I could rest a little easier leaving him behind.

Though he'd said he should leave, he stayed on the bench beside me, as if he couldn't pull himself away. I knew how he felt. I had work to do—though, if this was my last day in Williamsburg, did I want to use the time working? Mayhap Mama and I would close the shop today and spend our time with Rebecca and Hannah.

"I must go, Libby." He kissed my forehead.

I wrapped my arms around him and held him close, trying to savor this moment, knowing I would hold this memory with me forever.

He returned the embrace, holding me tight. "I don't know when I'll return from Edgewater Hall, but I'll try to send you a note to let you know."

I nodded as we both rose from the bench.

"Good-bye, Libby."

"Good-bye, Henry."

He touched my cheek and then placed a gentle kiss on my lips. "I love you," he whispered.

"I love you, too."

And then he left me. He put on his tricorne as he moved down the path we had just walked together, but before he left through the back gate, he turned. This time he didn't wave at me but simply smiled.

I returned the smile, forcing myself not to cry until he was gone so I could see him clearly for as long as possible.

I don't know how long I wept after he was out of sight, but eventually I wiped my cheeks one last time. I would not spend my last day in Williamsburg crying.

Mama was by the window in the sitting room, staring outside, when I entered. Rebecca and Hannah were not with her, so I assumed they hadn't come down yet.

She turned at the sound of my entrance and stood. "Did you do it?"

I remembered my resolve not to cry, so I pressed my lips together and nodded once.

"Oh, Libby." She rushed across the room and pulled me into her arms. "My dear, selfless Libby."

I held her for a long time, not wanting to let her go. She was my constant source of support and encouragement. What would I do without her?

"Do you know," she finally said, pulling back, wiping her cheeks with her apron, "from the day I first held you in my arms, I knew you were special. Not only because of your mark, but because of your heart. It's not easy being a time-crosser. It made my mother an angry and bitter woman, but I refused to let the same thing happen to me—or you. I've always admired how you handle your two lives. I know it was very difficult being raised by Mother Wells, but you held onto hope, and you kept your sweet spirit." She took my hand and pressed it to her heart. "Please, Libby, do not let anything turn your heart to stone. Do not let anger or bitterness take root in you. If you do, all of this was for naught. Instead, use what you've learned from me and from this life to do good and further God's kingdom in the time you occupy."

I nodded, unable to speak.

"Did you say good-bye to Henry?"

"Aye." I swallowed the grief threatening to choke me. "It is done."

She gently removed a tendril of hair from my cheek. "You are not the first person to lose the love of your life, and I know you won't be the last. I promise there will be a day when your heart has healed, when it will feel like you can breathe again. It might not happen soon, but it will happen."

I clung to her words, though they were hard to comprehend.

"You will face difficulties, I'm certain." Her eyes dimmed with something I could not identify. "After World War One, there will be a devastating pandemic. Then there will be peace for a time, followed by a worldwide depression. Another man will rise up in Germany in the late 1930s, and he will put the world through another war. But take heart, the best is yet to come."

"Another?" I struggled to understand. "Isn't the Great War the war to end all wars?"

"Freedom isn't stagnant or guaranteed. It lives and breathes and must be defended constantly. Don't take it for granted. Fight for it, both in the public and private spheres of your life. And always look for ways to help," she continued, almost feverish in her instructions. "That is one of our greatest purposes upon this earth. To be the helpers."

I nodded again, wanting her to know I understood.

She placed her hands on either side of my face. "And remember how very much I love you. I will think about you every day for the rest of my life, and one day we will see each other again, when our time on earth is at an end."

"I long for that day, Mama."

"You will be just fine, Libby." She smiled through her tears.

"You're strong and brave, and you have more courage and faith than anyone I know. God will use you in powerful and mighty ways if you'll allow Him. And you'll be a good mother. I wish I could meet my granddaughter, but I know you will teach her about me, and through you, she'll know me."

"She will know you as well as if she had met you." I wanted to reassure Mama, who seemed desperate to give me all the wisdom and advice she could think of. "You have taught me well. You've lived by example, and you've been selfless and loving every day of my life. I won't forget. I promise. I will hold your words here"—I pointed at my heart, where the mark resided—"every day of my life."

Mama's smile was bittersweet. "Let's not say good-bye then, Libby, because it's not good-bye forever. It's only until we meet again."

I returned to her hug and held her for a long time. "Until we meet again, Mama."

Hours later, after I had kissed my sisters good-night, said good-bye to Mariah and Abraham, and even gone to wave good-bye to Sophia through the window of the wig shop, I climbed into Mama's bed to fall asleep in her arms, praying that by some miracle we were both wrong and I would wake up in Williamsburg once again.

She sang me to sleep.

# 26

WHITBY, NORTH YORKSHIRE, ENGLAND
MAY 29, 1915

I slowly opened my eyes, and the first thing I saw was the window looking out to the wild and stormy North Sea. Tall waves rolled across the water while rain splattered against the thick windowpanes.

Inside my bedchamber, it was dark from the overcast sky, and I shivered under the covers protecting me from the chill. My hand slipped down to my stomach and rested over my baby. I curled into a ball around her, hugging her and drawing strength from knowing she was there and she was safe. She moved beneath my hand, and I smiled despite the pain aching within my heart. I still wanted to believe that when I went to sleep tonight, I would wake up in Williamsburg, but I had no guarantee. Everything Mama and I knew to be true about the time-crossers in our family told us that I would never go back.

I didn't want to think about what Mama was facing there, waking up with me lifeless in her arms. It was too much.

Yet if I did not go back, then that meant 1775 was in the past. All the people I knew and loved were truly gone. I took comfort in knowing they had led long and happy lives. I imagined Hannah and Rebecca fully grown, married, with families of their own. And Mama. It eased my heart, knowing she and Mister Goodman would be married and she would have a second chance at true love.

But what about Henry? It was easy to picture Mama and the girls, but it was harder to imagine what Henry's life looked like after I left. Had he taken over Edgewater Hall? Had he married, had children?

Edith entered the room and quietly laid a fire in the hearth, probably assuming I was still asleep. When she finally came to my bed, she smiled. "You're awake early."

I nodded as I sat up to accept the breakfast tray she had brought for me. I didn't have an appetite, but I needed to eat something for the baby, and I didn't want to alarm Edith. The buttered toast was the only thing that looked appealing, so I nibbled on it while Edith put another log on the fire and then went to my dressing room to find something for me to wear.

It was hard to find any reason to get out of bed. A long and uneventful day spread out before me, and the weight of my grief threatened to send me into despair. The only comfort I took was in thinking about how Mama had gone through this very thing and how she had survived. One day this ache would dull and I would find joy and purpose in this life. I might even find a way to accept my marriage to Reggie. My heart would forever belong to Henry, but that didn't mean I couldn't be a good wife and mother. Mama had found a way. There was some consolation in that. I was not destitute nor desperate. I could find joy in helping through the war and in my work for social reform. And when the baby was born, I would take pleasure in being her mama.

I would put one foot in front of the other, remember to breathe in and out, and take one day at a time. I could survive this grief if I gave myself the grace to get through it.

"How about the grey one?" Edith asked as she walked out of my dressing room with one of the few gowns that had been altered to fit my growing waistline.

I nodded, smiling at my friend, thanking God that she was still a part of my life.

"What would you like to do today?" she asked. "Will you work in the conservatory?"

"I think I will." I finished my toast and drank my tea, and then I allowed Edith to remove the tray so I could push the blankets off my legs.

Edith helped me dress and styled my hair. I sat at the vanity, my back straight, and looked in the mirror. I had not noticed how much I had grown to look like Mama. I could see her in my green eyes and in the slope of my nose. When I smiled, it almost felt like she was smiling back at me, and it lifted my spirits.

After Edith had left to take my tray downstairs, I slowly turned away from the mirror. The Virginia book still sat near the bed on the side table. I had avoided looking at it earlier, waiting for Edith to leave before I allowed myself the pleasure of opening its pages.

I retrieved the book, then held it against my chest as I grabbed a knitted blanket and went to the window seat overlooking the sea. The storm continued to blow, but I was warm and safe near the fireplace.

Wrapping the blanket around me, I curled up in the window seat and opened the book, wondering how much history I had changed with my actions. Nothing around me appeared different. The book had the same title, *A Complete Account of America's Sons of Liberty, Founding Fathers, and Fallen Heroes*. So America had still won the fight for independence. I flipped through the pages and discovered that Peyton Randolph's biography had not changed, and neither had Thomas Jefferson's or George Washington's. I didn't notice anything unusual or strange.

I took a deep breath and turned to the *m*'s. Leaving Mama three weeks early had broken my heart, but knowing it was worth the sacrifice allowed some joy to mingle with the pain. The hope I felt at what I would see lifted the corners of my mouth, and I began to read.

Henry Montgomery was a merchant, burgess, and American Patriot. He was born on August 16, 1750, at Edgewater Hall along the James River near Williamsburg, Virginia. Montgomery served as a spy for the Committee of Correspondence, first in Williamsburg, using his connection to Governor Dunmore, and then on two separate missions from Virginia to Massachusetts, gathering and sharing intelligence among the colonies to aid in preparation for war. It was on this second mission, at daybreak on June 17, 1775, during the Siege of Boston, that Montgomery was captured by the British army. . . .

I paused as my eyes tracked over the words again to make sure I had read it correctly, but I didn't understand.

Nothing had changed.

The book said exactly what it had said before I told Henry not to go on his mission.

I straightened, and the blanket fell off my shoulders and pooled at my waist. Didn't Henry heed my warning? Had he still gone? But why, when he told me he wouldn't?

Panic filled my chest, and I frantically flipped through the book to see if I had missed something important. Yet the book looked exactly the same.

I had tried to change history, and it hadn't worked.

But if it hadn't worked . . . had I really forfeited 1775?

A strange sense of hope took hold of me, banishing the panic. If I hadn't forfeited 1775, then that meant I would wake up there again tomorrow. Mama wouldn't have to say good-bye to me yet, and I could still stop Henry—couldn't I? Perhaps he hadn't left Virginia yet. Maybe he had gone to Edgewater Hall with his father and would leave in a day or two. I could go to him and convince him it was foolish to travel to Boston.

It wouldn't be easy, and he'd be shocked to see me, but I had to try again and again, until he listened to me.

I stood, needing to find something to keep myself busy. It would be a long wait until I could fall asleep tonight and try again tomorrow. I could imagine Mama's surprise when she woke up and found me still with her. It would prolong our inevitable parting, but it would be wonderful to spend one more day with her and the girls.

After I set the book on my side table, I left the room to work in the conservatory.

My heart was anxious to return to Williamsburg and find Henry. I had to stop him.

⁂

The next morning, it was still dark when my eyes flew open. It took a moment for me to fully wake up, but as my eyes adjusted, a sinking sensation filled my heart.

I was still in Cumberland Hall.

Perhaps it wasn't yet midnight and I'd just awoken too early.

I pushed aside the covers, the chill of the room making gooseflesh rise on my arms and legs. The wool rug scratched my bare feet, and the rain still slashed at the windows.

Edith had banked the fire before she left me for the night, so there was a little glow to the coals. Just enough for me to make out the hands of the clock sitting on the mantel.

It was four o'clock in the morning.

I stood there for a long, long time, staring at the clock. It felt as if time stood still, yet I watched the second hand tick-tick-tick away the minutes.

I was in Whitby for good. It was the first time in my life that I'd been in the same path for two consecutive days, and it meant that I was now like everyone else. I would go to sleep and wake up without crossing over again for the rest of my life. It was final. Complete.

Yet—

I raced to the side table and grabbed the book, then went back to the fireplace and knelt to stoke the flames, letting light pour forth. I frantically opened the book to Henry's name and looked down at the words one more time, hoping and praying they had changed.

But they hadn't.

Henry had still gone to Boston, things had still happened as God ordained, and I had given up my last three weeks with my family for nothing.

The book slipped from my fingers, landing on the rug near my feet.

"Why?" I cried out to God as the tears came. "I don't understand." My heart felt like it was being torn in two, breaking in ways it had never broken before. "Why would you allow such a thing to happen? Didn't his life mean anything to you?"

Silence echoed in the void of my chest.

Henry's life meant something to me.

I wrapped my arms around my knees, though the growing child made it difficult, and laid my head on them. Nothing about my life had been fair. Nothing about it felt like a gift, as Mama had always told me. How would I teach my own child that her life was a gift, especially if she was a time-crosser? How could I look her in the eyes and promise her that God had it all under control when it felt like everything was chaos and He had abandoned me?

This didn't feel like a gift. It felt like a burden, one I wasn't strong enough to bear. It proved to me, in a taunting, mocking voice, that I was weak and inadequate, and now it reminded me that I was all alone in the world. No one in 1915 cared for me like they did in 1775. There was no one I could lean on for support and encouragement, no one who loved me so completely that it felt as if I was whole.

The ache in my heart soon turned to anger, and I railed against God for the unfairness of it all. Weren't my hopes and dreams pleasing to Him? Then why did He tear them away from me and keep them out of my reach? Was I being punished for something? Was it all a big joke at my expense?

Slowly, Mama's voice filled my heart and mind. She had begged me not to grow angry and bitter.

If she had come through this, couldn't I? Where would I be if she had allowed herself to become resentful? I wouldn't know the joy and love I had always felt from her, and I wouldn't be the person I was today. Mama had left me with a legacy of grace and love—wasn't I obligated to pass along that legacy? Didn't I owe the same to my child?

And what about my faith? Hadn't Mama taught me that God was a good and faithful father, that He knew the plans He had for me, and they were plans to prosper me and not to harm me? If she had lived through the grief and despair I was feeling and had clung to her faith, living by the very things she'd taught me, then couldn't I trust that God *was* faithful and loving and that He knew what was best for me even when I couldn't see it for myself?

It was hard to comprehend, but perhaps all of this did have a purpose, even if I couldn't see it now. Even if I didn't feel like being positive and hopeful. Even when my heart longed to be angry and upset.

I had a choice to make, and I had a feeling I would be called to make it over and over again, day after day. I had before me life and death, blessings and curses. I would need to choose life. If I couldn't do it for myself, then perhaps I could do it for my baby.

My hand found my stomach again. "I will not become bitter or angry, and I will choose to trust God. I will live to see His goodness."

I slowly pulled myself off the floor and picked up the book. It no longer felt like a friend, and it no longer brought comfort to my lonely heart. But perhaps one day I could open it again and find joy in the memories of those I had once known.

That day was not today. From now on, I would focus only on that which brought healing and joy to my life. I would mourn and long for everyone I had left behind, but I wouldn't torture myself by purposely focusing on the past.

I had a life to live—a new life, in many ways—and I would see it as the gift it was. For me and for my unborn child.

It was the only way I knew how to honor Mama's and Henry's memories.

And it was the only way I knew how to survive.

# 27

## WHITBY, NORTH YORKSHIRE, ENGLAND
## SEPTEMBER 17, 1915

The pains began while Edith and I were walking on the moors.
A carpet of purple heather filled the dips and valleys of the
magnificent landscape, and I had come here every day for the
past month to bask in the beauty. It was here that I felt most at
peace with the path I had followed.

My entire abdomen tightened, and the pain radiated from
my back, wrapping around to my front. I stopped to take a
deep breath as wind played with the folds of my gown and the
tendrils of hair at my cheeks.

"Is it time?" Edith asked.

It took a moment for the contraction to pass, and I took
several more breaths before turning on the rocky path to walk
back to Cumberland Hall. "I think the baby is getting ready
to make her entrance."

Edith's hazel eyes widened as she put one gentle hand on my
back. "I'll help you to the house, and then we'll send Williams
for Dr. Aiken."

"Thank you."

It had been four months since I'd left Williamsburg. Four months of grieving, of remembering, and of choosing to focus on a future that looked much different from the one I had imagined. The time had gone by quickly since I no longer lived two separate paths.

Today would be the beginning of something new and profound. I would finally meet the child who had decided my fate, and I would learn whether or not she was marked.

As we walked toward the conservatory's rear entrance, I began to pray that she was not a time-crosser. Though I had come to terms with my own path, I didn't want to pass on this gift to another human being. It didn't seem fair that we somehow had to carry this burden. And it didn't seem fair that if she were a time-crosser, she would soon be born to a different mother in another time and place—one I knew nothing about.

It was such a strange reality, and it connected me to Mama in a new way.

We were almost to the top of the newly carpeted stairs in Cumberland Hall when the next contraction banded around my midsection. I had to stop and cling to Edith for support until it passed, leaving me breathless. I'd had no idea it would hurt this much.

"Just a few more feet," Edith told me as she helped me from the hall into my room. "I'll find Mr. Wentworth and then return to help you into a nightgown."

I nodded, thankful to have her by my side. She helped me sit on the bed and then left.

"Just a little while longer," I told my daughter, "and we will finally meet, and I will show you the wonders of this great, big, beautiful world."

Reggie's most recent letter was on my side table. Edith had brought it that morning, but I hadn't taken the time to open it. His letters were few and far apart. In my last correspondence to him, I'd finally told him about the baby. No doubt he had much to say on that topic.

I picked up the letter and opened the seal. It was the shortest letter he'd ever sent.

*August 15, 1915*

*Libby,*

*We are on the move soon, so I don't have time to write a lengthy letter. But I could not leave here without responding to your magnificent news. I confess, your last letter has taken me by surprise and delight. I wish I had known earlier, but I'm happy I know now. The trenches here in France are detestable, and though we live better than anyone else, it is still unfathomable. Despair and melancholy are a constant companion to us all, but when I read that I was to be a father and Cumberland Hall would have an heir, it was the greatest moment of my life. I know I have treated you abominably, and I cannot pretend that you love me, but I look forward to the day I might return to you and show you I am an honorable and worthy husband. Our marriage is the thing that sustains me on my darkest days, and it brings me great joy, knowing that when I come home to Cumberland Hall, it will be to a wife and child.*

*I pray your confinement is easy and that the child is healthy and strong. Please give him my love and affection until such time that I may offer it myself.*

*Yours affectionately,*

*Reggie*

Another pain stole over me, and I clutched the letter in my hand as I closed my eyes, lowering my head. I breathed in and out until the pain passed, my fists pressing into my thighs. When it was over, I set the letter back on the side table and collapsed onto my bed in exhaustion.

I'd only had three contractions, and I was already fatigued. How would I withstand hours of this?

Reggie's letter made me wonder if he would be a good father. Could we find a way to move past the tragic way our marriage started? Had Mama felt these things toward Papa in the early years? If she had found a way to love him, could I find a way to love Reggie? It didn't seem possible, yet he was my husband, and I would have to find a way to live with him once he returned to Cumberland Hall. If not for my sake, then for our child's.

Edith returned and helped me into my nightgown. By the time Dr. Aiken arrived several hours later, my body was spent, and my energy was flagging. The pain was unimaginable, but each contraction brought me closer and closer to holding my child in my arms.

"It won't be long now, Lady Cumberland," Dr. Aiken said after he had examined me. "You're doing splendidly."

"It doesn't feel splendid."

He smiled. "I would wager most mothers feel the same as you at this point. But when the child is born, you'll be amazed at how quickly the memory of labor recedes."

I hoped he was right, but I doubted him.

It was after dark when I began to push. Now more than ever, I longed for my mama to be at my side. I could almost imagine her there, comforting and encouraging me, holding my hand when it hurt the worst or when anxiety threatened to overcome me.

I didn't have Mama, but I did have Edith. She stayed with me through the whole ordeal, wiping my brow, whispering encouraging words, and rubbing my arm when I whimpered in pain.

Finally, I gave one last push, and the baby was born.

I cried out in both pain and relief and fell back against the pillows.

Dr. Aiken held the baby, and I opened my eyes to get a first glimpse of her.

"It's a boy," he said with a broad smile. "A large, healthy baby boy."

"A boy?" My mouth slipped open at the announcement. In all my dreaming and anticipating, I had not once contemplated my child being a boy.

"A fine heir for Cumberland Hall," Dr. Aiken said as he rubbed the baby with a clean towel. My son started to cry, and his strong voice filled the room and my heart.

"A boy," I whispered, my joy just as complete as it would have been had the baby been born a girl.

"And a fine, handsome boy he is." Edith wiped a tear from her eye as she smiled down at me. "Well done, milady."

"Thank you, Edith. For everything."

"It's my pleasure."

It took a bit of time for Dr. Aiken and Edith to care for all our needs. Edith gave the baby a sponge bath and then wrapped him in a warm blanket before she finally brought him to me. I was overwhelmed as I took him into my arms for the first time and looked down into his darling face. I knew, even before I looked, that he would not be a time-crosser. There had been no male time-crossers in my family. But I checked, just to make sure.

His chest was unmarked, free and unblemished. Just to be sure, I checked the back of his head as well, with the same result. And he was mine, all mine.

Tears of relief gathered in my eyes, and I pressed him to my shoulder in a hug unlike any other I'd ever given in my life. This baby was a part of me. My own flesh and blood. He was my new family, and I would love and cherish him until the day I died.

"What will he be named?" Edith asked.

"Henry Theodore Reginald Fairhaven," I whispered, almost more to my son than to my maid. "But I shall call him Teddy."

"Future Marquess of Cumberland," Dr. Aiken said as he came up beside Edith to look down at my son. "His future is laid out for him, is it not?"

"Nay," I whispered. "No future is certain."

## WHITBY, NORTH YORKSHIRE, ENGLAND
## OCTOBER 10, 1915

I could hardly take my eyes off Teddy. Every day he was a little different, growing quickly and eating well. He had just turned three weeks old and did little more than sleep and eat, but he was still fascinating. I spent hours just looking at him. Edith often teased me for my attentiveness, claiming that most women in my position would have already sent him off to the nursery and only seen him for an hour each day between tea and supper.

But not me. I had not hired a governess and wasn't certain I would. I had little to occupy my time as it was, and Teddy filled me with joy and purpose. Taking care of his needs was the greatest job I had ever been given, and I wasn't about to hand it off to a stranger.

We were in one of the drawing rooms on a dreary, blustery day, and I was pacing the floor with Teddy, who had been fussy that afternoon. I'd tried to feed him, but he hadn't wanted to eat. I'd changed his nappy, but he still fussed. The only thing that soothed him was bouncing as I walked back and forth across the carpeted floor. This was one of my favorite parlors, near the front of Cumberland Hall. It faced the sea, which was the reason I loved it, and it gave me a good view of the rocky cliffs down the shoreline.

An automobile appeared on the front drive, surprising me

a little. The wind and rain had kept everyone at Cumberland Hall inside today, and it seemed strange that someone would purposely come out in this weather.

Teddy was finally asleep, so I laid him in the pram I kept on the main level for when he napped. Rarely was he away from my side. I knew the staff talked about this, probably writing it off as my strange American ways. I had long since stopped caring what they thought of me.

A fire crackled in the fireplace as I sat on the sofa with a book Edith had retrieved for me from the library. It was still difficult for me to enter that room, though it had become a little easier as time passed and my love for Teddy grew. Had that terrible night not occurred, he wouldn't be here. It didn't erase my pain, but it smoothed the rough edges.

Several minutes later, the door to the drawing room opened, and Mr. Wentworth appeared. His body was stiff, and his long, narrow face was devoid of emotion as he addressed me. "A telegram has just arrived for you, Lady Cumberland."

Everything became still as I met his gaze. I had never received a telegram at Cumberland Hall before. There had been many letters from my parents and friends in America, and even a few messages from people who had stayed here after the raid, but never a telegram.

He crossed the room and lowered a silver tray with the telegram lying upon it. I didn't want to take it, but I could not avoid its news forever.

I slowly set aside my book and reached for the missive, taking the letter opener Mr. Wentworth had placed on the tray beside it. My eyes scanned the envelope, and my heart beat erratically. It was from the Post Office Telegraph and had the word *Telegram* in big bold letters across the front. My hands shook as I slipped the letter opener through the seam and tore it. Paper fibers floated on the air as I slowly set the opener on the tray.

Mr. Wentworth straightened and started to turn away, but I

held out my hand. "No," I said just above a whisper. "Please, don't leave me."

His gaze softened. We'd come a long way, he and I, and he now felt like an ally. Someone I wanted nearby. "As you wish, your ladyship."

I dipped my fingers inside the envelope and pulled out a small piece of white paper folded in half. Setting the envelope on my book, I gently unfolded the telegram, praying with each breath I took. I read it aloud to Mr. Wentworth.

"'To Anna Elizabeth Fairhaven, Marchioness of Cumberland. I regret to inform you that your husband, Captain Reginald Fairhaven, Marquess of Cumberland, was killed in action on October 5th near Champagne, France. A letter to follow.'"

The telegram fell to my lap as I stared straight ahead. Reggie was dead? I felt numb at the news.

"I'm sorry, your ladyship," Mr. Wentworth said. "Deeply sorry for your loss."

I found myself nodding in response, though I hardly knew what he had said. Reggie wasn't supposed to die. He was an aide to the commanding officer. His job was safe, wasn't it? He was only there as a figurehead to recruit more soldiers. How could he have died?

Teddy began to fuss, pulling me out of my daze. I rose and went to him, lifting him into my arms and holding him close.

"Is there anything I can do for you?" Mr. Wentworth asked, his tone gentle and sympathetic.

"No." There would be much to do in the days ahead, but right now all I could think about was comforting my son and coming to terms with the news I'd been given. "Please inform the staff. We'll need to go into full mourning."

The words felt hollow, even to me.

Mr. Wentworth slipped out of the room, and I began to bounce Teddy. I couldn't believe Reggie was gone. I'd sent him a letter the day after our son was born. Had he received it? Had he known he was a father and there was an heir for Cumberland Hall?

"You're the new Marquess of Cumberland," I said to my son as I paced to the window. "And I'm now the dowager."

It seemed strange to say these things to the infant in my arms. He was so tiny and helpless, so incapable of bearing the weight and responsibilities of his title. But I would be there to bear it for him.

"You'll never know your father." A soft breath slipped from my mouth as I said, "I never really knew him, either."

Sadness filled my heart, but not grief. At least, not in the way it had these past few months after leaving Williamsburg. I felt so desensitized to loss. It was all around me, seeming to lurk near every corner.

I held Teddy closer, praying that he would live a long and healthy life. I didn't deserve this favor from God, but I was confident He loved me and would do what was best. Yet I had learned that what was best wasn't always what was easy. In the days following the knowledge of Henry's death, I had asked God to forgive me for trying to change history. I still didn't understand why He had allowed Henry to die, but I had decided to trust God. I would have to leave Teddy in His hands, as well, and trust that He would take care of my son.

Edith soon arrived in the drawing room, her face pale and her eyes wide with sorrow. "I just heard the shocking news. I'm so sorry. What will you do?"

My hand ran over my son's back as I contemplated my options. The fabric of his sleeping gown was soft and warm from his small body. There was only one thing I truly wanted, one thing I was now free to do as a widow and in control of my own life for the first time.

"I want to go home, Edith."

"Home?"

"To America."

Her eyes lit up with joy for a moment, but then they dimmed again. "Will you want me to accompany you?"

"If it pleases you. Do you have other plans?"

Pink tinged her cheeks as she toyed at the edge of the carpet with her shoe. "Williams asked me to marry him."

"Did he?" I smiled, not surprised. "I'm happy for you, Edith."

"I was scared to tell you, because he's been wanting to go to America. I thought I'd have to choose between you."

"And now?" I asked hopefully.

"Now I can tell him we'll all go together."

I nodded at the idea. "I'll need to wait until Teddy is a bit older and I can get all of my affairs in order concerning Cumberland Hall. I'd like to keep some staff here to maintain its operations until Teddy is old enough to choose what he'd like to do."

"Do you think we'll leave this year?"

I considered how long we would be in mourning and how long it might take the solicitor to organize all the details. I also needed to consider the war and Teddy's ability to travel by ocean liner. From what Mama had told me, America wouldn't enter the war for another year and a half. I had my concerns about ocean travel, but there had been no real threats to passenger vessels yet. If we were going to go before America's entry into the fight, we would need to go in the spring. "I think it's safe to say it might not be until May or June."

"That will give us enough time to plan the wedding once our mourning period is over." Edith nodded. "Do you need anything right now?"

I shook my head. "You may go share the news with Williams. I'm sure he'd like to know."

"I will." Edith smiled and left me alone with Teddy.

"Well," I said to him, "it seems we have a new path to take."

I longed to return to America, especially with the war continuing to rage for the next few years. I could be useful there, especially now that I controlled Teddy's fortune.

It would also be good to return home to see my father, and even my mother. I could find my own home wherever I wanted to live. I could come and go whenever I pleased, and I could associate with the people I chose. I could pursue my work with the suffrage movement and campaign for women I wanted to represent me in state and federal legislatures. Perhaps one day I might run for office myself.

A new horizon spread out before me, and though I would miss Cumberland Hall, with its storm-tossed sea and breathless moors, I missed home even more.

It was time to return.

# 28

NEW YORK CITY
JUNE 19, 1916

My parents' brownstone mansion on Fifth Avenue had never looked so welcoming as when we pulled up to the front door on my twenty-second birthday. Edith sat with Teddy and me in the back seat of the automobile, and Williams sat in the front with my parents' driver, who had come to the harbor to collect us. I had loved seeing the Statue of Liberty, the Brooklyn Bridge, and St. Patrick's Cathedral again, but it was the familiar sight of William Tecumseh Sherman's statue on the corner of Central Park that really made me feel at home.

"I'll see that your things are returned to your old room," Edith said.

The driver opened the door for me, and I stepped out of the automobile holding Teddy, who was now nine months old. He had my green eyes and my curly brown hair. There was very little about him that reminded me of Reggie, for which I was grateful. I had resolved to put the past behind me and look to the future, and it was easier to do without constant reminders.

"Lady Cumberland," Mr. Pierson said as he opened the front

door for me, "welcome home." His gaze lit on Teddy, and he grinned. "And look at this young chap. Why, he looks just like you."

"He does, doesn't he?" I smiled. "It's good to see you, Mr. Pierson."

"And you, my lady."

"None of that," I said. "Miss Libby will do."

"I could never." He straightened, appearing to take offense, but I knew otherwise.

I entered the receiving hall, and all the sights and smells of the house returned to me. The dark wood gleamed and the rugs looked new, but everything else was exactly the same.

"Libby?" Father came out of the library down the hall. "Is that you?"

"'Tis me." For I truly felt like Libby again.

He grinned as he held out his arms to embrace Teddy and me in a hug. "And is this my strapping grandson?"

I presented my son to my father. Teddy was teething, so he had his hand in his mouth and drool dripping down his chin, but when he saw his grandfather, he pulled out his hand and grinned, waving his fist in excitement.

"He's a handsome, fine young fellow," Father said, reaching for him. "What an honor to meet him."

Father had aged in the past two years. He was greyer about his temples and had more lines around his eyes, but he looked hearty and hale.

I had never been so happy to see him in my life.

"Oh, Libby," he said as he put one arm around me, "I've missed you more than you'll ever know. It's so good to have you back. You'll stay with us, won't you? Permanently?"

I shook my head, a sad smile on my face. "Only until I can secure my own home. I think it would be best if Teddy and I had some space to call our own."

He studied me for a moment and then nodded. "I won't press

you any more on the subject. You just let me know what I can do to help. Do you know where you want to live?"

"I'm not certain," I conceded, "but I don't think I'll stay in the city. I'm drawn to smaller towns and villages, and I miss the ocean already. I'll know the place when I find it."

Mother Wells appeared at the top of the stairs and paused as she looked down at us. Our gazes locked, and my old insecurities tried to gain control of me again. I forced my chin up and my shoulders back. The entire voyage across the Atlantic, I had anticipated this moment of reckoning, for that was precisely what I had in mind. I did not intend to remove my hat or gloves until I addressed the past. It was the only way to move beyond the pain and heartache she had brought into my life.

Something in her gaze shifted, and she frowned. Had she noticed the change in my attitude and demeanor? Did she recognize the determination in my eyes?

She descended the stairway in regal style. "Hello, Elizabeth," she said when she reached the bottom.

"Hello, Mother." There was no affection between us. Like my father, she had aged, but she wore her age with grace and dignity, carrying herself well.

"And is this Henry?" she asked.

"I call him Teddy."

She let out a puff of air. "Oh, you and your pet names. I don't see why you would name him one thing and call him another."

I smiled to myself. "Yes, me and my pet names."

Mother didn't offer to take Teddy, but she did put her hand on his head. "He is a beautiful child."

"Thank you."

"He looks like you."

I didn't know if she realized she had complimented me, but I decided to accept it as one.

"How long do you plan to stay in America?" she asked.

"Indefinitely."

Her eyebrows rose. "You won't return to Cumberland Hall?"

"There's nothing there for me. One day, if Teddy chooses to return, I will gladly go with him and visit, but I want to make a life for us here."

"Whatever for?"

It was remarkable how much had changed in me since I left here almost two years ago. No longer did Mother Wells have control over my future or the plans I made. And no longer did I worry about what she thought of me. She couldn't win any more battles.

"America is home," I told her. "This is where I belong and where I want my son to grow up."

"But he's English."

"He's Teddy," I amended. "And he will be free to choose whatever he wants to be."

Mother huffed at my statement but could not refute it. The first battle had been won.

"You'll live here with us, of course," she said next.

"Only until I find my own home."

"You are welcome to stay here as long as you like," Father said, handing Teddy his watch fob, a grin on his face.

"There will be so many luncheons and social engagements for you," Mother said. "Everyone will be eager to host the Marchioness of Cumberland."

I wasn't eager to attend those functions, but I would if it meant building connections with people at the forefront of causes that mattered to me. Now that I was in charge of my own fortune, I would have the luxury of donating to the organizations that did the most good. But I wouldn't limit my work to writing a check. I planned to be in the places where people gathered and where they needed help.

"I will attend the events that suit me," I said.

"You mean to say you will attend the events that are the

most advantageous for you and your son." She clasped her hands together. "I've been compiling a list. I'll tell you which ones to prepare for."

The staff had gone their separate ways, and it was just Mother, Father, Teddy, and me in the front hall. The moment had come, though this might not be the ideal place to broach the subject. How did I convey a lifetime of hurt? How did I tell her what she had done to me in one short conversation?

"Your list won't be necessary." I lifted my chin and addressed her directly so she wouldn't misunderstand me. "From this moment on, I will be the one in control of our future." I licked my dry lips and forced myself to continue. "You spent my entire life dictating my every move, never once asking me what I wanted, but that will now stop."

She stared at me but did not make a move to respond.

I looked at Father, and he gave me an almost indiscernible nod to continue.

"I don't know if we will ever move beyond the past," I said to her, "but I would like to try. For your grandson's sake, if not ours. The best way to start is for you to realize you do not control my life any longer."

She did not say a word, but her jaw tightened, and I knew my words had upset her. How could they not, after so long in control?

"If you want to be a part of our lives," I continued, "then you must let me do what I think is best for Teddy and me."

It was her turn to lift her chin. "Everything I did, I did for your happiness and promotion, Elizabeth. I never once intended to hurt you or cause you pain. If I did, then I'm sorry."

My mouth slipped open as I studied her. She had never apologized to me before. And though she did not take responsibility for her actions, she had conceded that she might have caused me pain.

It was a start.

## NEW YORK CITY
## JUNE 30, 1916

"You must relax," Mother said as I fidgeted in the automobile next to her and Father.

"I've never left him alone before."

"He'll be fine. Edith is like a second mother to him."

I sighed. Mother was right. It had been almost two weeks since we'd returned to New York, and this was the first night I'd agreed to attend a social function with Mother and Father, a dinner party at the home of John and Abby Rockefeller. I'd never left Teddy in anyone else's care for longer than an hour or two and had never left him to travel to another location. Not that the Rockefellers' home on West Fifty-Fourth Street was terribly far. Less than seven city blocks separated us, but it felt like an ocean.

"You need to enjoy yourself," Mother said to me. "You're much too attached to that child. It's not healthy for either of you. You'll need to secure a governess as soon as possible. But first and foremost, you must start to look for your next husband."

I readjusted my long white gloves. My diamond bracelet caught on the fabric, and I had to disentangle it. "Remember, Mother, I am in charge of my own future, and I have no wish to marry again."

"Nonsense. Every woman wishes to be married."

I shook my head. "Every woman wishes to be loved, but that doesn't necessarily mean she wishes to be married."

"You and your newfangled ideas." She harrumphed. "You've let your freedom go to your head. Don't you want a home and a family?"

"I have a family," I said. "And someday soon, I'll have a home."

"Don't you want companionship?"

It was Father's turn to harrumph, and I smiled.

"I long to be loved, Mother." I laid my hands in my lap as the driver pulled up to the most impressive mansion in New York City. The Rockefellers had finished it three years ago and had spared no expense. It was enormous and beautiful.

"You must always be thinking of your social status, Elizabeth."

"I'm the Marchioness of Cumberland," I responded. "What more could I want where social status is concerned?"

"You exasperate me to no end."

I laughed, enjoying this newfound banter with my mother. Over the past two weeks our relationship had started to shift. When she reverted back to her old ways, I simply reminded her that she no longer had the power to control my destiny. She still tried, but it was easier to foil her attempts.

With her need to oversee every aspect of my life out of the way, she had begun to relax—just barely. And I was slowly beginning to discover some of the mutual interests we shared.

Father seemed to enjoy this ease in tension, too. As he got out of the automobile and offered me his hand, he gave me a wink.

The party was a glittering display of wealth and the height of society. It was good to be back among people I'd known most of my life. Everyone was eager to hear news of the war in England and my life as an aristocrat.

There was talk of America entering the European fray, but opinions were strongly divided. Some felt we should put America first and not worry about wars in foreign lands, while others felt that joining the war was imminent, and we should get involved now, before it escalated further.

Daily life in New York had not changed, but there was a heaviness in the air, much like I had experienced in Williamsburg leading up to the American Revolution. Fear and uncertainty tainted almost everything we did. This night at the Rockefeller home was no different. There was a weight upon the evening, though several people tried hard to push the conversation to the wayside whenever it was brought up.

At dinner, I was seated next to Mr. Rockefeller, indicating I was the highest-ranked guest at the event. It was an honor, but one I didn't deserve. There was nothing special about me except that I was forced to marry a marquess. In my heart, I was nothing more than Libby Conant, a public printer from a small press in Williamsburg, Virginia. I hadn't even been important enough to be considered a suitable wife for Henry Montgomery. But here, in this time and place, I was seated at the right hand of one of the wealthiest and most influential men in America, elevated above the likes of the Vanderbilts, Roosevelts, and Astors.

"Lady Cumberland," Mr. Rockefeller said as the meal began, "how do you like being home?"

I hadn't spoken to him much before we sat down to eat, but I had his full attention now—and the attention of several other men present.

And why wouldn't I? I was a wealthy widow—a wealthy *titled* widow.

"I've enjoyed it very much," I said. "I missed America."

"I'm quite fond of her myself," he said with a smile. "Though there is much we can do to help her."

John D. Rockefeller Jr.'s philanthropic work was widely known and celebrated. He gave millions to social reform and had recently established the Bureau of Social Hygiene to research issues pertinent to the health and well-being of New York citizens. I found myself talking to him about several causes I wished to champion. The conversation was invigorating and stimulating, and he told me I must talk to his wife, Abby, who shared many of my passions.

"Your work goes beyond New York, if I'm not mistaken," I said to him.

"Yes." He smiled as he took a sip of his water. "I've recently been approached by a man named Reverend Dr. Goodwin. Have you met him?"

"I'm afraid not."

"He's an Episcopal priest and author. An extraordinary man. He lives here in New York but was a rector in Williamsburg, Virginia, for several years and oversaw the restoration of the Bruton Parish Church some nine or ten years ago."

My attention was sharpened at the mention of Williamsburg and the Bruton Parish Church. I had never heard of the Reverend Dr. Goodwin, but I was very interested to learn more.

"He is passionate about Williamsburg," Mr. Rockefeller continued. "He's taught me so much. I was impressed to learn about Jefferson's and Washington's connections to the town and their involvement in the days leading up to the war."

"I'm quite familiar with the history," I said with a wide smile, knowing my face was glowing at the mention of my old home.

"I'm happy to hear it. Our young people must never forget our past. Dr. Goodwin and I both share a passion to preserve our history. Many of the original buildings and homes in Williamsburg are beginning to deteriorate, and several have already collapsed. It would be a travesty to lose such an important piece of our past."

"I couldn't agree with you more. Does Dr. Goodwin have a plan?"

"He does, though it will be a long process, if it succeeds at all. He envisions creating a foundation to restore the town and one day hopes to operate it like a large museum or living memorial."

"Truly?" My pulse sped up at the idea. "Is he looking for sponsors to help?"

"He is always looking for financiers and has spent years soliciting for help. J. P. Morgan was one of his early supporters when he was restoring Bruton Parish Church."

"I would love to become involved." The idea sparked a fervor in my breast that I hadn't felt since I'd left 1775 behind.

"Splendid. We have a trip planned there next month. Dr. Goodwin would like to give Abby and me a tour, and I've invited some other possible investors. If you'd like to join us, I would be happy to introduce you to Dr. Goodwin."

Excitement bubbled up in my stomach, and I found myself nodding like an enthusiastic schoolgirl. I could not wait to return to Williamsburg, though I cautioned myself that it would be much altered and perhaps difficult to accept. One hundred and forty-one years had passed since I'd lived there with Mama and the girls. Time and the elements would have done a lot of damage, but the essence of the town would still be intact, and so too would my memories.

I began to count down the days to our visit, starting to understand the reason for my return to America and the purpose my life would take in the years ahead.

# 29

## WILLIAMSBURG, VIRGINIA
## JULY 21, 1916

If I had thought leaving Teddy behind and traveling seven blocks was difficult, it was nothing compared to leaving him in New York City while I traveled to Williamsburg with John and Abby Rockefeller three weeks later. Though Abby was twice my age, she and I soon became boon companions.

We traveled by rail to Virginia and slept at an inn on the outskirts of town. The next morning, the Reverend Dr. Goodwin arrived with two automobiles to take us into the heart of historic Williamsburg.

There were two gentlemen with Dr. Goodwin, one of whom was a pleasant surprise.

"Congressman Hollingsworth!" I said with delight when we were reintroduced. I couldn't believe it was him.

"Miss Wells—or should I say Lady Cumberland?" The congressman took my gloved hand in his and grasped it affectionately. "How good to see you again, my dear. I have thought about you often since our time on the RMS *Olympic*."

Though it had been over two years since we traveled together, he had never been far from my thoughts. Now that my path was secure, there was so much I longed to discuss with him, though it would have to wait until we could speak to each other alone.

He had come as a possible financier and representative from Virginia, along with another man, Mr. Gartshore, who was a financier from Philadelphia. Mr. Gartshore was short and direct, with a nervous tic in his left eyebrow, whereas Congressman Hollingsworth was just as warm and congenial as I remembered him.

They couldn't have been more different.

The inn was just over a mile from Duke of Gloucester Street, and it would take us very little time to get there. I pressed my hands together as we drove, pretending to listen to Abby but fully engaged with the sights and sounds around me. The weather was nearly perfect, with a bright blue sky and a smattering of clouds.

The automobiles came to a stop near the Wren Building of the College of William and Mary, not far from the Palace Green. I was shocked to see how the campus had changed in the years since the American Revolution. There were several new buildings alongside the older ones. It was still a glorious institution and the second-oldest college in America.

After a lengthy tour of the campus by Dr. Goodwin, he directed us to eat luncheon on the lawn outside the Wren Building, facing Duke of Gloucester Street. It was a splendid day to eat out of doors, with nary a breeze, and I wore a comfortable walking suit with a large hat to keep the sun out of my eyes. I wanted nothing more than to get into the heart of Williamsburg and see the town, but I didn't want to be rude. I had waited this long. I could wait another hour or two.

I was seated between Congressman Hollingsworth and Mr. Gartshore, while Abby was seated between her husband and Dr. Goodwin. While the Rockefellers and Mr. Gartshore spoke to Dr. Goodwin, Congressman Hollingsworth engaged me in conversation.

"What a treat it is to see you again," he said as he removed his napkin from the table and laid it on his lap. "I've followed your journey in the newspapers and was surprised when I learned of your marriage to the Marquess of Cumberland soon after we returned to New York. I had the pleasure of meeting your husband when I was in England."

"Really? I had not realized your connection to him." There was so much I longed to say, but with the others close by, it would have to wait.

"Our acquaintance was brief, only a meeting or two." He nodded at the waiter who placed a bowl of tomato soup in front of him. "How is Lord Cumberland?"

I pressed my lips together for a moment. "I'm afraid he was killed in battle."

"Oh, my dear." His voice was stricken as he gently touched my hand. "I'm so very sorry."

"You have no need to be."

"That must be the reason you've returned to America."

I nodded.

"Have you been to Williamsburg before?"

"I have," I said, relieved that he had changed the subject. "But it's been many years, if you know what I mean."

"Ah." He nodded with understanding. "I do, indeed."

I dipped my spoon into my steaming bowl of soup and smiled, unable to contain my excitement at the idea of sharing more with him.

"It's wonderful that you've taken an interest." The congressman's blue eyes were admiring, though in the same fatherly way he had regarded me on the *Olympic*. "I imagine this project is very dear to your heart."

"Very much so." I took a sip of my soup. It was thick and creamy with a bit of a tanginess to it. "How did you get involved?"

"My son is a professor here at William and Mary, and he's

good friends with Dr. Goodwin. He was the first to tell me about the idea that Dr. Goodwin and Mr. Rockefeller have hatched."

"I'm eager to hear more of their plan." I longed to share Williamsburg with the world.

When we were done with luncheon, Dr. Goodwin suggested we walk into town, and my heart began to pound with anticipation. Congressman Hollingsworth walked beside me, his interest in Williamsburg almost as keen as mine.

"I thought perhaps we'd start with one of the properties currently for sale," Dr. Goodwin suggested, "and then walk down the length of Duke of Gloucester Street, with a stop at the Magazine and courthouse."

We walked past the Palace Green, and I glanced toward the palace, thinking about the balls I had attended there. My heart broke when I saw that the once-glorious building was gone.

"What happened to the Governor's Palace?" I asked Dr. Goodwin.

Everyone turned to look where I was indicating.

"After the last Royal Governor, Lord Dunmore, fled from Williamsburg on June 8, 1775, the place became home to a colonial mayor. After that, it was home to the two post-colonial governors, Patrick Henry and Thomas Jefferson, until the capital was moved to Richmond in 1780," Dr. Goodwin explained as we walked. "It burned a year later while it was being used as a hospital for American soldiers during the revolution."

"How horrible." It was but the first of several buildings I would find much altered or destroyed, I was sure.

We drew closer to the print shop and my old home. I saw a glimpse of it, and my heart soared. It was still intact, though run-down and in need of attention. Thankfully, the roof looked sound, the windows looked sturdy, and the brick was still holding strong. Weeds grew up from the foundation, and the lawn was overgrown.

I could almost imagine the wassailers at Christmastide, the busyness of merchants up and down Duke of Gloucester Street while the burgesses met, and the loud noises and intense smells on market day. Everything was coming back to me as if I were here just yesterday.

"This is the house I was referencing," Dr. Goodwin said as we came to a stop outside my old home. "It was originally built in 1755 by planter Philip Ludwell and then later purchased by Edward Conant, public printer and owner of the *Virginia Gazette*."

My chest filled with pride at hearing Papa's name, but even more so when Dr. Goodwin spoke about Mama next.

"When Mr. Conant died in 1774, his wife and daughter, Theodosia and Elizabeth, took over the press and became the first female public printers in Virginia."

Abby gave me a look that indicated she was impressed with the idea of female printers. I could only smile.

"Sadly, Elizabeth died the following year, and Mistress Conant remarried a cobbler, selling the printing press to her journeyman, Louis Preston. He was run out of Williamsburg during the war, and the house was sold to the Paradise family after that."

So Louis had not made a success of the newspaper. I couldn't say I was sorry.

"Do you know what happened to Mistress Conant and her family after they left here?" I asked, knowing it would be unlikely that Dr. Goodwin was familiar with their history.

"I do, indeed." He pushed his glasses up the bridge of his nose. "It's quite remarkable, actually. Mistress Conant, who married Alpheus Goodman, left a detailed diary dedicated to her daughter, Elizabeth, whom she called Libby. She wrote it as if she were writing a long letter to Libby after Libby's death. It's kept at the College of William and Mary. It's full of the most amazing details and is one of the books we've studied at great length to learn the history of Williamsburg. Congress-man Hollingsworth's son, Dr. Hollingsworth, has preserved it and keeps it in his office. I'm certain we could arrange a special viewing of it, if you'd like."

I stared at Dr. Goodwin for several moments, absorbing the things he'd just said to me. Mama had left me a diary? A letter written to me after I left them? Tears gathered in my eyes, and I had to bite my lips to keep them from trembling. I was torn between wanting to continue the tour and wanting to run back to the college to read her book.

But Dr. Goodwin had already moved on. "I've arranged for us to tour this building today," he said. "I believe I can purchase this property for a reasonable sum if we decide to pursue this venture."

He opened the door, and a thousand memories flooded my mind. I almost expected to see Mama standing in the hallway to greet us with a wide smile. But as we stepped inside, there was no one to receive us but shadows from the past.

It was bittersweet to walk through the dusty office, into the sitting room full of cobwebs, and up the stairs to the room I shared with Hannah and Rebecca. I stood at the window in Mama's room, looking out at the town, reliving the best years of my life and counting down the minutes until I could see her diary.

Dr. Goodwin meandered through the house with the others, but I stayed back in each room, taking my time and allowing my heart to reconnect with the space. The printing room had long since been turned into a modern kitchen, Papa's handprint painted over. Gone were the press, the rags, the paper and ink. But it was not difficult for me to see it all in my mind. I closed my eyes and could almost hear the thumping of the press, smell the moist paper, and feel the sticking of the ink pads against the type.

When the others went out to the backyard, I followed them.

The kitchen building was gone, looking like it had burned at some point, but the large elm tree still stood, tall and proud.

It was there that Henry came alive to me. A day had not passed that I had not thought of him and longed for him. My heart still ached at his memory. I recalled the last time I saw him over a year ago, as we said our final good-byes and he'd walked down the back path to the gate.

The yard was now a tangled mess. I pushed aside some weeds and found remnants of Mama's tulips, irises, and roses. Touching them felt like a soft caress from her gentle hands. The vegetable gardens were now fields of waving grass, with little to mark Mariah and Abraham's work.

"I'm quite taken with this place," Abby said as she stood beside me and looked back at the house. "I've been looking for a place to house my American Folk Art collection, and what better place than this? Many of the pieces were created right here in Virginia."

"It would be remarkable," I said, not knowing what else to add. It seemed strange to think of our home as an art museum.

She followed her husband and Dr. Goodwin as they walked back around the side of the house. Mr. Gartshore and Congressman Hollingsworth followed at a slower pace, talking to each other in low tones.

But I wasn't ready to leave my home just yet. I needed a minute to indulge in the memories. In a way, this project Dr. Goodwin had proposed felt like a bridge between my two paths. I would return here often, I was certain, but seeing time wear away at this place was a good reminder that my work should not simply be material and earthly, but for eternity's sake.

I stood under the elm tree and looked up into its leaves, allowing a wave of emotions to envelope me. They no longer held grief and sorrow alone but were mingled with joy and gladness.

A movement caught my eye, and I lowered my gaze to look

toward the back of the property where a man walked down the narrow path from the old, broken gate.

There was something familiar in the cut of his shoulders and the confidence in his stride. He was tall, with dark brown hair under his grey fedora. His shoulders were broad, and his figure was trim. He wore a grey suit and carried a briefcase in one hand.

The closer he drew, the more my heart pounded and the less I believed what I was seeing.

At the edge of the backyard, he came to a sudden halt, and his brilliant blue eyes met mine with a stunned expression.

I was looking at Henry Montgomery, and he was looking back at me.

# 30

We stared at each other for a long time. The wind blew against me like a gentle kiss, but it all seemed like a dream. This couldn't be Henry. Henry was long gone.

But he looked just like Henry, and the way he studied me, as if he were seeing an apparition, told me that he recognized me too.

We moved toward each other, seemingly drawn together by an invisible string. We met near the trunk of the elm tree, and I held my breath.

"Libby?" His voice sounded so much like Henry's—and he knew my name. A frown tilted his brow as he shook his head. "Is it you?"

I couldn't seem to find my voice, but I nodded.

"How? Am I dreaming?" He looked around the backyard and then turned his beautiful blue eyes on me again. "Are you truly here?"

"Henry." His name finally released from my mouth on a breath, and I rushed into his arms.

He dropped his briefcase and wrapped me in an embrace so powerful, it took my breath away. I didn't know why or how he was standing here, but I didn't care. It was Henry, and he was alive and well.

"Libby," he said again as he pulled back and put his hands on my face. "My dear, sweet, beautiful Libby."

"What is happening?" I asked him with a disbelieving laugh. "Why are you here?"

"I'm here to join a tour group with my father and the Rockefellers."

"Your father?" I was so confused.

"Congressman Hollingsworth."

"Congressman Hollingsworth?" I asked on a hushed breath. Did that mean . . . ? "You're a time-crosser?"

His gaze was incredulous. "How do you—? Are—are *you* a time-crosser?"

All I could do was nod.

"Until a year ago," he said, "I lived both here and in 1775."

"Until your death, you mean. You died in 1775."

His eyes filled with an aching sadness. "You died in 1775, as well, Libby. I thought you were gone forever. I had no idea you were here too."

I put my shaking hand to my head as I tried to make sense of this miracle.

He studied me, disbelief in his voice and gaze. "All this time, we were both crossing between the same years."

"And we never knew." I thought back to the first time I'd met Henry and how I'd felt drawn to him from the start. Our bond had been inexplicable, and now I knew why.

He drew closer to me. "I thought I lost you forever, Libby. You don't know how I've mourned this past year. Your mother wrote a diary for you, but I've kept myself from reading it for years, not wanting to know what happened to you, afraid I would try to change history. But since you died, I have spent the past year reading every page, over and over again. I keep it in my office."

351

"Your office?" I blinked several times. "You're Dr. Hollingsworth—the professor who works at the College of William and Mary."

He nodded.

Everything was happening so fast, and I struggled to fully grasp it all—but one question rose above the others. "Why did you go to Boston when I told you not to?"

"How did you know I shouldn't go?"

"I read about your death in a history book. I forfeited my path three weeks early to try to stop you."

"Oh, Libby." He brought his hand up to my cheek, caressing it with his thumb. His eyes were shadowed under the brim of his hat. "I had to go. I had foreknowledge about my death and knew I could not change my fate—and the truth is, I didn't want to. Not after you died that very next day. I learned about my death while attending college at William and Mary. It's why I fought my love for you so strongly. I knew I would die and you'd be left to grieve me, and it wouldn't have been fair to you. But I couldn't deny my love for you, Libby. It was eating away at me, and I knew if I didn't tell you, I'd regret it for the rest of my existence."

"I knew I was leaving, too. I had planned to stay—wanted to stay, but—" How could I tell him about Teddy? Would he understand? "I was forced to marry in this path, and I discovered I was going to have a baby."

Henry stiffened and lowered his hand, his eyes filling with anguish. "You're married?"

I swallowed and quickly said, "I'm widowed. I didn't want to marry Lord Cumberland, but I had no choice. I was going to leave him on my twenty-first birthday so I could stay in 1775, but then I learned about my son, Teddy, and knew I couldn't. My husband died last year, fighting in France." The words tumbled out in a rush. I wanted desperately for Henry to understand.

He took a step away from me, appearing to grapple with the information.

"I didn't love Reggie. I didn't even really know him." Frustration at the whole situation boiled up within me. "My mother forced the union, and we were parted just days after our wedding when the war broke out." I licked my lips, suddenly feeling parched and desolate. I had caused that pain in Henry's eyes. Pain and disappointment. For the first time, I understood why he hated disappointing me. It was a dreadful feeling. "I didn't want the marriage, or to get pregnant." Memories of Reggie's misuse of me threatened to swallow me again. Tears burned the backs of my eyes as I whispered, "It wasn't by my choice."

"Oh, Libby." Henry returned to me, gathering me in his arms.

I pressed my cheek against his chest, hoping he could forgive me, though I had not been at fault. At least, not for my marriage or pregnancy.

But another thought made my heart stop. "Are you . . . married?"

"Nay." He hugged me tighter. "I have never loved another, and I was content to remain a bachelor for the rest of my life."

"I have a son," I said, love for Teddy filling up the void Reggie had created. "His name is Henry Theodore Reginald Fairhaven."

"You named him after me?" He pulled back, his voice filled with wonder.

"I did. I call him Teddy. He's ten months old and is in New York with my parents. When my husband died, I was left with a fortune, which I'm managing for my son until he comes of age, but I want to invest some of that money here, in Williamsburg. That's why I've come."

"Your husband's name was Lord Cumberland?"

I nodded.

"I remember reading about your wedding in the newspapers. I can hardly believe that was you."

"And I can hardly believe you're you." I smiled as the full understanding finally hit me. "And we're here, together, with nothing standing in our way."

He cradled my face in his hands and kissed me there, under the elm tree in my mama's backyard. For a moment, it felt as if we were in 1775 once again—but we weren't. We were in Williamsburg in 1916, and we were both free. Free to love, to marry, and to spend the rest of our days together.

"Just think," Henry said. "If you had not become pregnant, you would have remained in 1775, and I would have died, and we would have never found each other again. Or if I had listened to you and avoided the path God ordained for me, I would have remained there, and you would be here."

The truth was overwhelming. I thought back to all those hours of grief and mourning when I had railed at God and cried out to Him in my agony, asking why those events had transpired. He had been faithful to listen to me and to hear my cries, yet He had known the end from the beginning. He had known Henry and I would one day cross paths again and that we would do it here, in a time and place where both of us were free to be together.

And in the process, I had been blessed with Teddy.

"God is good," I whispered to Henry. "So very, very good."

He took my hand and drew me along with him. "I want you to meet my father," he said. "He'll never believe I've found my Libby."

"I've met your father, and I have a feeling he knew more than I realized."

---

Henry didn't let go of my hand as we stepped onto Duke of Gloucester Street. We'd never walked down this road hand in hand, yet it felt as natural as if we'd been doing it all our lives.

I still had so many questions for Henry, but there would be time enough to answer them all. I especially wanted to ask him about Mama's diary, but he had other plans at the moment.

Congressman Hollingsworth was standing in front of the Magazine's brick walls, looking over the structure that had already been turned into a small museum, while the others stepped inside.

"Father!" Henry called.

Congressman Hollingsworth turned, and a wide grin lit his face. "I see you've found Libby."

I couldn't suppress my grin, nor did I want to. "You knew, didn't you?"

"I had my suspicions when we met on the *Olympic*," he conceded, joy in his blue eyes—eyes that were remarkably like Henry's. How hadn't I noticed before?

"Why didn't you tell me?" I asked.

"It wasn't my place." He lifted his hands. "If I've learned anything, it's that we must not try to usurp God's plans. Had I told you about Henry, it might have caused both of you to seek your own paths. I knew that if God intended for you to meet again, you would."

I shook my head, marveling at his faith. He was right. Had I known about Henry in this path, I would have made far different choices. I wouldn't have married Lord Cumberland, Father would have been ruined, and Teddy wouldn't have been born.

"What about your son?" Henry asked, as if he knew the course of my thoughts. "Is he a time-crosser?"

"No. He doesn't bear the mark."

"Do you have a mark, as well?"

"I have a sunburst over my heart, the same as Mama and her mother before her."

"Our mark is here." Henry took off his fedora and lifted the hair at the nape of his neck.

"I know." I smiled, recalling how I had realized Congressman Hollingsworth was a time-crosser.

"We are given until the age of twenty-five to choose which path we want to keep," Henry added.

I had wondered, since he had been twenty-three in 1775. "And now we are free to talk about our other paths together." Congressman Hollingsworth put his hand on Henry's shoulder. "I think I should leave you two alone. I'm sure you have a lot to discuss." He approached me and took my hands in his. "I'm so happy you're finally here with us, Libby. I've heard so much about you, and I look forward to getting to know you better."

After he entered the Magazine, Henry and I just looked at each other. I couldn't get enough of him, and I still struggled to believe what had happened. So many memories filled my heart and mind, and I thought about that day when we had said our farewell in Mama's backyard. What if we had known then what we knew now? How differently our paths would have played out.

I was happy I hadn't known.

Henry took a step closer to me, shaking his head in wonder. His eyes were so beautiful and so full of hope and love. He was exactly as he'd been in 1775.

"I want to marry you, Libby. As soon as possible. I don't want to spend another day apart."

"I want the same." I swallowed the worry that suddenly crept up my throat. "But what about Teddy?"

He took my hands and laid them against his beating heart. "I want every part of you, Libby Conant. The joy, the sadness, the blessings, and the pain. I can't wait to meet Teddy, because I know I'm going to love him with all of my heart. He's an extension of you, so how could I not?"

My heart expanded at his words, and I had to force back the tears threatening to fall.

I was done crying. From now on, my life would be one of laughter and joy. I wasn't naïve enough to believe that we would be immune to hardships, but I was confident that if we had survived a separation in 1775 and still found each other in Mama's backyard one hundred and forty-one years later, then there was something much larger than us at work.

We were walking on the path God had ordained, standing in the center of His perfect will, and I never wanted to be anywhere else.

# Epilogue

## WILLIAMSBURG, VIRGINIA
## JANUARY 1, 1921

"It's time, Henry." I placed my hand on his arm, while the other rested on my stomach as a contraction subsided.

He looked up from the paper he was reviewing and took off his spectacles. "The baby?"

"Yes. I think he's going to make his entrance on New Year's Day."

Henry wasted no time in helping me up from the chair I'd been sitting in, reading Mama's diary once again. She had filled it with every detail she could think of, communicating with me in ways that others would never understand. Whenever I missed her, I filled my heart with her words. The book was beginning to fall apart from how much I had handled it.

It was a diary spanning fifty years, until Mama's death in 1825. She'd told me about her happy marriage to Alpheus, Mariah and Abraham's work at the cobbler's shop, Hannah's and Rebecca's growth and eventual marriages. She'd even populated the diary with news about others I had known and loved in Williamsburg. Sophia and her father had eventually changed their minds and supported the Patriots' cause after the

Declaration of Independence had been signed. My dear friend had married and moved to Philadelphia with her husband.

The last page had been written by my sister Rebecca upon Mama's death, and she had inscribed a note sharing Mama's heart.

> She died on this day, March 29, 1825, after living a long and prosperous life. Theodosia Conant-Goodman was a woman of deep and abiding faith, loved and respected by all who knew her. Her joy was contagious, and her belief in all that was good and right inspired us daily. Until the moment she died, she kept the memory of my sister Libby alive for all of us. This book was her love letter to the child she lost too soon.

Henry set aside the diary and walked me out of the study, through the parlor, and up the stairs to our bedroom. The floors creaked as we went, reminding me how old this home had become. We had purchased the Montgomerys' house on the Palace Green and had spent years returning it to its former glory. The study was our favorite room and where we spent the most time together. It was a little haven in our simple world, with a beautiful view of the back gardens that we tended together.

"Send for Edith," I told him, "and Dr. Hutton, please."

"How much time do you think we have?" He gently helped me into our bed, positioning the pillows before taking off my shoes. "Anna arrived less than three hours after your pains began."

"There's no way of knowing." I placed my hand on his cheek and rubbed the worry lines around his mouth with my thumb. "Do not fret, husband. I've been through this twice before."

Teddy and Anna had already been put to bed for the night. At the ages of six and four, they were easily tired from a long day of play. Edith had taken them to the park, and Teddy had tried out the new roller skates he'd received for Christmas, so he was especially exhausted and had barely made it through supper without falling asleep.

"You know it's impossible for me not to worry," Henry said. "Are you certain you wouldn't like to go to the hospital this time?"

"I'm most comfortable at home. This is how Mama had me and her mama before her. I'll be fine. And besides," I continued, "something tells me this won't take long." I hadn't admitted to him that the pains had started about an hour earlier. "Please get Edith and send for the doctor."

He kissed me and then left the room.

I settled into the bed, trying to make myself comfortable for the ordeal ahead. The Montgomery Home, as it was called by those who were working to restore Colonial Williamsburg with us, was the perfect house for our growing family. We were not far from the ocean I loved, and we were close to Henry's work and the buildings we were helping to acquire for the foundation. The Rockefellers had been generous contributors, and it looked as if Dr. Goodwin's dream would become a reality.

As for Henry, I sometimes pitied that his students, both male and female now, had no idea they were being educated about the American Revolution by a man who had lived and breathed the start of the war and had been hanged for treason. He taught his class with passion and zeal, but no one would ever be able to guess where it originated.

Nor would they ever guess that I had been there too. I was simply Libby Hollingsworth now, the content wife of a professor, a passionate supporter of women's equality, and the mother of two beautiful children.

Soon to be three.

Another contraction wrapped around my waist as I thought about this child. Would he or she be a time-crosser? Neither Teddy nor Anna had been born with the markings, much to our relief. If we continued to have children, we might not be so fortunate with all of them, yet we longed to fill our home and lives with children. They were one of life's greatest blessings and a natural extension of the love we shared. I prayed for this child fervently, that no matter what God chose for his or her life, they would know and trust Him.

Another contraction came just a minute after the last. I was getting close. There might not be enough time for the doctor to come.

Edith appeared with fresh towels and a basin of water. "Are you ready?"

I nodded as the contraction gripped me.

She set down her things and came to my side to push back my hair, her own pregnancy noticeable. I was so thankful she had been with me at each birth. She and Williams had taken a home nearby, and she came to work for me during the day. I had insisted she stop calling me miss or milady and asked her simply to call me Libby. We were friends, first and foremost.

I labored for another half hour before Henry returned with Dr. Hutton, and with Henry on one side of me and Edith on the other, I brought our second daughter into the world.

"It's a girl," Dr. Hutton said as he held her up.

My exhilaration fell at seeing her chest. There, over her heart, was a sunburst birthmark. The reality crashed upon me harder than I expected.

"She has your marking," Edith said with a smile, not comprehending what it meant.

Somewhere, in a place I would not know until she was old enough to tell me, she was being born into a different family in a different year.

I looked up at Henry, and he gave me a slight nod, understanding, love and compassion filling his gaze. Tears gathered in my eyes as Dr. Hutton took care of our needs and Edith cleaned the baby.

"It will be okay," Henry said, sitting close to me on the bed and rubbing one of my hands. "God is sovereign, Libby. We know that full well."

I drew strength from him, choosing to believe what he was saying.

The doctor was soon finished, and everything was put to rights. Edith wrapped the baby in a blanket and brought her to my arms.

"You'll never guess," she said with a bit of wonder. "I found another mark on her."

I cradled my daughter in my arms but looked up at Edith in alarm. "What do you mean?"

"There." She pointed to the back of my daughter's head. "She has the exact same birthmark."

My heart pounded wildly as I gently lifted my daughter to examine the back of her tiny head—and there it was, another mark, just like Henry's.

"I'll leave you in privacy," Edith said, then stepped out of the room.

"Well done, Mrs. Hollingsworth," Dr. Hutton said. "Take your time and get plenty of rest. I'll return in the morning to check on both of you."

Henry rose to shake his hand and then closed the door behind the doctor. He stood for a moment and just looked at me.

"What does it mean?" I whispered.

"I don't know." He came back to the bed and sat down beside us. "And I don't think we'll know for many years to come."

I held our daughter as I gazed down at her. She was beautiful, with dark hair and a perfect complexion. Her eyes were closed, but her lips pursed into a little pucker, revealing identical dimples in each of her cheeks. My heart filled with love overflowing, yet I couldn't shake the uneasiness in my spirit over the marks she bore.

It was one thing to carry a single birthmark—but to carry two of them?

"What will we call her?" Henry asked as he caressed the baby's cheek with the back of his finger.

"Margaret Theodosia Hollingsworth," I told him. "But we'll call her Maggie."

"Maggie." Henry smiled and then leaned down and placed a kiss on her cheek. "May God bless and keep you, Maggie. May God's face shine upon you, may He be kind to you and give you peace."

We sat there, memorizing the lines of her delicate face, looking in awe at the perfection of her fingers and toes, and marveling at the gift of her life.

Neither one of us broached the subject of her markings again. Not for a long time.

# Author's Note

I wrote the first draft of *When the Day Comes* in December of 2020 while ill with COVID-19. Thankfully, my illness was mild, and I was able to write for hours on end, with nowhere to go and nothing else to do. While I was sick, though, I discovered a tumor at the back of my throat. My doctor told me that tumors like mine are cancerous over fifty percent of the time and that we would need to remove it as soon as possible. Because of the holidays, I had to wait several weeks for the surgery, and then a week after that for the biopsy results.

Amidst the worries and fears of those difficult weeks, I finished the last chapters of this story. As you read *When the Day Comes*, you saw the sovereignty of God permeating the pages, especially at the end. I had the story plotted long before discovering the tumor, but as I wrote the final scenes, God spoke to my heart, just as He spoke to Libby's—reassuring me that no matter what happened, His perfect plan would still be in place, and even if it didn't turn out how I hoped, I could trust Him.

Finishing this story was one of the hardest things I've ever had to do, but it was also one of the most beautiful experiences of my life. As I laid my fears at God's feet and offered up my words as an act of worship, He met me on the page. I was able to weave together the finishing touches while He infused hope into my heart.

I was so thankful when the biopsy came back benign. Though the news isn't always good for everyone, I've learned that no matter the path we are called to take, God does not leave us or forsake us. That is the hope we hold dearest of all.

As I reread this story during edits, and now share it with the world, it is yet another reminder that my time is in His hands. I pray that you are comforted by this same knowledge.

# Historical Note

When people hear the premise of *When the Day Comes*, many ask me what genre it falls under. Is it split-time, speculative, time-travel? Yes, I suppose it is all of those things, but to me, it's historical fiction—times two.

One of the reasons I chose to set this book in Colonial Williamsburg and Gilded Age New York and England is because of their contrast. In 1774, Libby is fighting for independence from England, and in 1914, her mother is trying to reestablish a foothold in the English aristocracy.

I tried to keep both eras as accurate as possible, but there were a few liberties I needed to take. First, Libby and her mother were inspired by the first female public printer in Virginia, Clementina Rind. The Rind family lived in the Ludwell-Paradise House, which is the house I use for Libby and her mother, and ran one of the many *Virginia Gazette*s. When Clementina's husband died in 1773, she was left to raise five children on her own. In May 1774, on the eve of the Revolution, she was awarded the public printing contract by the House of Burgesses, and was the first to print Thomas Jefferson's pamphlet, *A Summary View of the Rights of British America*. Sadly, she died in late 1774. After her death, her printing rival Purdie & Dixon, who ran another *Virginia Gazette,* memorialized her with this: "[she was] a lady of singular merit, and universally esteemed." From all accounts, Clementina was an amazing woman. I hope I was able to honor her through Libby and Theodosia Conant's characters.

Henry Montgomery is completely fictional and should bear no resemblance to a real person from history. I did, however, try to create a strong hero who could move comfortably alongside men like Washington, Jefferson, and Governor Dunmore. I chose for Henry to be the Clerk of Court, so he could have more interaction with Libby, however, the real Clerk of Court during the 1774 meeting of the House of Burgesses was George Wythe. Wythe was a lawyer and the clerk from 1768 to the Revolution. He went on to represent Virginia in the Continental Congresses in 1775 and 1776, and became a signer of the Declaration of Independence.

Just like in the story, restoring Colonial Williamsburg was the lifelong dream of Dr. William Archer Rutherford Goodwin. In 1905, as the rector at Bruton Parish Church, he began the restoration of the church building. In my story, I have the Rockefellers visiting Williamsburg with Libby and Dr. Goodwin in 1916. Though Dr. Goodwin had dreamed of restoring the whole town as early as 1905, he didn't meet John D. Rockefeller Jr. until 1924, and Rockefeller didn't visit Williamsburg with Dr. Goodwin until 1926, when he and his wife Abby brought along their five sons. Later that year, on another trip to Williamsburg, Rockefeller finally agreed to help Dr. Goodwin realize his dream. Over the past century, Colonial Williamsburg has become a leader in living history museums and programming.

The other bit of history that needed a little alteration is in Whitby. I love that region, and I wanted Libby to live there and experience the bombardment on December 16, 1914. I could not find a manor house on the cliffs of the North Sea, so I created Cumberland Hall. It is inspired by Flintham Hall in Nottinghamshire, complete with the Crystal Palace–inspired glass conservatory and two-story library.

One more piece of history that completely enthralls me is the American Dollar Princesses. Those who enjoy *Downton Abbey* might remember that Lady Grantham was an American heiress who married Lord Grantham and brought a significant amount of money into their marriage to save Downton. In Gilded Age America, this was an increasingly common practice for the newly rich who were trying to break into high society—and for the British nobility who were losing their homes and fortunes. It's estimated that over two hundred American heiresses married into the British aristocracy, bringing with them over twenty-five billion dollars in dowry. Some were love matches, but the majority were arranged marriages where the bride had little to no say. One of the most famous was Consuelo Vanderbilt, who was the inspiration for parts of Libby's story in 1914. Consuelo married the Duke of Marlborough on November 6, 1895. She was in love with another man and wept under her veil at her wedding. She eventually divorced the duke in 1921. It's interesting to note that Winston Churchill's mother, Jennie Jerome, was an American Dollar Princess, as was Princess Diana's grandmother, Frances Ellen Work.

As an author, I love to write a compelling story. As a historian, I long to share real history in a way that intrigues people to dig deeper. It is my hope that I have done both in *When the Day Comes*.

# Acknowledgments

Most authors claim that writing is a solitary pursuit, and while that's mostly true, it's also a little misleading. Yes, as I write the story, I am usually sitting alone at my desk with just my thoughts and my computer, but I am never truly alone. I could not write without a community of friends, family, and colleagues who stand by my side. There are so many people who help an author get their books into the hands of a reader, but for brevity's sake (if you know me, you might be laughing at that), I will only name a handful.

My road to publishing this story was long and winding, but it allowed me to cross paths with some of the most amazing people I've ever known. I want to say a special thank-you to Erica Vetsch, my museum partner, writing buddy, and "person-I-tell-everything-to." To Lindsay Harrel, Alena Tauriainen, and Melissa Tagg, my early critique group and retreat buddies. To Susan May Warren and Laura Frantz, who spoke life into my writing and mentored me from the start. To my agents, Mary Keeley and Wendy Lawton of Books & Such Literary Management, who believed in me and have represented me and my writing with pride. To the countless other friends, both writers and readers, near and far, who cheer me on and read my stories, and my MN NICE ACFW group. I truly couldn't do it without you.

I want to say a big thank-you to my team at Bethany House! It's been a dream of mine to work with Bethany House since I first read *Love Comes Softly* at the age of eleven. I'll never forget turning that book over, seeing the Bethany House logo for the first time, and being excited that Bethany House was in Minnesota where I lived. I spent a lifetime looking for that logo on the spine of all the books I checked out at the library, and it's an honor to know it will be on my book next. To my editors, Jessica Sharpe and Elizabeth Frazier, my marketing lead, Brooke Vikla, and the others who work behind the scenes: thank you for this opportunity.

I want to offer a special shout-out to Colonial Williamsburg and the amazing job they do of preserving such an important piece of our nation's history. If you haven't had a chance to visit, it's well worth the trip. I went there in the spring of 2019, not knowing that I would set a story there, and was completely enthralled. *When the Day Comes* was written during the height of the pandemic, and the videos and livestreaming events Colonial Williamsburg hosted were priceless for my research. They're still available online, so be sure to check them out.

And finally, on a more personal level, I would like to thank my friends and family who are not part of the writing world but are part of the fabric of my daily life. I want to especially thank my dad and mom, George and Cathy VanRisseghem, who have always taught me that I could do anything I set my mind to, and my good friends and neighbors who listen to me prattle on and on about my passion for history and writing around the campfire.

My biggest thank-you is reserved for my husband, David,

and my four children, Ellis, Maryn, Judah, and Asher. The only dream I've had longer than being a writer was being a wife and mom. To all their sacrifices, encouragement, hope, and prayers, I owe everything.

And to my heavenly Father, for whom I write.

**Gabrielle Meyer** grew up above a carriage house on a historic estate near the banks of the Mississippi River, imagining real and made-up stories about the occupants who had lived there. She went on to work for state and local historical societies and loves writing fiction inspired by real people, places, and events. She currently resides in central Minnesota on the banks of the Mississippi River, not far from where she grew up, with her husband and four children. By day, she's a busy homeschool mom, and by night she pens fiction and nonfiction filled with hope. Learn more about Gabrielle and her writing by visiting www.gabriellemeyer.com.

# Sign Up for Gabrielle's Newsletter

Keep up to date with Gabrielle's news on book releases and events by signing up for her email list at gabriellemeyer.com.

---

# You May Also Like . . .

Natalia Blackstone relies on Count Dimitri Sokolov to oversee the construction of the Trans-Siberian Railway. Dimitri loses everything after witnessing a deadly tragedy and its cover-up, but he has an asset the Russian Monarchy knows nothing about: Natalia. Together they fight to save the railroad while exposing the truth, but can their love survive the ordeal?

*Written on the Wind* by Elizabeth Camden
THE BLACKSTONE LEGACY #2 • elizabethcamden.com

# More Compelling Fiction

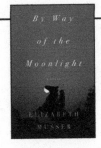

Allie Massey's dream to use her grandparents' estate for equine therapy is crushed when she discovers the property has been sold to a contractor. With only weeks until demolition, Allie unearths one of her Nana Dale's best-kept secrets—about her champion filly, a young man, and one fateful night during WWII—and perhaps a clue to keep her dream alive.

*By Way of the Moonlight* by Elizabeth Musser
elizabethmusser.com

British spy Levi Masters is captured while investigating a discovery that could give America an upper hand in future conflicts. Village healer Audrey Moreau is drawn to the captive's commitment to honesty and is compelled to help him escape. But when he faces a severe injury, they are forced to decide how far they'll go to ensure the other's safety.

*A Healer's Promise* by Misty M. Beller
BRIDES OF LAURENT #2
mistymbeller.com

Del Nielsen's teaching job in town offers hope, not only to support her three sisters but also to better her students' lives. When their brother visits with his war-wounded friend RJ, Del finds RJ barely polite and wants nothing to do with him. But despite the sisters' best-laid plans, the future—and RJ—might surprise them all.

*A Time to Bloom* by Lauraine Snelling
LEAH'S GARDEN #2
laurainesnelling.com

**◆BETHANYHOUSE**

# More from Bethany House

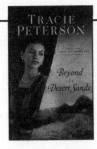

After living an opulent life with her aunt, the last thing Isabella Garcia wants is to celebrate Christmas in a small mining town with her parents. But she's surprised to see how much the town—and an old rival—have changed and how fragile her father's health has become. Faced with many changes, can she sort through her future and who she wants to be?

*Beyond the Desert Sands* by Tracie Peterson
LOVE ON THE SANTA FE
traciepeterson.com

Within months, Isabelle Wardrop lost her parents, her fortune, and her home, and with no qualifications, is forced to accept help from Dr. Mark Henshaw—the very man she blames for her mother's death. Mark has hopes of earning Isabelle's forgiveness and affections, but an unexpected incident may derail any hope they have of being together.

*A Feeling of Home* by Susan Anne Mason
REDEMPTION'S LIGHT #3
susanannemason.net

When her brother dies suddenly, Damaris Baxter moves to Texas to take custody of her nephew. Luke Davenport winds up gravely injured when he rescues Damaris's nephew from a group of rustlers. As suspicions grow regarding the death of her brother, more danger appears, threatening the family Luke may be unable to live without.

*In Honor's Defense* by Karen Witemeyer
HANGER'S HORSEMEN #3
karenwitemeyer.com